hidden roots

CITRUS COVE
BOOK 3

CLIO EVANS

Copyright © 2025 Clio Evans

Cover Designed by Emily Wittig

Dev Editing: Samantha Ninmo of Serpent & Sword Author Services

Line Editing: Emily in the Archives @emilyinthearchives

Art: Jess @dalooch__

All rights reserved. No part of this book may be reproduced or used in any manner without the prior written permission of the copyright owner, except for the use of brief quotations in a book review.

No part of this book was written with Artificial Intelligence. I support human creativity and will never use generative AI.

clioevansauthor.com

To being loved just the way you are

content warnings

- Parental death
- Animal injured (no animal death)
- Stalking
- Coping with grief
- Assault
- Gun violence
- Stabbing
- Kidnapping
- Discussions of difficulty getting pregnant
- *Detailed* sex scenes including: shibari, spanking, pegging, dub-con voyeurism, breeding kink, use of sex toys, role playing, anal, rimming, and more.

If you have any questions regarding content warnings, please reach out to me via Instagram **@clioevansauthor** or via email clioevansauthor@gmail.com

emma

Three Years Ago

"OH GOD, I'm going to die."

Not only was I going to die, I was going to die in the middle of fucking nowhere at night on a two-lane road surrounded by nothing but hills and sheep. Or cows. Or whatever animal Texas had in their stupid fields.

My car sputtered as I eased into the tall grass, rolling to a full stop. I put it in park, throwing my head back against the seat with a dramatic groan.

I'd underestimated the amount of gas I'd need on this last stretch to Citrus Cove, and now I was going to pay for it. I was hangry, needed to pee, and was so damn close to the small town that it only made me more upset.

I snatched my phone out of the cup holder and shook my head. No signal.

"Son of a bitch," I sighed.

I looked back at Donnie—my small, ancient dog. He was curled up in a tiny ball in his little carrier, sound asleep without a care in the world.

The only reason I ever considered moving to a place like this was because of Haley. She was my best friend, my ride or die, and after the hell she'd been through with an *actual* serial killer—I wanted to be there for her. I'd even make room for her new man too, though reluctantly. I didn't like sharing.

Come on, Emma. Think, think, think. The empty gas tank sigil burned in the dark, a glowing symbol of my untimely demise. I could see the headlines now. *Sexy City Girl Mauled by A Texas Cow.* I leaned forward, peering out the window for any sign of said beasts.

Despite my fears, my gaze lifted to the sky. The stars were pretty. I'd been in one city or another my entire life and couldn't remember a time I'd seen them like this. The vastness of it above me brought my panic down a notch.

I really didn't want to walk all the way into town. It was almost midnight and that sounded like a great way to end up murdered.

Headlights flashed in the rearview. My heart leapt in my chest. I grabbed my purse from the front seat, opened the door, and waved my hand erratically to get their attention.

Maybe I could hitch a ride. I had a taser and knew how to use it. Then there were the multiple years of martial arts. I could take out a grown man if he tried anything stupid.

A truck slowed down and pulled off the road in front of me. I pulled my taser out of my purse and turned it on, hiding it next to my side as I got out of the car—just in case.

The truck's driver side door opened and a man stepped out. Fuck, what the hell did they put in the water down here? Even from his silhouette, I could see he was tall and muscled. *What if he's also a serial killer?*

2

Driving all the way from Baltimore had made me tired, unhinged, and paranoid. Over twenty-four hours in the car was a long time to be alone with my thoughts. But I decided I couldn't be too careful.

"You okay?" he drawled.

"My car ran out of gas," I said.

"Are you all alone out here?"

What the fuck kind of question was that? That was one a psycho asked. "None of your fucking business," I snapped.

A sound echoed from him. Did he just *grunt* at me? I narrowed my eyes as he opened the back door of the truck and reached inside.

Oh god, oh god, oh god.

I aimed the taser at him in case he pulled out a gun. He leaned in deeper into the truck and then straightened, pulling out a red gas can. What kind of person kept a can of gas in their car?

He turned and froze, slowly setting the gas can back on the seat. "What the hell are you doing, woman?"

"Well, I got paranoid that—"

My finger slipped.

I squealed as the taser launched the two probes straight towards the stranger. It hit him in the stomach and his whole body stiffened on impact, the buzzing sound louder than the crickets chirping.

I dropped the taser with a scream. "Oh god, that was an accident!"

He hit the ground with a heavy thud, followed by a moan.

"Fuck!" I ran over to him and knelt down in the grass. "I am so sorry!"

"What the fuck is wrong with you?" he wheezed. I reached for the probes and yanked them free, earning another yelp from him. He swatted at my hands. "*Seriously?*"

"I'm sorry! There's been a serial killer in this area and I'm fucking tired and you're a stranger and I'm just trying to get to Citrus Cove and escape the woman-eating cows."

He grunted again and rubbed his jaw. Up close, he was far more handsome than I could have ever guessed. Shadows danced over his short beard, dark hair, and searing gaze. I couldn't tell what color his eyes were, but they were pretty, too.

He was also covered in mud and dirt.

And glaring at me like I was the last person in the world he wanted to see.

"I just need to get to 129 Hummingbird Lane," I said quickly. "If you can drop me off, I've got twenty bucks I can give you."

"Why the hell do you need to go there?" he asked.

"What do you mean?" I glared at him.

"That's where my soon to be sister-in-law's sister lives."

I stared at him as he stared at me. His expression slowly pinched.

The realization hit me. "*No*," I said.

It must have hit him too, because he groaned. "For fuck's sake. You've got to be fucking kidding me." He shook his head, his brows drawing together in a scowl.

"Don't you dare tell me." I stood up with a scoff.

Of course the one motherfucker I'd run into on my way to Citrus Cove was *him*.

He rubbed his face. "I should have recognized your annoying voice," he muttered as he sat up.

"Excuse me," I snapped. "I'm right fucking here."

"Oh, I'm well aware. You're really Emma?"

I crossed my arms. I certainly had no regrets about tasing him now. "I sure as hell am. Not so nice to meet you, I'm Emma Madden."

He snorted as he slowly got up. "Hunter Harlow."

"Oh, I know. I recognize your *annoying* voice."

Hunter rolled his eyes. "How in the hell does one run out of gas? Did you just not notice? Are you really that careless?"

Ugh, this guy could fuck all the way off. "I miscalculated when I needed to fill up. Just give me the gas can and I'll be on my way."

"It's empty. I was going to suggest we run to the closest gas station, but it may be easier to leave it for tomorrow."

"Okay. Are you going to give me a ride or what, then?"

He sighed, looking at his truck and then my car. "Yeah. Then you're Haley and Sarah's problem."

"Fine by me."

"Fine."

"*Fine*," I said again.

He narrowed his eyes on me. "You're one of those women who feel like you always have to have the last word, aren't you?"

"I'm one of *those women* who will happily taser you again and then grind your balls under my heel if you don't check your fucking tone," I said pleasantly.

His gaze slid down to my shoes, and he shook his head. "You're not gonna last here more than a month. Did you really drive all the way here wearing those?"

"It's only a three-inch heel. But of course you'd think three inches is a lot," I scoffed, my eyes flicking down to his crotch.

He raised a brow and got to his feet, towering over me. "How about you grab your purse and get in my car, *princess*?"

Yuck. I hated that nickname more than anything else. "Yeah, just what I need. A hillbilly knight covered in mud."

Heat flickered in his gaze. "Grab your things and get in the damn truck."

"Are you going to help me?"

"Nope." He turned and slammed the back door and then slid into the front seat. "Hurry up. It's late."

He shut his door before I could snap at him. Shaking my head, I stomped back to the car to grab my keys, purse, suitcase, and Donnie's carrier, before hauling it all to the truck.

I fought to open the back door to the cab of his giant truck and tossed my suitcase in. I decided I'd take Donnie out of the carrier to let him judge Hunter with me.

"What the hell is that thing?"

Hunter was twisted in his seat, looking back at us.

"This is Donnie," I said. "My dog."

"He's a rat."

"Oh, then you must be related." I opened the passenger door, and grabbed the ceiling handle to pull myself in. It took some maneuvering while holding Donnie, but I finally managed to settle into the seat before I turned to him. "Who even needs a truck this big?"

"Someone who works on a farm."

Donnie sighed, staring at Hunter with the same amount of disdain I harbored in my heart.

"Just drive," I snapped.

"As you wish, *princess*."

CHAPTER ONE

emma

Present Day

"I'M NOT WORKING WITH *HIM*."

I crossed my arms and gave Haley and Sarah *the look*. The one that said I wasn't changing my mind and there was absolutely nothing the two of them could do about it, despite how much I loved them.

Sunshine warmed the three of us around the table in my yard. My favorite sundress hugged my body. Red roses bloomed across the soft fabric while my broad-rimmed hat protected my face and shoulders. I wiggled my bare toes and slid my sunglasses down my nose so they could see my glare. Donnie basked next to me, tongue lolling, and eyes gleaming with a peace I dreamed of.

There wasn't a single cloud in the sky, and it would have been the perfect day if my two best friends stopped trying to make me work with Hunter Harlow.

Haley raked her fingers through her abundance of blond curls and leaned back in the hot pink camp chair. She gave Sarah a look I knew all too well—the one that told me they'd definitely talked about this before coming to me.

"You've been plotting against me," I hissed at them. "I'm shocked Alice isn't here too."

"Honestly, she would have been, but she had to be at the cafe today. She's waiting for our text updates."

I shook my head in disbelief. "Traitors. It's never going to happen."

"Hunter is easy to work with, Em," Sarah said.

"Easy for you, maybe. Sarah, you have *two* husbands. Why can't I work with one of them?"

Last spring, we celebrated Sarah, Colt, and Sammy getting married. Their wedding was absolutely beautiful, and I still teared up thinking about it. The way they looked at her like she was the center of their universe always left me feeling wistful, dreaming that one day someone would look at me that way.

At this rate, it would never happen. All the good men were either taken or dead, and pickings were slim in Citrus Cove.

Haley laughed and Sarah shook her head at me. "You know why you can't work with Sammy or Colt. They already have their hands full."

She wasn't wrong, but that didn't mean I'd go down so easily.

The Wildflower Festival was an annual event in Citrus Cove. Our entire family had been dragged into running it by Lynn Harlow and Honey, Haley and Sarah's grandmother. For some reason, they decided we'd be the best at it, and with their collective social influence, convinced everyone else in Citrus Cove too.

The thing was, they were right. Between all of us, we could run a festival easily. Cowboy Ciders—the new name for Cam and Colt's winery—would provide the alcohol. Sammy and Sarah would bake delicious treats and bring in other local businesses for more food options. Hunter had all the connections needed to bring in vendors to actually fulfill the 'wildflower' aspect. Then there was me—someone who had multiple years of experience in marketing to draw in the crowds.

It was all happening on Main Street. I wanted to highlight the historic buildings that gave this town all its charm. The Old Spur Museum, the Old Bank, the Victorian house-turned-bookstore. Citrus Cove was a slice of southern heaven that I could sell to anyone craving a homestyle bite.

I didn't know shit about wildflowers, but I could market like I did. Fresh flowers, raw honey, garden-grown vegetables, and decadent breads—*the perfect bounty for spring! A fun date or an outing for the whole family!* I had the entire marketing plan down at this point. The Wildflower Festival was on its way to being a crowning achievement, except for one problem.

Everyone wanted Hunter and I to be the face of the festival together.

When I'd agreed to help run it last fall, that had never been brought up. If anything, I distinctly remembered telling *everyone* I would help so long as I didn't have to work side by side with Citrus Cove's most annoying, ridiculously handsome, asshole grump.

It was Colt's fault. He said we were both 'single and hot,' so that would bring more people in our age range out to the festival. It was absurd. While Hunter *was* attractive, he had the most abysmal attitude ever bestowed upon a man.

Now that it was the end of March, we were a month out from the festival—and I was digging my heels in over the idea of having to interact with him more than I already did. I'd lived here for almost three years, had spent all holidays around him, saw him at least once a week, and still hated his guts.

Well, hate was a strong word. *Strongly* disliked.

"Hunter is the only other person who will have free hands that day," Haley said. "Cam, Colt, and I are running the drink stands. Sarah and Sammy are selling Bentley Bakery treats with the boys' help, and Sarah will be baking her ass off the days leading up to it. Everything else will fall into place, but we need someone in charge of the big picture. Which is why you and Hunter have been named co-captains. We're only a month out, Emma, and we need this to go well."

"I don't need a co-captain," I argued, folding my hands over my lap. "I'm perfectly capable of telling that man what to do. We all agreed to help out, but I never signed up to work with Hunter. I thought I'd be running it with Honey and Lynn. And you're right, we are a month out, and we've already done so much work. I do *not* need Hunter ruining it all."

"Honey and Lynn are running the contests and games. Hunter has done his part by reaching out to vendors, making sure we'll have tents, a stage, and all the other random things we need. Can't the two of you just get along? What made you dislike each other so much, anyway?" Sarah asked.

I narrowed my eyes on her, but it was hard to glare at Sarah. I loved her just as much as I loved Haley, and I liked seeing her happy. She wore shorts and a T-shirt, her dark waves gathered in a loose bun, her skin carrying a golden glow that definitely came from loving and being loved. It was night and day between this woman and the Sarah I'd met when I first came to Citrus Cove.

What else could I say? Hunter Harlow was an asshole. I'd thought so since the moment we'd first spoken on the phone years ago. We were oil and water. He always had something to say, always got on my damn nerves. He drove me up the wall.

"He's an asshole," I muttered.

"He says the same about you," Haley snorted.

"Hey, you're supposed to be on my side."

"We are," Sarah insisted. She leaned forward in her chair, giving her sister a helpless look. They were really trying hard to convince me, weren't they? "Sometimes, the two of you remind me of the boys when they have a tiff. But also..."

"You're both adults," Haley said, raising a brow at me. "My *darling* angel of a friend. Please call a truce with him for the good of us all so we can throw the best festival this town has ever seen. I refuse to allow anyone else to outdo us. This has also been good for forcing the gossip in Citrus Cove to become more positive about us."

Ah, the gossip. I loved gossip so long as it had nothing to do with me. Hell, I was the queen of it. Unfortunately, Haley was right.

Because of Thomas Connor, all of us had been the source of small town speculation and sidelong glances for over two years. When Sarah, Colt, and Sammy started dating, it added a whole new layer of whispers. On top of that, a whole storm of danger had erupted around them too.

Things had finally smoothed out, though. Spring was upon us, I'd survived another mild winter in Citrus Cove, and had a brutal summer to look forward to. I'd learned to enjoy March, April, and May before I melted into the dirt for the rest of the hot Texas months.

I pressed my glossy lips together and turned my gaze to the quiet street. Half of the house burned down last year, thanks to a crazy couple who had gone after Sarah, Sammy, Colt, and the boys. Since then, they'd moved into Colt's home together, and I'd bought this place from Haley. Now I lived alone in a pleasant, charming, and sometimes annoyingly quiet neighborhood. Hummingbird Lane was the perfect picture of a small, cozy town.

I'd painted the house pastel pink after the renovations. It

was everything I'd ever dreamed of, with the bonus of horrifying my father. I'd made certain to print holiday cards with a photo of me sitting in front of it with Donnie to send to him and some board members of his company.

It was worth the ten angry emails I'd received asking when I was going to stop fucking around and come home.

The answer was never. I'd managed to stay away from my father and step-mom when I lived in Baltimore, and it was even easier now that I was in Citrus Cove. I was certain he'd never step foot in a small town like this, not even to see me.

Especially not to see me.

"Are the guys having the same convo with Hunter right now?" I asked.

Sarah winced, a dead giveaway. Haley smiled softly, her wedding ring glinting as she took a sip of sweet tea. "Maybe."

"You bitch," I sighed. "Fine. I will make nice with the biggest dick in Citrus Cove."

"*Emma*," they both hissed.

"But I'm not going to like it. Not for a single moment."

Haley smiled victoriously. "Thank you. Now, I do think the two of you might need to set up some meetings..."

I groaned and squeezed my eyes shut for a second before giving her a fresh glare. "Ugh. You owe me one. You both do. I'll text him, I guess. I hope he knows what he's in for."

"Just go easy on him," Haley pleaded.

I gave her a sharp smile. "Oh, you know I will be *so* sweet."

Neither one of them believed me.

Sarah mustered up a nervous chuckle. "It'll all work out. There's really nothing we can't handle. Right?"

Some of the tension I initially had deflated at that. I could never stay mad at either one of them. "You're right. It'll be fine. And if it gets out of hand..."

"Cam and Sammy can step in," Haley said. "They can reign Hunter in."

Could they? I wasn't so sure. But I kept that thought to myself and nodded.

The Harlow brothers were something else. All the Harlows were, in fact. They always had each other's backs, and were always willing to do whatever was needed to help each other.

It made me wonder what my life would have been like if my sister hadn't died. When she was still alive, the two of us were close like that. She'd been the only person I could talk to, and she understood how fucked up our family was. Our mom died when we were young, and our dad raised us to compete against each other, but we'd always risen above that.

I came from a world of private jets, dinner parties, and keeping up with the Joneses in a way that would put Citrus Cove to shame. My dad was the founder of a computer chip company based in Sacramento known as Madden Enterprises. It was one of the last semiconductor companies that hadn't been bought up by a larger conglomerate. I could safely say I got my stubbornness from Michael Madden—my father and source of most of my woes.

I hadn't lived up to his expectations and never would.

I was envious of the Harlow family, even though they'd basically adopted me. I was part of their holidays, daily lives, and more because of Haley. Despite my reservations about accepting Cameron, he'd grown on me. Seeing how much he loved Haley made me love him all the more and now he was like an older brother. Sammy won me over quickly. Colt too, despite his dumbass idea to have me and Hunter work together.

I loved Sarah's boys, my honorary nephews. I loved Honey, too. She was my *Golden Girls* buddy and if Sarah or Haley were busy, I often found myself at her house, devouring a home-cooked meal and watching Rose annoy Dorothy. She was the grandmother I'd never had.

Bob and Lynn Harlow were beyond kind as well. It wasn't uncommon for me to end up at their house for dinner once a month. Everyone was so enmeshed in each other's lives here, it felt natural to be a part of it.

Each of them had become an integral part of my life. They'd accepted me, loved me, and made me feel at home.

Really, Hunter was the only thorn in my side. A sexy, rough-handed thorn. But a thorn, no less.

Haley pushed her chair back and stood up to stretch. She twisted left and right, then planted her hands on her hips. "I have a few errands to run and then I'm going to steal Cam away before the bar opens later. Emma, are you still up for working a shift next week?"

"Yeah," I said. "I can help out, unless Sarah needs me."

"No, no, it's okay," Sarah blurted out.

I snorted. "You just don't want me baking anything because I'm so bad at it."

"You put baking soda in my muffin recipe instead of baking *powder*." I wrinkled my nose at her. Sarah flashed me a grin. "I love you. But no, unless you just want to keep me company. I think the bar could use your help more."

"I miss living together." *Where did that come from?* I winced, not wanting to make her feel guilty. I did miss living with her, but sometimes it was more about not wanting to be alone. None of my friends were alone except for Alice, but she was following a strict 'no dating' rule until her life was less busy.

Sarah's eyes softened. "Come over next week. It's tight quarters, but everything's coming along with the construction on the new house."

"Okay," I said. "I'll pop over at some point. Maybe I can pick up the boys next Tuesday."

"I mean, I won't argue if you want to." Sarah smiled at me and I felt a moment of pride, knowing how much healing she'd done.

"We need a girl's night soon," Haley said. "One with no testosterone."

"Except Donnie is allowed," Sarah said, casting him a smile.

"The best man in my life," I teased, leaning over to ruffle the tiny patch of fur on top of his head.

I watched as a small red car slowed past the house before continuing down the street. Probably one of the nosy neighbors. Then I heard the *rumble*. *Ugh*. Haley and Sarah craned their heads as Hunter's unfathomably large truck pulled in to park behind my car.

Cameron hopped out of the passenger door, and Hunter slid out of the driver's side.

"Speak of the devil," I sighed. "This will be good."

Haley raised a brow at her husband as he approached us, holding his hands up. Then he grabbed hold of Haley and spun her close, kissing her on the lips. "I come in peace."

"Is Haley peace?" I asked.

Sarah blurted out a laugh and covered her mouth. Cam's cheeks turned beet red and Haley shook her head at me, lips upturned into a sly smirk as she leaned into him.

God, they were smitten. Sarah, Colt, and Sammy were the same way. They all looked at each other like the sun rose and set out of their Texan asses, and here I was—lonely and bitter and withering away like a bluebonnet at the end of spring.

They reminded me that I'd managed to somehow go on dates with ten different men over the last year, and every single one of them had been a bust. I'd briefly had a steady boyfriend, but the fucker dipped right before the holidays.

That had to be a record, right?

"Hunter had better be ready to compromise," Haley said to him.

"Yeah, so about that..." Cam trailed off as his older brother stomped across the yard to our group.

Donnie lifted his head, his tail wagging at Hunter. I scowled, completely disappointed—my own son had just betrayed me.

Hunter wore brown overalls with a navy T-shirt, cowboy boots, and a backwards baseball cap with the Cowboy Ciders logo on it. He crossed his arms, his biceps popping as he tried to appear tough. I wasn't sure if he actually hit the gym or if he was just ripped from working in the vineyard.

The vein in his forehead throbbed as his attention landed directly on me. He planted his feet in the grass. "Not happening."

"Oh, come on," Haley groaned. "Emma agreed to work with you!"

"I did," I said, flashing him a fake smile. "Because I'm an adult and can act like one. Can you say the same?"

Donnie sat up, drawing Hunter's gaze, his tail thumping. Hunter sighed and knelt down, running his fingertips over Donnie's head. "Hello, rat." He looked up at me. "This is absurd anyway. What do we even need to do? We're still a month out."

"We need two people to head all of the coordination, set up, wrangling vendors, and then be around to help people if they have questions. To make sure things run smoothly," Cameron said. "You'll be in the newspaper, too, with your pretty faces. Come on, man. Emma is great."

"It just seems like a lot to have two people running this together," Hunter said.

"You're right. I can handle it without you," I retorted.

He scowled at me and started to stand back up, but Donnie rolled over onto his back. I glowered at the little traitor. Hunter almost smiled, and remained crouched as he spoke. "Well, that's too damn bad. I'm going to run this thing with or without you."

"Oh, so now you're on board?" *Dammit.* Maybe I shouldn't have challenged him like that. He was as stubborn as me.

Hunter's gaze never left mine. Unlike his brothers, his eyes were a rich shade of brown, but they were just as piercing. "Afraid you can't get rid of me now. Are you sure you don't want to back out?"

He would drive me absolutely insane. But now, there wasn't a chance in hell I was going to back down. "Oh, I'm sure," I said sweetly. "Also, Cam, you might want to clear out a patch of dirt to bury your brother's ego in."

"It can be buried right next to yours," Hunter quipped.

"Okay, okay," Sarah said, holding up her hands as she stood up. "*Children.* I need to go do *things.* Love you all, talk to you later."

I shook my head as she darted for her new car. My expression soured as she got in, waved at us, and backed out of the driveway. I already knew she was calling Colt and Sammy to update them on this little exchange.

"Everyone is betraying me today," I sighed.

Haley winked. "It's for the good of Citrus Cove, right?"

Was it? I had a feeling it wasn't. Everyone was up to something, but I wasn't sure what. I couldn't imagine why they'd try to pair me with Hunter, unless they were trying to force us to be friends.

That wouldn't happen in a million years. Pigs would fly

and hell would freeze over before I would ever enjoy being in his prickly presence.

"Alright," I mumbled. "We'll make it work. Get out of here, you two. You're making me nauseous with your ridiculous standards of stupid love. Hunter, I suppose you can stay if you'd like to have some sort of meeting now. "

"We can set one up another time," he bristled. "I was bombarded right when I was about to get some stuff done at the vineyard. Unless you want to come trim vines with me."

"And ruin my manicure? I think not," I said. "We'll meet later. Now, get off my lawn."

Haley chuckled as she made her exit, giving me a hug and Donnie a scratch before heading toward her car with Cam in tow. Hunter stood awkwardly for a moment and turned to follow them.

"Just so you know, I'm only doing this for them," I said. "And I'm not going to make it easy on you. You can come over tomorrow morning for our first order of business."

Hunter didn't even spare me a glance. "See you in the morning, princess."

CHAPTER TWO
hunter

OUT OF ALL THE people I'd met in my life, no one had ever managed to make me feel the way Emma did.

Everyone was under the impression that I hated her.

Even Emma believed it.

But I didn't hate her.

I was fucking obsessed with her.

I sucked in a deep breath, her scent still clinging to me. God, she smelled so fucking good. She rotated through three different perfumes, but the black violet and saffron one was my favorite.

Seeing her sitting there in a sundress, her deep chestnut-brown hair curling down her petite shoulders, lips painted crimson—a weaker man wouldn't have been able to even speak in her presence.

Emma had tased her way straight to my heart. Since that night almost three years ago, she'd become the center of my every waking thought. She was often in my dreams too. I couldn't fucking escape her.

I knew more about her than anyone. I knew about her

family, her history, the men she dated. I also knew the reason why she'd never managed to keep a boyfriend longer than three months.

Well, that part was maybe my fault.

I'd threatened every single man who dared to date her. Most of the time, they lasted a week. A couple of them I'd intercepted on the first date. Then there was *Kyle*, who'd held out for three months before caving around the holidays.

My bad. Maybe I should have felt guilty about sabotaging her love life.

But I didn't care.

It wasn't like any of them were good enough for her anyways.

I stayed far, far away from Emma Madden for two reasons.

One, she brought out a part of me that I didn't like. A twisted, possessive part of me I always kept hidden.

Two, she drove me absolutely crazy with that smart mouth. Every time she was sarcastic, I wanted to haul her over my shoulder, carry her to my bed, and fuck the sass right out of her.

She made me act like a caveman.

I thought I was more evolved than that. Really, I did.

But when Emma was in my presence, all civilized thoughts turned *primal*.

I slammed my hand on the steering wheel as I sped down the gravel road that stretched around to the back of the farm. Sunshine splashed over me across the front seat. A perfect breeze ruffled my hair through the rolled down windows. Summer would be here before long, but for now, I was enjoying the mild weather.

If I looked to the left, I could see the Harlow tree up on the hill, a place that had been in our family since we settled here.

Bluebonnets sprung up in the distance, the scenery cradling our home.

There was nowhere else quite like the Hill Country. It was home to me. The rolling hills, the countless oak trees that twisted up towards the clear blue skies, the wildflowers a colorful patchwork quilt. This was where I'd lived my entire life and it was where I planned to stay forever.

The Harlow house was on the other side of that hill. I glanced over before refocusing on the gravel road. I'd taken the back route because I couldn't deal with Pops right now.

Without fail, if I were irritated or annoyed, he always found me and made it worse. It was a goddamn talent.

I couldn't avoid him forever, but I could manage until this evening, at least. I needed to stop by and fix one of the leaking faucets Mom had texted me about.

Add it to the list.

My to-do list was already a mile long without throwing Emma and this damn festival into the mix. It had to be some sort of joke that Colt had looked at me and thought 'Yep, Hunter should be the face of the festival.'

Maybe it was payback for something I'd forgotten about. Then again, probably not. That wasn't really Colt's style. If he had a bone to pick with me, he'd solve it with a good punch to the jaw and cracking a beer together afterward.

But still—why me? Why Emma?

Well, I could understand why her. She was good at planning—but so was I. When we'd agreed to help out with the Wildflower Festival, something I'd been dragged into, it was no secret to everyone in the family that we didn't want to work together. It was the silent, unspoken rule that if they put us in a room together, we'd drive each other up the wall.

They all knew how busy I was, and yet no one stopped to consider that maybe asking me to do more might not be okay.

In addition to the upcoming festival and my duties on the farm, I was always the go-to for anyone who needed a favor or some help. It came in handy, especially since it meant I'd made a lot of friends over the years. At first, I'd gone out of my way to make connections to prove a point to Pops that I could do things without his name. But the good folks of Citrus Cove appreciated the little tasks I'd done for them, and they would jump at the chance to pay it forward. I'd help a neighbor fix their car, and suddenly they'd put me in touch with a friend of a friend.

Over a decade of those types of friendships meant that whenever there was trouble, I knew someone who could help.

Too bad not a single one of them could help me purge Emma from my thoughts.

I needed a damn vacation. Or a hot, kinky fuck. I thought about the rope I had in my closet, along with the blindfolds, and bondage tape. I loved spanking a good ass too, but preferred to do it bare-handed. As much as I appreciated paddles and other implements, there was nothing quite like my rough palms on smooth cheeks, turning them crimson with each smack.

My cock jerked at the thought of Emma tied up and helpless over my knees, and I quickly shoved that image out of my mind. I didn't have time to think about a vacation or kinky sex— I had work to do.

Plus, that could never happen with her. Even though she made me feel things, getting into a relationship would be too sticky. At this point, she was as much a part of the Harlow family as I was, and I'd done a thorough job at making her dislike me.

The tires kicked up gravel as I rolled to a stop, parking behind another truck. What our farm lacked in acreage, we made up for in efficiency. Keeping up with everything had me working longer hours than a regular job ever would. Apples, grapes, and a patch of veggies we shared with neighbors and the guys who worked here.

We had three part-time employees; Ezra, Aaron, and José. I'd hired them a while back to alleviate some stress. Eventually, I wanted to have Ezra and José on full-time so I could *maybe* have time for a hobby. Like macraméing more plant holders for my house.

The good news was that this year's grape crop was promising. We'd have pinot grigio and malbec grapes ready to harvest in August. The orchard was mostly in good shape, too. I was glad I'd pushed for us to trellis some of the apple trees a few years back, because some of the older trees were having production issues. I worried about a potential soil infection, but so far it seemed like we were in the clear.

Then there was a concern about the demand we'd have once Cowboy Ciders was up and running, but the money that would bring in meant we could hire more people. I knew eventually they'd outgrow our current apple crop, so I was already putting out feelers to other growers.

I liked the rebrand. I had to give it to Emma, she was really good at marketing, and now Cam and Colt had a fresh logo that would stand out on grocery store shelves. We'd already made hats, shirts, and coozies and I proudly owned one of each so far.

I was proud of them—all of us, really, since we were all involved in one way or another.

My phone buzzed in my pocket. I drew it out and sighed. *Pops.*

I answered begrudgingly. "Yep?"

"That's how you answer the phone?" Pops grumbled.

"It is when I'm busy. What do you need?"

"I was just checking in."

"Okay. Well, Ezra is here. I'm about to get to work. Holler if you need anything."

"Alright."

And that was that. I hung up and slumped against the seat, sighing as I gathered the willpower to start my day.

The truth was, Pops wasn't going to be able to do this for much longer. The other issue was that the bastard was too stubborn to hand me the reins just yet.

Did I even want them? I wasn't sure.

My whole life, I'd always been told I'd take over the farm one day, and that this part of the Harlow legacy would be mine to have and to hold. As I'd gotten older, I'd started to resent how much rested on my shoulders.

Those expectations hurt my relationship with Pops in a way that probably would never recover. Ever since our blowout fight three years ago, right before Haley came back to Citrus Cove, nothing had been the same.

What if I didn't want this? What if I wanted to do something else? Cameron had always loved this place. Sammy—well, he didn't really care about it. I was stuck somewhere between the two of them, but I was the oldest so I'd always been expected to pick up the slack.

I knew a lot about a lot of things, and if I didn't have a solution for it, I knew someone who did.

Now, if I could only find someone who knew how to make me forget about Emma, that would be great.

She was nothing like me. I'd been so certain she wouldn't last long in Citrus Cove, but I'd been wrong. I'd underestimated her based on her love for all things pink and glitter, but she was a force to be reckoned with.

I got out and waved to Ezra. He wore a green ball cap, sunglasses, and a shirt streaked with dirt. Like me, his skin was tanned from being out in the sun. Unlike me, the bastard never wore sunscreen, which made him look older than he was. I could see the burn from this morning's rays already creeping up the back of his neck.

"Brother, you need some SPF," I called.

"We're out," he rebutted.

Sunscreen. Note to self, stop by the store and buy more soon.

He walked over as I pulled down the tailgate at the back of my truck. "I'll pick some up this week," I told him. "How's everything looking today?"

"Good, but we need to do some pruning."

I nodded. "Yep. We can split the vineyard."

"Sounds good, boss. Oh, also... Well, your dad came by earlier."

Of course he did. I'd been doing this since I could walk, but he still didn't trust me to get things done. "Oh boy. Did he try and tell you how to do your job?"

"Yeah," Ezra chuckled. "I don't really mind him. He's been doing this for his whole life, you know."

"Oh, I'm fully aware." He liked to remind me all the fucking time. "Let's knock out some work and I'll order us lunch."

"Aw, such a sweetheart. How are you single, huh?"

Because I'm obsessed with a woman who hates me. "Just too busy to date."

"Sure. You know all the single women in this town eye you like vultures."

"I know. My mother has tried to set me up with almost all of them at some point."

He chuckled. "My wife even asks. 'What's the last Harlow doing? Is he dating?'"

"Well, tell Rachel I said hi. And that's my business and my business alone."

Ezra snickered as he helped me unload the fertilizer out of

the back of my truck. By the time we were done taking everything to the barn, the two of us were covered in a sheen of sweat.

One of the better updates with all of the rebuilds over the last year was moving the wine and cider processing to a warehouse we'd added behind the barn. I no longer had to haul goods all the way over to the old barn that burned down, which used to be located at the very front of our property.

It'd been a crazy three years, but I was thankful for it in a weird way. Well, thankful everyone I loved was safe, but also happy we'd had the chance to make some positive changes that helped the farm.

Lemons into lemonade, as Mom liked to say. In this case, they were murder lemons, but things had still worked out for the better.

Where the old Harlow barn used to stand was now a new one built to serve our community. It was a place where we had live music, a variety of ciders and wine, and space for food trucks. Cam had finally hired some people to work at the bar, although I sometimes liked to jump in to help.

It might have officially been Cam and Colt's business, but we all had a hand in it. And at the end of the day, I was a people person. Even if Emma didn't believe so.

I rolled my shoulders, cracked my neck, and retrieved my canteen of water from the truck. I took a few swigs, raising a brow at Ezra. "You better be drinking water, man. I'm not dragging your dehydrated ass back to your wife this summer. She'll kill me."

"I'll be fine," he said. "I have gatorade. Stop being a mother hen."

I couldn't help it. Perks of being the eldest child, I always worried about others before myself.

I carried my canteen with me over to the vine trimmer. It

was a large—*expensive*—piece of equipment that helped keep the rows of grapes neat and in line.

Concern sat heavy on my chest over the apple crop, but I tried to push that out of my mind. Instead, I thought about Emma and how often I'd have to be in her presence over the next few weeks.

Only until the festival, at least. Then we could go back to normal.

One month.

Would it really be so bad? I couldn't decide.

I wanted to spend every moment with her.

I also wanted to never see her again.

The Wildflower Festival would be good for all of us, in theory. Good for Citrus Cove, for local businesses, for our family and friends. So long as Emma and I managed not to burn it all down with our arguments.

I sighed as I cranked the vine trimmer on. It was mindless work, which was nice considering Emma was once again plaguing my thoughts. I rolled out of the barn and steered my way towards one of the first red grape rows. I looked out over the fields, spotting José and Aaron in the distance.

Sometimes I wished Cam and Sammy were interested in this part of our family business, but I was glad they'd found their own passions. Cam loved running a bar and vineyard, Sammy loved... food. Or whatever the hell he did. I occasionally wondered if I would have picked up something else if I wasn't the oldest, but at the end of the day, I did love the farm. Regardless, I would have ended up working with the earth somehow. I loved the dirt, the plants, and seeing something grow because of my care.

My phone chimed in my pocket. If it was Pops again, I was going to lose my shit. I pulled it out to check my messages and sighed.

Emma: Be here tomorrow at ten. Not earlier or later. K, bye.

So bossy. My fingers hovered over the letters but instead of typing what I wanted to say—*why don't you clear the whole day for me, princess?*—I sent a thumbs-up.

I slid my phone back in my pocket, pulled my gloves on, and focused my attention on anything but Emma.

CHAPTER THREE
emma

THE ONLY WAY TO start the day was with an iced cold brew. I topped off my glass with oat milk, stuck a pink metal straw in it, and settled down on the couch. Yesterday had flown by, and admittedly, it was partially because I'd done everything to put this damn meeting with Hunter out of my mind.

I'd lied about having work meetings this morning. I just wanted to annoy him, and by the way he'd stalked off yesterday, I'd clearly succeeded. Since then, I'd made a checklist for us to go through.

My real job was with a woman-owned marketing firm based in Baltimore. All work was done remotely, although they occasionally liked to try to get me to visit the office. The company was one of the best, and I was proud that I'd worked my way up without using my Madden name for clout.

My father didn't understand why I'd chosen to work for another company when I could have everything I wanted with his. But I didn't just want my career handed to me. I wanted to earn it. I didn't want to be beholden to his power or his secrets.

Secrets were currency in the Madden world. Unfortunately, I had many. Haley, my best friend of almost a decade, still didn't know how bad things were with my family, only that we weren't close and my sister died when I was young. Alice and Sarah didn't know either.

I didn't keep things from them because I didn't trust them. It had become a default and I liked pretending my father didn't exist. My stepmom unfortunately fit the shitty stereotype, and had never cared about me. She'd only married my father for the money, and always made sure to belittle me. So, I ignored her. I ignored both of them.

I worked hard, collected a well-earned paycheck, and lived my life being the single, hot best friend to the three women I loved dearly.

There was a lot I disliked about living in a small town, but nothing would ever take me out of it now. I had my real family here. Honey, Haley, Sarah, Alice, Cam, Colt, Sammy, and the boys. Hell, even Bob and Lynn. All of them were there for me when I needed them in ways I'd never experienced before.

The first sip of coffee hit and I released a contented sigh. Donnie hopped up onto the sofa and burrowed into a knit lilac throw blanket. I leaned over and snatched my laptop from the art deco table I'd thrifted from a place in Austin.

After everything that happened last year, Sarah and the boys moved in with Colt and Sammy, and they started building a new house. Haley used the insurance money to rebuild the back of this house and I'd bought the property from her. She'd given me a damn good deal, too.

Having my own home gave me a reason to pick up a couple of random hobbies aside from karate, which I'd been practicing for over five years now. I'd started thrifting furniture, refurbishing it, and reselling it online to fund my manicures and facials. I'd also taken a couple classes in Austin to learn how to fix things, because owning a house meant that random repairs were always required. With Hunter being the go-to handyman for everyone in Citrus Cove, it only made sense to learn how to do it myself.

Besides, if he could do it—I could do it.

Now, I got to live in a little pink house with my cute little dog. I had my found family, hobbies, and...

Still was not as happy as I wanted to be.

Maybe it was because I hadn't been laid in months. I was dying. The nether regions were drier than the Sahara and I couldn't find a single motherfucker in the entirety of central Texas who could find the clit *and* stick around for longer than one date.

I pulled up my Wildflower Festival spreadsheet on my laptop. There was no way Hunter could think of more than I already had. I'd started to make a checklist to share with each vendor attending the festival, along with compiling necessary waivers and a few other documents. I had a playlist in the works, along with an email ready to be sent about renting a sound system.

I even had some social media accounts up and running, and put together a small budget for ads. We were getting followers and gaining interest online. It was going to be a success.

A month out now, all of us just needed to do our part, and it would go well. I didn't need Hunter at my side.

A knock rapped on the front door. Donnie lifted his head, and I gave him a dirty look when he didn't bark. I glanced at the clock as I got up.

Surely it wasn't him. I was still in pajamas. My hair was a mess.

If he's here already, I'm going to lose my mind—I opened the front door and crossed my arms. This son of a bitch. "You're an hour early," I snapped. "What the fuck?"

Hunter's gaze swept over me. A molten heat rolled through

my core as the corner of his mouth tugged. *Whoa, what am I thinking?*

"Maybe I'm on a different time zone."

The southern pull of his accent sounded way sexier than it should have. Hot or not, Hunter was still an asshole. "You drive me insane," I seethed.

He leaned against the doorframe. The hem of his shirt pulled up ever so slightly, a sliver of his toned stomach peeking out. *Get a grip, girl, this man is your enemy.*

"You gonna leave me on the front porch?"

"I should," I said. "But come in. I'll run upstairs and change."

"You don't have to," he drawled. "I like the casual look."

"Good thing I don't care about what you like."

I moved aside to let him in and shut the door. I darted up the stairs to my bedroom and locked myself in. God, I wasn't even wearing a bra. I ripped my shirt off and stepped out of my shorts, changing into a T-shirt and leggings.

Actually, no. If he was going to drop by unannounced, then I was going to take my sweet time getting ready. I snatched a pink blouse and denim overalls from my closet and headed to the bathroom, flipping on the shower.

I heard his frustrated sigh all the way up here.

An hour later, I went downstairs with two minutes to spare until our *actual* meeting time. I had a fresh face of makeup, my hair dried and straightened, and the perfect outfit on.

And froze on the bottom step.

This *bastard*.

Hunter was in *my* spot, with *my* dog, *my* laptop, and *my* coffee.

"You got to be fucking kidding me," I said.

He turned his head and arched a dark brow. His eyes trailed down my body, something burning in his gaze that made me want to run. Sparks skated across my skin. I wanted to tell him to stop looking at me like that, like he wanted to devour me—but, I kept my mouth pressed into a thin, cranky line.

"Well, you were taking your sweet time getting ready, so I got cozy."

My god, the audacity. How did everyone else love this man? All of our friends thought the sun shined out of his well-toned ass. Not that I'd checked out his ass before. Okay, maybe I had. "Well next time, show up when I say to. It's rude."

"It's polite to show up early," he rebutted. "Didn't someone teach you that?"

"Okay, by like ten minutes. Not a full hour."

"Live in Texas long enough, you'll learn eventually."

Never had a man tempted me to grab him by the ear and drag him out of the house before Hunter. I walked over to him and leaned across the couch, reaching for my coffee as he took a sip. This close up, it was almost funny seeing a pink straw between his lips, the rough stubble of his face a masculine contrast.

I let my gaze linger. And dammit, his arms were long too. He held the cup out of my reach with an ease that absolutely infuriated me.

In a combination of overconfidence that I could snatch the coffee and stubbornness not to let him have it, I yelped as I lost my balance and tipped forward.

"Fuck," he barked, his arm looping around my waist.

Hunter caught me, my face an inch from the floor, and hauled me back as the coffee glass shattered against the hardwoods.

"Noooo!" I yelled.

Hunter's arms wrapped around me like a vise, his breath quickening. We both stared at the shattered glass and the coffee splattered everywhere. I closed my eyes, counting to five before I lost it.

"This is already a disaster," I seethed. "Why would they pair us together? Why the fuck would they think we can be in each other's presence without strangling each other?"

"I can repair the wood," he said quickly.

"Hunter," I growled. I looked up at him and then became *painfully* aware that I was in his lap. I moved against him, my ass rubbing over something hard.

"Emma," he gritted out. "Stop."

Oh. Fuck. Had I just rubbed on his dick? Oh god. Oh god, oh god, god, that is Hunter Harlow's dick and oh god, it's big??? What the fuck— "Let me go."

His arms tightened around me before I could wiggle free. "There's glass on the floor and you're barefoot. For fuck's sake, stop wiggling."

My head whipped to the side to see where Donnie was, but he was sitting a few feet away, eyes pinned on us in a judgmental way.

"Alright, let me up," I said, moving again.

With heroic ease, Hunter lifted me and set me on the back of the couch slowly enough that I could drop my feet to the other side. My cheeks were red hot, the heat of embarrassment spreading through my whole body. I kept my attention on anything but him as I tiptoed across the floor to slide on my rose-gold sandals.

Hunter cleared his throat, stood up on the cushion, and swung his legs over the back of the couch to stand. His face was as red as mine felt. "Sorry, Emma. I didn't mean for that to happen. I'll clean up," he said, quickly moving past me. Neither of us made eye contact. "Unless you moved the broom closet."

I raked my fingers through my hair, my heart pounding. Hunter was already in the kitchen, his back to me. I stared at the way the fabric stretched over his muscles a little too long. *Snap out of it.*

"Have at it," I said.

I snatched Donnie up and carried him upstairs, plopping him in my office. He plodded over to his bed and curled up in a patch of sun, which was his usual place most mornings. I shut him in the room as a knock echoed from downstairs.

"What now?" I muttered to myself.

I hurried down the stairs, shaking my head as Hunter mumbled in the kitchen.

I'd just sat on that man's dick.

Everything was a mess. Coffee, ice, and broken glass spread over the hardwood. The edge of my rug was soaked with coffee, too. Damn it. This wasn't how I'd planned for this to go.

I glanced at my reflection in the mirror and attempted to make my expression more serious. I smoothed my hair and opened the door.

A familiar face was on the other side—one I'd hoped to never see again.

"Emma. Oh good, I was right about this atrocious pink house being yours."

I tilted my head and plastered on a fake smile.

My ex-husband stood there looking like he'd walked off the front page of a business magazine. Perfect jaw, perfect blue eyes, perfect blond hair, perfect teeth. Perfect *everything*.

My worst *perfect* secret had just shown up on my front porch.

"Josh." I crossed my arms and leaned against the doorframe, my heart thumping in my chest. Although my thoughts were still on Hunter, I tried to completely focus on the disaster that was Joshua Martin, soiling my pink doormat with his designer oxfords. "What on earth are you doing here?"

"The lawyers sent me," he said with a grim smile. He wore

a navy blue suit and held a leather briefcase, his watch glinting and out of place against the backdrop of my neighborhood.

In fact, everything about him was out of place here.

All the reasons why I hated him came rushing back as I processed his words. We'd been married for fourteen months when I was twenty, and it was the reason I'd moved to Baltimore.

I'd seen pictures of him over the years, of course. My dad and stepmom never cut him out of their lives the way I had. Seeing Josh in person made me feel like throwing up right on him.

"So is *this* really where you're living?" he asked, raising both brows. He glanced around with a look of disgust that gave me flashbacks to the disaster of our short-lived marriage. "Emma? You there?"

What the fuck am I going to do? "The lawyers sent you. Why would they do that?" I asked, trying not to think about my outfit or house or *life*. "My dad has my phone number and my email address. He can send urgent matters there. I can't see why the lawyers..."

He winced and for a moment, actually had a human expression instead of the lizard-person mask he wore so often. "Can we maybe talk inside?"

A thousand knots twisted my stomach. "What happened?" I asked.

"*Emma?* Where the fuck is the broom?" Hunter's gruff voice called from within my house.

Damn it, Hunter.

"Hold on," I muttered to Josh. "It's in the closet!"

"Emma, why do you have pink trash bags? Since when do they even make pink trash bags? Oh god, they smell like cherry blossoms."

His grumblings continued and Josh raised a brow. "Is there a handyman in the house or something?"

"What? Like it couldn't be a romantic partner?" I scoffed.

He shrugged his shoulders and gave me a haughty smirk. "Last I heard, you haven't dated anyone long term since me. Guess I was always the one, right?"

This fucker.

"Honestly, part of the reason I'm here is because I think it's time we remarried, Emma. This whole separation was just to let you have some fun in your twenties, but it's gone too far."

"Emma, even your broom and mop are pink—"

I turned right as Hunter came around the corner.

A flash flood of panic washed over me. I said the first thing that popped into my mind—the one thing that could match Josh's venom with the same intensity he was using on me.

"Oh, there you are, baby." I grabbed Hunter and hauled him close. "Josh. Meet my boyfriend, Hunter."

CHAPTER FOUR
hunter

BOYFRIEND.

Boyfriend?

Alarm bells rang in my head. Shock sank its teeth in, then shifted into something else entirely.

"I'm actually her fiancé," I corrected, holding my hand out to whoever this douche was. *Red alert, red alert, this is breaking the rules? What am I doing?* "Hunter Harlow. Nice to meet you."

He shook my hand—*he's got soft hands*—but it wasn't him I was focused on.

Emma's expression was priceless. Her eyes widened, her perfectly arched brows drawn up before forcing another smile.

Maybe it was childish, but if she was going to spring dating on me as some sort of ploy to mess with this jackass, I was going to take it a step further.

I refocused all my attention on the displeased Ken doll. His icy vulture eyes flickered to her hand, noting the absence of a wedding ring. I already knew what he was thinking.

If we were going to play pretend though...

"Her ring is being custom made," I said, sliding my arm around her shoulder. Her scent washed over me and my mouth watered. Damn, she was wearing my favorite one. "Only the absolute best for my princess here."

Emma let out the fakest laugh I'd ever heard in my life, her red acrylic nails digging into my back so hard I wondered if it would leave a mark. I kind of wished they would. In another life, maybe she'd leave her marks on me and I'd punish her by tying a vibrator to her. *Get your head out of your ass.*

"Interesting," Josh said flatly, releasing my hand. "I was unaware Emma was engaged. I don't think anyone knew, including her father before his... Emma, we really need to talk. And you should probably sit down."

"Just tell me what you need to say," she snapped.

Now I was concerned. She didn't like this prick, and the way she'd pulled me in—all of my protective instincts were kicking in. "Go on," I urged.

Josh almost rolled his eyes. "Have you even met her family?"

"Hunter is my best kept secret," Emma said smoothly. "And our engagement is new."

"*Very* new," I agreed with a smile. "We had the most beautiful proposal last night, actually. The sun was setting just right, the sky the color of ripe peaches. Got down on one knee, popped the question, and my future wife said yes. Happiest day of our lives yet."

"You proposed to Emma Madden on a Thursday?"

I was torn between laughing and punching him. "Yeah. And?"

His eyes flickered from me back to Emma. "Never pictured you with someone so..."

"Handsome?" Emma smiled, leaning into me.

Who the hell was this guy? Emma was uncomfortable and stiff, but not because of me. I'd never seen her like this with anyone before.

"Yep. Her handsome future husband. What was your name again?" I asked. "Can't remember it."

His cheeks turned crimson, brows drawing together. "Joshua. I'm here on behalf of—"

"Wow, would you look at the time?" Emma interrupted. "Hunter and I have an appointment to get to, so we'll have to do this another time Josh."

"Emma, I need to talk to you. It's fairly urgent and I'm not leaving until we talk. Preferably somewhere private—"

"Not gonna happen," I said, tightening my grip on her. Was she shaking? Fuck, she was actually shaking. My temper boiled hotter. "Emma and I need to get to our naked yoga class, so this will have to continue another time."

"Naked... yoga? But Emma hates yoga."

"It's not the type of naked yoga you're thinking about, bud." I made sure to draw out my Texan accent.

I wasn't sure which was better. The way his face contorted or the way Emma had to physically withhold a snort.

"Now, if you'll excuse us, you can send her an email to schedule a meeting. Goodbye, farewell."

I started to close the door, but the tip of his shoe jammed forward. *Who the fuck does he think he is?*

"Emma, your father is dead."

I was about to slam the door hard enough to break his foot, but stopped short. Emma went still next to me, her eyes widening as the door slowly swung back open.

"What?" she whispered.

Josh let out a slow breath. "He's dead. He passed away yesterday."

"*Wh-What?* How? How did he die?"

"They aren't sure yet," he said gravely.

"*Why* didn't anyone call me?"

"You have everyone's phone numbers blocked. And clearly you've been ignoring your email. I hopped on the first flight I could so I could tell you in person."

Jesus christ. This was not what I'd expected to be pulled into. And what kind of family *emails* about someone's death?

I took a step closer to Emma, unsure of what to do. Her eyes were wide, a haunted expression overtaking her pretty face that twisted every part of me with worry. I'd never seen her like this.

"Can I come in now?" Josh asked.

"No," she whispered. She swallowed hard, cleared her throat, and then smoothed her hands down her sides. "No, you need to go. Thank you for flying out to tell me. I'll handle the rest."

"Emma, there's other urgent business, though. Contracts and—"

"She said to leave," I growled. "You just told her that her dad is dead. Contracts can come later."

I started to shut the door, but he shoved at it. I opened it just a smidge, enough to give him a glimmer of hope—then shoved him so hard his expensive suited ass hit the porch. I slammed the front door and locked it.

"Who the fuck does that asshole think he is?" I hissed.

Emma blew out a breath and leaned against the wall. I immediately sucked in a breath, cooling my temper.

"Emma, I am so sorry. Are you okay, princess?"

"God, don't call me that, please," she rasped, doubling over. "Josh used to call me that and I hate it. I *hate* it. I hate being called princess. I'm not the type of girl who needs saving. If anything, I'm a motherfucking queen."

Fuck. "I'm sorry, I won't say it again. Emma, I need to know if I need to go kill that guy, or make you a new coffee, or... I don't even know."

"Can you check if he's gone?"

I immediately leaned over and peeked out the window, watching as a very nice Lexus pulled away from the house. I made a mental note of the make and model. "He's gone."

"Then a coffee would be great. Oh god, I told him you were my boyfriend. Fuck—you told him you were my *fiancé*."

"I did." I slipped my hands in my pocket, rocking on my feet for a moment. "Emma, do you need to sit down? Do you need me to call Haley or Sarah or Alice?"

"No."

Okay, then.

She dragged in a breath, her shoulders sinking. I found myself briefly entranced by the golden shimmer on her eyelids, before snapping myself out of it. I didn't know what to do. "Emma..." I trailed off.

"I'm not telling you shit."

Spell broken. "No? But I'm your fiancé."

"Fuck off," she seethed. "Dammit. Dammit, this is bad. Give me a minute to think, please."

Bad felt like the understatement of the century. If someone told me one of my parents died, I wouldn't be able to breathe or stand. But Emma stood there, shaking her head like this was just an inconvenience.

"What can I do right now to help you?" I asked.

"You can clean up the broken glass and the spilled coffee."

"Okay." I studied her a moment longer and then went to the kitchen to continue searching for cleaning supplies. Once I'd gathered everything, I took it to the living room.

About ten minutes later, everything was cleaned up, but

Emma hadn't spoken a word. Instead, she stared out the front window, dark brows drawn together.

Why wasn't she crying? Or doing *something*? I'd never seen anything render this woman speechless, and it worried me.

Emma's phone buzzed on the coffee table. She turned around and grabbed it, sighing as she checked the message. "Dammit."

"I'm gonna make you another coffee," I said warily.

Her expression softened for a split second. "Thanks."

"But then I'm texting Haley."

"No, no, don't do that," she blurted out.

I went back to the kitchen and opened up every cabinet until I found the cups. Emma had reorganized things in a way that took me a moment to understand, but then I realized it was by color, not dish size. I had to admit, I liked how she'd changed things in the little house. It was colorful, alive, and full of warmth, and far more homier than my cabin on the farm.

Being here made me realize how much of a man cave I'd turned my place into.

I made us each an iced coffee and sat back down on the couch. "Where'd Donnie go?" I asked, glancing around for the little rat. He was usually glued to Emma's side if he wasn't in a slice of sun.

"He's upstairs," she said. "Okay. Hunter, I can't believe I'm saying this, but we need to convince everyone we're engaged now. Every family member and friend. Even Haley. Even your brothers."

"What?" *Had she lost her mind?* I stared at her, dumbfounded.

She rubbed her temples before hissing at me. "Why the hell did you tell him I was your fiancé?"

"You told him I was your boyfriend. I was rolling with it.

Also, I think there are more serious things to be concerned about?"

"Okay, well you rolled a little too fast and hard." She completely ignored my last question.

I held out the coffee. She sighed and reluctantly took it, settling down on the opposite side of the couch. She pulled her knees up, able to tuck in with ease, whereas my legs were too fucking long for such a seating arrangement.

"Are you sure you're okay, darlin'?" I asked, despite knowing how stupid the question was.

A frustrated groan peeled from her lips. "If you have to use a nickname for me, I want to pick it out. No princess. No darling."

Still ignoring the question about if she was okay. "What do you want me to call you?"

She sipped coffee through the straw, her cheeks hollowing in a way that brought dirty thoughts front and center. "I'll think about it."

We were still ignoring the death of her father, apparently, and I was going with it. "So who was that Josh guy?" I asked.

"What I'm about to tell you, you can't repeat to anyone. No one, Hunter. Not a single soul."

"Not even Haley?" I asked. "She's your best friend."

"She is." Emma turned grim. "So are Sarah and Alice. But there are things they don't know about me, that I don't want them to know."

"Such as?" I fished. I took a sip of coffee and hummed. It was good.

How crazy was I to think about how nice it would be to do this every morning? A house that smelled like *her*, iced coffee, sitting on the sofa...

Don't think about her on your lap again. Focus, caveman, focus.

Emma sighed and glanced at her phone, shaking her head. "I just got a text from Josh. He's staying in Citrus Cove until we can meet to go over contracts and inheritance and papers. *Fuck me*, this is so annoying. Why would they send him, of all people? My dad owns a computer chip company in California, and I don't speak to him or the rest of my family, except for when I have to. We haven't gotten along for a long time."

I didn't point out that she was still speaking about him like he was alive.

The thing was, I knew her dad owned the company thanks to the weird stalker tendencies Emma had brought out in me. I also knew she wasn't close with him, but didn't realize how severe it was until now.

Her head fell back against the cushion. "God, this sucks. I never wanted to see him again."

"Your father?" I choked on a sip of coffee and fought for my life to clear my throat.

"No, of course not... I should make you sign an NDA or something."

"Emma," I said, looking directly at her. "I'm not telling anyone. Contrary to your belief, I'm not a bad guy. I can help."

She studied me intensely. A strand of hair curled, framing her heart-shaped face. Her cheeks were still flushed, but she was calmer now. "First—will you *please* keep pretending to be my fiancé until I sort everything out?"

Was I really going to do this? Deceive everyone? Make them believe Emma was mine? I thought about it. My entire family prided themselves on honesty. Lies never went over well, no matter how small.

When it came to Emma, they were all protective too. She didn't have the Harlow name, but she had the Harlow squad in her corner. If we lied about this, it would complicate everything.

The other part of this was that I was breaking the rule I'd given myself when she moved to Citrus Cove.

Emma was off limits. She was Haley's best friend. She was loved by all. She wasn't someone I should try anything with in case things went badly.

Even *pretending* to date came dangerously close to breaking that rule.

Emma wouldn't ask me to do this unless she was desperate, though. She'd just learned her father was dead. She was a woman in need of support and how could I tell her no?

Every muscle tensed as I thought about the jackass who'd tried to cram his foot in the door. The fucker was lucky I didn't break his foot.

This was why Emma was a problem. The thought of someone trying to do that to her door without me here made me want to bury him somewhere in the vineyard.

"I thought you hated me," I said.

"I do. But I can't go back now. Josh thinks we're engaged."

"You want me to lie to everyone we love..."

"Yes." Her lip quivered.

Damn it. I raked my fingers through my hair. We were trapped in a bubble, and any wrong word could pop it.

"What happens afterward?" I asked.

"After what?"

"After the ruse is up? Unless you intend to actually marry me." I wasn't even teasing her, even though I knew that's how she'd take it.

She shook her head. "We just tell them the truth, and they'll move on with their lives. I need the buffer while Josh is here. I know it's a lot to ask, but I really need some time to deal with him."

And to grieve your father's death? I mulled it over. We both knew that's not how our friends and family would react once they found out the truth.

But I really wasn't the type of guy to leave a woman in distress.

I was a gentleman, right?

"Are you sure you don't want me to call anyone?" I asked. "Emma, this is... this is a lot to be thrown at you on a Friday morning. If you need me to call Haley, Alice, Sarah, or Honey—"

"I don't want you to tell a single soul about this."

I winced. It was a big ask.

"They'll be like bloodhounds," I said.

"I know. We'll keep it simple."

"They're going to think we've lost our minds."

"I know. Hunter, I know it's a lot."

Dammit. "Fine," I breathed out. "I'll do this under one condition."

"What condition?"

"You tell me everything. And don't spare the details. I need to know what I'm dealing with," I said. "So clear your schedule for today, and I'll text Pops to let him know I won't be making it into the farm. The guys can handle it."

"Deal."

She held out her hand. I took it and fought a smile when her grip tightened and she gave me a very firm shake.

"Deal," I said, releasing her. "Alright, wifey. Tell me what I need to know."

"*Wifey* is out of the question."

"Baby girl?"

Her cheeks turned almost as pink as the paint on her house. "No..." she giggled, her eyes tearing up.

Fuck. I leaned forward slightly, expecting her to start crying. I could handle her tears, right? Rules be damned, if she started crying, I'd be there for her. This entire situation was fucked.

It didn't happen. Instead she cleared her throat, her expression dropping back to unreadable. But her leg was bouncing up and down constantly, her fingers drumming on her thighs.

Keeping her distracted seemed like the right thing to do. I thought about nicknames again, and offered the first one that came to mind. "Taser?" I asked.

Her eyes darkened and she shook her head. "No. Are you ever gonna let that go?"

"No, I take personal enjoyment out of torturing you about it," I said. "To this day, I've never been tased by anyone else for giving roadside assistance."

Emma let out a soft laugh and tilted her head, as if seeing me in a new light.

The rule. Remember the rule. You want her to hate you. You want her to stay at arm's length.

"You've never told anyone," she said. "I know you didn't, or they would have asked me."

She was right, I never did. That night was still a fever dream in my mind. I took a sip of coffee before carefully setting it down on a coaster shaped like a pink flower.

I moved closer to her than we'd ever sat before. Her eyes were beautiful. A mesmerizing hazel, a kaleidoscope of greens and blues. I fought the temptation to cup her face so I could study the flecks of gold in there, too.

"How about my own personal hell?" I teased.

"Better." She smirked.

"Nah, doesn't have the right ring to it."

She *almost* laughed, but then it seemed to hit both of us that we were enjoying each other's presence. I leaned back and cleared my throat.

"Alright, quit stalling. Spill."

"I wasn't stalling."

"Emma," I groaned. "*Please*."

"Okay. I guess I should start from the beginning. The first thing to know is that Josh is on the advisory board for my dad's company..."

The suit made more sense now.

"And he's also my ex-husband."

CHAPTER FIVE

emma

WHEN I IMAGINED TELLING someone about all of my dirty little secrets, I never thought that someone would be Hunter Harlow.

But he listened without interrupting, even as his face turned three shades of pale and then three shades of red.

"When I was twenty, Josh and I got married. He was the guy my dad had approved of, and they expected him to rise up fast in the company. I was supposed to go to college and get a degree and eventually do the same thing, but that wasn't what I wanted. I was steamrolled by their expectations at the time, so I ended up going through with it and marrying Josh."

I relaxed into the couch, thinking about those fourteen months. I'd been a completely different girl then. Divorcing him and moving across the country was the best thing I could have ever done for myself, even if it was the hardest decision I'd ever made.

But then I met Haley. The two of us had become fast friends and she'd seen me go through my fair share of bad relationships. She was there with me through ups and downs. Now here I was, living in Citrus Cove with my own house and life.

Josh, my father, the rest of the family—none of them could take this away from me. My stomach twisted at the thought of my father. I did what I did best, and shoved every single emotion down, smothering it just like he'd taught me to do.

The pain radiated through my entire body for a split second and then evaporated as I focused on Hunter. Focused on the way he listened, on his rich brown eyes and the rough stubble along his jaw. I knew he had to be judging me right now for not having a breakdown. He'd never understand why I wasn't crying, right?

I picked at the hem of my shirt, looking down at a loose thread as I spoke. "It was awful. I used to be such a pushover. It was just how I was raised. And then after my sister died, I blamed myself."

Hunter cleared his throat. "I'm sorry," he said gently. He sounded genuine. He sounded the way I'd heard him talk to everyone else in our lives. "I can't imagine a loss like that."

My hand smoothed the ache in my chest. I missed Evelyn. Every year around the anniversary of her death, I was emotionally wrecked for a few days. Then it would pass, and I'd go back to living my life as normally as I could. It didn't matter that many years had gone by, there were moments where the grief felt fresh.

I knew she'd be proud that I'd taken charge of my life.

Now that my dad was dead, though, it was bringing up all the sadness I'd felt over my sister. Death felt so final. When was the last time I'd even seen my dad? It had been years.

"It was a long time ago," I murmured. "I miss her. She was the only family member I was ever close with. My dad tried really hard to divide us, but it never stuck. When she died, he blamed me, though."

He shook his head. "I don't know how she died, but I know it wasn't your fault. I'm sorry for ever calling you an only child. There's nothing wrong with being an only child, I was being a jackass."

"Thank you." He'd always said it as a way to pick a fight with me, and I'd always taken the bait even though I knew he wasn't aware of Evelyn. Still, I appreciated the apology. "You didn't know."

"I never asked," he said firmly. He rubbed the back of his neck. "And I should have. I'm sorry, Emma."

"I forgive you," I said, nudging him with my foot. I forced a playful smile. "Don't go getting soft on me. We don't like each other, remember?"

Something flashed in those deep brown eyes that I couldn't quite put my finger on. It was gone in a blink, and he offered a coy smile. "So how does pretending to date me help this? And why would they send your ex-husband to tell you?"

I wasn't entirely sure. The fact that he didn't even know how Michael Madden died worried me. If my dad passed yesterday, then it was entirely possible that Josh had just hopped on a plane, like he'd said. But then again, he'd also said we should get remarried. The timing felt gross to me. "Maybe they assumed I wouldn't immediately slam the door in his face. They all know I'm not close with my stepmom, so it makes more sense that he'd tell me, I guess." I shook my head bitterly. "What a bastard. Acting like we should get remarried. And that I'd been *allowed* my fun."

His brows drew together and he stiffened. "What the fuck? He said that to you? I'm gonna kill the guy."

Despite everything, Hunter managed to make me laugh. "No, no killing. We're better than he is."

He was amused. "Now it's *we*, huh?"

Ugh. I let out a groan and covered my face. This was a

nightmare. "Shut up. My god, the fact that it's *you* of all people I'm having to pretend with."

"I'm a good actor," Hunter said quickly, his lips tugging with the type of confidence I only ever saw on a man who knew what he was doing. "And a good kisser."

I wrinkled my nose. I didn't want to think about kissing him.

"What? You think the family will believe us if we don't kiss?"

Fuck. He had a point.

I didn't even know what kind of a boyfriend Hunter would be, but he *was* a Harlow. If I knew anything about the Harlows, it was that all of them were swoony as fuck when they were in love.

Which would be perfect for driving Josh absolutely insane. He deserved it, after the hell of our marriage. And the audacity of showing up on my doorstep to tell me my time was up, in the same breath that he told me my father was dead.

Distract me, distract me, distract me.

Hunter ran his fingers through his hair. Silver glinted at the sides, just a few stray strands that were sexier than I cared to admit. "So... while Josh is here, we'll pretend to be engaged."

I nodded. "That's the idea. But he's smart. Everyone will really have to believe it."

"I don't know, Emma. I don't know if this is a good idea."

It was the only idea I had. If Josh was going to stick around, then I wanted it to be clear I was off-limits. Hunter would be a good, buff, and tough shield. It would have been easier if he hadn't told Josh he was my fiancé, though. "If you don't want to, no pressure," I said. "I don't want to force you into this. And don't feel like you have to because my father is dead."

He winced. "I... Are you sure you're okay?"

"I'm fine," I lied. It was an easy lie, too. It was one I'd said so many times in my life, I'd lost count. "We weren't close. Clearly. This is no different than reading in the news about some random actor or politician dying."

He pressed his lips together. We both knew it was a lot different, but he let it go anyway. "Okay, then. If you need anything, let me know. But, I suppose I'll go along with the charade." He exhaled and readjusted the way he was sitting. "Will Josh talk to anyone else? Shouldn't we just meet with him soon and send him away?"

It was complicated. Way more complicated than that. Because Hunter said we were engaged, and that meant he was probably on the phone with the lawyers already. Marriage in the Madden family was a huge ordeal. Even if my father was dead, there would be plenty of complications.

None of this was a good thing.

The last thing I wanted was for my stepmom to show up. The best scenario was that Josh left, the lawyers called me to wrap everything up, and I never had to deal with her or Josh again.

I needed to think about the company and what I wanted to do with it. Assuming it was left to me.

"We should be prepared for anything," I said. "Hopefully he'll take the hint that I want nothing to do with him and leave."

"Is Josh dangerous?"

I pressed my lips together. "Not like Thomas Connor-level dangerous."

Hunter crossed his arms. "But he *is* dangerous."

"Our divorce didn't go well. After the papers were signed, I took off to Baltimore. He stayed in Sacramento and became my dad's right-hand man. I'm pretty sure everyone still thinks the reason we divorced is because I was being stupid and unreasonable. It wasn't long after I left him that I met Haley."

"Would he try to hurt you?" Hunter asked patiently.

"I don't think so." The truth was, I wasn't entirely sure. I didn't know him anymore. But for the moment, everything seemed to be fine. "He slapped me once, and then I divorced him almost immediately after. That was years ago. And well, he's an asshole, but I can't see him delivering the type of news he just did *and* trying to kill me."

"Okay." Hunter clapped his hands on his thighs and stood up.

"Where are you going?" I asked. "We still have festival planning to do."

"Do we really have festival planning to do?" He asked. "We're a month out and pretty much everything is on autopilot from here out. There are some loose ends to tie up, but I'm not sure it'll take both of us. Although your list was good."

I shook my head, exasperated. "We should at least go over it. Where are you running off to?"

"What do you mean? I'm going to go run the fucker out of town." He headed toward the kitchen with his coffee cup. "Fuck this guy, Emma. I don't want him here if he's caused you that much trouble."

Oh god. "*Hunter.*" I jumped up and followed him, stopping in the doorway as he put his cup in the sink and began to wash it. "Just put it in the dishwasher. Also, you're not running him out of town. You sound ridiculous."

"I have my ways," he said as he put the cup away, his voice strained. "Not my first rodeo."

"I don't need you to defend me," I said. "I just need you to pretend to be my pretty, small-town husband. That's it. Josh just needs to believe I'm firmly taken and realize I don't want anything to do with him, then he'll leave. Once we take care of whatever contract bullshit there is, once it's over, everything should be fine."

Hunter closed the distance between us in two long strides. "Should have chosen a different partner then, sparks."

Sparks. Butterflies erupted in my stomach as he *lifted* me out of his way and strolled out the front door.

Damn his long legs. I went after him, halting on the porch. "Hunter Harlow, I need you to behave."

He paused on the second step and sighed, turning around to look at me. "I can make him leave, Emma. I don't like the idea of you feeling threatened while you're at home. Not after this news."

"If you do that, it will make my life harder," I said. "The lawyers will send someone down here to try to bribe you to break the engagement. I just need you to be my fiancé until I find out what papers Josh is talking about. I'm sure he'll leave on his own. Once he does, we can call off the engagement and everything can go back to being sunshine and fucking rainbows."

Hunter blew out a breath, tipping his head back to look at the sky. It smelled like rain outside, even though there weren't any clouds above us.

He came back up on the step, his hands on his hips. "I have three other conditions for this."

"You already struck a deal," I argued.

"We didn't seal it."

"We *shook* hands!" I protested.

He surprised me by cupping my face. I went still, my eyes widening. "One, I need you to promise you will call me if he shows up unannounced. Two, I need you to promise me you will not schedule a meeting with him alone." He leaned in so close, I thought he was going to kiss me. *Is he going to kiss me?!* "Three, when we're not pretending to be engaged, I need you to stay as far away from me as you possibly can. Unless you have an emergency, of course. Otherwise, I want nothing to do with you."

My mouth fell open and he released me, taking the warmth with him. He turned on the heel of his boots and stormed down the steps, crossing the lawn to his truck.

"Send me the spreadsheet for the festival I saw on your laptop," he called. "I'll fill in some things. Otherwise, I think we're set there. And let me know when we're gonna start telling people."

"Are you going to keep my secrets?" I yelled.

"Yes, goddammit."

"Then where the hell are you going?" I called.

"To buy a fake ring."

Thunder rumbled in the distance as he got into his truck and drove off, leaving me speechless.

What the fuck? What the hell was I going to do? I was in absolute shock.

And there was no way he'd pick out a good ring. Right?

Fuck, fuck, fuckity fuck. Everything was falling apart. Fear rose up like a tidal wave, soaking my muscles in tension. All the things I'd never told the people closest to me, along with the guilt that came along with it, weighed heavily on my shoulders.

I'd worked so hard to become the person I was now. I was independent, smart, driven. I didn't need a man, contrary to Michael Madden's belief. I didn't need anything from anyone.

Haley was going to kill me when she found out the truth.

I could call Josh and tell him I lied to him about Hunter. That would be easier right? My ego would take a hit. He'd hold it over me forever. Hell, he'd probably try to blackmail me.

I mulled it over, but...

The way Hunter had put him in his place was beyond satisfying. I'd been wanting someone to do that for ages. Josh was accustomed to everyone in the room kissing his ass, not throwing him out on it.

So for now, we'd keep the ruse.

Even if Hunter was definitely going to drive me insane. Then again, maybe this was the distraction I needed.

I held my breath and waited for the tears to fall.

But they didn't.

Maybe I was broken.

I blew out a breath and stepped back inside, closing the door and locking it behind me. I heard a whine upstairs and cursed, rushing into the office to let out Donnie.

"Sorry, sorry," I said. "I can't believe you cuddled that man knowing he's my greatest enemy. How dare you."

Donnie gave me a slow, unbothered blink.

"Don't give me that look. Let's go outside before it rains."

'Outside' was one of the words he knew well. His nails clicked over the hardwoods as he trotted downstairs. I followed him to the backdoor and let him out into the yard I'd fenced in.

All the renovations I'd done to this house had really improved it. On my new back porch was a rocking chair, like a real southern gal, and even some potted plants. Although they were struggling, they were also still alive, so I considered that a win.

Thunder shook the house this time, the air heavy and still.

It was all too much for one day. I mentally replayed the conversation with Joshua. I should have kicked him in the balls. Hell, I should have kicked him in the balls *and* broken his nose. I *should* have told him to fuck all the way off.

Instead I'd dragged Hunter into Madden drama, which wasn't going to be good for anyone.

He'd give my father a stroke if he wasn't already dead.

"Fuck," I wheezed, letting out a broken laugh.

I waited for the tears again. But, nope. They weren't coming.

Mentally I scolded myself and rolled my shoulders, trying to not spiral.

Once Donnie finished his business, he came back inside and I threw myself on the couch with a groan. It went from sprinkling to a downpour within a matter of seconds as I flipped on the TV, grabbed my laptop, and got comfy.

I ended up staring at the screen as my thoughts went haywire.

Was I losing it or had Hunter almost kissed me? I'd definitely sat on his junk. His very hard, very large junk. I'd called him the biggest dick in town and now that had a whole new meaning to it.

Then he'd told me to stay far away.

Unfortunately for him, I wasn't going to make his life easy.

CHAPTER SIX
hunter

I'D TOLD Emma I was leaving to buy a ring, but I wasn't just yet. First, I had to get a security camera system for her house.

I beelined through Lowe's, straight to the home security section, shaking my head as I thought about the predicament we'd put ourselves in. I still felt inclined to tell Haley that Emma needed her, but I had to trust Emma to call her.

When Sarah and the boys moved in with Colt and Sammy, we'd uninstalled the security system since Emma insisted she didn't need it. I'd disagreed—of course—but was overruled.

They all should have listened to me, dammit. This was the perfect reason why.

I'd make this Josh guy leave. The fact that he'd made a comment about them needing to get remarried in the same breath as announcing her father's death infuriated me. Even with our rocky history, I needed to make sure Emma was safe.

In some ways, I was probably worse than him. The obsession was sinking in and I was trying to shake it free. This was why I didn't date unless it was casual, but nothing about this arrangement felt *casual* with her.

Sparks. It was the perfect nickname for her. Not only because she'd tased me the first time we'd met, but also because she sparked something inside of me that I'd never felt before.

"Hunter?"

The voice was somewhat familiar. I turned around and saw the face of a woman I recognized, but couldn't put a name to. "Uh..."

"It's Louise," she said with a broad smile. "Remember me?"

Oh yeah. Vaguely.

I'd gone to high school with her and we reconnected briefly last year. And by briefly, I meant we had a one night stand, she started acting a little strange, and I told her I wasn't interested in anything further. I was honest about it, but she still seemed to pop up sometimes. Now, I went out of my way to avoid her.

"Yes," I said quickly. "I remember. Nice to see you, Louise."

I ducked down an aisle with plumbing fixtures and realized she was following me. I glanced over at her again.

"Did you need something?" I asked bluntly. I picked up my strides, heading to the end of an aisle and looping around to the one with cameras.

She struggled to keep up. "Just wondering if you're seeing anyone, I guess. I know it's been awhile but—"

"I am actually," I said. "We're pretty serious too. Engaged."

"*Engaged?*"

Fuck.

"Oh, hey Hunter." I turned around to see Cam standing behind a blue shopping cart with a birdhouse, three huge bags of birdseed, paint, and other random items in it.

What was it—national go to the hardware store day? Why the hell was everyone here?

Sometimes I hated living in a small town.

Cam raised a brow, his eyes sliding to the wall of cameras.

Dammit. Panic rolled through me at the thought of lying straight to his face. I forgot about Louise standing there and the way she was staring at me like she'd seen a ghost.

For a moment, I thought about telling him what had happened with Emma, but I promised to keep her secrets.

I'd told her I'd go along with this fake engagement.

For better or worse, right?

"I thought you had enough of these," Cam teased as he approached. "Also, I thought you were meeting with Emma today? Or did you already meet up?"

I flexed my hands, annoyed. "Yeah. I met with her." *I met with her, she found out her dad died, and now we're engaged because her ex-husband is an asshole.*

He walked around the shopping cart and braced one hand on the end, the other on his hip. "What's wrong?"

"Nothing." I glanced over at Louise and she gave a partial wave, crossing her arms and wandering down the aisle a few feet, but still within earshot.

Cam snorted. "You can't lie to me."

Oh, I definitely could.

I just hoped Emma was ready for all the consequences of this ruse.

Here we go. I couldn't believe I was going along with this. "Emma and I are engaged. I'm buying her a home security system."

"What?" Cam blurted out. He barked a hard laugh and then his expression warped with confusion when I didn't laugh with him. His skin started to flush red, his blue eyes sharpening into two daggers. "Wait. You're not serious."

"I am," I said.

"No," Cam said. His knuckles whitened as he gripped the edge of the shopping cart harder. "No, you're not. What the fuck do you mean you're *engaged*? You aren't even dating. You can't even stand each other."

"Well, things happen. We're together. Engaged," I said shortly. "Getting married." Fuck, this was a disaster.

"But Emma hates you."

"Not as much as you think." He was going to kill me. They were all going to kill me, and rightfully so. This was exactly why I'd made sure to keep Emma at arm's length. Exactly why I'd gone out of my way to stay on her shit list for three years. "We've been... dating behind everyone's backs."

There was a flicker of hurt there, and I felt the guilt that followed. I never lied about things like this, not to Cam. We had our differences, but he was my brother, and I loved him.

"You're lying," he whispered.

"I'm not," I said. "I'm going out to buy the ring after this."

He stared at me for a moment and I saw the temper flare up. Shit, I didn't want to fist fight my brother in the middle of a Lowe's.

Cam moved fast though, grabbing a bag of birdseed and smacking me with it in the gut. I grunted as the weight of it knocked the breath out of me. The bag ripped open and seeds scattered across the aisle. Cam lunged forward, throwing the first punch. I let him hit me in the jaw because I felt like I deserved it. But then I grabbed his shirt, and we tumbled into the shelves, knocking shit to the floor.

"Goddammit," he snarled, punching me in the stomach.

My boots slipped over the seed and I fought to remain on my feet. The two of us nearly toppled to the floor. I grunted and landed a punch back, only to hear a shout down the aisle.

A couple of strangers ran up and pried us apart. I shoved them away and cursed under my breath, wiping blood from my nose as I stepped back from Cam.

He jabbed a finger at me. "Family meeting. Half an hour. If

you're not on my doorstep, I'm going to slash the tires of the vine-trimmer."

I scoffed as he wheeled his shopping cart around and stalked off, shaking his head.

"Don't tell Haley yet!" I shouted.

"I'm fucking telling her!" he yelled without looking back.

I breathed out, shaking my head furiously. Dammit, this was already a mess. I shouldn't have told Cam. I could have probably made sure no one knew about this situation at all if I would have kept my damn mouth shut.

Hindsight was twenty-twenty, but there was no going back now.

I ignored the sidelong glances and mumbles from other people in the store. My jaw ached as I quickly grabbed a camera set off the floor and headed to the front.

Cam shot me a dirty look as we both went through the self-check out, and headed for the door. It was pouring rain outside, but I still followed him to his truck. Thankfully, I almost always wore boots, so running through the puddles didn't get my socks wet.

"Listen," I said, trying to keep up with him. The fucker could move faster than me sometimes. "Cam, goddammit."

He spun around. Rain soaked the two of us as he shook his head angrily. "What the *fuck*, Hunter? Why would you keep that a secret? Emma is already part of our family."

I blurted out the only thing that would soften his anger. "I love her."

His eyes grew wide and his mouth fell open, but no words came out.

"Call off the family meeting," I pleaded. "If you haven't sent the text out already, don't. Emma and I want the space to tell everyone on our terms."

"This is *insane*," he sputtered. "This is the craziest shit I've ever heard, Hunter. And I've heard some crazy shit. I've been through some crazy shit. But this takes the cake."

I clenched my jaw. "Are we gonna keep standing out in the rain, or what?"

He threw up his hands, looking around the parking lot. Water rolled down his face as he sighed. He scrubbed the scruff along his jaw and shook his head. "Fuck. Alright. Haley is at Sarah's right now. Come over so we can talk."

"Alright," I said, relaxing a fraction. At the end of the day, I knew Cam, and wasn't surprised he was giving me a chance to talk first. "I'll meet you there."

"Yeah, yeah." He shook his head as he got in his truck.

I crossed the parking lot and slid into the seat drenched, putting the bag of cameras on the floorboard. I blew out a breath and decided to text Emma.

Me: Ran into Cam. Told him we're engaged. Not happy.

Emma: Damn, that was fast. Does Haley know?

Me: I don't think so. Not yet... I'll keep you updated. We should probably get our story straight.

Emma: Keep it simple. No need to make this bigger than it needs to be. We just need to do this while Josh is here and then it's over.

Me: Great.

She sent back a thumbs-up and I smiled like an idiot. It wasn't even flirting, but...

We were texting. Texting wasn't breaking my rule, was it?

Cam honked at me and I sighed, starting up my truck. I flipped the windshield wipers to the highest setting and slowly backed out, following him over to his house. The weather made for a slow drive, but eventually we both parked in his driveway. I hopped out and hurried inside behind him.

"Boots off," he muttered. "I'll grab an extra T-shirt and jeans."

"Thanks."

He ran upstairs as I kicked off my boots. I should have known that telling him would mean I'd end up here, but maybe it was for the best. Maybe I could get ring advice from him.

Ideally, I could ask Haley...

I had to remember this was all fake. It wasn't like I could drop a lot of money on a ring for Emma to sell this lie. Well, I could—but did I want to? We were rushing into it so fast, my head was spinning.

Cam came back downstairs a few minutes later, shoved a set of clothes in my hands, and stalked towards the kitchen with tense shoulders. I used the guest restroom to change, and found him with a bottle of whiskey and two glasses.

"You have to tell me everything," he said. "The only reason I'm not calling Haley right now is because I'm assuming Emma wants to tell her, and I'm not ruining that."

"There's not much to tell," I said simply.

He slid a glass to me. "Not good enough. Emma is Haley's best friend, she's like a sister to me. You're lucky I didn't knock you the fuck out."

"First of all, you could fucking try."

He narrowed his eyes on me. "Do you want to test that theory?"

Damn, he was really mad. I'd underestimated how big of a deal this would be to everyone.

They'd be devastated when we broke it off.

I buried the guilt under a gulp of whiskey. "Alright," I exhaled, my throat burning. "We've been dating for a few months. We've kept it quiet because we knew everyone would be up in our business."

"But she hates you," Cam said. "And you hate her. She's been here for almost three years and I've never seen the two of you interact in a positive way. Even at holidays, the two of you stay as far away from each other as possible. Hell, even Davy and Jake talk about the two of you like you're mortal enemies. Jake literally drew a comic where you were Godzilla and she was Mothra and you were fighting."

I chuckled. Jake was pretty damn funny. "It was easier to keep it up while we figured things out," I said.

He shook his head, still not buying it. "I don't know man. Are the two of you in trouble? Is there something wrong?"

"Nothing's wrong," I lied. "We just realized we couldn't keep it a secret anymore... because of the festival. And Colt suggesting we work together."

Cam pressed his lips together silently.

Fuck, was he even believing a single word? "We hooked up at your wedding."

His mouth fell open. "That's more than *a few* months ago! Are you serious?"

"Yeah. Had a one night stand. Didn't talk about it for a while. Then hooked back up."

"Is that why all her dates fail?"

"I'm certainly the reason for that." It felt good to get that off my chest, even if it wasn't the whole truth.

"Damn. This is crazy. Sammy, Colt, and Sarah were a surprise but this is like... This is something else. I really thought the two of you would never like each other. We all did. I can't believe you lied to all of us."

I sighed. "I'm sorry, Cam. You know I've always been private about who I date."

"No, you just don't date," Cam snapped, leaning over the counter. He studied me with a sour expression. "And I know that's a fact. You only do casual hookups. If you treat Emma this way, I will be bound by my wedding vows to Haley to bury you for hurting her best friend."

"I won't hurt her," I said. "I just want her to be safe and happy. Hence buying cameras."

"I thought Emma didn't want cameras around," Cam said. "We had a whole conversation about it."

"She changed her mind."

"Hmm."

"Look," I growled. "You can disapprove all you want, but this is happening. Now, are you gonna help me pick out a ring?"

"I thought you proposed already? Please don't fucking tell me you proposed to *Emma* without a ring. There's no way she said yes, unless you have her under a spell."

My jaw set. "She said yes."

Cam scrubbed his face. "This is the craziest shit I've ever heard. Yeah, brother, I'll help you pick out a ring. Better yet, we should ask Haley. Or Alice. Or Sarah. Oh god, they're going to be livid."

"Do you think Sammy will try to punch me, too?" I teased.

"I hope he fucking does. You deserve it. This is a big deal. This changes a lot."

"Like what?" I asked.

"Everything, Hunter. Why are you being so fucking annoying about this?"

"I said I love her. What else do you need?"

Cam scowled. "This type of thing isn't just about love. I love Haley more than anyone else. But sometimes, I have to be her friend, sometimes I have to be able to talk things out, even when things are hard. She's seen me at my worst. She's literally brought me wipes for my ass after food poisoning because I shit so much. I've held her hair while she projectile vomited all over the place. It's knowing we can both fart in bed and then laugh about it later, before having mind-blowing sex."

"Okay, noted. I didn't need to know all of that, though."

Cam sighed. "My point is, I don't see how this will work. Why get engaged if you didn't even pick her out a ring first? If you didn't even tell your family about the woman you want to spend the rest of your life with? Are you ready for that kind of relationship when you've never dated someone for more than three months? Oh my god, wait. Did you get her pregnant?"

I glowered. "Okay, now maybe I should punch you."

"Why else would this be happening so fast?!"

"We live in a modern era, Cam. Plan B is a thing," I said. "No, Emma isn't pregnant. And no, we haven't done this the traditional way."

Dammit, I was really fighting for my life.

Cam shook his head and poured us each another glass. "Okay. Well. Congrats."

"Now you're being a dick," I said. "You didn't even mean that."

"I have a hard time meaning it when I've never even seen the two of you smile at each other."

"We do more than smiling."

"Stabbing, too?"

I fought a laugh. "I never told you about the first night Emma and I met."

He cocked his head, clearly interested now. "No, you didn't. Do go on."

"Okay, well. I was driving down the old country road. It was almost midnight. I see a sports car pulled over on the shoulder, clearly stranded. I pull over to help, as usual. I get out and ask her if she's okay, she says she ran out of gas. We didn't recognize each other. So I go to get gas out of the back of my truck, and she *pulls her stun gun on me*."

Cam's shoulders relaxed and he chuckled. "Yeah, that sounds like her."

"So I'm laying there on the ground, thinking what the fuck

just happened? She runs up and we start bickering. Then we each realized who the other was."

"Damn. So then what?"

So then I became super obsessed with your wife's best friend. "So then I drove her to Sarah's house. She's been unforgettable ever since."

My brother scrutinized me for a few seconds and then hummed. "Alright. I'm buying it now. But, be prepared for even more interrogation once everyone finds out."

"I'm ready," I said.

I absolutely was not ready.

CHAPTER SEVEN

emma

I HADN'T HEARD from Hunter since our texts yesterday, and Haley had yet to call me.

I hoped that meant Cam was keeping our secret.

I groaned as I rolled over onto my stomach. An empty ice cream pint sat on my side table next to a half-eaten bag of Doritos.

Sadness settled in like a heavy, dark cloud. I still hadn't cried, though. I'd even watched *Marley and Me*, a movie that usually made me sob.

Except it hadn't worked this time.

I couldn't even remember how many years it'd been since I'd seen my dad. Nine? Ten? We didn't talk, hardly kept in touch. Whenever I spoke about him, which was rare, I basically called him my sperm donor because that's all he'd been to me after I'd divorced Josh.

Grief was all too familiar. I knew what it felt like to lose someone you loved. I knew what it felt like for everything to stop moving, for your entire body to twist so painfully around your heart that you felt like you were dying, too. I knew grief, but *this* felt different.

I wasn't mourning my father, exactly. I was mourning the relationship I'd wanted. I was mourning the father I never had. In a perfect world, maybe the two of us could have reconnected later in life. Maybe we could have shared real conversations and feelings and could have patched up the broken road of our past.

But now, he was gone. I'd never get that chance. And instead of feeling sad, I was relieved.

I was relieved I'd never have to try.

Wasn't that selfish? Didn't that mean there was something wrong with me? I should have cried or screamed or curled up in a ball, but instead I just...

I just felt annoyed. I resented that Josh was the one to tell me. I hated that he'd come to my town, to my doorstep, and then stood there with his damn smug face thinking that he was *still* better than me.

I hated that my father had always taken Josh's side. That after our divorce, he'd even graced me with a phone call to tell me I was being absurd for taking off to Baltimore. That my job was to get married and have plenty of children so the Madden name could carry on, especially since my sister was dead.

I was too much. I was too little. I'd never been who he wanted and never would be. Rage bled all over whatever grief I felt, turning it into ugly resentment.

A knock echoed from downstairs. I lifted my head and stared, my heart lurching in my chest. If it was Josh again, I was going to kick him in the balls this time. I owed that much to myself, right?

My entire body felt like lead. I'd planned to rot in bed with my bad decisions today, but the knock came a little harder.

Donnie leapt off the end of the bed and followed me downstairs. I unlocked the door and opened it.

Haley and Sarah stood on the other side.

Both of their expressions told me they knew. *Fuck*. Should have known better than to even consider Cam would hide something this big from Haley.

"Oh boy," I breathed out. "He told you."

"Yeah, he did. Emma, *what the fuck?*" Haley seethed.

I wrinkled my nose and leaned forward, plucking my mail from the box next to the front door. There were two letters and a bill. I frowned at one of the envelopes. My name was the only thing written on the front, nothing else. I glanced up as a red car drove by slowly, but then turned to Haley and Sarah.

"*Really?*" Haley asked.

Her arms were crossed, her curls drawn up into a top knot. Sarah's hair was in a similar style, her lips pressed into a disapproving line. Both of them were in leggings and T-shirts which made me think they'd found out this morning and immediately rushed over.

This was somehow worse than I'd expected.

"Well," I sighed. "Come in. Might as well talk." I stepped aside to let them both in, tucking the mail under my arm.

The right thing to do would be to tell them the truth, but now that felt harder than rolling with the lie.

"Can I at least make coffee before we start?" I asked.

"Um, no," Sarah said. "You have a lot of explaining to do. I'll make the coffee."

I winced as I followed them to the kitchen. Haley turned around to glare at me. "We've been friends for almost a decade," she started. "And I hear from my *husband* that you're engaged to his brother? Do you know how shitty that feels? I didn't even know the two of you were dating."

"It's new." I couldn't help but sound dejected.

"He said you've been dating for *months*. And that you hooked up at our wedding."

Goddammit, Hunter, what the fuck? This yarn was spinning out of control. We definitely hadn't hooked up at her wedding, though I'd considered it. I remembered drinking a little too much that night and thinking his ass looked good in a suit. But nothing ever happened.

I bit the inside of my mouth, deciding what to say next. "Well. Yeah... Okay, so we've kept it a secret. But there's just been so much going on and..."

"Emma, *nothing* has been going on," Sarah said. "Aside from my wedding and all the construction, it's actually been normal for the last year. Why didn't you say anything?"

"Because I knew it would be a big deal. I'm not used to having everyone up in my business all the time."

Haley gasped. "Are you serious? *That's* your excuse? I tell you everything!"

"I'm sorry," I said quickly. "To both of you. But yes, Hunter and I are engaged." *Liar, liar, silk pajamas on fire.*

"When did he propose?" Sarah asked as she started the coffee maker. "And where's the ring? Cam said there was no ring. It doesn't sound like you to say yes without a ring."

Dammit. I should have called him last night to get our stories straight. Now, I had no idea what they knew and didn't know. I tossed the mail onto the counter and leaned against the fridge.

"He showed me the ring. It's being custom made," I said.

"I was asked about ring opinions," Haley said flatly. She blew a stray strand of hair out of her face and shook her head at me. "Not buying it. This whole situation is weird."

"Okay, so maybe this was a whirlwind decision," I said defensively.

"Do you love him?" Sarah asked.

Silence settled over the kitchen. The storms of yesterday had passed, but that didn't mean I didn't feel like I was trapped in the eye of a hurricane.

"Yes," I lied. "I love him."

"You, Emma Madden, *love* a grouchy, muddy farmer. Hunter Harlow. The man you've supposedly hated from day one." Sarah crossed her arms as the coffee maker beeped. "I have doubts."

"I didn't have doubts about you, Sammy, and Colt," I protested.

"Yes, you did," Haley said. "Didn't you threaten both of them?"

I definitely had. Then again, I'd also seen Sarah go through so much and it wasn't just one guy, it'd been two. "You can threaten Hunter if you want," I said with a shrug.

Haley frowned. "Don't shrug at me like that. This is a huge deal. Cam said Hunter was casual about it, too. We're all in shock."

Sarah nodded in agreement. "Also, this is *Hunter* we're talking about. He's like Superman around here. Everyone knows and loves him, *except* for you. For almost three years, you two have fought, argued, and hated each other."

"Things can change. Is it really so outrageous that we're in love?" I massaged my temples as a headache threatened to settle in.

"Yes? It is? Because we all thought you hated each other?"

"Blame my ADHD for forgetting to tell you?"

Both of them shook their heads at me. "Emma, that's the lamest excuse you've ever given," Haley scolded. "I've known you for so long. I know how your brain works. You forget things like closing the fridge, putting a clip on bags of chips, folding your laundry."

"Or you hyper-fixate on random hobbies, like thrifting,"

Sarah said. "I did live with you for a while, so I know how your brain works, too."

"I like thrifting," I mumbled.

"I know. But you've gone through a lot of hobbies since I've known you. My point is, it's things like that—not forgetting to mention a whole-ass relationship," Haley continued.

I was feeling shittier and shittier about this. "I don't know what to tell you."

"We'd hoped that maybe the two of you could be friends, but now you're engaged and have been dating behind our backs. It's just... I don't even know," Sarah added.

"I need more caffeine before we continue this. Why aren't you guys happy for me?" *It's not real.* I had to keep reminding myself.

Maybe this was a terrible mistake.

I opened my mouth to tell them the truth and snapped it shut when I heard a knock. "I got it," I said, spinning and fleeing. I bolted to the door and opened it. "Josh."

Fuck my life. Not now. Now was not the right time.

Josh stood there looking just as put together as he had yesterday, but far more irritated. He was wearing a different, far more expensive suit, which meant he was pissed.

"Hey, Emma," he said. "Listen, we really need to talk—"

"Now isn't the right time, Josh," I said firmly.

He rolled his pretty blue eyes. "Then give me a time—"

"Emma? Is that your *fiancé*?" Haley called.

Dammit. The last thing I needed was for her to meet Josh. She'd start to suspect something was even more wrong.

At some point, I'd need to tell her about my dad, too.

Everything just felt too difficult right now. All my secrets were a tornado and everything was getting caught in their path.

"Emma?"

I could hear the snap in her tone. "Nope!" I called, stepping outside. I shut the door behind me. "I need you to go," I said to Josh "Like I said, now is not the time. I told you to send me an email to set something up, not show up uninvited again."

"Then, when? I can't stay here forever, Emma. The lawyers are breathing down my neck."

God, I wanted to fucking kick his nuts. "Come by tomorrow night at six, I'll make dinner. What papers do you need me to sign?"

"I can't just give you a rundown here," he said. "Let me in."

"No," I said. "I have guests. Go away."

He sighed, clearly even more agitated. He put his hands on his hips. "I'll tell you tomorrow, then," he said, shrugging. "Tomorrow at six."

"Yep," I said dismissively.

He went down the steps to his car. His body looked so stiff, I wondered if there was a stick up his ass. Then again, he'd always been too lame to let me peg him.

"Bye," he called.

I bit my tongue before I shouted *'farewell motherfucker'* at him in the middle of my neighborhood. I stepped back inside and slammed the door quickly.

I really, really hated him. Like, truly hated him.

It made me realize I didn't actually hate Hunter.

Not like that, anyway.

Time could heal all wounds, sure, but that didn't mean they healed without ugly, jagged scars. Every time I saw Josh, I felt nauseous, angry, and sad all over again.

At the end of the day, my dad had chosen him over me, right? Maybe that's what hurt most of all.

My eyes started to water and I sucked in a breath. Was this it? Was I going to cry?

They dried up before any tears could fall. "Dammit," I whispered.

I pulled my phone out of my pocket and sent Hunter an angry text.

Me: You should have fucking told me what you told Cam yesterday. He told Hal, she told Sarah, and they're both over. WHAT DID YOU TELL THEM????

Texting bubbles popped up and then disappeared.

Me: HUNTER HARLOW I need info now! Also Josh came by again. He's coming over for dinner tomorrow.

Hunter: I'll be there in five, stall them.

That was even worse. I looked like a drowned rat right now. My face felt puffy from sleeping like shit, my hair was an absolute mess.

I walked by the kitchen and held up a thumbs-up, saying the only thing that could get me out of this mess temporarily to Haley and Sarah.

"I'm going to take a shit."

They both snorted, all too familiar with my hot girl tummy troubles.

"I'll be back."

"Take your time," Haley said.

I planned to take all the time I needed until Hunter got here.

CHAPTER EIGHT
emma

I DARTED UPSTAIRS, almost face planting on the top step, and barely managed to slam the bathroom door behind me. Letting out a breath, I leaned against the wall. My stomach was feeling especially bubbly, but that wasn't shit-related, it was shitty situation-related.

This was way harder than I'd thought. How long could we possibly keep this up? We needed Josh to leave Citrus Cove ASAP.

I decided to wash my face and brush my hair, listening to the kitchen sounds and murmurs downstairs. I heard a knock at the front door, followed by Hunter's voice.

Thank god.

I stepped out of the bathroom and looked over the rail, meeting his gaze for a brief moment.

Help, I mouthed.

I've got this, he mouthed back before he continued into the kitchen.

Haley's voice echoed a little louder and I knew she was

giving him hell. I took another deep breath, getting myself into the right mindset.

Hunter was my fiancé.

Hunter Harlow was mine.

I could do this. Right? I could do this.

I squared my shoulders and headed back downstairs to the kitchen. Hunter turned around as I came through the doorway, giving me a smile that stopped me in my tracks.

Hunter had dimples.

Had I just never noticed before? Or had he just never smiled at me?

"Morning, sparks," he said casually. His long arm darted out and he pulled me into a hug, kissing my forehead. I was speechless as he turned back to face the scrutiny of Sarah and Haley. "See? We actually like each other."

Hal pressed her lips together. "Hmm."

"You know, your husband made a similar noise when I told him," Hunter said.

"Was that before or after he made your nose bleed?"

My mouth fell open and I craned my head back to look at Hunter. His hair was still wet and he smelled good. Really good. "Cam punched you?"

"Well, he nailed me with a bag of birdseed first. But yeah."

Sarah narrowed her eyes. "Okay. I suppose I believe this. But only a little. Honey believed it immediately."

"What?" I hissed. "You told Honey?"

"I called Honey to see if she knew," Haley said. "I called Sarah first, then her. And Hunter, Cameron can't keep a secret from me to save his life, by the way. Don't try that again unless you plan on taping his mouth shut."

"Noted," Hunter sighed. "He's too much of a simp. You've changed his brain chemistry."

Haley smirked. "Yeah, maybe."

"What did Honey say?" Hunter asked.

We were both interested. Mostly because Honey usually knew everything. She could be tough and stubborn, but was sometimes sweet enough to give me cavities.

"She said she saw it coming from a mile away. And she saw the looks you gave each other at *my* wedding."

Did she mean murderous looks? I bit my tongue and Hunter tightened his hold on me. I became painfully aware of how my shirt had hiked up slightly and his hand rested on top of my hip, his thumb brushing my bare skin. Slow tantalizing circles sent a shiver up my spine.

"Okay, so pop quiz. The two of you have been dating for how long?" Haley asked.

"Months," Hunter answered.

She crossed her arms. "How many months?"

"Six."

"Okay. What's Emma's favorite shampoo?"

"Nope, we're not doing this," I said. "We're not playing twenty questions."

"If he's been dating you for months then he should be able to answer some basic questions," Sarah said sweetly.

"This is a trick," he snorted. "She orders a custom shampoo and conditioner. She also rotates through three different perfumes. My favorite is the black violet one."

What? How did he know that? *Why* did he know that? Haley and Sarah both looked as shocked as I felt.

"Okay. Her favorite ice cream?" Sarah shot.

"Oh, come on," I groaned. "This is silly."

"It's not. Answer the question," Haley demanded.

Both of them glowered at Hunter in a way that made me feel loved and terrified.

"Wild Blueberry Shortcake or vanilla."

I stifled a gasp. *How does he know?*

His thumb brushed back and forth, my heart rate kicking higher.

"Drink order?"

"Bar or restaurant?" Hunter countered.

"Bar."

"She likes the super sweet wines or dirty martinis. She always eats the olive first."

What.

The.

Fuck?

"What's her job?" Haley asked.

He snorted. "Do you even know?"

She fought a smile. "Not answering that."

"She works in marketing. Clearly, considering the new cider logo." Hunter let out a dark chuckle. "Anything else?"

"Yes. Why have you two acted like you've hated each other? We've been dealing with your shit for years," Sarah said. "I'm still not buying this."

"It's complicated," he said lightly. "But, do you mind if I have a moment alone with Emma?"

Haley and Sarah nodded and then both gave me a prying look. I didn't have a moment to get a word in before he was *manhandling* me out of the kitchen. His rough hands slid around my waist and lifted me, practically carrying me to the back porch.

The moment he shut the door behind us, I slammed my bare heel on the toe of his boot and yelped.

"What the fuck?!" I wheezed.

He caught me before I fell over, pain radiating up my leg.

"I'm wearing steel toed boots," he said. "Did you seriously just stomp on my foot?"

"I did because you *manhandled* me," I snarled. "You can't just move me around like I'm—"

"You're short and tiny and I needed to get you out of there before you gave us away."

"I am not tiny," I growled. Now my foot hurt and I was mad. "Why didn't you call me last night and tell me what you spilled to Cam? I thought we agreed to keep this simple."

"Well, I thought my brother would actually keep a damn secret. And I had shit to do yesterday."

"Like what?"

"For starters, I bought you some security cameras."

"Hunter. I don't need that."

"You're living alone," he said. "You're a woman."

"Okay, that's sexist."

"Emma, are you really going to keep arguing with me after what we've seen Haley and Sarah go through? Even I have security cameras at my house. I just want you to be safer while your ex-husband is hanging around. Also, I did some digging on him. And you." His eyes sharpened and he stepped closer. "I'm starting to doubt that you're actually safe."

"We'll have him over for dinner tomorrow night and he'll leave," I said. "We just need to make it through the weekend. That's it, okay? Then we can call off this ridiculous act."

He shrugged his shoulders. "Fine."

"*Fine.* Also how did you know those things about me?"

He raised a brow. "What things?"

"My shampoo? My perfume? My favorite drinks and ice cream?"

"I've known you for almost three years now and we see each other at every fucking family event and holiday. It's not hard to notice things about you."

My heart leapt to my throat. He made it sound so damn casual, but I couldn't think of a single person I'd dated who could ever rattle off those facts about me.

I wasn't sure how to feel about any of this after that.

Hunter's gaze slid past me and he blanched. "Oh my god. What are you doing to these poor plants?"

"What?" I hissed. He shouldered past me to one of the plants on the porch. I didn't know what the hell it was called. I'd put it in a pot and watered it, but the long leaves were yellow. "Hey, it's still alive."

He shook his head in horror. "Do you even know how to care for it? You're overwatering it."

"Okay, plant man," I said. "Noted."

He looked at the next one and shook his head. "You're a plant murderer."

"Hunter. We've got to focus," I said. "You can repot my plants later, if you're so determined to save them."

"I'm going to steal them all and take them home."

"Oh my god," I sighed. "You're so dramatic. Hunter, please."

He hesitated and turned to look at me, casting me a worried look. "Are you doing okay?"

I swallowed hard. The shift in subject caught me off guard. It was easier to deal with when no one asked how I was. The truth was, I didn't really know. "I haven't cried yet, if that's what you're asking."

His lips thinned. "You can grieve without crying. I don't know if it's healthy, but—"

"We need to get back in there before they think of a thousand more questions," I interrupted. "You can rescue my plants later. And don't worry about my feelings, I'll be fine. I'm tough."

"Okay." His eyes roamed over my body, the corner of his mouth twisting. "I like the pink."

Heat spread through me like a wildfire, but I rolled my eyes. "Whatever. Let's go."

The two of us went back inside. As we walked into the

kitchen, Haley handed me a cup of coffee and before scooping up Donnie, peppering kisses on top of his scruffy head. Sarah was seated at the table, holding her mug close to her chest.

"I have a proposal," Hunter said.

"You mean one with a real ring?" Haley asked.

"My god, you'll never let that go," he chuckled. "There will be a real ring. But no. How about we all go on a triple date?"

What?

"Hmm. I think that's a good idea," Haley said.

"I'm sure Honey will watch the boys," Sarah said. "I'll check in with Colt and Sammy, but I think next Saturday would work for us."

Haley nodded. "That would be good. And weird."

We all hummed in agreement. It would be super weird.

"She's finally letting me install some cameras around the house," Hunter said.

Damn this man.

"Yep," I said. "I want to be safe and... all that."

"Good," Haley said.

"I agree," Sarah said. "Citrus Cove is a small town, but we all know how people can be. Well, I guess we should leave the lovebirds alone, huh?"

"Yes," Haley said. She let Donnie down and pointed at me. "Brunch on Monday."

"Yes, ma'am," I snorted as she pulled me into a hug. I held onto her for a moment, shoving down the wave of guilt. I hated lying to her. "I'll see you then."

Sarah got up to clean out her coffee mug but I shook my head. "Leave it in the sink, I'll take care of it."

"Alright," she sighed with a smile. She gave me a big hug too. "We'll see you soon."

I nodded and leaned against the counter, going still as the

two of them left. The front door clicked shut, and the sound of their cars starting and driving away filled the silence.

"Welp," Hunter said.

"I would like to kill you right now," I said.

He smiled, flashing those stupid dimples. "I'm gonna get to work on the cameras."

"I'm going to go take a hot shower and pretend you don't exist."

CHAPTER NINE
hunter

KNOWING EMMA WAS UPSTAIRS, naked and wet, was a special kind of torture. The last twenty-four hours had been a shit show and our fake engagement was proving to be a bigger problem than anticipated.

Not only was my cock unreasonably hard, but I was losing my fucking mind. The questions I'd answered without batting an eyelash gave Emma a glimpse into my little obsession with her, which was dangerously close to pulling back the curtains on a bigger lie.

The one I'd let Emma believe from the start.

I reached into my truck to dig out my tool bag and the cameras. I was taking my sweet time despite my rule to stay far away from her. Knowing that her ex was hanging around made me anxious.

I hadn't run him out of town.

Yet.

If he stepped a toe out of line tomorrow night, then my fist would be going straight down his throat.

My brows drew together as another wave of worry for

Emma swept over me. Any time I asked her how she was, she avoided the question like the plague. But maybe it was stupid to be asking that, anyway. I knew she wasn't okay, and she wasn't supposed to know I cared.

I was also concerned about her plants and would absolutely be stealing them. With some TLC, I'd have them thriving, and then I'd bring them back with a care guide.

I slammed the door and returned to the porch, setting everything down on the wood. I heard a whine and sighed, cracking the front door to take a peek at Donnie.

The little rat was my buddy, even if Emma disapproved.

"Can I let Donnie out on the porch with me?" I called.

"Sure!"

Her voice rang from the bathroom. I inhaled the scent of black violets and saffron that filled the entire house, and shook my head to clear it. Donnie trotted out and found a patch of sunshine to curl up in, and watched as I started unpacking my tools.

"What do you think?" I asked him as I opened a box. "Am I being too much?"

Donnie let out a soft, contented sigh.

"Maybe I am," I said. "I don't know."

The good news was I'd never uninstalled all the wires that were in there from Sarah's security system. Really, it would only take me an hour but I planned to draw it out as long as I could in case that jackass showed up again. I was curious about what papers Josh wanted to go over with Emma. Flying all the way from California for something that could have been an email seemed unlikely.

The research I'd done hadn't given me much insight. The only thing I knew was that when Emma was married to him, there were complaints filed by neighbors about overhearing their fights. I didn't want to make assumptions, but given how

Emma kept dodging questions about him, I was assuming the worst.

Which gave me all the more reason to send his ass packing.

Already, this was turning into one of the wildest things I'd ever done. And I'd done plenty of wild things in my life. But lying to my family about who I loved was way harder than I'd expected.

The way Haley and Sarah looked at me was a knife to the heart. Mostly because after some talking, they believed it.

And because I wanted to believe it, too.

There was a very real part of me that wished all of this was real—that I had an amazing ring for Emma, that she didn't hate me as much as she claimed she did.

Regardless, if Josh didn't leave after this weekend, I would definitely need to pony up for a ring to keep this up. Or alternatively, I'd commit a crime and he'd end up six feet under an apple tree at the farm. The good news (for him) was I already had a ring picked out, even though it would take a pretty chunk out of my savings.

My mind continued to wander as I focused the cameras around the outside of the house. Once finished, I gave Donnie a low whistle, opened the door, and we both headed inside.

Emma stood at the top of the steps wearing nothing but a towel.

"Fuck!" she yelped, scampering to her bedroom.

I caught a glimpse of her ass, and nearly fell to my knees.

"What the fuck, Hunter?" she yelled from her bedroom.

"You knew I was here!" I adjusted my poor, touch-starved, desperate-for-her cock.

I heaved a breath and leaned against the wall. I could hear her grumbling over my blood pressure, but couldn't tell you a single word she said.

Damn this woman.

She was gonna be the end of me.

Emma came back out wearing leggings and a shirt that I could see straight through. Her dark brown hair was piled into a bun, her lashes still wet from the shower. She planted her hands on her hips.

"Are you finished?"

Not even close, nor in the way I wanted to be.

One breath. Two. "I still have the inside cameras to put up. What's our plan for tomorrow?"

"We'll see what he wants, I guess."

"What did he say?" I asked, trying to force small talk. Because if we didn't keep talking, then my eyes would stray from her face to her tits.

"He said the lawyers are pressuring him. That's all I know."

"Is there anyone you could call for more info?" I asked.

She sighed, her shoulders deflating. She made her way down the stairs and collapsed onto the couch, throwing herself at the cushions with a dramatic flare only she could pull off. "Technically, I could call my stepmom. We aren't close."

"I'm sorry. It seems like they all missed out on knowing you, and that's their loss." I was thinking clearer now. I shifted from the wall to the couch and plopped down on the opposite side.

She gave a slow nod, staring off into space. "You know what? Yeah. They did miss out. I am pretty cool."

"You're more than cool," I said.

It was a rare instance where I'd complimented her and she hadn't immediately told me to fuck off.

"Thank you." She sank into the cushion, studying me. "My family isn't like yours. There's been a lot of times I've felt jealous."

"But you're part of the family," I said. "You should have seen Cam at the store, Emma. He was about to throw my ass to the wolves for you."

She smiled. "I know I'm part of it. I know people care for me. But it's still... I just feel like an outsider sometimes. Because I am one."

And my attitude towards her over the years probably hadn't helped.

"When I moved to Baltimore, I was cut out of my dad's life. Monetarily, too. He eventually let me work for a marketing agency he owns... owned... but that's about it. All of my credit cards were cut off. And any money I made from the company stocks was put into an account I don't have access to. Everything I have now is what I built up for myself. Which is saying something, considering I didn't know how to do a damn thing when I left."

"You were so young," I said, frowning. "What were you? Twenty?"

"Twenty-one," she said. "I used my degree and my last name to gain access to some circles, got a good job, and that eventually led me to work for the agency I'm with now. At first, I thought it would be a bad idea, but my father never interfered with anything. His name was just attached to the agency on paper. Then, I met Haley. She stepped into the role of sister for me, and I did the same for her. And I'm proud of who I've become, even without those people in my life."

I smiled. "They don't deserve you, Emma."

Her eyes softened. "Yeah. They don't. And I really don't want to call my stepmom. The very idea of it makes me want to throw up. So I'd rather deal with Josh's bullshit and see what papers he has for me to sign, then put this all behind me."

"It's strange," I said. "I can't imagine opting to fly across the country rather than send an email."

"A flight to Texas is nothing for Josh," she said with a shrug. "I'm sure sitting in first class to deliver bad news to me got him off. That bastard is loaded. After we divorced, he became even closer to my dad. I'm certain he married me just for the proximity to him."

She was probably right, unfortunately.

"Tell me something about you," she said. "In exchange for this very secret and private information I've shared so freely."

I chuckled. "Our rivalry isn't transactional."

She nudged me with her foot. "Come on. Tell me something no one else knows."

"Hmm." I thought about it for a moment. There were countless things, really. But I wasn't used to anyone asking about them. "I don't know."

"Oh, don't do that. I know there's something."

"Okay. Well. I don't want the Harlow farm some days, but because I'm the oldest, everyone thinks I do. And they expect me to just take over. Not a single soul has ever asked me if I want it. But if I don't take it, no one else will."

Oof. I'd never vocalized that before.

"Why don't you talk to your brothers?" she asked.

"I don't want them to feel like it's their problem."

"Like you do?"

Double oof. I didn't like this game. "Cam is happy with the winery. Sammy has his own thing going between having a family now, his online stuff, and helping Sarah get her business off the ground. Neither of them have time to run a farm. They also don't have the same amount of knowledge. Cam can keep things floating for a bit, but he can't really run it like I can."

"Then you can't blame them," Emma said.

"I never said I did."

"No, but you resent them for doing something else, without the pressure you feel. But you've never said anything to them about it. I would be mad if I were you, because you didn't ask for those responsibilities. But you also haven't told anyone that you didn't want them."

I wrinkled my nose. "What are you, a therapist?"

"No," she snorted. "Far from it. I just know how it feels. When my sister died, the expectation was that I'd be the one to rise through the company. That I'd go to school, get all the degrees I needed, shadow him. If I didn't, then I was supposed to get married and have children so they could follow in his footsteps. But I didn't want any of it. I've never been interested in running the company. He was never home, always working. Like a corporate ghost. He missed my graduation, my birthdays, everything. And he didn't like to hear me gripe about it, because that made me ungrateful."

"My dad is like that sometimes," I mumbled. "Not nearly as bad, of course. He was there for all the milestones. But he doesn't take feedback well."

"It sucks," she said.

It did.

"I don't mean to complain," I said. "I'm lucky. I love my family. They're everything to me."

"You can love someone and still be mad at them," Emma said. "God knows, they'll be furious when we tell them the truth."

I gave a dry smile. "Yeah."

"Then we can put this whole thing behind us and go back to hating each other."

"Right," I said.

Like I wasn't sitting on the couch with her.

Like I hadn't just told her something I'd never told anyone before.

Like I didn't want to worship every part of her body and make her scream my fucking name.

"Well, on that note, I'm going to finish installing the interior cameras and then head home," I said, standing up. "The cameras outside are up and working. I'll text you about how to set up the app on your phone. If that bastard shows up—"

"I'll call you," she said. "I doubt he will, though. Plus, I can always take him down. I've got skills. Are you sure you don't want to go home and enjoy your afternoon?"

"It won't take long," I said. "I'm putting one in here and one faced on the backdoor."

"Great, now you can watch me all the time," she snorted.

"Oh, so you like being watched?" I teased.

"Yes, I do."

What the fuck did she mean by that? Was she trying to chase me away? I shook my head, grabbed my bag, and headed to the other room, releasing a breath once I was out of earshot.

Nothing was going to be the same after this weekend. I couldn't go back to pretending.

But I had to. Everyone would expect me to.

CHAPTER TEN
emma

WHY THE *FUCK* had I just told Hunter I liked being watched?

I thought about that while he finished the final camera. It wasn't until he walked out the front door, started his truck, and drove off that I let myself entertain more all-too-horny thoughts. Thinking about him spying on me was the kind of wild distraction my brain needed, apparently, because I was way too turned on for my own good.

It *had* been a couple days since my last good orgasm.

I looked up at the camera in the living room and chewed on my lower lip.

It was just a fantasy.

Hunter hated me. I hated him. But that didn't mean I couldn't imagine him watching me while I played with myself, right?

I ran upstairs to my bedroom and yanked open the second drawer of my dresser, revealing my abundance of sex toys.

After the fucking hellish forty-eight hours I'd just had, I was gonna have some fun. What Hunter didn't know wouldn't hurt him, and I was going to let my mind wander about him in a way I'd been fighting for years.

There were things I hated about Hunter.

He was an asshole.

He was grumpy.

He was rude, and incorrigible, and always went out of his way to annoy me.

There were also things I (sort of) liked about Hunter.

His ass looked insanely good in denim.

He was always willing to help someone out, even me, his enemy. *I am his enemy, right?*

He had dimples.

He also had agreed to be my fake fiancé, even though he hated me.

I picked out my glass tentacle dildo, a bullet vibrator, and some lube. "I can't believe I'm doing this," I muttered, my cheeks flushing.

I'd done way crazier things in my sex life, though. Not that this was even all that wild. All I was planning to do was masturbate on my couch and imagine him watching me like some horny creep.

I grabbed a towel and carried my goods back downstairs, laying them out on my coffee table. Then I double-locked my front door.

If my ex-husband dared to show up on my porch and interrupted this, I was going to stab him with my tentacle dildo.

I turned on the TV and pulled up Pornhub, scrolling until I found a video that was so cliché, I felt disappointed in myself.

A hot neighbor plumber came over to fix her sink. Corny one-liners followed by unrealistic fucking. It was exactly what I needed.

I slipped out of my leggings as I sat down on the towel, spreading my legs as I looked up at the new camera on the wall.

Oh my god, I was really imagining this. This was so, so wrong in so many ways, and that made it all the more tantalizing.

My breath caught as I slid my fingers down to my pussy, my moan mirroring the woman on the screen as she took the sexy plumber's cock into her mouth. He had rough hands like Hunter.

A bolt of desperation shot through me. I groaned, thinking about the way his thumb had felt on my skin earlier. It was nothing, it was absolutely nothing. But even now, I felt his lingering touch and the thrilling *infuriating* way he'd picked me up and hauled me to the back porch.

I hated being manhandled, unless it was consensual. But once it was agreed upon, I wanted to be manhandled all the way. Pick me up, pin me down, toss me over your shoulder or on the bed.

I hiked my leg over the back of the couch, spreading myself further with a quiet moan. I reached for the lube and glass tentacle dildo.

Hunter would probably think a tentacle dildo was too much.

Or maybe, he'd think it was perfect. Maybe he had all sorts of kinky secrets under that prickly exterior.

I lubed up the dildo and myself, sliding two fingers in. Pleasure erupted, my nipples hardening against my shirt. I sat up quickly and yanked it off, tossing it to the floor.

"Fuck," I rasped.

I looked over at the TV right as the plumber bent her over the counter, his palm slapping her ass. He grabbed a fistful of her hair as he lined up his cock with her pussy, the two of them groaning together as he shoved into her.

Then my eyes went to the camera, my imagination going wild.

Fuck. I was losing it. I was so touch-starved that I was imagining being watched by him, and I couldn't find a reason to stop myself. It felt good to let go, and I realized just how badly I needed the release.

The tension between us was too much. It was already fucking with me to think that there might be a shred of real desire between us.

There wasn't, I reminded myself.

My body didn't believe it, though.

I moaned as I arched against the couch, pushing the cool ribbed glass tip inside myself. I was so wet that it slid right in. I closed my eyes, thinking about the camera again. Thinking about him angrily pulling out his cock and stroking himself as he watched me, because he couldn't help himself. The tension between us was driving me insane.

I grabbed the vibrator and turned it on, holding it to my clit as I worked the tentacle in and out. My voice pitched as I got closer and closer to coming, need curling inside of me, growing with each pump. Moans echoed from the TV but my gaze settled on the camera.

"Hunter."

His name felt too damn good on my lips.

"Oh god," I groaned.

I turned up the setting on the vibrator and squealed as it rocked my whole damn world, pleasure popping like a thousand fireworks. I arched as I clenched around the tentacle dildo, every muscle in my body tensing as the gush of pleasure and release followed, washing over me and chasing all my inner demons away.

"Fuck," I rasped, melting into the couch.

I panted hard, my chest rising and falling. God, that was... that was exactly what I'd needed.

I looked back up at the camera. Hunter was too good, he wouldn't be watching me...

Maybe the hardest part of this situation was realizing he wasn't as bad as I had thought.

I glanced over as the plumber and woman started into another position, one I wanted just as badly.

Well. It was Saturday, and I had no plans.

Round two it was.

CHAPTER ELEVEN
hunter

MY HOME WAS A SMALL, well-kept cabin on the other side of the farm with a perfect view of the rolling Hill Country. Bluebonnets were starting to pop up, and soon there would be blue skies and blue fields as far as the eye could see.

After I'd left Emma's house, I'd stopped by the store to grab some food, sunscreen, snacks, and Gatorade for work before driving home. I pulled my truck to a stop and got out, walking my groceries up to my front porch.

I unlocked the door and stepped inside. The silence was heavy. I'd become so used to being alone, but Emma was starting to ruin that.

Suddenly, I wanted to actually have a smart, sassy fiancé. One who painted everything pink and had a rat for a dog.

There'd been so many times over the last day where I'd thought about telling the truth. Lying didn't come naturally to me. I could bend the truth, sure, but telling everyone I loved that Emma and I had been dating behind their backs? It made me feel awful.

Then again, selfishly, I was enjoying certain parts of this. Mostly the way Emma's eyes widened when I surprised her. Or the way she bit her bottom lip when the tension between us became unbearable.

Unless I was just imagining the tension.

I set everything down on the counter and looked around. Everything was clean, lived in, and cozy. But it was lacking something. I couldn't quite put my finger on what.

My living room had a nice leather couch and a couple of plush chairs, a big TV for watching games, and a coffee table with a stack of books about farming. I kept countless plants in the house, each one feeling like part of my bloodline at this point. Some of the plants hung from the ceiling, cradled by rope I'd used to create macrame holders. Plus, it kept my rope tying skills from becoming too rusty.

My gaze lingered on the knots and patterns for a moment. Emma would look really fucking good in a chest harness. Maybe in a rope tie that would cradle her entire body, with a knot resting over her clit. If I tugged the rope at the back, it would tug down there too—the idea of her squealing, of her being at my mercy...

Stop. Don't even go there.

My thoughts were already there, and this time they lingered longer than they should have.

Most of the time, I was dominant. I especially liked rope and breath play. The idea of tying her down to my bed, my hand around her throat as her lips formed my name, her rich brown eyes full of lust and need...

She'd be a brat in the bedroom.

Or maybe she'd be completely submissive.

Hell, if she were dominant, I'd even be willing to submit to her. That's how far gone I was.

I shook my head. I was desperate to know what she would be like, but she was off-limits. This entire fake fiancé situation was making me too comfortable.

Once we got through the dinner with Mr. Jackass, I'd be able to put this all behind me. I could go back to pretending to hate Emma, and my life would feel less empty again.

I drew in a deep breath, trying to steady myself. The scent of grapefruit wafted through the air. Grapefruit?

I didn't like that scent. At all. I turned my head, scowling. I didn't wear cologne, nor did I keep candles that smelled like fruit—so where the fuck was it coming from?

"Hello?" I called.

Surely, someone hadn't broken in. That would be absurd this far out of town. Citrus Cove was barely a dot on the map, and my cabin wasn't exactly the most luxurious looking place out here.

Nothing seemed to have been touched. My front door had been locked. *What about the back door?*

The hair on the back of my neck stood up. I opened up a kitchen drawer, pulling out a knife. Call me crazy, but after all the shit I'd seen happen to the rest of my family, I didn't think it was paranoid to grab some sort of weapon, especially since my gun was in the side table in my bedroom.

"Hello?" I called again, listening for any sort of rustle. I didn't hear anything.

I crept down the hallway and paused in the doorway of my office, kicking the door wide open. I stepped inside, but there was no one in here either. My heart pounded as I yanked open the closet door.

My shoulders deflated. Nothing.

Was smelling grapefruit cologne a sign that I was losing my mind?

I sighed and scanned my bedroom next. Again, nothing

appeared to have been touched. I lowered my knife and shook my head, quickly checking the bathroom before moving on to the final bedroom with a door that opened to the outside. I usually kept it blocked and locked, but the boxes looked like they'd been shifted out of the way.

"Son of a bitch," I muttered.

I turned the knob and pushed the door open with ease. Who the fuck would have come into my house? And why? I kicked the boxes aside and stepped out the back door, looking at the field that stretched toward the hills. There was no important shit back here. I didn't have anything valuable in the house, aside from my laptop and TV. All of my expensive things were in the barn.

I planted my hands on my hips, my stomach twisting.

It looked like I'd be taking my own advice and installing cameras around my house, too. I did a quick walk around the yard before going inside through the back door. I slammed it shut, locked it, and piled the boxes again.

I ran through a mental list of who could have done this, and the only person who could be stupid enough was Josh. If it was him, I was now even more concerned for Emma's safety.

My nerves were rattled.

I searched through the house once more, scrutinizing the bare walls and plants I had in each room. Satisfied that nothing else was touched, I made my way back to the kitchen. There were countless photos on the fridge of Cam, Sammy, Colt, and me. Pictures from holidays we spent together, and of me officiating Haley and Cam's wedding.

My gaze swept over them. All I wanted for our family was for everyone to be safe and happy. I reluctantly included Emma in that, too. If Josh had really broken into my house, I couldn't trust that he was going to leave Citrus Cove without a fight.

I unloaded my groceries, grabbed my laptop, and settled

down on the couch with a beer. I turned on the TV for some noise as I opened a browser.

I'd done some basic research on Josh, but now it was time for a deeper dive. If Alexa were still alive, I would have called her to see if she could find anything on him using police resources. I rubbed the ache in my chest, trying not to think too much about her.

The events that surrounded Haley and Cam had been horrific. We'd been lucky to get to Haley in time before Thomas Connor could kill her, but he'd still taken out Alexa. She'd been the only cop worth her salt in Citrus Cove, and it hadn't been the same since she'd been gone. They hadn't done shit when David Connor came to town, and while I was happy he was dead, I felt like they could be blamed for his death.

What if Josh had waited for me to leave Emma?

I felt a flicker of guilt for what I was about to do, but it was just to check in on her safety. I pulled up the security camera app, logged in with the info I was supposed to send to her, and pulled up the feeds.

The front porch was clear, so was the back of the house and the back door, but I didn't spend more than a second analyzing those feeds. My eyes were immediately glued to the living room camera.

Fuck.

I immediately looked away, every thought evaporating as my cock hardened.

Fuck. *Don't look, don't look. Shut your laptop like a gentleman. You're a good man, you're a good man, you're a—*

My eyes widened as I stared at the camera feed. Emma was sprawled out on her couch, her legs spread and pussy facing the camera. Her fingers circled her clit, her other hand cupping her breast as she arched, her lips parting for an inaudible moan.

There wasn't a single good thing I could do after this

moment to save my soul. I was going to hell, and I knew that, accepted it—and then unbuckled my jeans and pulled my cock free.

This was so wrong. It was so fucking wrong. She didn't know I was watching her, didn't know I could see her pussy glistening in the afternoon light, or that I was so fucking hard for her I could barely breathe.

Her words came back to me. I'd teased her about being watched, and she'd said yes, *she liked it*. Was she doing this on purpose? Had she thought I would look at the cameras like some horny freak?

I was better than this. I had to be better than this. Everyone in my life knew me as someone with good morals, always willing to lend a hand—safe and kind and good.

But I wasn't good enough to look away from her.

Fuck, she made me crazy.

I gripped my cock and groaned as I stroked myself. I watched her every movement, the way her fingers worked her pussy, imagining that I was there with her. This was a perfect lesson on how to make her come, and I had always been a good student.

Fuck, was that a tentacle dildo? Jesus. That only turned me on more.

One day, I owed her a fucking apology on my knees for how insane I was around her. But today was not the fucking day.

I grunted, thrusting my cock into my grip, imagining her cunt wrapping around me, milking me.

Emma's perfect ass jiggled as she adjusted her position, putting her leg over the couch. I wished I was sitting there with her.

"Fuck," I whispered as her fingers moved faster.

She was a dream I couldn't wake up from. Or a nightmare,

depending on how I looked at it. Regardless, every thought was about Emma.

We'd talked more in the past couple of days than ever before, kindling a desire for more.

A few minutes with her wasn't enough. I wanted hours, days, *forever*.

My palm was rough as I stroked myself, her name chanting in my mind as pleasure branded me. *Emma, Emma, Emma.* Fuck. What the fuck was I going to do? Nothing could pry her out of my mind or heart, no matter what I did. I didn't want to touch another, kiss another, fuck another, breathe around another. I just wanted her.

But I couldn't have her. Right? I was too obsessed with her. I probably needed to go to therapy and figure out why the hell she'd become all I wanted.

Denying myself felt so wrong. So what if I wanted to get on my knees and eat her pussy until she came on my tongue?

I grunted, stroking myself faster and harder. I imagined her riding me, my fingers digging into her ass as her head tipped back, her perfect lips parting with a scream—

"Fuck!"

Emma arched the same moment I came. I couldn't hear her, but I could see her pleasure in her movements, the way her face twisted. My release shook me to my core, my muscles trembling. I panted as I melted, sinking into my sofa. My thoughts cleared as I blinked.

Damn, I'd made a mess. Cum streaked my jeans, dripping down my cock and over my hand. I panted as I stared at my laptop, watching as she came down from the high of her orgasm too.

Fuck. What the hell was I doing? I leaned forward and quickly logged out of the app, closing the page down, and wiping my laptop's search history.

I threw my head back against the couch and stared at the ceiling. At this point, I needed to call up a pastor to exorcise her from me.

My phone buzzed in my pocket. I winced and got up, pulling off my clothes and heading for the bathroom. I washed my hands before pulling it out of my pocket.

Sammy: Dinner tonight?

I sighed. I wasn't really sure I could handle being grilled again. I leaned over the sink, staring at myself in the mirror. I felt the urge to jump in the shower and scrub myself raw, as if that could wash away this feeling from the voyeuristic masturbation session.

Sammy: I'll bring food over to your place?

I grit my teeth. Fuck it. I couldn't avoid my family. I sent him a text back.

Me: Sure

I wondered if it would just be Sammy or if he'd bring Colt, too. Or maybe he'd bring my nephews.

Me: Just you or..?

Sammy: Me, Colt, and the boys if that's okay?

Maybe getting some uncle time in would be good for me. And whatever Sammy made would be way better than anything I would have come up with for dinner.

I was sure everyone thought Emma and I had lost our minds. They'd be right on my part.

I sent Sammy a thumbs-up and flipped on the hot water Steam swirled through the air as I stepped under it, the heat permeating my muscles.

If Josh had broken into my house, I should be able to tell during dinner tomorrow. We'd see what he needed to show Emma, then he'd be out of our lives. Everything would go back to normal. We'd be safe and sound, and I'd try to start dating again like a normal man in his thirties...

There wasn't a chance in hell for me and Emma to make anything work between us. She was too much of a damn princess, and I was the furthest thing from a knight in shining armor.

She deserved the best.

Better than I could ever give.

CHAPTER TWELVE
hunter

"HELLO, HEATHENS."

My nephews clunked up the porch steps. They were shooting up like weeds, getting taller every day. While they were twins, Jake and Davy thankfully wore their hair differently. They were even starting to get a couple pimples here and there.

I did not envy them. The teen years sucked.

"Y'all are getting too tall," I protested.

"Mom thinks we'll be taller than her next year," Jake said, clearly excited.

"I'm sure," I agreed.

"Maybe we'll be taller than Sammy one day," Davy said.

"Maybe. Although he's really tall." I chuckled as they slid past me. Colt and Sammy got out of the truck carrying several bags.

"What the hell are you cooking up?" I asked. "There's only five of us."

"Three grown men and two pre-teen boys? Don't you remember how much we ate at that age? They're horrifying. I got enough vegetables and chicken to feed the entirety of Citrus Cove," Sammy said, raising his brow at me as he came up the steps. "Also, you don't have enough pans. So we brought some of mine. I'm here to get info too, of course."

"Mmhmm. Naturally. Hey, Colt."

"Hey, Hunter," he greeted. "Still mad about me suggesting you and Emma work together?"

He was too smug about it. I bit my tongue as his smirk broadened, following Sammy inside.

"Should I text Cam?" I called as I shut the door behind all of us.

"He's working the bar," Sammy answered.

Made sense. While he wasn't working as many hours as he used to, he was usually behind the bar a few nights a week.

Jake and Davy plopped on the couch, immediately making a grab for the remote. They were quick, and soon *One Piece* was on in the background. I joined Sammy in the kitchen as Colt went over and sat next to the boys, the three of them chatting.

I smiled. He and Sammy were damn good dads. I envied them in a way. While I loved the idea of being a dad one day, I was terrified of being awful at it. Maybe because of how complicated my relationship was with my own dad.

"So," Sammy said quietly. "What's wrong?"

A lump formed in my throat. I crossed my arms and leaned against the counter.

Like Cam, Sammy could tell when I was lying. The difference was that Sammy had an unnerving ability to pinpoint exactly what was going on. He was quieter, more observant, and more blunt than Cam.

He wouldn't hit me with a bag of birdseed. But he would draw the truth out of me if I wasn't careful. I didn't know which was worse.

"Nothing's wrong," I said.

Sammy heated up oil in a pan. "I'm making fried chicken with some baked veggies and biscuits."

"You're a hero," I said, my stomach grumbling in response.

"Being a dirty liar works up an appetite, doesn't it?"

My jaw dropped and I scoffed. "Really? That's how we're starting this?"

Sammy smiled. "I love you. You know that. And I haven't said what I'm thinking to anyone else yet. I listened to what Sarah and Haley had to say. And Cam too, for that matter. Hunter, none of this is sitting right with me."

"Do I have to give you the same spiel?" I muttered. "Convince you that Emma is who I love?"

"I'd rather know what's wrong, actually. You and Emma haven't gotten along for years. Why? I have no fucking clue. She's kind, cool, smart. And arguably, so are you."

"Gee, thanks," I muttered.

Sammy reached to turn on the oven, then started chopping away. Warmth filled my little kitchen, and he moved like he'd done this a thousand times. Laughter floated from the living room and I glanced at them before stepping away from my brother.

"Am I in the way?" I asked.

"Nope. You can stay there and talk."

Too damn intuitive for his own good. "I love her," I said.

"No, you don't," he said smoothly. "If you loved her, you wouldn't have hid anything from everyone. You would have had a ring already. You would have known that she's someone who deserves everything good in the world."

"I fucking know that," I growled.

"Then what—"

"Can you drop it, please? I don't want to do this. I'm tired. I'm tired of everyone always expecting me to be perfect. If I didn't do this how all of you expected, then so be it. But it wasn't for you. It's not for any of you, it's for her."

Sammy pressed his lips together as he shoved a pan of veggies into the oven. I was hardly paying attention to what he was doing, keeping my gaze fixed on the fridge.

Uncomfortable silence settled between us as he dipped the chicken in buttermilk batter. I scrubbed my face and started to move out of the kitchen, but he *tsked* at me.

"Nope. Not running away," he said.

"Either punch me or leave it be," I snapped.

He snorted. "It's been a long time since we've thrown punches and I'm not interested in kicking your ass."

"I've let you and Cam get way too fucking cocky about that," I said.

He laughed. "I mean, one of us has silver in his hair and the other one doesn't."

"I grayed early because of you fuckers."

He grinned. "Grab me a beer, will you?"

"Yeah." I sighed, the tension finally melting. "I stocked the fridge with some sparkling water for the boys."

"That's sweet. I'm sure they'll appreciate it."

I went to the fridge as the oil started to pop. I grabbed two sodas and three beers, taking the sparkling waters to the boys first.

Davy perked up. "Oh, my favorite."

"So I've heard." I handed him one can and the other to Jake.

"Thank you," they both chimed.

Colt craned his head back as I gave him a beer. "How kind of you, sir."

I physically bit my tongue before I told him to fuck off, and narrowed my eyes on him instead. "Did you bring your children as a buffer, Colton Hayes?"

"I sure did."

Damn him.

He cracked the beer open as the pirate kid on the screen stretched like a piece of gum. I frowned. "What is this?"

"It's *One Piece*," Jake said. "We're on episode six-hundred-something."

"Six hundred? Jesus. How many episodes are there?"

"Over a thousand," Colt strained.

My brows shot up. "Damn. That's a lot." I watched the screen for a few moments and it dawned on me that I'd seen some of it before. "Sammy used to watch this, I think?"

"Yep," he said from the kitchen. "Greatest show ever."

I chuckled as I headed back to the kitchen.

"You don't want to sit next to me and watch Luffy take down his enemies in a heartfelt way?" Colt said sweetly.

It was either that, or be trapped in the kitchen with my too-insightful brother. I was between a rock and a hard place.

"I'm going to let Sammy torture me some," I decided.

"Good luck."

Davy gave me a curious side glance. "Is it because of Emma?"

Not the kids, too. "Yes."

"And how you're engaged?" Jake continued.

"Yep."

"But you love her, right?" Davy asked, studying me. He was like Sammy, always observant.

"Yeah..."

"Then it's fine. Right?" Jake asked.

"You'd think," I said.

"We all love Emma," Colt said. "So we're being a little over-protective, maybe."

"But Hunter is great." Jake frowned at Colt. "He's always working or helping someone. So isn't he good for Emma, too?"

113

I nodded, crossing my arms. "Yeah. Exactly. Exactly that."

Colt and Sammy glanced at each other, but said nothing. I went back to the kitchen and handed Sammy his beer. Now I was the smug one.

"So glad you brought them over," I teased.

Sammy sighed, his expression softening. "I just want you to be happy. And I want Emma to be happy, too."

"Me too," I said. "That's all I want, Sammy."

"Then I'll stop giving you shit. But if you fuck this up, there will be hell."

"I know there will be."

CHAPTER THIRTEEN

emma

I TURNED onto Honey's street and slowed to a crawl, eyeing the vehicle behind me. I'd seen the little red car around recently, and wondered who it belonged to. I parked next to Honey's yellow truck and watched it go by, shaking my head.

"Weird," I said to Donnie.

His tail thumped against the seat in excitement as I got out, opening the door for him. He jumped out and sniffed around the grass before following me up the steps.

Honey opened the door right as I went to knock, a silver brow raising. "About damn time. You've been keeping secrets."

My cheeks burned red hot. I should have known she'd have expected some news by now.

It was Sunday morning and I'd slept like shit last night. It didn't matter how many times I'd masturbated (which had been a lot), I couldn't get Hunter Harlow off my mind. The plumber porn had only made things worse.

I needed to be planning a festival and readying myself for snappy responses to whatever bullshit Josh said tonight at dinner.

My stomach twisted at the thought of Josh. Him being here in Citrus Cove was a problem. I needed to hear him out and then kick him out.

With my dad's death, there were probably things I had to do for a funeral, right? Hell, I hadn't even thought about that. I wasn't sure I even wanted to go, and that only made me feel worse.

But really, who would I need to pretend to be the perfect daughter for? No one.

After tonight, Josh would leave. Hunter and I would tell everyone the truth. All would be right in the world.

"I can keep secrets," I quipped.

Honey snorted. "Yeah, sure. Come on, lunch is almost ready. Hello, my sweet darling Donnie." She leaned down to give him a few pets before he trotted inside, finding his place on the sofa in the living room.

Most Sundays, I found myself at Honey's. Alice was always busy on Sundays. And since Haley and Sarah were now happily married, it was harder to drag them over to my house and away from their sexy men. Honey had her own beau, but Mr. Johnson only came over on Mondays. She claimed the distance made their sex lives more exciting, which was way too much information, but also goals.

If my golden years weren't full of the best sex of my life, I didn't want them.

I shut the door behind me, kicked off my shoes, and followed Honey to the kitchen.

"How's everything going?" she asked.

"It's going," I said.

She made a drawn out hum, shaking her head. "Uh huh."

Maybe I'd try to redirect her. "Is there anything I can help with?"

"Nope. You can tell me about your little secret. Along with the truth, if you don't mind."

My mouth opened and then clamped shut. "We've been seeing each other for a few months."

Honey shook her head. "You know, I told Haley I could have guessed. The two of you were always griping at each other, and that tension can turn into something else. But getting engaged without breathing a word to any of us? Just doesn't seem like you."

Because it wasn't. According to the Emma Life Plan, I would date a man for three years before he would plan an extravagant engagement, one that would absolutely sweep me off my feet. One that would leave me breathless and swooning. Then, he'd propose with a gorgeous diamond ring inspired by my Pinterest mood board. I'd say yes, plan the most *perfect* wedding, and then we would live happily ever after.

Hunter Harlow didn't exactly fit into that picture. I doubted he even knew what a marquise cut diamond was.

"It just felt right," I said.

Honey fixed her silver hair in a bun and grabbed a set of oven mitts, pulling a pan of enchiladas out of the oven. It didn't matter that it was still morning time, the two of us had decided a while back that enchiladas for breakfast was a fine way to start the day. My mouth immediately watered.

She set it on the stovetop. "Darling, I've known you for some time now, and I just have to say—it's a shock. That's all. Now, I've known Hunter Harlow all his life, and there's a very real part of me that's thrilled for the two of you. He's a great man who's smart and kind—with a great ass, too."

"Honey," I hissed, fighting a giggle.

"What? Have you seen those Levi's on him? Can't get much better than that. All that aside, working the Harlow farm is what he seems to want to do with his life. He'll always be here in Citrus Cove, just like he's always been."

"Do you think I don't want to be here?" I asked, frowning.

"I don't know. Some days, I think this place is perfect for you. Other days, I wonder if you'll get tired of it. It's the same thing all the time, save for all the little dramas that pop up. Everyone knows each other and leans on each other in hard times, but there's nothing glamorous about it."

"I don't want glamour," I said. "I'm glamorous enough as it is. I want to feel like I'm home and loved. I want to care about—and be cared for by—people who really know me. Who love me for who I am. I didn't get that growing up." My eyes teared up. It felt stupid to say all of this out loud, even if I meant every word. But the relationship with Hunter wasn't real, and eventually we'd disappoint everyone with the truth. "I just want someone to see me, you know?"

Honey's gaze softened as she slid her oven mitts off and pulled me into a hug. I leaned into her and shut my eyes.

Was this it? Was I finally going to cry?

"You've got people who love you, and I'm one of them. Whenever Haley and I talked on the phone over the years, she'd always tell me about you. Emma this, Emma that. I always felt happy she had someone close by who loved her when we couldn't. And then I got to actually meet you and know you, and I want you to stay here forever. But I also want you to do what feels right."

The tears dried up. *Dammit.* Maybe I'd never cry again. "Thank you," I said softly.

"Marriage is a big commitment. And I just worry you're diving in too fast, with Haley and Sarah both being married now."

"It's not because of them," I said. "And no, I'm not pregnant."

"Well, good. Because that's certainly not a reason to get married either." She pulled back and pointed at the stove. "Now grab the plates and I'll serve us some food. I got some chips and queso and *The Golden Girls* all ready to go."

"You're the best," I said.

"I can be. And Emma, whatever this is with Hunter, I'm happy for you. But my instincts are telling me that something ain't right here. Hidden roots always get dug up, darlin'. When you're ready to tell me the whole truth, I'll be here."

I winced and decided I'd give a small concession. "I'll tell you eventually. That's all I can say for now."

Her lips pinched but she nodded. We served ourselves and headed to the living room, queueing up season five. Donnie burrowed himself in a blanket, completely blissed out. I ate slowly, trying to focus on the show, but my mind kept drifting to the plans with Josh later tonight.

I'd hear him out, kick him out of town, and then be done with it.

I soothed my uneasy stomach with chips dipped in queso.

Hunter and Josh being in the same room for more than five minutes would be difficult. I wished Hunter wouldn't have told him he was my fiancé. It made everything so much more complicated. If Josh already told the lawyers about Hunter, I wouldn't be surprised if they showed up here too.

Josh expected me to fall in line and turn into the perfect trophy wife again, but that would never happen.

I wasn't the girl he married all those years ago. His audacity at suggesting we remarried was disgusting. I wrinkled my nose, thinking about all the work I'd done to become a better and stronger person. It'd taken me years to undo the beliefs he'd instilled during those fourteen months. Haley had seen me go through several toxic relationships in the first few years we knew each other, because I'd still held onto all the damage from my marriage.

He'd had a terrible taste in home decor. We were doomed from the beginning.

"Next Sunday, bring your fiancé over for lunch," Honey said.

Dammit. "Okay," I said. "I'll see if he wants to."

"I'm sure he will. If he doesn't, let him know I'll be showing up on his doorstep to interrogate him in person."

I snorted and stole a glance at her over my shoulder, clocking her smirk. I narrowed my eyes on her, but didn't say anything else.

It was worth the chaos, I reminded myself. Josh would be gone soon and Hunter and I could clear the air, and they'd all be fine with it. Right? Surely they'd understand why we'd started a fake relationship.

All I could do was hope they would.

CHAPTER FOURTEEN
emma

I SMOOTHED my hands down my dress, fixed my lipstick, and then headed downstairs right as Hunter knocked.

He was right on time. Which meant, according to his logic, he was late.

I'd already put Donnie in my room with a couple of chew toys and ordered take-out. I planned to plate it up as if I'd cooked it. I even put on my battle armor—otherwise known as my favorite shoes. They were bright red and gave me an extra three inches of height. The stiletto heels were a great weapon, if needed. And right now, I could use every bit of protection possible.

I'd been mentally preparing myself for this meeting. I could do this.

I shook out my hands before opening the door.

My mouth went dry. Hunter stood at the threshold, the last of the sun's rays splashing brilliant scarlet light over him. He was wearing a dark denim button-down shirt with jeans and boots.

A devilish cowboy was on my doorstep.

His cheeks reddened, his gaze sweeping over me. My heart pounded, my brain short-circuiting as I processed just how damn hot he was.

"Hi."

"Hey, sparks," he said.

"I'm incredibly anxious right now," I said, forcing out a short laugh.

He offered a gentle smile. "It's okay. He won't be here long, I'm sure. Then we're done."

Done. Just like that.

I swallowed hard and nodded, ignoring the ache in my chest. Just as I stepped aside to let him in, Josh's car pulled up. Hunter shot him a dark look.

"He's early," I sighed.

"Want me to hold him off?" He flexed his hand.

"No, of course not," I said. "It's fine, it's fine, it's fine—"

Hunter took a step closer and held my face in his hands. "I'm here. You'll be okay. He can't do anything to harm you. Okay?"

"Okay," I breathed out. "Kiss me to make it look real."

He gripped me a little harder. "No," he said. "I won't kiss you."

"Oh, come on," I hissed. "It's not like you'll turn into a frog."

His face contorted between surprise and anger and something else. He dragged me close to him, his body lean and muscled.

Fuck. I'd underestimated how touch starved I was. His arm looped around my waist as he lowered his lips to mine.

Oh god, oh god, oh...

Our lips brushed, gentle at first. But then it was harder, needier, *hungrier*. The softest moan escaped me and suddenly he was pushing me against the wall, pulling my legs around his waist. His fingers knotted in my hair, every touch rough and desperate. Every swipe of his tongue seared me with need.

I gasped as he deepened the kiss, melting against him.

Oh my god, I was *kissing* him.

I couldn't tell you what day it was. I couldn't tell you *where* I was. All I knew was Hunter Harlow was kissing me, I was kissing him back—and I *needed* more.

The sound of Josh clearing his throat loudly tore us apart. Hunter dropped me and took a step back, wiping his mouth with the back of his hand. So much for the lipstick I'd just touched up.

Now, that ache in my chest stung a little more.

"Got carried away," he muttered.

Note to self, Hunter actually did hate me and this wasn't real. That might have been a damn good kiss, but it was fake.

It didn't feel fake, though.

Josh was furious. He held a briefcase up, his body tense and blond brows furrowed. "I brought all the documents we will need."

"Great," I said. *Focus.* It was difficult now that every nerve ending in my body was alive and hot.

Hunter didn't take his eyes off me. An awkward silence settled over the three of us, but I was still recovering from whatever the fuck that was.

"Done any driving around the Hill Country while you've been here?" Hunter asked, attempting to make small conversation.

Josh shook his head. "No."

"Not much of a sight-seeing guy, huh?"

"There's really not much to see here. You have two gas stations. Can we go inside?"

Hunter's dimples flashed. "Aw, that's not fair. We have a grocery store too."

I strangled a laugh. "Come on," I said. I let them both in as I reminded myself that I was in control, I could kick Josh out at any time, and I should probably hear him out. "Hunter, will you show him to the dining room?"

"Sure thing. Follow me."

Hunter headed for the dining room with a clearly distressed Josh in tow. The moment they were out of sight, I went to the kitchen and braced my hands against the counter, forcing myself to breathe.

I squeezed my thighs together, trying not to think about how it'd felt to be pinned against the wall by Hunter.

Dammit, this entire plan was going to shit.

The takeout containers sat on the counter. I pulled out plates, making sure to pick the pinkest, craziest design I owned just to piss Josh off. I arranged the food on them and managed to carry all three to the dining room.

"I'll get the drinks," Hunter said, squeezing by me as I set the plates on the checkered table mats.

I'd put Josh across from us. My dining table was a beautiful birchwood find off Facebook Marketplace. It had an inlaid mirrored panel which reflected the midnight blue velvet chairs around it. A vase of fake flowers sat between us, which I decided to push to the side so we weren't having to glare at each other through plastic sunflower petals.

Josh eyed the food. "Didn't poison this, did you?"

I really wasn't sure if he was joking. "Do you want me to chew it up and spit it in your mouth to prove otherwise?"

He blanched. "I'll just trust you're not up to anything suspicious."

"Why would I be? I want you gone," I said. "Legally gone, not dead."

Hunter came back with glasses of iced water and lemons. He sat them out and then pulled out my chair for me.

"Thanks, babe," I said.

"Anything for you, my lovely fiancé," he said sweetly.

Maybe before our kiss, I would have thought about telling him to fuck off. But now, it took all my strength not to think about him pushing me up against a wall again. About the heat of his lips on mine, the way my entire body felt so damn right against his.

The fact that I maybe sort of *wanted* Hunter Harlow was starting to eat away at me.

I crossed one leg over the other, forcing myself to appear relaxed.

Josh's jaw tightened, the vein already throbbing in his forehead.

Sitting here now, I wasn't even sure why I'd offered dinner. Having my ex-husband across from me and my small town enemy-turned-fake-fiancè to my left felt like a level of ridiculousness I wasn't prepared for.

Nerves rolled through me as he pulled papers out of his briefcase. He pushed his plate aside, but it didn't offend me. If anything, I was more than ready to just get this over with. No niceties or bullshit. What could he possibly be here for?

"Wonderful, we'll just get right into it," I said. "Why are you here? Really?"

"Well, you've complicated things now that you're engaged," he snapped, giving Hunter a dark look. "But I suppose we'll start with why I came here initially."

Hunter leaned back, the chair creaking as he slid his arm behind me. He appeared relaxed, but every muscle in his body was as tense as mine.

"As you know, your father has passed away—"

"Did you find out the cause?" I interrupted.

His expression tightened. "Not yet. But, his lawyers have been busy preparing his estate and what will ultimately be your inheritance. Before I knew about Hunter, I planned to ask you to marry me again. I mean, we're perfect for each other and—"

"Drop that nonsense right now," Hunter quipped. "Emma is mine."

Mine. My cheeks heated. *He doesn't really mean that,* I reminded myself. "Continue, Josh," I said.

He shot Hunter a dirty look. "Well, anyway. Emma, you don't want this company. You never have. Your father didn't want you to have it either. You know, he was grooming me to take over. I know how to run it, and know how to lead it in the direction he envisioned. And you never fit into that vision."

Ouch.

"Now, if you were Evelyn, it probably would be different—"

"New rule," Hunter interrupted. "Stop being a fucking asshole before I rip your tongue out."

"I'm just being candid." Josh drummed his fingers on the table impatiently.

"*Candid* is corporate speak for you're being an asshole."

"Josh. Get to the fucking point," I said.

"Now that Michael Madden is dead, you are the owner of Madden Enterprises. The entire company is in your name. But I want it, Emma. I want the company. I deserve it after all the work I've done."

I was completely stunned. This motherfucker. He'd lost his mind. I wasn't going to hand my father's company over to him without talking to lawyers. Even if they were present, there was no way in hell this was going to happen.

I cleared my throat, pushing past the discomfort of dealing with a childish, entitled man. "First of all, you are mistaken if you believe we're signing anything here today. Where are the lawyers? Why aren't they here with you?" I asked. "And what about my stepmom?"

"She inherited a small portion of money, enough to comfortably live on."

That wasn't a *small* amount then.

"And the funeral?" I asked, furrowing my brows.

His shoulders stiffened. "It already happened, Emma."

Well, then. It'd already happened. My throat burned as I digested that bit of info. For some reason, it almost hurt more than knowing he was dead.

"That's fucked up," Hunter said. "That's really, really fucked up. You didn't think to call Emma? Email her? They really had a funeral so quickly?"

Josh held up his hands. "I'm not the one who called the shots in regards to that. Don't shoot the messenger."

Hunter's gaze burned with fury. He looked over at me before leaning back in his chair. "I have a lot of things I want to say right now, but I'm gonna bite my tongue."

I opened my mouth to speak, but Josh beat me to it. "I think we can all agree you would ruin the company, Emma. I think you should do the right thing and sell the company to someone who cares, and that would be me. I've worked there for almost a decade. I was his right-hand man."

"And yet you couldn't call Emma about his death."

"Shut up, you fucking hillybilly son of a bitch," Josh snarled. "This is none of your business."

I snapped my fingers like he was a dog, rendering him speechless. "If you fucking speak to him like that again, I will see to it that you don't get a fucking dime, Joshua. Do you hear me? I know I can run that company a hell of a lot better than you ever can."

"Your father wanted me to—"

"He's dead," I said. "So it doesn't really matter what he wants, does it? It matters what I want. And I do *not* want to sell."

His expression contorted with seething rage, the type of anger I'd seen towards the end of our marriage. But then, just like that, he was back to being calm and semi-professional.

"Emma," he said. "How would you even run it from here? From Texas? And you're marrying *him*. He's probably just in it for the money."

"No, Josh, that's what *you* were in it for," I said.

He sighed as if I were the dramatic one, as if I were the problem. Nevermind that he was the dumbass who flew all the way to Texas just to be told no. He'd been so sure he could manhandle me, that he could tell me what to do. That he could control me.

I'd forever revel in the fact that I was able to pluck all of his dreams out of his grimy smooth hands.

"You don't do anything for the company anyway, so why be part of it? Why own it?" he continued. "You don't care about it. Just let me buy it. I'll give you a decent amount. You wouldn't have to worry about anything financially again, especially if you're staying in a place like this."

I plastered a smile on my face. "No."

"*No?*"

I held his furious gaze. "You can't imagine someone telling you no, can you? Especially me. You thought you could fly all the way down here and force me into submission. I'm not a stupid girl, contrary to your belief. The audacity to tell me my dad is dead and then to try and make me hand his company to you is—" A laugh bubbled up. "It's really just so silly. Childish, even."

God, his face was red. His ears were the color of crushed

tomatoes, sweat glinting on his forehead. His carefully crafted mask had cracked. "He trusted and respected me, which is more than I can say about how he felt about you."

Hunter's muscles rippled as he leaned forward, mouth tugging into a growl. "Watch your fucking mouth."

Josh snorted. "You just wait, Hunter. You'll find out what kind of woman she is eventually. I doubt she'll stay with you more than a few months. Just a good fuck until she decides to get off elsewhere."

Hunter's chair screeched as he stood up, but I burst out laughing. My voice rang like a wicked witch through the whole house. "Oh, Josh. Bless your heart. You were never a good fuck. You don't know the difference between rubbing a clit and rubbing the labia."

Josh's face flared even redder, almost purple. "You'd much rather be at the salon than in a boardroom. I mean, just look at this ridiculous house. Everything pink and gaudy."

My grin turned sharper. "Oh my god, *look*. Another man who's threatened by a color because he thinks it's girly. God forbid you ever stray outside of the misogynistic, asinine box you've built for yourself."

"Your own father didn't even want you," Josh seethed. "He wanted me to take over. He wanted me to be in charge. He never found you competent, never loved you. He thought you were just an entitled little bitch, and he was right."

Hunter blew out a slow breath. "Emma."

I heard the warning in his tone. The tension in the room was teetering on the edge of nuclear.

"I can handle this," I said to him. Fury rolled through me and I crossed my arms, focusing on Josh. "So, let's cut to the chase. I'm not signing this. I refuse to. I'm not selling you the company. I'll be in touch with the lawyers and we'll see what your position looks like in the future."

"Are you threatening me?"

"No," I said. "I have no need to threaten a man as small as you."

Josh sat back in his chair. "Emma—"

"No," I said. "Ms. Madden. No more first name basis with you. I am not selling anything. I'm not handing over anything to you."

"Why are you making this so difficult? This is just like you. You think—"

"Okay," Hunter muttered under his breath. "I don't think he's going to get it by himself. He's a little dumb, isn't he?"

Oh boy.

Hunter stood up and towered over Josh, the air crackling with electricity. "Emma said no. Crawl back to California now or I will make you."

"You can't force me to leave," he scoffed. "What are you going to do? Fight me like some ogre?"

"You either leave on your own or I break your kneecaps and send you crawling back to California."

I fought a laugh. Nothing about that was funny, but hearing him say it gave me a visceral vision of Josh on his knees, and well... I did like seeing a man put where he belonged.

Josh glowered at me, his voice lowering. "When they lost your sister, they lost the child they cared about. You were always an afterthought."

His words cut straight through to my heart.

Hunter moved in a blur, his fist landing against Josh's nose. His head snapped back with a crunch, blood splashing onto the table.

"Dammit, my birchwood," I hissed.

"Get the fuck out," Hunter demanded. "Emma isn't signing shit and you're not welcome here."

He cupped his nose as blood dripped over his snarling lips.

"You fucking idiot. Do you even know what you're getting into with her?"

I stood up. "Get out. Now."

He wiped his nose and grabbed his suitcase, standing up. "I'm not leaving Citrus Cove. Not until you sign these damn papers."

"You have three seconds," Hunter said calmly. "Three fucking seconds to get out. I know you went to my house. Your grapefruit cologne smells like cow shit, by the way."

Josh blanched. "I... I don't know what you're talking about."

"You went to his house?" I whispered, shock rattling me. "What the fuck, Josh?"

"I think this whole *thing* is bullshit!" Josh exploded.

"Three," Hunter said.

"But why would you do that?" I yelled. "Why would you go to my fiancé's house? Did you break in? What the hell were you thinking?"

"I was thinking of you! That man doesn't have a single photo of you in his house. And you're engaged? I don't believe it. This is some fake shit to—"

"It's not fake!" I shouted.

"Two," Hunter said. "I'm being really generous right now."

Josh snatched his briefcase from the table. "You will sign these papers. Maybe not tonight, but you will." He raked his fingers through his blond hair, but it was slick with gel and not a single hair moved out of place.

"One," Hunter said. "Time's up."

Before Josh could protest, Hunter went around the table, grabbed him by his jacket, and hauled him out of the dining room. I followed behind them, my mouth open as Hunter literally *tossed* him out the front door.

He slammed it shut and locked it.

I stared at him. My heart thrashed, drowning out all other

sounds. I'd never wanted to kiss him so badly as I did right now. *What if we did? What if I kissed him—*

Hunter turned around, his gaze dropping to my mouth. "So the ruse isn't over."

"No," I blew out a shaky breath. "Fuck."

"Fuck indeed."

CHAPTER FIFTEEN
hunter

I PACED BACK AND FORTH, trying to keep myself from hopping in my truck and taking off after that stupid son of a bitch.

The things he'd said to Emma and the way he'd spoken to her enraged me. She'd handled it better than anyone could have, strong and calm. I respected the hell out of her for it.

Emma groaned, laying her head on the dining room table as she stabbed her fork into her rice. "Are you going to keep pacing? Or will you help me eat some of this?"

I put my hands on my hips. The truth was, I shouldn't be anywhere near her. Not after kissing her on the front porch.

For a moment, I'd lost myself to her. Just a few blissful seconds, her lips had been locked with mine and I'd kissed her the way I'd been wanting to for years.

"I need to go," I said.

"You can't go yet," she protested. "We have to talk about this. And that it's not over yet."

She was right.

I sat next to her at the table. I'd never met someone with velvet dining room chairs, but after hearing the way Josh spoke about her house, I'd mentally taken a step back from critiquing her. It was her home and when I wasn't trying to think about how to avoid her, I had moments where I could appreciate her eye for color and design.

Her little pink house was absolutely beautiful. It was warm and inviting and unique and purely *Emma*.

I grabbed the plate of fried rice and chicken and dug in. I hadn't realized how hungry I was until now. Threatening that son of a bitch had worked up an appetite. Emma straightened in her chair and started to eat too, eyeing me with the same uneasiness.

"Want a drink?" she asked.

"I've got water."

"And I've got whiskey."

I snorted, thinking about it. "Yeah. I'll take some."

"Old fashioned?"

I nodded. "I think the situation calls for it."

"Agreed."

"I can make them," I said, both of us getting up at the same time.

"Don't be silly. I offered."

"Yeah, but that asshole said some pretty shitty things. So just sit. I'll find everything."

Emma sat back down with a sigh and returned to picking at her food. I went to the kitchen and rummaged around the cabinets until I found everything I needed.

I raised a brow as I pulled out a tiny vial of edible glitter.

Of course she had glitter for her drinks.

I smiled and decided to stir some into hers. After adding a cherry and an orange peel garnish, I was sitting back down with two old fashioneds.

Her eyes lit up when she saw the glitter. "Oh god, you're too sweet."

My heart leapt. I liked hearing her praise a little too much. "Seemed like it would be nice," I chuckled.

"Thank you. And thank you again for helping me."

"Mmhmm." I took a sip and relaxed a fraction. "So, what's our plan, sparks? Can I run him out of town yet?"

"No," she sighed. "That would make things worse."

"I can't see how things could get much worse," I said. "I mean, we had to kiss."

Her smile dropped and she shrugged. "I mean, kissing me can't be that bad."

Fuck. That wasn't what I'd meant. But also, what the hell was I supposed to say to that? She had no fucking clue how much I wanted to kiss her again. Or how I wanted to kneel between her pretty thighs and make her see stars.

I shifted in my seat. "You know what I mean."

"No, Harlow, I don't," she snapped.

I held up my hands. "I'm not saying it was a bad kiss."

"Then what are you saying?"

"That we shouldn't be kissing in the first place. You're Emma. I'm Hunter. Remember?" I growled.

"Oh, how could I forget? You're the dumbass who told him we were engaged to begin with."

I glowered as I sipped my drink. "I'm finishing this and then leaving."

"Good riddance," she mumbled, snatching up her glass and plate. "Have fun, I'm going upstairs."

My fingers tapped on the side of the glass as she stood and turned to leave. I hadn't exactly been very smooth there. I sighed and leaned back, staring up at the ceiling.

The way she'd fit against me during that kiss. I'd be thinking about it for the rest of my life.

"Emma, I'm sorry," I called, my voice echoing through the house.

"Good for you!" she shouted back.

I fought the urge to laugh. If only she knew how I really felt, then maybe she'd understand why I'd been so callous about our kiss. If she ever knew that I'd ruined her dates and watched her masturbate, she'd kill me.

And she'd have every right to do so.

I couldn't leave her angry at me. But I also couldn't tell her the truth.

I finished off my food and drink, cleaned everything up, and then slowly crept upstairs. Her room door was wide open and she was sprawled over the bed, her face buried in the blankets. Her ass faced me, her dress hiked up her smooth thighs.

Jesus Christ.

My cock hardened and I turned around, gripping the stair railing. I closed my eyes, trying to sort through the way all my thoughts went to sex. I wanted to bury my face against her pussy and make her forget everything else. *Fuck me.*

"Emma," I grunted. "I just want to say I didn't hate the kiss. That's all."

She didn't respond.

"And also that Josh is an awful, pathetic man. You are so much better off without him and I'm glad the two of you weren't married for long. I'm sorry your family is so shitty. Are you going to be okay?"

"One day," she sighed. "One day, I'll be okay. You don't need to hang around."

But I wanted to. God, I wanted to. But if I did, I wouldn't be able to stop myself from kissing her again.

"Call me if you need me," I grunted.

"Sure thing, *fiancé*."

I never looked back at her. Instead, I rushed down the

stairs, threw the front door open, and bolted for my truck. My cock was hard in my pants, begging for her. For a touch, another kiss, *something*.

I took one last look at her house before driving away.

As if I could escape her. It wasn't possible.

I drove well over the speed limit until I was finally pulling up to my cabin. "*Why?*" I sighed as I slowed, parking next to my dad's truck.

Pops sat on the chair on my front porch, rocking slowly. I got out, thankful that the drive had given my body time to relax, and waved grimly.

"Hey, Pops."

"Howdy," he returned. "You got some explaining to do, son. Your mother is losing her mind over at the house."

"I'm sure she is."

I'd never intended for either one of them to find out about this. My hope had been that after tonight, we'd put everything to rest and move on like normal, but now...

My parents had clearly heard about Emma, Josh was still in town, and I was fucked.

Whiskey wasn't enough. I needed a tranquilizer.

"I don't really want to chat right now," I said tightly.

"Well, that's too bad," he said, standing up from his chair. "What the hell is going on?"

Dammit. "Who told you?" I asked.

"Your mother."

"Who heard it from...?"

"Her Facebook group."

Oof. That was bad. I unlocked my front door and waved him in. "Might as well come inside."

He followed me in and went straight for my favorite chair, taking a seat. "Emma?"

"Yeah," I said. I kicked off my boots and beelined to the

liquor cabinet. I got down two glasses, a bottle of whiskey, and poured one for myself first. "Emma."

Pops blew out a long sigh. "What the hell are you thinking?"

"What do you mean?" I asked. I slammed the shot, and poured another. I took a moment, letting the burn center me. Talking to Pops was always hard, but right now was the worst time for him to show up. I poured him a shot and took our glasses to the living room. I handed him one and sat down on the edge of the couch. "Emma is smart, gorgeous, and—"

"Yes, and why would she want to date you?"

I was speechless. It was jabs like this that had led to our last big fight. A low laugh left me and I leaned back. "Well, Pops. We're not dating. We're engaged. Maybe ask her why she wants that, but I'm not very inclined to explain anything to you."

"I've seen the two of you at the holidays. You're always at odds," he said. "And supposedly the two of you have been secretly dating for months? Why wouldn't you just tell us?"

"Because," I said. "We wanted privacy. And because that's what felt right for us."

"But—"

"Pops, I don't want to argue with you about this," I said. "I've had enough from everyone the last couple days."

He snorted. "Heard Cam decked you in the hardware store."

"He did," I said slowly. I threw back the second shot and leaned forward, studying him. "Why don't you think I'm good enough for her?"

"This is Emma we're talking about. Haley and Sarah's best friend," he said. "She's part of the family. I've heard about how much you dislike each other for months and then suddenly you're engaged? Do you really see someone like her being the wife of a farmer?"

My temper boiled hotter and hotter. "You know, Emma is tough. She's smart and talented and able to do anything she sets her mind to. I can't imagine a world where she'd choose someone who didn't fit what she wants."

"And *you're* it?"

There he went again. I grit my teeth, biting my tongue. "Yep. I am. Have you ever thought about asking what I want?"

He looked at me in surprise. "What do you mean?"

"Exactly that," I snapped. "Have you ever thought about asking me what I want?"

"Is this about the farm?" he sighed. "Are we really doing this again?"

"You never talk to Cam or Sammy this way," I said. "Ever. You're always so fucking proud of them and everything they do and meanwhile I have been busting my ass to keep this farm running. You never thank me. You never say you're proud of me."

He threw his hands up. "Well, thanks for doing your job. How does that sound?"

"Not very good. I think you should leave."

He scoffed but stood up. "You always do this. I don't understand why you won't just talk to me."

"I just tried to talk to you, and you were an ass," I said.

"But, I *am* proud of you Hunter. I just don't understand why you need to hear it."

"Because it's nice to hear sometimes!" I yelled, startling him. "Because I'd like to think you love me as much as you love Cam and Sammy. Meanwhile, the reality is you're always disappointed I don't do everything the way you would."

"That's not true. You're being unreasonable," he said, shaking his head.

Everything bubbled over and I couldn't take it anymore. I stood up, throwing my hand at the door. "Get out before I say something I can't take back."

"And what the hell would that be?!"

"Get. Out."

He sighed in disappointment and headed for the door, but not before pausing to look back at me. "That girl deserves someone better."

I bit my tongue so hard, the copper taste of blood filled my mouth. He slammed the door, leaving me alone.

"*Fuck*, man," I breathed, blinking back tears.

He would never listen to me. It didn't matter what I said, he always went on the defense. I could never get through, could never tell him how I felt.

I'd tried. I'd tried so many times. And maybe I was saying things wrong, but I got some of my gruffness from him. Since our blow out, nothing had been the same, and I wasn't sure it ever would be.

All because I'd suggested he retire.

My entire life, I'd been told the farm would be mine. I'd worked my ass off for it and knew how to do everything, how to run everything.

The suggestion had come after he fucked up one of the vine trimmers by not paying attention. I'd told him I wanted him to retire, he'd told me I wasn't good enough yet to run the farm alone, and we'd yelled until I'd taken off for a few weeks.

When I got home, Haley was back in town, and all of our lives changed. My relationship with Pops had only grown more tense. I could barely stand in the same room with him without hearing something that pissed me off.

But this? This was too much. I could almost understand him resisting retirement to the point of us fighting, but him telling me I wasn't good enough for Emma hurt deep.

My throat burned with tears. I didn't fight them, though. Instead, I let them come as I spread out on the couch and turned on the TV, flipping absentmindedly through movies as I tried to distract myself from everything that happened today.

I landed on *Practical Magic*, pulled a blanket around myself, and wished Emma was curled up next to me.

CHAPTER SIXTEEN

emma

SABRINA CARPENTER BLARED on the radio as I pulled up next to Haley's car in the parking lot of the Citrus Cove Cafe. I sat there for a moment, trying to wake up.

I'd barely slept last night. After Hunter left, I couldn't get him out of my head. There was too much to say, too many words that just wouldn't come out of my mouth, and that kiss hadn't helped at all.

For now, Hunter and I would keep pretending to be engaged. All I could do was hope Josh would leave soon. Him showing up to try and force me to sell the company to him was insane, but not unexpected. He'd always expected everyone to do what he asked.

There was no way he could even buy me out if he wanted to. Not unless my father let him get closer than he should have.

More than once, I'd felt the temptation to pick up the phone, only to realize I couldn't. My dad was dead. There wasn't ever going to be a phone call. And that made me start to sweat in places I forgot existed.

Then there was also the whole not crying thing. Not a single tear had fallen. Maybe I was broken.

I drew in a shaky breath and leaned over, snatching my bag from the floorboard. For now, Hunter and I would have to just keep this going.

God, he frustrated me.

I got out and waved at Haley through the cafe window. Flowers bloomed in the boxes beneath it, the air balmy with the promise of summer. I pushed my sunglasses on top of my head as I stepped inside. The bell above the door rang and I smiled when I spotted Alice, giving her a wave.

She was putting food down at a table, but still shook her head at me.

Dammit. That meant the whole town knew. I forced a smile as I darted to the table where Haley was seated with a coffee mug, steam twisting into the air. Sunshine warmed her skin through the window, and she wore a denim jumpsuit that I would have stolen if she wasn't several inches taller than me.

"Good morning," I chirped as I slid into the booth.

"Morning," she said. I frowned, noticing the circles under her eyes. She looked like she'd been crying. "For the record, Alice already knew, because Colt told her when he stopped by on Saturday."

I sighed. "No one can keep a damn secret in this town."

"Correct," she snorted. "How was dinner yesterday?"

I was glad I wasn't eating yet, because I would have choked. "Dinner?"

"With Hunter?"

"Oh. It went well." My cheeks turned red. I tried not to think about how much of what Josh said was a knife in the back, or how Hunter kicking him out had turned me on.

Both were equally unsettling.

Alice waltzed over to our table with two coffee cups. Her

apron was tied around her waist, her hair styled in loose curls. She wore a plum red lipstick today that was gorgeous, highlighter dusted over her dark brown skin.

"Hey, beautiful," I said. "I need to know what lipstick that is."

She shook her head at me. "I'll tell you once you get your head out of your ass. Scoot over, Em."

I made room for her, giving her a pleading smile as she slid in next to me. "Angelic Alice to the rescue with caffeine," I said.

"Nope. Don't try to charm me. You've been holding out," Alice said. "What the hell is this all about?"

I laid my head on her shoulder. "Should I beg for that cup of coffee or are you feeling generous?" I asked.

She snorted and slid the mug over, drumming her nails on the table top. But, she leaned her head against mine for a moment before sighing. "I thought we were closer than me hearing the news from Colt. And don't get me wrong, I adore that man. But he's a friend, not a friend-friend like you are."

"I thought the same thing," Haley said. "Apparently they've been keeping it a secret. Which makes sense for Hunter, maybe, but not for you. You don't keep secrets like that."

"*Interesting*," Alice hummed.

"It just happened," I said, sitting up. "Do you want to come over this week and co-work? I know you have admin shit to do."

"Nope, we are not changing subjects yet," Alice laughed. "Nice try. I want details. Timestamps. Dates. Information about how he is in bed."

I fought a laugh. "It's not that big of a deal. We got together."

"At my *wedding*?" Haley hissed. "I swear you were with me the whole night."

Fuck. I definitely had been. Was I really going to gaslight

my best friend? Once again, I felt the weight of our lie on my shoulders. But I really needed to keep this going until Josh was gone for good.

"When you and Cam left, Hunter and I somehow fell into each other's arms," I said.

"And that led to you falling on his dick?" Alice asked.

Haley stifled a laugh. I glowered as I took a sip of coffee, praying the caffeine would help me lie better. The thought of falling on Hunter's dick made me think about the couch situation, and my imagination took it in a much more feral direction. Now, I was imagining—*stop. I can't go there.*

"That's exactly what happened," I said.

Alice took a slow, thoughtful sip of her coffee. "Hmm. So what's he like? He's really helpful around town. Everyone knows who he is but no one really knows him, huh? I have so many questions."

"He's... I don't even have words," I said.

"That would be a first, knowing you. How about you try to find them?" Alice asked a little too pleasantly.

Dammit. My friends knew me too well.

I took another sip of coffee, using the moment to try and catch up with my thoughts. What the hell was I supposed to say about Hunter? I certainly had more to say about him now than I used to.

For a moment, I decided to pretend like he was someone else. Like he wasn't Hunter Harlow. Like he wasn't my best friend's brother-in-law, the well-known handyman farmer of Citrus Cove, and absolutely infuriating man.

I pretended he didn't hate me.

"Well, first off, he's really good in bed. Because he's so tall and strong, he can really just manhandle me in a way that is really sexy."

"Oh god," Haley said. Her mouth fell open, her expression

making me want to smirk. "I don't know if I need to know about all of that."

"Oh, come on," I said. "You've told me what you and Cam do."

Alice stifled a laugh. Haley took a sip of coffee and then grinned. "Yeah, I have. Okay. So he's good in bed, which isn't really a shock to anyone. Hunter is thorough about every job you give him."

The three of us burst into a fit of giggles. I covered my mouth, trying not to think too hard about what it would actually be like in bed with him. Especially after that kiss.

"What else?" Haley asked.

What else? This was the furthest thing from keeping things simple, but I was just going to roll with it at this point.

"Aside from being great in bed, he's just really sweet. He makes breakfast in the mornings, gives me massages, takes me to get pedicures or manicures. He'll wash my hair in the shower, make our bed, and is always just so thoughtful. He makes me feel seen and loved."

God, I was really laying it on thick. Maybe I needed to make this seem a little more realistic, or they would be more suspicious. Was there a man alive who could actually fulfill all those things I yearned for?

Haley nodded, surprising me. "I can't say I'm surprised. Hunter is a great guy. I've been telling you that from the beginning, although I guess you've known for a while. He's just a little rough around the edges sometimes. I think it's because he feels like he has to parent everyone."

"Yeah," I said. "I know he feels that pressure of being the oldest in the family."

Haley nodded. "I love Lynn and Bob, but Bob is much harder on Hunter than Cam or Sammy. I really don't know why. They're good parents, but there's just something there. Cam worries about it, but doesn't know how to fix it."

"It's not really something he could fix," I said.

I thought about everything Hunter had shared with me, and kept it to myself.

"All I know about him is that he is always willing to help out. So it makes me happy if he makes you happy. I just can't believe you hid it from us. I don't know if I can ever forgive you for that," Alice said, bumping my shoulder with hers. "You know you can tell us anything, right? No matter what it is?"

I sighed, giving two of my best friends an earnest look. I hated this, I realized. I wished it were real. I wished that Hunter really was all of these things and that I was telling them about the dreamy relationship I craved.

"What if I murdered someone?" I asked. "What then?"

"I mean, at least give us time to get the shovels," Alice said.

I laughed, but then the guilt returned. "We were just getting to know each other and we knew it would be a big deal. And we were wanting to have our privacy while we tried to understand what was actually between us in case it was just a fling."

Alice thought about it for a moment, and then nodded. "Okay. I get that."

Haley was more reluctant. I could see her weighing all of my words. "I guess. I just don't know why the two of you had to pretend to hate each other so much."

"He's as easy to hate as he is to love," I said.

Haley and Alice accepted that. We kept chatting until Alice eventually brought brunch to the table. As usual, she had the cafe running like a well-oiled machine, but she still jumped in when it got busy. I tried to keep her with us, but one of the new waitresses needed her help.

I took a bite of French toast, looking out the window at the picturesque Main Street that would soon be bustling with people visiting for the Wildflower Festival. I let my mind wander, enjoying the break from my problems.

I needed to send Hunter the spreadsheet. I'd completely forgotten to do that. The two of us needed to make an effort to plan since we were now seen as a team with our engagement.

Then again, he didn't want to be around me.

"Earth to Emma," Haley pulled me from my thoughts. "What are you thinking about?"

"The festival," I said. "I need to get some planning done for that this week."

"Well, that's a good excuse to bring Hunter over, isn't it? You know, spreadsheets and spreading sheets?"

I barked out a laugh. "Oh god. You're not wrong."

"I'd tease you about how long it's been for you but you've been supposedly dating Hunter for months and I imagine that man has quite the appetite."

Heat crept through my cheeks. Our kiss came roaring back, along with the thought of sitting on his lap again and feeling how damn big he was. I clenched my thighs. "You are ridiculous," I hissed, glancing around at some of the other cafe patrons. None of them were paying attention to either one of us though.

"Okay. I have two more questions and then I'll sort of stop giving you hell," Haley said.

"Good. Go on."

"One—you've dated other people since you've supposedly said you started seeing each other? I know you're both monogamous, and aren't looking for a situation like Sarah, Sammy, and Colt have. And you and Hunter are probably both a little possessive."

I certainly was.

Hunter definitely was too.

"Those guys were to help keep you off our trail," I said lightly. "That's all."

"But isn't that kind of shitty to those guys? I mean I know most of them weren't even good first dates, but I just can't imagine Hunter being okay with you going out with someone if you were actually coming home to him."

"Is that your second question?" I asked.

Haley sighed, scowling as she scooped up a bite of biscuits and gravy. "Okay, okay. Second question—when's the wedding?"

I feigned a dramatic gasp. "You're making a pretty big leap there."

"He's your fiancé. What—were the two of you going to have a ten-year engagement?"

Dammit. Why did Hunter have to go with the fiancé thing? Why not boyfriend? It had made everything so much more complicated.

"Maybe," I said. "You never know."

She shook her head with a smile. "Alright. Okay, I give up. I believe you and this wild story, and I'm excited for you. I've always wanted you to find someone who loves you the way you deserve, and if that's Hunter, then I'm thrilled."

"Thank you," I whispered.

She reached over and grabbed my hand, giving me a squeeze. It was moments like this I could tell Honey raised her. I squeezed her hand back right as the back of my neck prickled.

I glanced over my shoulder and immediately swiveled my head back to my food.

Josh was sitting at a booth in the cafe, his eyes focused on the two of us.

Fuck. The last thing I wanted was for him to approach us

and talk to Haley. She didn't know I even had an ex-husband, and this was not how I wanted her to find out.

Haley frowned, her eyes flickering past me. "Do you know that guy?"

"No," I lied.

"Hmm." She scowled. "Should I tell him to stop staring at us like some creep?"

"It's fine," I said.

"Okay, now I'm worried about you. You never turn down a chance to fight a man."

"I didn't sleep well last night," I said. "I'm not in the mood."

Haley frowned. "Are you sure you're okay?"

"I swear I'm fine," I snapped. "Can you please stop asking me?"

She looked away, her eyes tearing up. I winced, realizing my tone had been way too harsh.

"Hal, I'm sorry. I didn't mean to snap at you. It's just been a really weird few days. And I haven't even asked about you. Are you okay?"

"Not really," she whispered.

Now, I went into best friend mode. I immediately got up and went to her side of the table, sliding into the booth. "What's wrong? What happened? Did Cam do something? I will bury him. I will take him out."

Haley's blue eyes glistened with tears. "Cam and I have been trying for months to get pregnant. For *months*. And it hasn't happened. I feel like a failure. I feel..."

"Fuck," I whispered, wrapping my arms around her. "You're not a failure, my love. You are one of the most amazing people I know, Hal. I'm so sorry you're hurting."

"I started my period yesterday," she sniffled, wiping her eyes. "I really got my hopes up that this could be the one. I was a couple days late and really thought this would be it. And

Cam is so supportive. He's so fucking sweet. I cried, and he held me and got us ice cream. He's just the best. But I want a family. I'm ready for a family. I just don't know if it's ever going to happen."

"Have you made an appointment with your doctor yet? I'll go with you. We can make it a date," I said. "See if they have any recommendations for you, and I can get a pap or something."

"You are the only person who would get a pap smear to make me feel better," she snorted, leaning into me.

"Well, I love you. I love you so much. You're my best friend and the whole reason I came here to begin with. And now I have Alice, Sarah, Honey, and everyone else."

"Hunter," she reminded me.

Hunter. "Yeah," I whispered. "Hunter, too. It's going to be okay. There are so many ways to make a family."

"I know," she sighed. She wiped her eyes and sank back against the booth. "I'm sorry I sprang that on you."

"What are you talking about? Don't be sorry," I said. "We tell each other everything."

As soon as I said that, my gaze flickered up to Josh. He got up from his table, tossing cash down next to his plate. He stole one more glance at us before leaving.

"Sure you don't know him?" Haley asked cautiously.

"Maybe we went on a date once," I said.

"A scorned lover of the past, devastated that you slipped through his unreasonably smooth fingertips and into the rough and ready hands of Hunter Harlow."

We burst out laughing. I bumped my shoulder against hers and stole a piece of bacon off her plate.

"Are we still going on that triple date this week?" Haley asked.

"Yeah," I said, an idea starting to formulate. "What if

instead of a triple date we turned it into a little party? We could invite Alice, Katie, and Anna too."

The more people we had, the easier it would be to escape scrutiny.

"Ohhh," That was Haley's noise of approval. "Okay. I mean, that could work. I feel like we need to set Alice up with someone."

We both looked over at our friend and I nodded. "Know anyone hot?"

"I'm sure one of us does. I'll ask around."

"Excellent," I chuckled. "Time to force Hunter to be social with all of us."

"And to finally let the whole world know the truth about you two."

I felt nauseous all over again. "Yep. That too."

CHAPTER SEVENTEEN
hunter

THE GROCERY STORE was more packed than usual. I smiled at a few familiar faces and did my best to steer clear of anyone who'd want to chat as I cleared out the shelf of beef jerky and then rolled my cart towards the meat section.

My phone rang and I picked it up without looking. "Hello?"

"Hey, darling. It's Mom."

I fought a laugh. "Hey, Mom, it's your son."

She snickered. "Are you? Are you my son? Why have you been holding out on me about Emma?"

I winced as I rolled up to the fresh cuts of steak. What the hell was I supposed to say to her? Lying to Lynn Harlow was never a good idea.

"There's a lot of reasons," I said vaguely.

"Hmm." Oh god, I knew that tone. She wasn't buying it. "You know, I found out on Facebook. Facebook, Hunter."

"I know," I sighed. "I'm sorry. There's been a lot going on recently."

"You clearly have my phone number, don't you? And just so happen to live on the same farm. Not only are you my son, you're also my neighbor. Last time I checked, your phone and truck work just fine."

"They do." I grunted as I added a couple steaks to the basket. "Do you need anything at the store?"

"Yes. How about you pick up some chicken and potatoes and come by and explain what the hell is going on?"

Dammit. I really didn't want to do that. I could lie to everyone else, but my mom? She'd know. Lynn Harlow knew me, Cam, and Sammy better than anyone else and there was no getting shit past her. We'd all learned that time and time again.

"I can't," I said. "I was gonna—"

"I know how long your to-do list is, and yet, I'm not asking. Pops is out of the house for a couple hours so you don't need to worry about him. I'll see you in half an hour."

She hung up before I could argue. I stared at my phone screen for a moment and cursed, sliding it back into my pocket. Fuck. I really didn't want to do this, but I had no choice.

Well, I technically had a choice. But if I didn't show up, she'd show up on my doorstep instead. And that would definitely not be a situation I wanted to happen. I'd never hear the end of it for as long as I lived.

I traded steaks for chicken and then headed to the vegetables for potatoes. Once I had them in the basket, I went to checkout. The lines were slow moving, but that was part of being in a small town sometimes. I sighed as I joined one, leaning against the bar as I waited patiently.

"This place is awful."

My hackles raised and I closed my eyes for a moment, finding every shred of willpower I had. Then I turned around to see Josh standing there with a hand basket, a sneer on his ugly face.

"Then leave," I said.

"Have your fiancé sell me the company, and I will," he said. "Don't you want a good little wife who isn't running a Fortune 500 company? Someone to have your hillbilly kids?"

"I'm going to give you a sound piece of advice," I said. "Which is to either shut the fuck up or I'm going to beat the shit out of you in a grocery store."

"You wouldn't," he snorted. "I'm just telling you the truth. Trying to save you some trouble. I can't see Emma sticking around here long."

"So which is it? Are the options that she leaves to run the company or she stays here and sells it to the smallest man on the planet?"

His eyes lit up with fury, cheeks reddening. "You don't know the real Emma."

"I know her more than you do," I said. "I know she's smart and capable. I know she can do anything she sets her mind to. I know she's better than you will ever be. I can't see why she ever married you, but I can sure as hell see why she divorced you."

Speaking of her divorce. Now I remembered that this son of a bitch had slapped her.

"She'll do the same to you. She'll just move on to fucking whoever—"

I threw the first punch. And god, was it satisfying. Josh's perfect nose crunched under my fist as it landed, and his head whipped back. He hit the tiled floor and was out cold.

Well, then.

I hadn't expected him to go down so easily. I scratched my head, not sure what to do now.

"Hunter Harlow, what the hell are you doing?"

I looked up to see Bud, the sheriff. It was clearly his day off, because he was in velour joggers and his wife stood next to him, her eyes wide. She was clearly fighting a laugh.

"In my defense, I didn't expect him to be knocked out," I said. "I thought he'd at least punch me back once."

Bud shook his head. "Goddammit. I'm off today, Harlow."

"Yeah, so look the other way? You do it all the time anyway."

"We're in the middle of the grocery store, in the middle of the day," he griped.

I glanced around at everyone staring. "This man said some unkind words about my fiancé, Emma Madden." I announced. "He's her ex and a no-good son of a gun, so I couldn't just let him walk away after what he said."

Murmurs followed. Bud's eyes lit up with anger as Josh started to come to.

"Bud, I didn't see anything." The woman in front of me said.

I realized I knew her. She was Lee Zeller's girlfriend. Lee was a local electrician I'd helped countless times over the years. Most recently, it'd been showing him how to keep his tomato plants from dying.

She winked and then turned to look at the cashier. "Did you see anything?"

"No, ma'am, I did not."

Bud's wife gave his arm a tug. "You would have done the same damn thing."

He let out a grumble under his breath.

"And you are off today," I reminded him.

"What the fuck?" Josh mumbled, slowly sitting up. "You broke my fucking nose! You stupid country cunt!"

Lee's girlfriend scoffed.

I held up my hands in feigned innocence. "Didn't touch you."

His face contorted with rage as blood dripped down his

butt-chin to his eighty-dollar T-shirt. "Everyone saw you punch me!"

"I didn't see shit," she said. "Anyone else?"

"Nope," the cashier chimed.

"I didn't either," Bud's wife said. "You look a little lost, though, honey."

"Don't *honey* me, you hag."

Bud's expression soured. "On second thought, I think I am working today."

"Good luck," I told Josh. "Also, after this, you need to get the hell out of Citrus Cove. If you ever speak that way about Emma or anyone else in this town, there will be hell to pay."

I turned around and ignored the chaos that followed. By the time I managed to pay for my groceries and get out to my truck, a cruiser had pulled up and Josh was arguing with Bud and another officer.

Bud was shit at his job. Over the last two years, I'd seen him fuck everything up countless times and had nothing positive to say about the police, but this had worked out. I smirked at Josh, gave him the bird, then loaded up my truck and left the parking lot.

I'd been wanting to punch that guy since he'd tried to force his way through Emma's front door. My knuckles smarted, but it was worth it. I smirked as I headed home, but my stomach knotted up as I went down the driveway to my parent's house.

I parked and sat back, readying myself. I wasn't ever going to be ready for this.

I grabbed the bag of potatoes and chicken, and hopped out of the truck. The front door swung open as I went up the steps. I gave Mom a kiss on the cheek.

"Took you long enough," she chided.

"I punched a guy at the store," I said.

"Oh lord. Why?"

"He's Emma's ex," I explained, leaving out the ex-*husband* part. "Nasty. Deserved it. Then he called Bud's wife a hag."

"Oh. That was a poor decision. About one of the only things that'll make Bud get off his ass is an insult to his wife."

"Agreed." I took the bags to the kitchen and sat them on the counter. I glanced at the sink and cursed. "I forgot to fix this."

"Pops already fixed it," she said.

"I'll double check," I said, already kneeling down. I opened the cabinet and peeked under, humming to myself. She was right though, he'd patched it up. I double-checked a few things and got back up, meeting her all-too-knowing gaze.

"So," she said, giving me the *look*. "Spill."

"I don't know what to tell you," I said. And that was the damn truth. I didn't know how to do this. I'd made a promise to Emma to keep her secrets, but now standing here, I felt the weight of that burden. "I don't have much to say, Mom. I love her."

"This is *Emma* we're talking about." Her eyes narrowed on me with superhero perception. "Emma, who you've been arguing with until you were blue in the face since she moved here."

"I know," I said.

"So you're telling me that was all an act? Or what? The two of you can barely stand in the same room together, even during the holidays."

"I'm aware," I said. "And all I can tell you is that I love her."

"What do you mean that's all you can tell me?"

"That's all I'm going to say," I said firmly. "Everyone is getting up in our business and I just want some privacy."

A long, drawn-out sigh. "Hunter, this is just so out of character for you. I love Emma, I just never thought the two of you would end up together given how strongly you seemed to dislike each other."

All I could do was shrug, which made her shake her head.

"Out of all my kids, you're the one who made me gray first," she muttered.

I couldn't help but chuckle. "Is that where I got my grays from?"

She shook her head at me, but smiled. "Probably, unfortunately. I'm gonna let all of this go for now, but I want you to know, I'll get the truth. None of you can hide a damn thing from your mother. Honey and I have already been talking about this, and I know what you look like when you've been caught with your hand in the cookie jar."

I grimaced. I appreciated the reprieve, though. "At least you didn't say I don't deserve her, like Pops did."

She pressed her lips together. "He's... I don't know, Hunter. I'm sorry. I love your father, but he's always been tougher on you. When I first found out, I was a little hurt and hysterical because I felt like you keeping this from us was big."

"I'm sorry," I said. "But I have my reasons. And I need you to trust that I'll tell you those reasons when I can."

"I can do that," she said. Her eyes narrowed. "Are you taking care of yourself? You look tired."

"I *am* tired," I said. "I'm doing my best. You don't need to worry about me."

"I'm always gonna worry about you," she said.

"I'm pretty sure I got my ability to worry about everyone else from you, too."

"Probably. Just promise you'll tell me if you need something."

"I promise," I said immediately.

She nodded and seemed to relax a fraction, her shoulders

softening. "Alright. Well, I'm going to cook up some dinner if you want to hang around."

"I think I will," I said. "Need anything else fixed?"

"You can take a look at the washer if you want. It's been rattling recently."

"You got it."

CHAPTER EIGHTEEN

emma

I MANAGED to avoid Hunter for a few days, but Saturday came around, and we had to go back to being the world's worst actors.

I knocked on his door, pushing my sunglasses up as I waited. I decided to leave Donnie at home and take the initiative to show up on Hunter's doorstep, knowing that otherwise he'd claim he was busy. And truth be told, he probably was. But we needed to talk at some point, right?

He was the one that suggested this triple date to begin with. Now that it was a small party, we needed a good, solid game plan. One that was good enough for our closest friends and family to believe we were engaged.

Why am I doing this again? And why can't it be real?

I tapped my foot nervously. There'd be food on the grill, drinks, games, and hanging out like usual at Cam and Haley's tonight. This time, the focus would be on us and how we interacted, scrutinizing our engagement.

Basically a nightmare.

"Hunter!" I yelled, knocking again.

His truck was here. What the hell was he doing? It was almost noon.

I knocked rapidly until I heard his curse. The door flew open and he stood there, dripping wet, a towel around his waist. My gaze traced the hair on his muscled chest, the tan lines from being out in the sun. The V of his hips and the bulging outline under the towel.

Fuck. Why was I here again?

"For christ's sake, sparks," he growled, immediately slamming the door.

"Wait!" I yelled, my cheeks now the color of a fire engine. *This is fake, this is fake, I don't like him, he's not the sexy plumber, he's just Hunter.* "We need to talk!"

"Why the fuck didn't you call?!"

I opened the door and stuck my head in. He turned around, the towel at his feet.

He had the most perfect ass.

My mouth fell open.

He was staring at me over his shoulder, his jaw stiff, vein ticking in his forehead. "Did you want to see the front too?"

"Um," I squeaked. "Um..."

"Love of my life, creature spawned from hell to torture me, woman who literally tased me the first time we met—either come inside and sit on the couch like a good girl, or leave."

My brain short-circuited as he left the towel on the floor and continued down the hall, shaking his head and muttering under his breath. He slammed his bedroom door behind him.

Well.

I wasn't leaving.

I stepped inside and shut the door, looking around his house. I don't know what I'd expected, but it definitely wasn't so many plants. All of them were thriving, blooming, soaking up the sunshine that poured in through the windows. The whole cabin smelled like citrus cleaner and whatever soap he used.

My stomach did a slow flip.

We could do this. We could make it through tonight.

We had no choice.

HUNTER PARKED his truck behind Cam's. It looked like everyone was already here. Sammy's car was parked in the grass, Katie's big-ass truck and Alice's Jeep parked next to it.

My heart raced as Hunter looked over at me. "Are you sure we have to do this?" he asked.

"This was your idea!" I hissed. "Why did you make this suggestion if you didn't want to do it?"

"I thought Josh would be gone and this would be done by now," he said. He blew out a breath and raked his fingers through his hair. "I may have forgotten to mention something about Josh."

Oh god. "What do you mean?"

"I may have punched him at the store."

"Hunter," I hissed. "*What?*"

He shrugged his shoulders. "He confronted me. Said some nasty things. I punched him. He was knocked clean out. Bud saw it all and was gonna just let everything go, then Josh got up and called his wife a hag."

"Dammit," I sighed. "He hasn't talked to me again."

"Well, good. Okay. Alright. Glad I told you."

I shook my head at him and fought a smile. I shouldn't be laughing at the idea of Josh getting knocked out, and yet... "One punch really put him down?"

"Yep."

"Kind of wish you took a picture of that."

"I know the manager at the store if you want..."

I stifled a laugh and took a deep breath, holding his gaze. "We've got this," I said softly.

He nodded. "We've got this. We're good actors."

"Are you going to kiss me again?"

"I'm gonna have to, aren't I?"

"Oh come on," I hissed. "It's not a chore."

The momentary charm went up in smoke. I glared at him as he got out of the truck, waiting for him to come around and open the door. I squeaked in surprise as he reached in the truck and grabbed me, lifting me out of the front seat with an ease that made my stomach flip.

Thunder rumbled in the distance. Both our gazes turned to the dark clouds gathering before I realized his hands were still on me, and mine were on him.

"Damn spring storms," he muttered. "Remind me to check the radar. If it's a bad one, I might need to run to the farm to check on things."

"Okay," I said. "Let me know if you need help or anything..."

He raised a brow slowly. "You're offering to help me on the farm?"

"I mean... no. Of course not." Why in the hell had I just offered exactly that?

"You'd look good covered in mud," he teased.

I swatted his chest. "Stop that."

"Stop what?"

"Flirting," I hissed.

"You were flirting with me."

"I was not," I growled.

I definitely was.

Hunter tightened his grip as he looked down at me. The dark stubble along his jawline had been neatly shaved, and he smelled like the best kind of aftershave. His brown eyes softened. "We can do this, sparks," he whispered.

"Yeah," I said. "We can. I'm sorry."

He shook his head. "No, no need for that. I don't need you to apologize. I just need to know you're safe. And until Josh leaves and this is over, I just don't think you will be."

"We could tell them tonight," I said softly. "We could walk in there and tell them now."

"No," he said. "I agreed to do this with you. I made you a promise. We're going to see it through."

"Are you sure?"

He nodded. "Surer than anything."

"Okay. I trust you."

Hunter flashed his dimples. "Big mistake, sparks."

I rolled my eyes. "I need a nickname for you. Like..."

"Cowboy? Sir? *Daddy?*"

None of those worked, but then it hit me. A wide grin spread across my face as I looked up at him.

"Dimples."

His lips tugged as he tried to maintain his manly demeanor. "You cannot call me dimples."

"I sure can."

"I am a tough man who farms and fixes things. You cannot call me *dimples.*"

"Please?"

He let out a deliberate sigh. "Fine. Come on."

He released me and held out his hand. Our palms slid against each other as I took it, his callouses making my pulse spike. He gave me a gentle, reassuring squeeze and we made our way to the front door.

We paused. "We've got this," I whispered.

"It's fake," he reminded us.

"Yes. So fake. Nothing we do means anything."

"So... might as well kiss a lot."

"Right," My heart was pounding. "I'll make sure to eat a lot of garlic."

Hunter squeezed my hand again and then opened the door, his body language shifting. "We're here," he called.

Everyone's voices merged together as we were greeted. He led me to the kitchen, a kitchen I'd been in countless times with people I loved so fucking much it hurt. Sarah was leaning against Sammy with a gooey smile on her face. Colt was on the other side of her, his brow slowly raising.

"Well, well, well," Colt said as he crossed his arms. "They don't have knives at each other's throats."

Katie had a beer in one hand, her wife, Anna, standing next to her. "They're even holding hands," she teased.

"Ha ha, very funny," I said.

Alice and Haley came into the kitchen, their attention turning to me.

"Well, well," Alice chimed. "The happy couple is here."

"And still no ring," Cam pointed out.

"Oh my god," I said dramatically. "There will be a ring. You're all being way too hard on Hunter." I meant that, actually. While I'd done my fair share of convincing, it seemed like everyone was tougher on him about the situation. It was starting to piss me off.

Hunter tugged me close, kissing the top of my head. "See? We're more than cordial."

Haley crossed her arms. "Wow, a head kiss."

I sighed and turned to face Hunter. I leaned up on my tip toes, grabbed his head, and pulled him down into a kiss.

Heat flashed in those dark brown eyes as he brushed his mouth against mine, and then yanked me completely against him, kissing me hard enough to steal my breath. I felt dizzy as he released me, smiling like an idiot as everyone clapped.

"Y'all are assholes," Hunter snorted. "What are we doing?"

"We've got all the food and alcohol possible, good music, and each other," Cam said. "Dig in."

Hunter gave my hand another squeeze before releasing me to the wolves. I winked at him before grabbing a cider off the bar and going to hug Alice. I spotted a gorgeous red-haired stranger and raised a brow.

"Who's that?" I asked.

Alice lowered her voice to a whisper. "That's who they tried to set me up with."

Oh yes. I'd forgotten about my little side quest from Haley to find someone to introduce Alice to. "Is she your type?"

Alice wrinkled her nose. "Maybe. My type varies depending on the day."

"So... who is she?"

She shifted with some discomfort, which made me frown. "A well-known singer-songwriter who Sammy invited. Jenna Hart."

My mouth dropped. I knew that name. I wasn't too familiar with country music, but I still knew who she was. There'd been a song that went viral a couple years ago I could have sworn was hers. "Didn't she write that one song...?"

"About her ex-girlfriend? Yep."

I frowned at the bitterness in Alice's voice. "Do you know her or something?"

"Of course not."

"Oh." It was just like a Harlow to know someone famous. "She's gorgeous," I said.

Alice stared across the room and swallowed hard. "Yes, she is."

Jenna chatted away with Anna and Katie. She was tall with curves for days, vibrant red hair that fell in soft waves, and tattoos inking her arms, chest, and I assumed back. She wore a short black skirt with flats and a red top that showed off her sleeve of rose tattoos.

"Damn," I mumbled. "I'm no better than a man right now."

Alice snorted. "You and me, both. You're with Hunter though, remember?"

"Yeah, but I have eyes, ma'am."

Alice snickered at me and pushed her bouncy curls over her shoulder. Her gaze swept over to Jenna again before giving me a flat expression. "So was it Haley's idea to set me up with someone or yours? Trying to distract us from the main course, huh."

Dammit. Everyone knew me too well. "I may have contributed to the idea," I admitted. "I mean, I just suggested we find someone sexy to introduce you to, and they succeeded."

"You know I'm not dating right now," she hissed. "I have a cafe to run. And after... I just can't do anything casual."

I winced. I only knew bits and pieces, but the last person Alice had been with broke her heart. Whoever that bitch was, she'd lost out. Alice was the best of the best and was now one of my closest friends. "I'm sorry, I forgot you don't do casual. At least she's good eye candy. But noted, Miss Too-Busy-to-Date."

Alice swatted me. "I forgive you. And yes, she's beautiful *and* famous. Haley nearly had a heart attack when Sammy told her who was showing up. She even dusted the shoe cabinet."

I was surprised she hadn't texted me about it. A flicker of worry was interrupted when Haley appeared in front of us, eyes ablaze with curiosity.

"What are you two conspiring about?" she asked.

"We're talking about your failed attempt to set me up," Alice chided.

Haley's expression hardened with the challenge. "We'll see about that. Come on. Let me introduce you both."

"You didn't tell me about a hot songwriter attending," I said.

Haley grinned as she dragged Alice and me over to Jenna, Katie, and Anna. Katie winked at me, her arm sliding around Anna. They were always so cute together.

"Jenna, this is Alice Belrose," Haley said. "And Emma Madden."

Jenna's smile lit up the entire room. "Hi Alice." She held out her hand to Alice's and they shook, her mossy green eyes sweeping over her. She then glanced at me, holding out her hand. "Emma *Madden*..." she said slowly, humming.

Needles prickled on the back of my neck and I glanced back, seeing Hunter watching us. He narrowed his eyes before I turned my attention back to Jenna.

She tilted her head. "Your last name sounds so familiar."

"Oh," I said. "I mean it's... sort of well-known, I suppose."

"Wait, are you related to the Madden family?"

Heat crept up the back of my neck. "I am."

Her brows drew together in sympathy. "I'm sorry for your loss then. One of my cousins works for Madden in Sacramento. He said it's been awful since Michael Madden passed."

The blood drained out of my body. Haley looked over at me, frowning. "Wait? Isn't Michael your dad's name?"

"No," I said, my voice pitching.

Fuck. *Fuck, fuck, fuck.* I looked over at Hunter again and his gaze locked with mine. *Mayday, mayday, fucking rescue me, please.* He frowned and immediately left Cam and Colt for me.

Alice gave me a long *WTF is going on* look, but then she and Jenna started to chat with Katie and Anna again, their conversation smoothing over the awkwardness I'd caused.

Haley didn't take her eyes off me as she grabbed my arm,

pulling me to the side. "Emma," Haley whispered. "What is going on?"

"Nothing." I blinked rapidly, on the verge of tears.

This wasn't how I wanted Haley to find out about my dad's death. I didn't want to talk about any of this, not here. Not now.

Dammit. Panic started to freeze me, but then a broad, warm hand settled on my lower back. Hunter's scent hit me and I inhaled it like oxygen.

Hunter pulled me close. "Hey, sparks," he said gently. "Hungry?"

"Did you know about this?" Haley demanded, looking up at Hunter.

"Drop it," I growled.

"No, I'm not dropping this," Haley said firmly.

"I don't know what you're talking about," Hunter said smoothly. "But I could hear Emma's stomach growling from all the way over there, so I think I'll steal her for a bit."

Haley glared at us. She opened her mouth to speak, clamped it shut, and then spun on her heel, leaving the living room. I watched her go upstairs and wrung my hands together.

Hunter steered me towards the back door. We stepped out into the muggy night, the scent of rain heavy in the air as storms crept closer.

"What the hell was that?" he whispered.

"Jenna has a cousin who works for my father's company," I whispered back. "She offered condolences for my loss. And Haley remembered my dad's name."

"Fuck."

"I need to talk to her. Oh god, I'm panicking."

"Breathe," he whispered. "I'm here with you. It's going to be okay."

"I need a shot," I said. "We both need shots. Let's go get shots."

"Emma, you should talk to Haley," he said. "Haley is your best friend. I'm sure she's already hurt because she thinks we were dating behind her back."

"I can't do this today," I said. "I can't."

"I've never seen you back down from a confrontation."

"Then you've never seen how I act when I love someone," I said, my voice shaking. "I don't want to disappoint her. I don't want to hurt her. I..."

"Emma, sometimes we hurt the people we love. Sometimes we fuck up. Sometimes we say shit we don't mean and we do things we shouldn't. But running from it? Avoiding it? I promise that it doesn't help anything."

I stared up at him, wondering where the hell this man had been my whole life. Now, more than ever, I wished this was real. I wished that Hunter didn't actually despise me. I wished that...

"Shots," I croaked. "I want to do shots."

He studied me, but then nodded. "Alright, sparks. Let's go do shots."

CHAPTER NINETEEN
hunter

EMMA SLUMPED against me with a moan. I wobbled as I picked her up, holding her like a princess.

"You guys are staying the night," Cam said. "You can use the guest room."

"I'd be... Actually, yeah."

I could barely fucking see straight. Doing shots with Emma had been the worst idea in the world. She was a quarter of my size but could hold four times as much liquor.

It was midnight, and everyone had either cleared out or were staying over. Sarah, Colt, and Sammy had sandwiched into the other spare bedroom.

Which meant there was one left.

"Hunter," Emma crooned. "Hunter. I think you're really hot. But you're also such an asshole."

"I'll sleep on the couch," I grunted.

Cam raised a brow. "The couch?"

Fuck my life, man.

"Just kidding," I said quickly. "Uh... Goodnight. I love you."

"I love you," Emma sighed, burying her face against my chest.

I went still, looking down at her. My heart was beating out of my damn chest.

She was a ridiculously cute drunk.

Cam let out a low chuckle and clapped me on the back. "Alright. I'm going to lock up and head to bed. I left a couple water bottles on the side table because I figure you'll need it. I'm already looking forward to breakfast in the morning to cure these hangovers."

I nodded and carried Emma to the extra bedroom, kicking the door shut behind us. She grinned and opened her eyes, looking up at me. "Why do you hate me?"

"Emma," I said softly. "I'm gonna get you in bed."

"Fucking finally."

"Not... Not like that." My god. She was killing me. I let out a low laugh as she looped her arms around my neck, hanging onto me as I put her on the bed. She fell back, pulling me with her. "Emma. Emma, Emma... God, your grip is fucking strong."

She started to wrap her legs around my waist and I grunted, stopping her.

"Emma, no. I don't want this with you," I said sternly.

Her eyes widened and she went still, looking up at me. "Ever?"

I sighed, pressing my forehead to hers. "You're drunk. You're really drunk right now. It's a miracle you didn't tell everyone about everything."

"I can keep secrets," she whispered.

"I know. I want to get you cozy in bed so you can go to sleep. I'll sleep on the floor."

"You're too old to sleep on the floor. Just sleep next to me."

Goddammit. Why did there have to only be one bed? I thought again about going out to the couch, but...

"I promise I don't bite," she whispered. "Hard."

I grabbed hold of her again and moved her up the bed. I grabbed her heels and fought to unclasp the straps. Usually, Cam and Haley's house had a no-shoes policy, but they'd let it go for the party tonight. I wished they would have enforced it, because unclasping Emma's heels was way harder than it should have been. She giggled as my fingertips brushed her ankles, satin skin that I wanted to pepper with kisses.

"Do you need help?"

"Nope," I grunted.

"*Nope*," she mimicked. "So gruff. So grunty."

"Emma," I snorted, grabbing hold of her legs and holding them in place. Her calves felt damn good in my grip. "Stop wiggling. I'm drunk too, silly."

"If I vomit on you, will you still love me?"

The corner of my mouth tugged into a smile. She wouldn't remember anything I said right now, right? "Yeah, sparks. I'd still love you if you vomited on me."

I managed to get her heels off and tossed them to the floor. I kicked off my boots too and looked at her.

There really weren't any words to describe how beautiful she was. Whenever I looked at her, I felt the whole world stop. All I wanted to do was make her smile like that for the rest of my life.

She lifted her head, smirked, and then let it fall back into the pillow. "Can we get naked?"

"No," I said. "No naked."

"But why? I want you. I imagined you watching me the other day, you know? I even watched plumber porn since I figured he'd have hands like yours."

What? My cock perked up and I swallowed hard. "Emma. You don't need to tell me about that."

"Do you want to hear about it?"

"Not while you're drunk. I rather know you actually want to tell me. And you shouldn't want to."

"Why not?"

"Because you make me crazy. I'm not good for you."

"You're so good for me," she protested. She started to sit up, but I shook my head.

"Lay back down."

Her hand patted the space beside her. I sighed and crawled over, yanking the blankets back. She started to roll the wrong way and nearly went off the side of the bed.

"Fuck," I barked, grabbing onto her before she hit the floor. She laughed as I dragged her back up, cursing under my breath.

"I'm always catching you."

"I'm always falling for you."

Oh. Everything stopped for a moment. I swallowed hard and pulled the blankets around us.

"Do you get tired of catching me?"

"No," I said. "I never could. Now, get some sleep. We'll deal with everything else in the morning."

She turned over onto her side and stared at me. "I can't believe you did shots with me."

"I can't believe I did shots with you either."

"Then you kissed me a lot."

"I sure did. Goodnight."

"But what if we did more than kissing?"

"Emma. Go to sleep."

"Fine." But then she smiled, her eyes closing. "I'll just dream about you instead."

"Mmhmm."

"Goodnight, dimples."

"Goodnight, sparks."

MY EYES OPENED SLOWLY, painfully, then shut again. Sunshine poured through the window, filling the room with early morning light. All the storms had blown through without really hitting us, thankfully. *Fuck.* A soft groan left me and I tightened my arms around the body curled into me, her warmth...

Who the fuck was in my arms?

Emma.

She let out a soft hum, her face buried against my chest. At some point in the night, I'd lost my shirt, but otherwise the two of us were still clothed.

Which meant my cock was straining against the zipper of my jeans. I closed my eyes, willing myself to stop, but it wasn't working very well.

Emma stirred, long lashes fluttering. I expected her to scream at me or shove me away, but she looked up, her eyes softening.

"Hi," she croaked. "Oh god, my head."

"My entire body."

She smiled, but didn't pull away. Instead, she ran her finger tips up my stomach, her nails scraping my skin and only making me harder.

"Emma," I whispered.

"I'm not drunk now."

"Neither am I."

"And I want you even more than I did last night."

Fuck. I was losing control. Everything in me screamed for me to touch her. To kiss her.

"If..." I trailed off, unsure of what to say. "If we do this, we can't let it derail our plans to go back to normal."

"Deal."

"Are we really doing this?" I asked.

"Please," she whispered. "I want you."

Years of wanting her hit me like a damn truck. I rolled her onto her back, pinning her beneath me. Her eyes widened as she looked down between us, to the bulge of my jeans, and how fucking hard I was for her. The skirt of her dress hiked up over her smooth thighs, her lace thong short-circuiting my brain.

"Please fuck me, Hunter," she whispered. "I'm going insane. All I want is for you to fuck me for hours, over and over and—"

I crushed her lips with mine. It was clumsy at first, all of my nerves rattling as it hit me that I was touching Emma. I was kissing her, had her beneath me, in the same bed.

"Oh god," she moaned.

I clamped my hand over her mouth, my eyes widening. "We have to be quiet."

She nodded and moved her hips against me, grabbing hold of my other hand and guiding it to her breast. I cupped her and then tugged down her dress straps.

"You're beautiful," I whispered reverently as her breasts spilled free. Her nipples were light brown and hard, begging for me to suck on them.

I leaned down, my lips brushing her skin.

Knock, knock, knock.

"Rise and shine, kids. Breakfast is made," Cam yelled from the other side of the door.

We immediately broke apart, both of us biting back moans. Emma immediately pulled her dress up, her eyes vaulting daggers at the door. I shook my head in frustration.

"I'm going to kill your brother," Emma muttered.

"Get in line," I growled.

"Helloooo? Lovebirds?" Cam called.

"We fucking hear you!" I yelled, closing my eyes. "We'll be out in a few."

I heard his smug chuckle. That fucker.

"Breakfast," Emma said. "Food. And then..."

Her gaze searched mine. We were both sitting on the edge, ready to jump, and for once...

For once I couldn't stop us.

"After breakfast, I'm dragging you to my bed. Or your bed, if you need to go home for Donnie."

"Yes," she said. "Yeah. Okay. Food, then let the dog out, then my bed. Or your bed. Or the shower since we both smell like we were up until god knows when."

I sat back, straddling her hips, and held out my hand. She took it, and I brought her knuckles to my lips, kissing them gently. "Deal."

She smiled. "Deal."

CHAPTER TWENTY
emma

BREAKFAST PASSED BY IN A BLUR. The good news was that the bacon, pancakes, fried eggs, water, and coffee cured the two of us enough that we were ready to jump each other. We said our quick goodbyes and were out of there before Haley could dig in too much.

Was I avoiding her?

Yes.

Did that feel really shitty?

Also, yes.

But before I talked to her about anything, I *needed* Hunter.

He parked behind my car and we both got out. I fished my keys out of my bag, unlocked the door, and greeted Donnie as he ran up to us.

"Hi, rat," Hunter said, kneeling down to pet him.

"Outside?" I asked. Donnie took off for the back. I let him into the backyard, turning right as Hunter stepped up behind me.

He caged me in against the doorframe.

"Oh," I rasped.

He slid a finger under my chin, tilting my head back. "Are you sure you want this?" he asked.

"Absolutely sure," I said. "Are *you* sure you want this?"

"More than anything else."

"Then kiss me."

"I'm gonna do a lot more than kissing."

I smiled as I knotted my fingers in his shirt, giving him a light push. He raised a brow as he caught my wrist and yanked me forward, lifting me with an ease that had me internally swooning.

"I like it when you do that," I said.

"Do what?"

"Manhandle me."

He chuckled as he pulled my legs around his waist, opening the door as my dog trotted back inside. He didn't let me go as he took us in and pushed me against the first available wall, his lips crashing against mine.

I was starving for him.

He kissed along my jaw and neck, pleasure rocketing through me. He paused at my ear. "Can I tell you a secret, sparks?" he whispered.

"Yes," I rasped, moving my hips against him.

"I like it when your nails scratch me."

My breath hitched as he continued to kiss down my neck, gripping my hair and yanking my head back. I groaned and dug my nails into his shoulders, feeling his hips buck against me, his cock straining.

"Just like that," he grunted. "Fuck, Emma. I've wanted you for so long."

His confession shocked me, but I didn't have a moment to think about it. Instead, I grabbed hold of his T-shirt and pulled it up. He helped me toss it to the floor and then hiked my dress up.

"Off," I moaned. "I want clothes off. Now."

He put me down for just a moment. The click of his belt buckle being undone followed by the shuffle of clothes coming off turned me on. I started to pull my dress up, but he shook his head.

"No. Stay like that. I'll be the one to undress you."

His command sent a shiver of delight through me. Outside of the bedroom, I really didn't like taking orders. In fact, I never did. But here, in front of him, wanting him... I craved his dominance. I needed my submission.

His gaze never left me as he kicked his jeans to the side, just down to his boxers now. I could stare at him for days. The quick glance I'd gotten yesterday morning had really just been that—a mere glimpse. Now Hunter was in front of me, close to me, his eyes on *me*, our worlds finally crashing together.

For better or worse, this was going to happen.

We were both fucking liars. There was no way we'd go back to normal after this.

He took a step closer, and then another, until he was backing me up against the wall again. His fingers roamed over my body as he leaned down, kissing me gentler this time.

I'd been on the edge for days because of him. My lashes fluttered as he swept my hair back and looped a finger in the strap of my dress.

"Hunter," I whimpered. "I want more."

"Mmm, and I want to take my time."

He tugged it down over my shoulder, leaving a path of kisses that seared my skin. I sucked in a breath, groaning as I leaned my head back.

"Please," I begged.

"You drive me crazy, you know that?" he murmured, trailing more kisses over my skin. He continued to tug my dress down until the neckline was sitting right above my nipples. "Tell me to stop."

"No," I whispered. "I want you. I won't tell you to stop."

He closed his eyes for a moment as if he were fighting himself. I felt a flicker of worry that he'd stop now, that he'd turn around and walk out the door and never look back.

"You won't be able to get rid of me after this."

I breathed a sigh of relief. "I don't want to," I admitted.

"Normally I'd ask you what you liked first. And I'd get on my knees and worship you first and—"

"Hunter. I want you to fuck my brains out and then we can do all those things," I growled. "I want to know all your kinks and desires, but first, I want you to fuck me. Please."

He grabbed my jaw, forcing me to look him in the eyes. "Say please again."

I narrowed my eyes. "*Please.*"

"Mmm. Again."

"Fuck you," I growled.

I squealed as he spun me around, grabbing a fistful of my hair as he hiked my dress up, pressing his cock against me. "Again, sparks. Say please again or you're not getting this cock."

"Maybe I don't want it anymore."

"Liar," he chuckled. His hand slid between my thighs, two fingers rubbing against my clit through the lace I wore. I gasped, arching back against him. "You're so fucking wet for me."

I was. He was driving me insane. I needed him inside of me, I needed to feel his cock— "Please. Please fuck me. *Please.*"

He peeled my panties down until they fell around my ankles and I kicked them off. Desperation and lust swirled into a potent mix in my blood, thrumming as it hit me. I'd never wanted someone more than I wanted him.

His palms were as rough as I'd imagined. I moved my hips

against him and he grunted as he cupped my breasts, pinching one of my nipples.

"Fuck," I moaned. "Hunter, please. Please. I need you inside me."

"I know," he whispered. "I need it as much as you do. And as much as I'd like to just fuck you right now, I'm going to take my time first."

Dammit. "Now is *not* the time for you to be thorough," I growled. I reached back behind me, feeling the waistband of his boxer briefs. I tugged them down until his cock sprang free, slapping against him.

My eyes widened as I realized just how big he was.

God, he was going to skewer me.

He chuckled. "I think *now* is the exact right time for me to be thorough. Do you have lube?" he asked.

"Upstairs—"

I yelped as he lifted me and threw me over his shoulder. His palm slapped my ass as he carried me up the stairs. I laughed as I held on for dear life, my world spinning as he tossed me onto the bed.

"Second drawer," I said, pointing at my dresser.

He pulled it open and went still, and then it occurred to me that it wasn't just lube I kept in that drawer.

Oh god.

He pulled out a ball gag and turned to look at me, his gaze making my knees weak. "We'll come back around to this."

I nodded. "Okay."

He smirked as he went through my drawer, a couple of dark hums following. What was he doing? He pulled out a slender bottle of lube and then looked over his shoulder, his hands still in my drawer. "Condoms?"

"I had a STD and STI test recently and was negative, and I also have an IUD," I said. "Unless you want to use a condom, then I understand, and you don't have to do anything that makes you uncomfortable and fuck I'm rambling—"

He flipped the cap open as he came to the edge of the bed. He raised a brow as he climbed onto the mattress and knelt between my legs. "Am I making you nervous?"

"Maybe," I whispered.

"I also tested negative recently. And if you're saying yes to me filling your pretty pussy, then I think I'll oblige."

I swallowed hard. "I want you to fuck me."

"Mhmm. Why are you in such a hurry?"

Because I've been thinking about this all week and it's been far too long since I've had someone in bed with me and— I gasped as he shoved my knees further apart, his hungry gaze feasting on my pussy.

"Look at how fucking wet you are," he murmured. "And how perfect."

"Please?" I begged. "Please."

"Do you have plans today?"

"No. Hunter, for god's sake. My *plan* is to fuck you."

How was he just carrying on like this as hard as he was? His cock was right there, the veins bulging along the thick shaft. Pre-cum dripped from the tip. My mouth watered as I thought about worshiping his cock with my tongue.

He poured a generous amount of lube over his fingertips and then slowly, methodically, started to rub my clit. My head fell back as my hips lifted, desperate for more of his touch. Pleasure careened through me as he took his time, working the lube over me, until he gently slid a finger inside of me.

"Oh god," I groaned. His fingers were rough and thick, waves of need rippling through me as he worked one back and forth.

"Fuck, you feel so good," he whispered.

"More," I moaned. "More. I'm dying here."

"Patience," he said. "I promise I'll give you more than one. This is called *foreplay*, sparks."

My god, he was going to be the death of me. "I'm desperate, you bastard," I growled.

Another dark chuckle. He slid a second finger inside of me and I moaned as I clenched around him. He worked them slowly in and out as his other hand settled over my pussy, his thumb pressing against my clit.

I arched, my fingers digging into the blankets. My nipples hardened as he began to circle slowly, my hips moving involuntarily.

"That's right. Good girl. Fuck my hand, sparks."

Oh.

I kept moving my hips for him. The way he looked at my pussy milking his fingers nearly sent me over the edge. No one had ever looked at me like that.

He added a third finger and I shivered, running my hands up my body.

"Play with your nipples for me."

"Yes, sir," I whispered.

He groaned, circling my clit faster. I rolled my nipples between my fingertips, all of that pent up need building and building as I fucked his hand.

"Good girl," he murmured. "Keep going. Keep going for me."

A ragged cry tore from me as it kept building and building. He circled my clit faster, keeping the momentum as my muscles tensed.

"I'm so close," I moaned.

"I know. I can feel how close you are. Take what you need. You're fucking my hand so well."

My head spun with his sexy words. I screamed as I came on

his fingers, bucking against him as my orgasm washed over me. I panted, melting into the blankets.

Hunter withdrew his fingers slowly and then held them to his lips. My lips parted in surprise as his tongue darted out, sucking off the glistening essence. His eyes rolled back on a moan, more pre-cum dripping from his cock.

"You taste like heaven."

I was in heaven. He licked his lips and leaned down, swiping his tongue across my clit. I whimpered, so sensitive from my orgasm, and yet...

I pushed my fingers into his hair, holding his hot mouth there.

Hunter grunted against me, sucking my clit.

"Oh god," I groaned.

His hands grabbed hold of my hips and he dragged me towards him and lifted me, holding my pussy up like it was a platter for him to feast off.

His eyes met mine before he buried his face between my thighs, his tongue pushing inside of me. I gasped as he held me in place, his arm looping around my waist as he pulled my thighs over his shoulders, putting me in a position that made me thankful I did yoga semi-regularly.

"I want to taste you too," I rasped.

"Not yet."

He reached over and picked something up. I couldn't see what it was though and couldn't even think straight. Not with his tongue lapping at me, his arm clamped around me and holding me in place for him to devour.

I heard the vibration before I felt it. A shriek left me as he held the head of one of my vibrators to my clit, immediately sending me straight back to the edge of coming. There was no going anywhere, only submitting to the mindless pleasure. No escaping the cusp of ecstasy.

"Fuck," I gasped.

The intensity of this orgasm was deeper, longer, stronger. I gasped, tears filling my eyes as I came, still held in place by Hunter. He waited until I was a shaking mess before turning the vibrator off, releasing me.

I rolled to the side, gasping. He kissed up my thigh, up my stomach, until our lips met and I wrapped my arms around his neck, tasting myself on his tongue.

Fuck, he was hot. I couldn't remember a time when someone had turned me on this much. I reached between us, encircling his cock in my grip. I broke our kiss as I looked down. Even after two orgasms and lube, I wasn't actually sure he'd fit.

The size difference between us had always been overcome by my ego, but now...

Well, ego couldn't take a big cock.

"Now, do you see why I wanted to take my time?"

I grinned. "Are you bragging?"

"Maybe," he chuckled.

"Well, we won't know until we try, right?"

"Right."

"We'll make it fit," I said. "One way or another."

CHAPTER TWENTY-ONE
hunter

I PRESSED the head of my cock against her and slowly, carefully pushed inside. My blood roared as our gazes locked. Her lips softened on a mewling moan. Every sound she made was driving me crazy.

I was breaking all the rules. But after waking up next to her, after kissing her, I'd decided—fuck the rules.

Just for today.

Emma's eyes fluttered, her nails digging into my biceps. I huffed as her pussy clenched around me as she took another inch.

"Fuck," she groaned. "What the fuck?"

I kissed down her neck to her breasts. I took one of her nipples between my lips and sucked, feeling her response. I wanted her nice and wet for me. As I teased her, she moved against me—taking more of my cock. I sucked and tugged each nipple, feeding off the lust between us.

She dragged her nails down my arms and I cursed. It felt so fucking good. I was fighting for control right now, fighting every part of me that wanted to take this fast. She'd been begging for me to just fuck her, but I'd be damned if I wasn't going to savor our first and only time together.

"How far in are you?"

I looked down. "Getting closer."

"Give it all to me."

"Baby, I don't think you can take it all."

"Try me," she growled.

"I don't want to hurt you—"

She bucked her hips, demanding more of me. I planted my hands to either side of her with a growl as her legs wrapped around my waist.

"*Please.*"

"Damn it, Emma. Hold on to me."

I couldn't stop myself anymore. Not after her pretty little beg.

She tightened her grip on me as I kissed her hard. In that same moment, I thrust my hips, taking her exactly like she wanted. I caught her gasp between my lips, our moans melding together.

I'd never seen anything more beautiful than her expression as I fucked her. The way her brows lifted, her lips soft with tender cries, her eyes full of heat. *You're so fucking gorgeous.* Frenzied lust mixed with awe.

I pumped in and out of her relentlessly. The sound of our skin slapping together echoed through the room. She gasped, her nipples hard as she arched. I grabbed a fistful of her hair and looped the other arm around her waist, pulling her closer to me as I fucked her.

I'd been dreaming about this moment for years. Her pussy clenched around me as I fucked her harder, not giving either of us a moment to breathe.

"You feel so fucking good," I grunted. "You're *mine.*"

"I'm yours," she whimpered.

Her nails left a trail of scratches over my back, which only made my hips jerk harder. *Fuck, fuck, fuck.* I was so close to coming inside of her.

"Breed me," she gasped in my ear. "I want your cum dripping out of me."

A growl tore from my throat. I was so fucking close. I pulled out of her and pushed her legs back, enjoying her squeal as her ankles ended up by her head. Her eyes lit up as she held them in place, her pussy begging for more.

I held her gaze as I thrust into her again. Her scream melted into a breathless moan as I drove deeper, teasing her clit. She started to tremble as she bent in half, her eyes leaving mine to watch my cock slid in and out of her.

My blood rushed in my ears as I came to the edge. I gave a final thrust and buried my cock deep inside her, coming hard. Hot spurts of cum filled her, her moans heightening as she clenched around me, her orgasm following mine.

"Oh god," she moaned. "Fuck, I can feel it all inside of me."

"Do *you...fuck*," I panted, unable to form full sentences. "Breeding kink?"

"*Yes.*"

I closed my eyes. Sweat glistened on our skin. I stayed just like that, savoring the euphoria that flowed through my veins. My cock continued to pulse in place, trapping my cum inside her.

It hit me that I really wanted to get her pregnant.

The idea of it made my cock harden again. Her eyes widened. "What...?"

"I thought about getting you pregnant," I grunted, moving my hips again.

"*Oh.* Do you like the idea of that?"

"No. Maybe. *Yes.*"

"And claiming me as yours?"

"You are mine. At least right now, Emma." Another deep thrust, followed by her whimpering moan. "You're mine, your wet little pussy is mine. *Mine.*" I didn't care how fucking selfish I sounded.

"Yes," she panted. "Fuck. Just like that."

Every movement was deep and measured. My cum glistened on my cock, dripping down her cunt as I moved in and out. Her fingers dug into the backs of her thighs as she remained folded in half, her head tossing back and forth against the pillow as I took her again.

"I want you to claim every hole."

Fuck. I wanted that too.

"Your ass too?"

"Yes," she moaned. "Please. It's been too long—"

I pulled out of her again, enjoying her squeak as I flipped her over onto all fours. I pushed her knees apart and her breasts against the blankets, snatching a pillow and placing it under her stomach for support.

Now her pussy shined in front of me, my cum dripping from her just like she'd asked for. Her beautiful pussy ingrained into my memory—a sight I'd never forget for as long as I lived. My cock jerked. She was on display for me, *bred* by me.

"Fucking beautiful," I murmured, pushing some of my thick cum back in. "Let's keep that all in, huh?"

She shivered, pushing back against my fingers. I grabbed hold of her ass cheeks and spread them, looking at her hole, my cock ready to fill it.

First, I wanted to get a taste.

I moved my fingers in and out of her as I lowered my mouth to her, running my tongue over her. Emma let out a surprised whine as I rimmed her, all while fucking her with my fingers. I curled them down slightly, feeling for the rough pad of her G-spot.

My cock was painfully hard again. I drove my tongue with the same fervor I fucked her pussy with my fingers, finding a rhythm that had her squirming. She was fighting to remain still, her melodic voice singing louder as she took the pleasure.

If only I had my ropes. Then I could tie her in place and do this for hours. Edging her until she was so close to coming, only to deny her the pleasure and do it all over again.

I was lucky. I had my little goddess's pussy on my fingers, her ass on my mouth, and I wanted more. She was an addiction, an obsession, and it scared the fuck out of me how I was ready to toss my entire life away just to make her happy. She could call me dimples and bathe me in glitter, and I wouldn't bat an eye if it meant she was happy.

"*Hunter*," she moaned.

God, I'd never get tired of hearing my name on her lips.

I withdrew my tongue and rose up behind her. "Yes, baby?"

"*Please.*"

I'd also never get tired of hearing her beg.

I added more lube and then pressed the head of my cock against her ass, carefully pushing forward. There was a bit of resistance at first, but then she took me, our grunts blended as I slid deeper, until my balls were against her ass cheeks.

"Fuck," I mumbled, tipping my head back. I fought to breathe, fought for control.

I leaned over her, kissing her shoulders as I started to fuck her all over again. I watched her fingers dig into the blankets, her ass squeezing me tight with every pump.

"I'm going to come," she whimpered.

I kept the same pace, the brutal repetitive thrusts as her voice pitched higher, her muscles tensing. I felt the moment she was on the edge and watched in pure awe as she came, tightening around me like a coil as she rode the abandon.

I buried my face against her back as I gave a last thrust,

burying myself as deep as I could as I came again, filling her with all that I had. She moaned as she melted beneath me. I caged her in my arms, relaxing against her as much as I could without crushing her.

"You can lay all the way on me," she mumbled. "I like the weight of you on top of me."

I let out a soft hum and relaxed further.

The two of us stayed like that for a few minutes until Emma let out a soft, satisfied sigh. "Want to shower?"

"Yes," I murmured.

"Good."

"I also want to get my rope and tie you up."

That admission slipped out before I could stop it. I felt her tense in surprise.

"We should talk about that," she said. "Like... kinks. And things."

"Mmhmm." I kissed her shoulder again. "Emma..."

"No," she said. "Don't take that tone. We're not thinking about anything else right now. I want a shower and to hear exactly what you want to do to me."

I chuckled. "You're so demanding."

"I know what I want."

I smiled against her skin. "Alright, sparks. I'm pulling out."

"And then I'm running for the shower."

And she did exactly that. I pulled out and grinned as she darted for the bathroom, rolling out of bed and following her. She flipped on the hot water and I found myself feeling grateful she'd remodeled the shower with glass doors. I admired her as I pulled open one of the sink cabinet drawers.

"Toothbrush?"

"There's a spare in the bottom drawer."

I brushed my teeth and then joined her, squeezing into the shower. Her hair was already soaked, even longer when wet and curling down her back. I tipped her chin up as I planted a kiss on her lips, steam curling around us.

"Tell me," she said with a smirk. "What secrets do you have, huh?"

"So many," I said. "Let me under the water."

I reached up and adjusted the shower head so it would douse us both, and then started to knead her shoulders. She groaned, relaxing under my grip.

"I'm into shibari," I said. "I like playing with rope. Chest harnesses, suspension, all of the things. There are classes you can take in Austin that I go to occasionally."

"Whoa," she said. "That sounds like fun."

"I think so. I have a couple friends in the community I've learned from too." I grazed my knuckles over her chest, cupping one of her breasts. "I want to see these in rope."

"I've been tied up before," she said. "But only once."

"Did you like it?" I asked.

She nodded. "I did. I'd love to try it out with you."

"We can do that," I said. "Emma—what are we doing?"

"We're having sex," she said with a shrug.

"But that's all it is..."

"Yeah."

I pressed my lips together and nodded. My chest felt heavy, my heart sticky with feelings I didn't want to give time to.

"What else do you like?" she asked.

"Clearly I have a breeding kink. I don't know if I want kids though," I chuckled.

"I mean, those two things don't necessarily go hand in hand," she said with a grin. "But, that was hot. Hearing you say you want to breed me. That you want to get me pregnant."

Even hearing her say it now, my cock jerked to attention. I narrowed my eyes on her evil smirk. "I also like spanking," I said. "But with my hands. And I have bondage tape too. I'm interested in all the items I saw in your drawer." Her cheeks turned red. "Tell me what you like."

"All sorts of things," she said. "I like being restrained. I like submitting, although only when someone earns the submission. But it's nice to give into those desires and to let go of being in control. I'm used to having to make so many decisions in my everyday life, so giving up the reins for a bit is relaxing. It puts me into a good head space."

I nodded, understanding what she meant. Many submissives I'd met over the years were lawyers, CEOs, scientists, and such. Turning off their brain allowed other parts of their body to turn *on*.

"I like the idea of doing some role playing too," she said. "But I've never done that before."

"Want me to come fix your sink?"

The corner of her mouth tugged. "Maybe I do."

I reached for her body soap and quirked a brow. "Can I wash you?"

"Yes."

I poured some of the soap into my palms and lathered it up. Black violets and saffron filled the shower and I inhaled deeply, my mouth watering as I started to run my hands over her body. "If we do more, and especially if we start getting into BDSM activities, we need safe words," I said.

"I like the stop light system," she said. "Red for stop, yellow for slow down, and green for go."

"I like that too," I agreed.

"And if I'm wearing a ball-gag..."

Fuck. I needed to see that on her.

"Then I like to hold up one finger for green, two for yellow, and three for red."

"Perfect," I said. "What about spanking?"

Her breath hitched as I cupped her breasts, running my

thumbs over her nipples. They hardened as soap bubbles trailed down her body to swirl around the drain.

"Yes," she said. "We can try it. Also... well, never mind."

"Uh uh. Tell me. Ask me."

"CNC?"

Fuck.

"I've never done that before, but I've always fantasized about it. My turn with the soap." She grabbed the bottle and poured some of it into her palms, lathered it, and then pushed me against the tiled wall.

I narrowed my eyes on her. "Sparks. You're playing with fire."

"I know," she said. "But I like the burn, dimples."

Earlier, I'd promised myself that having sex with her today would be the one and only time. But now my thoughts were bursting with ideas of all the things we could do together.

She wasn't the only one playing with fire.

Maybe we'd just do this until the jackass was gone...

All my thoughts evaporated as Emma ran her hands down my chest to my cock. She knelt down before I could stop her, hot water streaming over us as she washed me.

"Come to the cabin with me," I whispered. "After our shower. I have rope there. And a mirror."

"Oh really?"

"Mmhmm."

"Should I maybe bring other things too?"

"You should."

She smiled as she cupped my balls. I groaned, my body shuddering. "*Emma.*"

She stood back up and winked at me. "Let's wash off and I'll pack a bag."

I cupped my hand behind her neck and kissed her once more, savoring the taste of her tongue against mine.

"Are all your towels pink?" I asked as we stepped out of the shower.

"Yep." She tossed me the fluffiest, pinkest one of all.

I wrapped it around my hips and shook my head, hiding a smirk.

I was getting in over my head.

But I couldn't stop. When it came to Emma, there was no turning back.

CHAPTER TWENTY-TWO

emma

HUNTER STOOD BEHIND ME, his tan muscles rippling as he reached for the cherry red hemp rope he'd pulled out of his closet.

After our shower, we packed up quickly and headed straight for his cabin. Now, here I was, naked in front of him again and wondering if we'd lost our minds.

I wasn't sure how long this would last. We were both nervous about crossing the lines we'd drawn, and yet neither of us had slammed on the brakes.

I wanted this.

I wanted him.

We stood before a mirror, our naked bodies reflected back at us. Hunter untangled the rope, his gaze occasionally meeting mine in the reflection.

He draped the rope over his shoulder and stepped up behind me. He gathered my hair and used a band on his wrist to put it up, leaning down to kiss my shoulders.

"Touch yourself," he murmured. "Watch yourself."

I nodded and did as he asked. My eyes widened as I looked

in the mirror, running my hands over my body as he created a loop with the rope.

On the drive over we'd talked about ties.

The one he was doing would wrap around my chest, torso, and hips. The rope would also go between my legs.

I sucked in a breath as I rolled my nipples between my fingers. Little shockwaves of pleasure followed.

"Turn to the side."

I turned for him. He stood in front of me now, towering over me. I tipped my head back to look at him as he created a loop of rope around my neck, loose enough that the center of the loop hit my upper back.

"Hold it here," he said, tapping right below my collar bone.

I pinched the ends of the rope, holding them in place as he created a knot.

"Now hold the loop on the back."

I reached around, holding it in place as he began to create a knot every three inches or so. I closed my eyes as the rope slid across itself. As they tightened, vibrations traveled over my skin, the sensations rippling through me. The rope pressed against my skin as he lowered to his knees in front of me, continuing to tie knots in a line all the way down my front until he came to my pussy.

"Spread your legs."

"Yes, sir," I whispered.

"Good girl," he murmured.

The praise washed over me as I spread my legs for him. I looked down.

"I like seeing you on your knees," I teased.

He let out a dark chuckle. "I'll remember you said that. This knot will sit against your clit. When I tug on the rope, it will rub against it."

"Okay," I whispered.

He tied the knot and pressed it against my clit, tugging the rope between my legs and pulling the ends up to meet the loop I'd held in place at my upper back.

I squeaked as he tightened it, the rope pressing against my clit. He grabbed hold of me and turned me with ease, pulling the rope ends around my chest. He threaded the ends through the space between the first two knots he tied, and pulled back around to create a diamond on the front.

I felt every vibration.

Every single movement.

My moan made him pause. "Too much?"

"No," I rasped. "It feels really good."

It was intense, but not too overwhelming yet. The rope made me feel like I was being hugged, cradled within its embrace. I was still sensitive from the orgasms I'd already had today, but this was a completely different kind of pleasure. It was a simmering heat, one threatening to boil over every time he tugged on the rope, adjusted me, bound me more. Eventually he rose up behind me, made me face the mirror, and started to tie off the work he'd done.

My eyes widened.

My body was displayed in rope, the diamond pattern down the front absolutely gorgeous. It dug into my skin in a way that made me wet, which...

"Oh. Fuck. What if I get the rope wet?"

"This rope is yours, sparks," he said. "I expect it to get wet."

He reached around me and grabbed my chin, forcing my eyes to the mirror. His fingertips left a trail of heat in their wake as his other hand moved around, grabbing hold of the rope right above my pussy.

Then he tugged.

"*Hunter,*" I moaned. He grabbed a fistful of my hair and

pulled my head back, holding me as he pulled on the rope again. I gasped, but if I moved, the rope moved too.

It was the perfect kind of torture.

I shivered in pleasure. In this lighting, his eyes were dark, his expression full of lust and reverence. He was going to destroy me. He was going to worship me. I arched against him, my eyes fluttering as he tugged the rope to the side and slowly circled my swollen clit.

"Watch," he demanded. "Watch what I do to you."

I couldn't look away. I rolled my hips, desperate for more, but he was taking his time, and there was no escaping his grasp. His lips traced the curve of my neck, his beard scraping against my skin.

"Hunter," I whimpered.

He tugged on the rope again, drawing another moan from me. I was unable to do anything but submit. I submitted to the pleasure he was giving me, to the overwhelming waves of sensation that refused to let me go.

Hunter slid his hand up my chest and around my neck. Having his palm there, the gentle squeeze to the sides of my neck, the way he controlled my breaths—I realized just how hot I found hand necklaces.

"Tell me about all the fantasies you've had. Including the plumber one," he murmured.

My cheeks turned bright red. I vaguely remembered telling him about that last night. I started to stiffen, but he tightened his grip, keeping me in place before I could escape him.

"I don't think so, sparks," he said. "Go on, tell me."

"It was nothing," I said. Which was a total lie. That fantasy had definitely been something.

"You're not as good at lying as you think you are," he chuckled. He kissed down my neck, and then sank his teeth into my shoulder.

"Fuck," I moaned. The pain shot through me, followed by a wave of pleasure that made me shudder with need. "Tell me."

"I like your hands," I whispered. "I like how rough they are."

Hunter sucked the spot where he'd just bitten me and released my neck, running his palms up my body.

I wasn't used to this type of intimacy. Any time I'd ever been with someone it was always about the guy. But with Hunter, his focus was on me.

"What else?" he murmured in my ear. "Tell me. I want to know."

I closed my eyes, my head falling back against his chest. "He was a sexy plumber fixing her sink and she thanked him."

"How did she thank him?"

I felt embarrassed, but then he gave me a wicked smile.

"My cum was dripping out of your pussy and ass earlier, and you can't tell me about your little fantasy?"

"Fuck you—" my mumbling curse was cut off by a cry as his fingers returned to my clit, rubbing faster this time.

"Tell. Me."

"She unzipped his pants and started sucking his cock," I gasped. "Then he bent her over the counter and fucked her."

He grabbed hold of one of my thighs and lifted, exposing my pussy more. I whimpered as he lined up the head of his cock with me.

"Then he ate his cum out of her," I gasped. "He was rough and dominant and—"

Hunter shoved into me in one smooth motion. I cried out as I watched our bodies meld together in the mirror, his expression twisting with pleasure. I gasped as the ropes tightened around my body as he held my leg up, his cock thrusting in and out of me.

"Fuck," I moaned. "*Fuck. Fuck.*"

It was the only word I could say.

"Look," he growled.

I looked in the mirror, feasting on the sight of us, which only turned me on more. My head fell back against him, my eyes narrowing into slits as he fucked me, his gaze holding mine through the reflection.

"You look so fucking hot taking my cock all tied up," he said. "Look at you. Look at how well you take me."

"Yes," I whimpered. "I take you so well."

I was begging for his praise. Every thrust made me moan as he pressed his mouth to my ear.

"My cock was made for you," he growled. "You feel so good, Emma. I could stay like this with you forever. I could fuck you every day for the rest of my life and it would feel like this every time."

My breath hitched as he thrusted deeper. The ropes tightened, squeezing me, his rough hands gliding over me as he held me still. I was so close to coming again, right there—right on the edge—

"I'm coming," I gasped.

He grunted as he fucked me through my orgasm. I tensed around him, moaning as my entire body shuddered in full body pleasure. He gave another pump and then stilled as he came, his head tipping back as his cum spurted inside me.

"Fuck," he sighed, relaxing. He rested his chin on top of my head and smiled at me. "Should I untie you?"

"Not yet," I croaked. "I like how it feels."

He nodded and slowly pulled out of me. Our attention returned to the mirror and I watched his cum slowly drip down my thighs.

He gave the rope a surprise tug, drawing a squeal from me. "You're such a sadist," I said.

"I can be." He smirked and kissed the top of my head.

"How do you feel about laying on my couch still in rope while I make us lunch?"

"I think that sounds like a dream come true."

CHAPTER TWENTY-THREE

emma

I HAD a stupid grin on my face that just wouldn't go away. It lasted all of Sunday, Monday, and now it was Tuesday and I'd been smiling so much, my cheeks were a little sore.

Ever since Hunter and I had sex, something between us shifted. It was starting to feel like less of a lie and more like a possibility, but maybe I was being too optimistic.

I stepped out onto my front porch and gathered my mail, going through the small stack as I went back to the kitchen. I leaned against the counter and hummed as I came to an unmarked envelope. Hadn't I seen one like this before?

I glanced at the even larger stack next to the microwave. Admittedly, I was terrible about opening my mail. All of my bills were on auto-pay, and typically, I let the paper gather dust until it overflowed, then I would purge it all at once.

I went through the stack until I found a similar envelope.

And then a third one.

"What the fuck?" I mumbled.

All three of them had nothing on the front except my name. I stuck a nail under the envelope flap and peeled it back. Inside, there was a piece of paper. I pulled it out and spread it over the counter.

My heart skipped a beat.

> *Emma,*
> *You don't belong in Citrus Cove. Everyone wants you gone. If you don't leave soon, there will be hell to pay.*

Well, then. My heart pounded as I ripped open the second envelope, pulling out another piece of paper.

> *Emma,*
> *How does it feel knowing that everyone around you hates you? You're nothing but a whore, and I know it. Want to know how I know? I've been watching you.*

A polaroid picture fluttered to the counter. My stomach lurched as I slowly flipped it over.

Oh god.

That was a picture of me. That was a picture of me in my house.

Sitting on my couch masturbating.

"Oh my god." My vision started dotted as I took a step back. What was going on? Who were these from? I turned around and put my hands on my head, forcing myself to breathe.

Could this be from Josh? Or was it someone else? My head spun as I tried to make sense of it, but there were too many possibilities.

After the confusion came a wave of horror. I felt violated knowing someone was watching me like this.

I raked my nails through my tangled waves and reached for

the third envelope. I tore it open and read over the most recent letter.

Emma,
Did him fucking you fix all your problems? You don't deserve him. He should be with someone else.

I dumped several photos out of the envelope and spread them over the counter. The hair on the back of my neck stood up as I flipped through them, facing them up. Pictures of me in my car, at the store, in my yard.

A picture of me and Hunter.

Kissing me on my doorstep.

It was even more horrifying knowing they'd gotten a picture of our first kiss.

Did this mean it was coming from someone other than Josh? I hadn't seen a camera on him.

But if it was from him...

"I can't do this right now," I whispered to myself.

I just couldn't. I couldn't think about someone watching me this closely or threatening me. It was giving me flashbacks to what Haley and Sarah went through. Nausea rolled through me as I thought about Haley's destroyed apartment in Baltimore, and everything I'd seen written on the walls.

I can't do this. I can't right now.

My hands trembled as I gathered all the photos up and stacked the papers together. I crammed them back into one of the envelopes, tossed it onto the pile, and took a steadying breath.

Maybe it was someone just messing with me. I'd seen email scams like this. Someone saying they knew everything about you and if you didn't give them money, they'd ruin your life or expose your secrets.

But those letters hadn't asked for anything.

They'd just been ominous and creepy and *ugh*. A chill licked up my spine and I washed my hands to get rid of the gross feeling.

Logically, I knew I should take them to the police station.

But I just didn't want that type of attention right now.

I glanced into the living room where Donnie lounged in a sliver of sunshine, tongue lolling.

"Lucky," I sighed.

He got to lay on the floor, not a single worry about weird stalkers and sexy farmers.

I glanced at the clock. I needed to get ready. I'd agreed to work a shift at the winery tonight to cover for one of the newbies. Cam and Haley hired a few college kids to take a load off all of us. But occasionally, I enjoyed jumping in. Seeing the locals was nice, and well—it made me feel like a local myself. And I liked that a lot.

That's what I needed right now. Just some regular bar time, chatting with people, and serving some good ciders.

I pulled my phone out of my back pocket and stared at the screen. I was tempted to text Hunter. We'd made a deal. But the deal had been about Josh, and well...

This was something else entirely.

I decided to wait to mention it for now. What he didn't know wouldn't hurt him, right? And I didn't want to add more to his plate. Not after all the problems with Josh.

The phone buzzed in my hand.

Dimples: what are you doing tonight?

My heart skipped a beat, but this time for a much better reason.

Me: working the bar

Dimples: Damn. Maybe I'll swing by

I grinned.

Me: Do you think they'd be mad if we fucked in the office?
Dimples: Only if they found out. Then again, that's what my oversized truck is for.

I snorted.

Me: Oh, I see. It all makes sense now
Dimples: I'll see you tonight ;)

Flirty Hunter was the kind of man I'd happily get on my knees for.

I was doomed.

A couple hours later, I parked my car behind the new Cowboy Ciders barn and got out. I recognized Sammy's voice singing as music floated through the air, the sunset turning the sky violet and fuchsia. The soft strum of an acoustic guitar melted into the hum of cicadas. I spotted Cam and Colt's truck as I grabbed my bag and headed for the back entrance.

The door slammed behind me and I hung my bag on one of the pegs. I was wearing jeans and a Cowboy Ciders T-shirt, the one with the logo I had designed. It had a simple cowboy hat with a western-styled font, and a rope twisting around it, and stars and trees in the background. Simple, recognizable, perfect for merchandise and their website.

I smiled as I pulled my hair back into a messy bun. I made my way to the bar, stepping out into the large space.

Music blended with the roar of voices. Different groups sat at tables or at the bar, chatting over drinks and food. I'd never seen the old barn in person, but I'd seen plenty of pictures. They'd modeled the interior design after it, but with more seating, extra space, and a bar placed more strategically. It featured vaulted ceilings with exposed beams, polished concrete floors that were easy to clean, and a perfect homespun southern vibe.

I slipped behind the bar, heading straight for Cam as he poured three glasses of wine.

"Hey stranger," he said. He was wearing one of the same

shirts and a backwards ball cap. "Or should I start calling you sister-in-law?"

"Absolutely not," I snorted. "I came in a little bit early. Figured it would be busy."

"It is for Tuesday," he said. "Hal said we had a video trending online, which I think is pulling people in. Go ahead and jump in whenever you feel ready."

I nodded and dove into the fray. Cam worked one part of the bar while Colt worked the other. He gave me a quick wave, but otherwise, we were all on autopilot. One of the new guys worked between the two of them. I took the opposite end, smiling as I took orders and poured ciders and wine.

This bar was a community place. During the week, it was mostly full of locals wanting to unwind with their family or friends. We had several regulars I recognized, knowing they were always here on Tuesdays.

This was the part about living in a small town that Josh would never understand. There was something very comforting about going to a bar and knowing exactly who would be there, because it was the day they always showed up. I was starting to recognize those patterns, and I loved it.

I took a tray of ciders over to a table, setting it in the middle. One of the guys obviously checked me out, his brow raising. He led out a low whistle, but I rolled my eyes, heading back to the bar.

Maybe I would have flirted with him any other time, but now that Hunter and I had sex... Things were different. And not even because of the fake engagement.

I looked around for Hunter, but he wasn't here yet. My gaze landed on a woman sitting alone at a table, her gaze pinned on me, tracking my movements. I ignored her as I fell back into autopilot, only occasionally glancing at her.

God, she was really watching me. Glaring at me.

I shot her a dirty look back as I returned to the bar. What the fuck was her problem? I thought about confronting her, but then a broad hand settled on my hip.

"Hey, sparks."

I jumped and turned, looking up at Hunter. He winked as he reached around me, grabbing a bar towel and slinging it over his shoulder. Then, he tipped my chin up and kissed me on the lips, earning a few whoops and a whistle from Cam.

I grinned. "Are you working too?"

He kissed my forehead and nodded. "Yeah. Seems like they need the help. I keep an extra Cowboy Ciders shirt in the truck."

And it looked damn good on him too. Once again, I couldn't stop smiling as we worked side by side, falling into a rhythm that kept the crowd manageable. He had the same stupid grin on his face too.

God, we were idiots for each other. He shouldn't have been able to make me feel the way he did, but here I was.

Once again, I found myself wishing our fake engagement wasn't fake at all.

BY THE TIME midnight rolled around, Hunter and I were done. Cam and Colt were going to close down and the last few customers were headed to their cars.

I followed Hunter to his truck.

"Who was that guy who kept checking you out?" Hunter asked.

"Which one?"

He chuckled as he pushed me against the door. "Touché."

"Did it make you jealous?" I teased.

"Sure did. But then again, I'm the one who got to kiss you

and touch you. And I'm the one standing here with you against my truck. Although I'm a little disappointed one of them didn't hit on you. Then I could have taken them down."

"Oh really?" I snorted. "What are you, an Avenger? I can take care of myself, you know."

"I'm aware."

"I have a black belt in karate."

"Yeah. You couldn't take me down though."

I couldn't tell if he was being serious. "I absolutely could."

He shook his head. "Sorry, sparks, but there's no way you could take me down. I know martial arts too."

I laughed. He was wrong. He was so, so wrong. "Okay. But do you have a black belt?"

"Well, no, but—"

"I've taken down men way bigger than you," I argued, my temper flaring. "I could do it easily. So easily."

"Never," he said.

"Do I need to take your ego down a peg?"

"I'm just saying..."

"Mhmm." I raised a brow at him. I was ready to put him in his place. In the bedroom, I might be getting on my knees for him, but outside of it? I wanted to rub his smug words back in his face. "I'll make a bet with you."

He arched a brow. "A bet?"

"Yep." I stabbed my finger at his muscled chest. "If I take you down, then you'll send me a ten-minute voice message of you whimpering."

"*What?*"

"You heard me." I tipped my chin up. "I said what I said."

"Why... what? Why would you..." He couldn't even finish his words until finally he got a whole question out. "Why the fuck would you want ten minutes of me *whimpering*?"

"Explaining why isn't part of the bet, but no one else would ever hear it. For my ears only."

He stared at me like I'd lost his mind. Surely, he'd say no. Right? There was no way he'd send me ten minutes of him whimpering.

I really wanted him to, though. I loved those audios online, they were hot as fuck. And maybe, secretly, the idea of him moaning my name the same way he had the other day was a huge turn on.

He crossed his arms, studying me. His eyes lit up with amusement. *Big mistake.* I didn't make a bet unless I knew I'd win.

"Fine," he said. "And if I win, then you send me ten minutes of *you* begging and whimpering."

"Deal."

Before he could react, I grabbed hold of his arm, kicked out his leg, and twisted him around, taking him to the gravel. He hit the ground with a heavy thud, fighting against me as I slid my arm around his neck. The moon shone high above us, the stars twinkling with the same amusement I'd seen in his pretty brown eyes as I put him in a chokehold.

"Fuck," he croaked. "Goddammit, woman. What the fuck?"

I tightened my grip as he tried to flip me over, holding onto him with the grip of an anaconda.

His hand slapped the gravel and I released him, feeling victorious. I rose up as he turned over on his back and then straddled his hips, grinning. I glanced up at the barn, but he'd parked far enough out that I didn't think anyone could see us if they were going to their cars.

"See," I said. "Told you I could."

"You cheated," he growled, his hands settling on my hips.

"A bet is a bet," I said. "Ten minutes, sir. Whimpering, moaning."

"Do you want me to beg you too?"

"Yeah," I said. "I want you begging for me to give my pussy to you."

His eyes darkened, gaze sliding down to the position we were in. I rocked my hips, feeling his erection between my legs.

Suddenly I couldn't even remember my name.

"Promise me," he said seriously. "My whimpers are for your ears only."

"I promise," I said. "For my ears only."

He nodded and his lips slowly tugged into a grin. "So that's what does it for you, huh? Me moaning your name? And plumbers. Can't forget about the hot, sexy plumbers."

I shoved his chest with a scoff, my cheeks flaming. "Oh, fuck you."

"Do you want to right now?"

"No," I said. "I want you to go home and record those ten minutes for me. Then we'll see if I'll bless you with my presence."

I got up and stood over him in a power stance for a moment.

"Mm. Alright," he said. "I'll get you those ten minutes, ma'am."

"Good," I said. I held out my hand and helped pull him to standing.

He backed me against the truck again and leaned in. "I don't actually know self defense," he whispered. "Just how to brawl with drunks."

"So you knew I'd take you down?"

"Sure did."

My lips parted in surprise. "You scoundrel."

He laughed and slid his hand behind my neck, rubbing the

muscles. My eyes nearly rolled back in my head. "Don't worry," he said. "I'll be good for you."

Fuck. "The power will go to my head."

"Mmhmm. And knowing that, I'll savor your submission all the more."

His damn mouth. My eyes widened.

"Goodnight, sparks."

He planted a kiss on me and winked, turning me around and giving me a gentle push towards my car. I shot him a look over my shoulder, shaking my head as I went to my car.

"Goodnight," I said, waving at him.

Hunter smiled and waved. He waited until I got in before he got in his truck. I sat there for a moment and giggled.

He was something else.

I was looking forward to hearing him whimper.

CHAPTER TWENTY-FOUR
hunter

I SPREAD out on my bed and stared at the ceiling.

My dick had taken control of every action and thought lately. Guilt was an elephant sitting on my chest. I wondered if Emma would still want me if she actually knew about all the things I'd done.

Ruining her dates, running off boyfriends, watching her on camera...

All reasons to hate me.

Yet, I couldn't keep my hands off her. Waking up to her on Sunday morning had been the spark that had set all the rules on fire. I closed my eyes and drew in a long breath, trying to release the pent up stress, but it didn't quite work. The only thing that was going to help me feel better at the moment was stroking my cock as I whimpered her name into my phone.

Through the entire bar shift, countless guys hit on her. Women too. She was the center of attention and she loved it, reveled in it.

It felt good knowing that she wanted *me*.

I laid there for a few more moments and pulled my phone out of my pocket. I found the recording app and stared at the screen.

I was really doing this, wasn't I?

Anything for Emma.

I unbuckled my belt and unzipped my jeans, then kicked them off to the foot of the bed along with my boxers. My cock sprang free, hardening at the thought of her sitting on my hips again.

I knew I was dominant in the bedroom, but there was something so fucking hot about her pinning me down in the parking lot which such ease. She was so much smaller than me, but was stronger than a damn ox. I knew that moment was going to live with me for the rest of my life, just like the memory of her tasing me the first time we met in person.

No one had ever asked me to do something like this. I didn't like losing bets, but I'd been too damn curious to see what she'd wager. I knew her well enough to know she wouldn't make a bet unless she was sure she'd win.

Which meant she really wanted to hear me moan her name.

I swallowed hard and circled the base of my cock with my hand, stroking myself. Fuck, I wished she were here with me. I should have asked her to come with me for inspiration.

Not that I needed her here to feel inspired. Just the thought of her was enough to make my cock harden, and I was dreaming of tying her up again and fucking her in front of my mirror. All we did on Sunday lived rent free in my head.

It had been a lot easier when we hated each other. Or at least, when we thought we hated each other. Now, all of those emotions from the last three years were rushing together, pushing us closer and closer.

Every time I was near her, I was fighting an internal battle. I should have kept her far away from me, but I couldn't any longer. I just couldn't.

"Alright," I mumbled to myself. "I can do this. I'm going to do this."

I pressed the red recording button. I let out a soft chuckle, slightly nervous, and I thought about Emma.

The way her long hair tumbled down her back. The way she looked with rope hugging her body, cupping her breasts and pussy. How fucking gorgeous she was when she smiled.

The fire in her eyes.

I thought about touching her, holding her in front of the mirror and gliding my hands up and down her body. My cock hardened in my grip, and I moaned.

"*Emma.*"

I whimpered, and it didn't take long before I truly fell into the headspace of *begging* for her. The sounds I made were unlike anything I'd made before.

I was so fucking desperate for her.

Desperate for her approval.

I'd never wanted anyone more in my entire life. Everything I did was because of her. Emma was the center of my universe, and that would never change, even if our lives spun out of control.

"Fuck," I gasped. "I need you. I'm so fucking needy for you."

I kept moaning and groaning as I stroked my cock. My hips bucked helplessly and the phone started to slide off my chest. I grunted as I caught it, rolling over to my knees.

I placed it below me and planted a hand on the blankets, pumping my cock relentlessly.

"I can't wait to fuck you again," I rasped. "I've been

dreaming about touching you for years. About having you in my arms. *Fuck.*"

A long roll of whimpers left me as I kept imagining her beneath me. My phone was a beacon in the dark, recording all of my filth, my begs, groans, whines. Pre-cum slicked my cock, lubricating every feral stroke.

"I want to *breed* you. I want to touch you."

Fuck, fuck, fuck.

"Emma."

"Emma. Emma."

"Fuck."

"Emma."

I was so fucking close, but I needed to slow down. I needed to stop before I came, and we were only five minutes in. I panted as I forced myself to release my cock, sitting back on my heels.

"Ah-ah-ah..."

I closed my eyes, imagining her before me in all her glory. I licked my lips, thirsty. My hand closed around my cock again and I glided it up and down, shivering all the way to my toes. I couldn't last much longer. The second ticked by as I continued to whimper and moan, lasting as long as I could until the last minute stretched before me.

Finally. Fucking finally.

"The next time I fuck you, I'm going to make you beg," I rasped. "You're going to be crying out my name the same way I'm saying yours now, sparks."

Her name was a melody rolling off my tongue as I stroked myself faster, huffing as my orgasm washed over me. I grunted as I came, my cum spurting in hot ropes. I groaned as my muscles relaxed, my eyes fluttering as pure bliss filled me.

I tapped the red button and ended the recording.

I rolled to the side, collapsing against the blankets. I'd made a fucking mess, but I'd clean up in a few minutes. Sweat coated my skin, my heart pounding.

I glanced at the clock and decided I was staying up late tonight. I was betting she'd be asleep soon, and I'd wait to send it.

Then my whimpers would be the first thing she woke up to tomorrow morning.

CHAPTER TWENTY-FIVE
emma

I WOKE up to a ten-minute voice message from Hunter.

My cheeks were bright red, heat flushing my body as I listened to him moan. Holy shit, he'd really done it. He'd really sent me ten fucking minutes of him moaning and groaning and whimpering my name, begging for my pussy.

Oh my God, this was the hottest thing ever.

I sat up in bed, staring at the screen. He sent this to me at 1 a.m. I shook my head, glancing over at my bedside table clock. It was early in the morning, and I needed to get ready for work. But I'd be thinking about him all fucking day.

A plan began to formulate. I got out of bed, pressed play again, letting Hunter's moan float through the house as I got ready for the day. I shook my head as I pulled my hair back, did my makeup, went downstairs and made a cup of coffee. *Fuck, Emma. Emma I need you. Emma I want to be inside you.*

As my second listen through ended, I took a sip of my coffee, a long thoughtful sip. Then, I opened up the cabinet underneath my sink, got down on my knees, and broke the pipe.

I grabbed my phone and snapped a photo, sending it to Hunter.

Me: Oh no. My sink is broken. Do you think you'd have time to fix it today? Maybe around lunch?

Dimples: Sure. I can work that into my schedule for you.

Me: Thank you, sir ;)

Dimples: Of course. Can't let you go a day with a broken pipe.

I grinned.

Me: Lunch is at noon :P

Dimples: Perfect, I'm starving for you.

"*Sir*," I hissed, setting the phone on the counter. I'd really lost my mind. I'd just broken a sink pipe—one I knew how to fix —just so he'd come over here and lay on the floor for me.

I was already turned on.

I suffered through meetings with my first two clients. Everything went smoothly, but they dragged on *forever*. Every minute that went by was torture.

My last call for the morning went by fast. As soon it was over, I snapped my laptop shut and ran upstairs. I changed into a short sundress that barely covered my ass. I pulled my bun out, letting my curls unravel.

I jumped when a knock echoed through the house. Donnie let out a couple of barks, following me as I got up and went to the door.

I opened it and swallowed hard.

Hunter stood there.

In gray sweatpants.

And a black shirt that hugged him in all the right places.

His dark hair was mussed, the silver flecks in his sideburns glinting in the sunlight. He held up a tool kit and a bag of supplies from the home store. "Hello, Ms. Madden," he said. His eyes fell to Donnie, who was wiggling with excitement.

He leaned down and gave him a few pets until he was content.

"Hi." *Fuck, I just want to jump him right now.*

Hunter smirked slowly and straightened. "Gonna let me in? Would hate to keep a busy woman like you from the rest of your day."

"Of course." I stepped aside and leaned up for a kiss, but he muscled past me like he was a professional plumber and not the man that had sent me whimpers and moans to wake up to this morning. "Kitchen is on the left."

He set the bag on the counter. I crossed my arms over my chest and leaned against the door frame as he knelt down, opening the cabinets. He let out a long hum.

"Wow," he said. "What an interesting break. Can't say I've ever seen anything like it."

"Yeah," I said, inspecting my nails. "Not sure how it happened."

He looked up at me and winked. "I'll get it fixed."

My mouth fell open as he started to pull out his tools. He rolled over onto his back on the floor. The hem of his shirt hiked up slightly, exposing his stomach.

I suddenly felt really fucking thirsty. I licked my lips as he let out a hum.

"Ma'am, do you mind handing me the bag on the counter?"

"Sure," I said quickly. I grabbed the bag off the counter and then stepped over him as he reached up, handing it to him. "Need any help?"

"Hmm. How about you hold the flashlight for me? That would be very helpful."

"I can do that," I said.

He handed me the flashlight as he pulled the pipes out of the bag. He then grabbed his tools from the box and got to work.

And I held the flashlight.

Am I being a good girl?

The question was on the tip of my tongue.

I looked down between us and my eyes widened. I could see the shape of his cock through these pants, and how hard he was. *Fuck. I want him. I want him so bad.*

"Can you angle the flashlight up?" he asked.

The only way I could do that was if I lowered myself, which meant I'd be sitting on him. I slowly lowered down until I was seated on his chest. I leaned forward, shining the light beneath the sink.

He just went back to work.

Fuck.

"Hunter," I whispered.

"It's Mr. Harlow, ma'am."

I narrowed my eyes on him. "*Mr.* Harlow."

"Can you lean in a little closer?"

I sucked in a breath and planted a hand on his chest, leaning in further. I watched as he finished securing the pipe and patched everything up.

"Thank you," he said. "You can get up now."

I didn't want to. I lingered for a moment and then slid back, grinding over his hard cock as I got to my feet. He slid out from under the sink and stood up, towering over me.

I fought a smile, looking at the erection straining against his pants. How in the hell was he keeping this up?

"Alright," he said. "Should be fixed up. How would you like to pay today?"

Oh.

I batted my eyelashes and took a step closer. "Well, you see, I'm on a really tight budget..."

He made a smooth *tsk-tsk-tsk* sound. "That's a shame, Ms. Madden."

"It really is... Do you take any other forms of payment?"

"Hmm." His eyes danced with excitement. "Maybe I can..."

I leaned past him and put the flashlight on the counter. I grabbed the hem of my dress and held his gaze as I pulled it up, tugging it over my head and tossing it to the floor. I wasn't wearing a bra, only a bright green thong.

My nipples hardened under the full weight of his attention.

"I can offer you lunch," I said with a smile.

"I see," he whispered. "I am starving after all that hard work."

"I can see that," I said. "You can use me however you want to."

"I think I'll have to do that," he said.

He moved in a blur. One second, I was standing in front of him, and the next I was squealing as he lifted me up, sitting me on the counter. I gasped as he looped his fingers in the thong and pulled it free, kneeling down as he cradled my calves.

"Show me how you're paying."

My breaths quickened as I spread my legs, running my fingers over my clit in front of his face. He kissed up my inner thighs until his tongue met my pussy. I gasped as he draped my legs over his shoulders, diving in.

Hunter Harlow was a man determined to die between my thighs. I gasped, pulling his hair as his tongue fucked me, his hands gripping my hips and holding me on the edge of the counter.

"Fuck," I groaned.

He drew back, licking his lips. "You're already so fucking wet, Ms. Madden."

"Will this payment work for you?" I moaned.

Hunter chuckled and turned his head, sinking his teeth into my inner thigh like a goddamn vampire. I arched against him as he sucked on the bite, his tongue chasing the pain with pleasure.

"This will do."

He drove his tongue back inside me, eliciting another cry. I held the edge of the counter, rocking against him as he fucked me with his mouth, sucking on my clit, tonguing my pussy. The orgasm burst through me out of nowhere. He held me in place, his tongue licking me through it.

"Fuck," I panted. "This is so hot—"

He pulled me off the counter. I stumbled forward as my feet hit the ground and he turned me around, shoving my breasts against the cool top. I gasped as I felt his cock against me. He lifted one of my legs, grabbed a fistful of hair, and shoved into me with ease.

I was so fucking wet for him. I grunted as he started to fuck me, every thrust rough and dominant. This was better than any fantasy or porn I'd watched. Every muscle in my body thrummed with the pleasure of being thoroughly fucked in exactly the way I craved.

He pulled my hair taut. "Begging for you last night was one of the hottest things I've ever done," he said.

I made a noise of agreement. "I've been wanting you all day."

"So you broke the pipe?"

"It was worth it," I moaned, my eyes rolling back.

He fucked me harder, our skin slapping together. I lost myself to him—his to use, his to fuck.

"Emma. Fuck," he rasped. "I need to see your face."

He pulled out of me and spun me around. I reached up, wrapping my arms around his neck as he lifted me. My legs tightened around his waist as he pushed into me again, our lips meeting in a fevered kiss.

I reached for his wrist, grabbing hold of it and guiding his hand to my neck. He growled as his fingers circled it, squeezing the sides gently as he continued to thrust in and out.

Pleasure continued to roll through me in relentless waves as he fucked me. He pressed his forehead to mine, our lips brushing with each pump. My breath shuttered between us, my entire body melting into his.

"*Emma.*" He gave a final thrust, holding me as he came. I closed my eyes, my head tipping back as I reveled in the feeling of him filling me.

His chest rose with heavy pants. He released my neck, kissing me again, running his knuckles up and down my chest. His touch was gentle and reverent.

I kissed him again, relaxing completely.

It was crazy to think now that I ever hated him. The more I got to know the real Hunter, the more I realized I was falling for him.

That scared the shit out of me.

In all the relationships I've had, I couldn't say I've ever truly been in love. Not the kind of love that made me feel like I was free-falling without a parachute. I hadn't felt like I'd found the person I wanted to spend the rest of my life with. I've never felt seen or loved or cared for, not in the way I so desperately craved. Not in the way I saw my friends be loved and cared for.

I wanted that with him. I wanted this to be real.

But I wasn't certain he would ever be open to the possibility of us being right for each other, when we'd been saying we were so wrong for so long.

He kissed my forehead again and let out a soft hum. "I have to get to the vineyard," he sighed. "But I want to see you again this week."

"We could have dinner Friday night," I offered. "If that works for you."

"It does," he said. "Or any night. I'm usually done working around dinnertime."

"Me too. I wish..." I trailed off and swallowed hard.

"You wish what?"

I wish you'd come over tonight. But that would be too much, right? "Nothing. I'll see you Friday."

He slowly pulled out of me and groaned, looking down between us.

"Shit," I mumbled. "Let me go get a towel."

I slid past him and ran upstairs, grabbing a towel for the two of us. When I came back down, he was over the counter, his brows drawn together in a scowl.

"Emma, what the fuck is this?"

Fuck.

The letters I'd gotten were spread out on the counter, the photos too. "Do you just go around looking through mail?" I snapped. I reached past him to grab them, but he shook his head, stopping me.

"Emma, what the hell? This is crazy. When did these start showing up? This is a fucking picture of us!"

My heart dropped. "Can you pull up your pants if you're going to scold me?"

"I'm not... fuck. Okay, hold on. Let's get cleaned up first."

An uneasy silence settled between us as we both cleaned up. He grabbed the towel and before I could protest, knelt down, spread my legs, and wiped up his cum. My cheeks turned three shades of red.

"I... I didn't want to burden anyone with those," I said.

He shook his head, his brows furrowed. "I'll throw this in the wash."

He was mad. I knew he was. I grabbed my dress and slid it back on as he left the kitchen. I heard the washer open and sighed, leaning against the counter. As I looked at the letters and the photos, my blood pressure shot higher.

Hunter returned to the kitchen and washed his hands, then redressed.

"You have to go to the vineyard," I said.

"This is way more important," he said firmly. "The vineyard will survive without me. Now, please, tell me. *What is going on?*"

CHAPTER TWENTY-SIX
hunter

EMMA SQUIRMED in front of me, avoiding eye contact.

I'd known her long enough to know that this was going to be hard. I didn't like that this was happening after the mind blowing sex we'd just had, since it was already hard to wade through the emotions I was feeling. More than anything, I wanted to soothe her, but I needed answers first.

Emma was like a porcupine when she was pissed. I could already feel the sting of her quills digging into me. She was stubborn, but I was stubborn too.

Her hiding this from me felt like a slap in the face.

All I could think was that we'd fucked up more than we'd realized. The pain of finding out she could have been in danger mirrored the pain the rest of our loved ones would feel when they discovered the truth.

I was angry, because she was in danger and no one fucking knew. After everything we'd seen our loved ones go through, I felt like a failure for not noticing something was wrong. I'd read through the letters and each one of them was strange and alarming, even without the photos.

And with the photos, they were terrifying.

"Emma," I said softly. "I'm worried. This scares me. This scares me for you and for everyone else. These are pictures of *you*." I looked back at the photos and letters, shaking my head. "And there's one of us. This isn't okay."

I already knew who to call. I could have the whole fucking police department here in five minutes. Bud would bend over backwards to try to help, especially after the bullshit job they'd done in the past with Sarah and Haley. The police never helped the way we needed them to.

Emma blew out a breath and threw up her hands. "I don't have a good answer to this right now."

"Walk me through what you know. Why didn't you tell me about this? When did you get them?"

"I don't always check my mail," Emma said defensively. "I don't know exactly when it started, but it's been a couple of weeks, I think. I opened them a few days ago, but I couldn't deal with it. It's been too much."

I forced myself to take a deep breath. "Could it be Josh?"

She didn't immediately answer. She chewed on her bottom lip nervously and looked away again.

"Emma," I pleaded. "Please look at me."

"I don't want to right now."

"We need to call Bud," I said. "This isn't okay. Whoever is doing this, they're unhinged. I'll call him right now, we can get them updated on what you do know, and then we can go from there."

"I don't want to," she said. "I don't want anything to happen. I don't want to call the police, especially after they were so unhelpful with Haley and Sarah. I just want to be left alone. It seems harmless, right?"

"No," I said. "It doesn't. Someone sent you three threatening letters and they took photos of you without your consent. That's not harmless, Emma. That's obsessed."

"It's fine," she said. "It'll be fine. I don't need your help."

"You can't just let this go on," I said. "And it's not even just about you. I'm in one of those photos, too. And the last letter was clearly about me."

"I don't want to do this," she said.

Goddammit. "*Emma*, for fuck's sake—"

"Don't take that tone with me," she snapped.

I bit the inside of my mouth and crossed my arms, looking away from her. Every single part of me demanded that I protect her. I had resources. I knew every single person in this entire town. I could figure out who was doing this and make sure they never did again.

"Could it be Josh?" I asked again. This time I couldn't hide the irritation in my voice.

"Maybe? I don't know. This is crazy. This is probably just someone being stupid and weird. I don't think he would do this."

Time to find the fucker. He was probably staying in the bed and breakfast downtown. It was a little more his style, unlike the couple of two-star hotels between here and Austin.

"I already punched him once," I said. "The fucker clearly didn't get the message."

"I don't need your help with this."

"Well, that's too bad."

"You're not actually my fiancé," she said. "I don't want your help."

"Well, everyone sure believes I'm your fiancé. So if we're going to keep up this stupid lie, we're doing this my way."

"You can't tell me what to do," she said. "That's not how this works."

"It is when you're being unreasonable."

She scoffed and glared at me. I glared back.

"This is exactly why we'd never work."

Ouch. My temper flared, and I crossed the kitchen to her, pinning her against the counter. Her eyes widened and she planted her hands on my chest.

"You can't get rid of me now," I said. "Don't you fucking get that?"

"I can get rid of you just as easily as I let you into my life," she snapped. "Leave. I don't want you here anymore. I don't need your help, I'll take care of it myself."

"You're being ridiculous," I said. "I'm trying to help! I'm trying to protect you."

"I don't want your protection!" she yelled. "I'm not one of your projects. You don't need to protect me."

"I clearly do if you're not going to tell the police, at least."

"What the fuck would they even do, Hunter? They wouldn't do anything. You *know* that. These are vague, threatening letters, and that's all they'll see them as. It's not illegal to send someone a letter. Anytime a woman reports something big, you know what we're told? Unless we're fucking assaulted, they can't do shit. That's the reality." She shrugged her shoulders angrily. "I'm not a man, so they're not going to listen. They won't care."

"Emma," I choked out. "We have to do something—"

"I'm done. Get. Out."

She meant it. I stood frozen, my heart thumping. I hated this. I hated the look on her face, the stress.

"Please let me help," I whispered. "Please. It's one of the only things I'm good at."

"No," she said. "Get out. *Get out.* I don't want you here right now."

I took a step back and grabbed my tool bag. "If you'd stop

acting like you're the only one in this, you'd see that a lot of people care about you and want to see you safe."

"And if you'd stop thinking it was your god-given right to always get in other people's business, you'd see why you're burned out and bitter."

My jaw stiffened. Her words fucking hurt. "You're so fucking stubborn all the time. It's exhausting to deal with."

"If I exhaust you so much, we can just go back to how it was before all of this. I never asked you to *deal* with me."

"You did when you told your ex-husband I was your boyfriend."

"You're the one who told him you were my fiancé!" she exclaimed. Her voice wavered, and she shook her head, crossing her arms. "Goddammit, Hunter! I'm so sick of you! You can't just take control of my life!"

Fuck. I was fucking up. I knew I was fucking up, but I couldn't find the right words.

"I just want to help you," I insisted. "That's all I'm trying to do. That's all I want to do."

"You're no better than Josh. He was the same way, always trying to control me."

"I don't want to control you," I argued. "I want you to be safe. That's all I want, Emma. I just want—"

"What about what *I* want?"

I scoffed. "This isn't about what anyone wants. This is about keeping you safe. Keeping *us* safe."

"There is no us. Not anymore." Emma threw up her hands. "Get out. Go. I'm not doing this. I'm not going to let you, of all people, tell me what to do."

"Fine."

"*Fine.*"

"Call me next time you need me to pretend to be your fucking fiancé."

I headed to the doorway and paused. I felt like I needed to do something, to say something. I couldn't just let her drive me away, but...

"There won't be a next time," she said softly.

My heart ached. I didn't look back at her the way I wanted to. I didn't apologize the way I wanted to or say all the things that sat on the tip of my tongue.

This was for the best, I reminded myself. It was better for her to hate me.

I tightened my grip on my bag and made my way to the door. I left quickly and climbed into my truck.

It wasn't until I reached the end of the street that the first tear finally fell.

CHAPTER TWENTY-SEVEN
hunter

I WAS DOING my best to avoid Emma.

It was hard. She was everywhere all the time. It was Monday, almost a week since the two of us had fought, and I felt like she was haunting me. If I went to the bar, she was working with Colt, Cam, or Haley. If I went to the store, she happened to be getting her groceries too. If I stopped by to see Sarah and the boys or Sammy, she was having a beer with them (and would blame her stomach and mysteriously disappear into the bathroom until I left).

Fate was fucking with us, that much was clear. Or maybe I was losing my mind. Maybe both.

The only texts we'd exchanged were if we knew we'd have to appear together.

I hadn't confronted Josh again the way I wanted to. I had been right about where he was staying. He'd booked a room at the bed and breakfast and with a small tip for the owner, I'd learned he'd booked the place for three more weeks.

Just another problem on top of fifty other things. The Wildflower Festival was getting closer, although everything was on track with that. It was one of the few good things happening.

Despite Emma telling me not to help, I'd decided to ask Bud to have a cruiser drive down Hummingbird Lane a couple times a day, in hopes it would help deter whoever was stalking Emma. She'd been right about them not being helpful beyond that. It pissed me off beyond reason to even think that if she'd gone to them herself, she might have been treated differently.

I was fucking miserable.

Every time we were in a room together, everyone looked at us closely. They expected us to behave a certain way. Meanwhile, I was trying my very best not to even touch her.

If I had to kiss her again, I wasn't sure I'd be able to stop.

I set my bottle of whiskey on the front seat and pulled out of the liquor store parking lot, taking Main Street towards the cabin. It was late and although I didn't plan on drinking tonight, a restock had been necessary.

I rubbed my eyes. My entire body ached. I'd been working overtime at the vineyard while actively avoiding my parents. The only reason my mother hadn't shown up on my doorstep yet to interrogate me again was because she expected me to come to her, and I would. Maybe. Eventually.

The road got darker as I drove out of town. I hummed to myself, taking it easy, keeping an eye out for deer or other critters that could dart into the road.

Headlights flashed behind me, and I scowled as they sped closer. Whoever they were, they could go around me. I wasn't going to accommodate some asshole who didn't want to go the speed limit. Perks of having a monster sized truck, I got to decide when to be an ass and when not to be.

They sped up until they were on my tail. I braked a couple times, giving them the equivalent of a driving middle finger. *Is that the fucking Lexus?* I couldn't quite make out what the car was, but it looked like Josh's.

Surely fucking not. He'd have to be stupid to try to run me off the road. My truck would crush his dumb ass.

I cursed under my breath as the car swerved into the other lane and picked up speed. I looked over and shook my head. It was definitely the Lexus.

I slowed as the car jerked in front of me. I gasped as something darted out into the middle of the road, but Josh didn't slow down.

Instead, he swerved further to actually hit the animal.

"What are you doing?!" I shouted.

I slammed on my brakes, skidding to a halt.

He drove the car to the other lane, taking off. My heart hammered as I saw an unmoving lump on the road.

"What the fuck?" I rasped.

Panic flooded me and I flipped on the hazard lights, immediately jumping out and rushing over.

Oh god, it was a dog. I knelt down, tears filling my eyes. It was still breathing.

"Fuck," I whispered. "That son of a bitch. Fuck. *Fuck.*"

The dog let out a soft, crying whine and tried to move. "No, no, buddy. Stay put. It's okay. It's gonna be okay."

I pulled out my phone and immediately called Anna. She was married to Katie Mays, our local vet, who we'd all gone to high school with.

She answered. "Harlow, this better be an emergency. It's nearly midnight and my wife is waiting for me."

"Anna, a dog has been hit and he's... fuck, he's in bad shape. Something's wrong and broken, I don't know. Fuck."

"Okay, breathe," she said firmly. "Where are you at?"

"About ten minutes from the farm," I said. "Should I move

him? God, this is fucking awful." The dog stared up at me, eyes glistening. He continued to cry, and I wiped the tears from my eyes. "I saw the son of a bitch do it and he just fucking drove off."

Josh was a dead man. A fucking. Dead. Man.

"I'm on my way. Don't move him, okay? But Hunter, if he's that bad, he might not make it."

"Okay," I whispered. "I'll be here."

Luckily, there wasn't anyone else on the road because it was so late. "It's going to be okay," I murmured softly, gently petting his head. He let out a soft whine, his tail giving a dejected thump. "You're gonna be just fine. You have to pull through because otherwise I'm going to feel obliged to turn that son of a bitch into roadkill."

I kept stroking the uninjured parts of him, talking to him softly until Anna's car pulled up. She hopped out and rushed over to me. Katie was with her, too.

"Aw, fuck," she sighed, kneeling down. "Okay. Katie, grab the towel. He's a sweet boy, yes, you are."

Katie rushed over with a towel and Anna took it, wrapping it around him.

"He's still a puppy. Looks like a blue heeler mix," Katie said, shaking her head. "Did they hit him on purpose? Should I call the sheriff?"

"He did," I said. "He had the whole road. And no, let's leave them out of this for now."

Anna nodded, crooning as she carefully scratched his head. "I'm gonna pick him up and we'll head to the clinic."

"What can I do to help?" I asked.

"Nothing, really. He looks like a stray, and you made the call. Someone probably dumped him."

I shook my head. "I'm coming with you. I want to know what happens."

She winced as she carefully picked him up. "Alright. I'll see you at the clinic."

"Right behind you," I said.

I watched as they loaded him up, then got into my truck and followed behind. Holding my phone as I drove, I finally decided to call the only person I could talk to about this.

The phone rang three times before Emma picked up. "What do you want?"

"Josh tried to run me off the road and then he hit a dog," I croaked.

"Holy shit, what the fuck? Oh my god. Are you okay? Is the dog okay?"

"Katie and Anna are taking him to the clinic, I'm going with them."

"Okay. I'll be there in a few minutes."

"No, you don't have to—"

She hung up as I pulled into the parking lot. Katie hopped out and opened the door for Anna. I followed them to the back door, which Katie unlocked for the three of us.

"Emma is coming over too," I said.

"Oh," Katie said, raising a brow. "Your *fiancé*."

"Yep," I sighed.

Anna nodded at the light switch. "Turn all the lights on, I'm gonna get him sedated and see what's going on. Hunter, honestly, just go sit somewhere. I don't need you hovering with your pretty-man tears."

Katie winced and flipped on the lights. "Sorry, she's going into doctor mode."

"No, it's okay," I said, wiping my face again.

"Katie, come with me!" Anna called.

"Oop. Okay. Um, just go wait up front and let Emma in when she gets here."

"Thank you," I said.

"What are you naming your new dog, huh?" she asked.

I opened my mouth to tell her he wasn't mine, but clamped it shut when Anna called for her again. Katie took off after her.

I went to the front of the clinic. Headlights flashed outside as Emma's car pulled in. I opened the front door as she got out wearing her silk pajama shirts, a tank top, and fluffy flip flops.

Relief flooded me.

She rushed over to me, her eyes wide. She reached up, her hands clasping my arms. "Are you okay?" she asked.

"Yeah," I whispered. "Fuck, Emma. He really hit that dog on purpose. He swerved right into it. He's a fucking monster."

Tears filled her eyes. "I'm so sorry. This is all my fault and—"

I reached up, sliding my hand around the back of her neck. "Baby, this isn't your fault," I said. "I am scared for you. I am scared he'd try to go after Donnie or harm you."

"I'll be okay," she whispered.

"I think we should go to the police," I said. "He broke into my house. Then you have all of those letters. And now this? I can't imagine anyone sane hitting an animal on purpose. There are so few things that make me see fucking red, but animal abuse is one of them."

She let out a shaky breath. "I don't want to go to them about this. They aren't helpful. After seeing what Haley and Sarah have gone through, I just..."

"Just think about it, please. At least so we can start a paper trail," I whispered. "Fuck. I'm sorry."

"Let's talk about that later. I'm just thankful you're okay and... is the dog...?"

"He's alive." My throat burned, and I wiped my face. "Anna has him in the back. Katie is with her."

"It's times like this I'm so glad you know everyone," she said.

"Me too."

I suddenly became aware that we were touching. And that we'd been touching for a few moments. My gaze swept to her mouth, everything inside me screaming to kiss her. To taste her.

I'd missed her so much it hurt.

"You don't have to wait with me," I murmured.

"I'm going to," she said. "I'm not leaving. I have Donnie in the car, though..."

"My favorite rat," I said.

She rolled her eyes and pulled out of my embrace. My hands fell to my side as I watched her go back to her car to get Donnie. He was tucked into a special purse meant to carry him, his head poking out. I ruffled his head and locked the door behind us, sighing as I glanced towards the back room.

Anna had told me to stay out of the way, but I really wanted to check on him.

"Are you sure you want to hang around?" I asked. "It's late and I don't know how long this will take."

"I'm sure," she said.

"Okay." I was too distraught to fight her. I started to pace back and forth, until I finally decided to ask for an update.

I went down the hall to one of the rooms and poked my head in. Anna glanced up and shook her head.

Fear bolted through me. "Is he okay?"

"He's okay," she said. "He's gonna be just fine."

I slumped against the door frame. "Fuck, man."

Katie offered me a soft smile. "So, did you decide on a name? And a budget for surgery?"

"Katie," Anna hissed.

"I'll pay whatever," I said.

Because yeah, even if I didn't plan on owning a dog, I certainly had one now.

"I don't care how much," I said. "And no, I haven't decided on a name."

Anna smiled. "I'm sure you'll think of one. I think he's a lab and blue heeler mix. He's about eleven months old and he's not chipped. He got lucky. His front leg is broken, and it needs to be plated. He's got some road rash too, but overall he's in better shape than I thought he'd be. I already called in my assistants and they'll be over soon. It'll be at least five hours, Hunter. And this will be pricey. Are you sure you want him?"

"I'm absolutely sure. I don't care how much it costs. And I'm waiting."

"I'll give you the friend discount. And like I said, five hours—"

"I'll be in the waiting room," I said.

She nodded as I ducked away, heading back to the waiting room. I sat down next to Emma and leaned back, my head resting against the wall.

"Any updates?" she asked.

"It'll be at least five hours. You don't need to wait with me, sparks."

"I'm not leaving you."

I blew out a breath. "Okay."

"Okay," she said, relaxing next to me. "Want to hold Donnie?"

"Yeah, actually."

"He's good at emotional support," she said as she unlatched her purse and pulled him out. She plopped him in my lap and he stretched up, putting his paws on my chest. I scratched his ears, fighting tears again.

"When I was ten, my dad and I were driving and someone hit a dog in front of us," I said. "But we got out to help and it didn't make it. And I cried so hard, my dad gave me Benadryl to calm me down instead of actually talking to me."

"What the fuck?" she whispered.

"He's changed a lot," I said, sniffling as I kept petting Donnie. "I don't know. Sorry."

"You don't have anything to be sorry for," she said. "*I'm* sorry. I don't know, Hunter. Sometimes I'm really stubborn."

"Me too."

Her hand slid over, her palm turned up. I slid mine against hers, giving it a gentle squeeze.

"I'm glad you were there to save him. I can't believe Josh did this."

"Unless it was someone else's silver Lexus."

We both knew it wasn't.

"Have you ever talked to your dad about how he treats you sometimes?" Emma asked. "I mean, I know your dad. He's so sweet, I just don't get it."

"I've tried, Emma. When he found out about us, he came over and made it clear I wasn't right for you. And that I could never be worthy of you."

She scoffed. "Well, good thing it's not up to him."

"He doesn't understand me," I said. "He never will. And any time I try to talk to him, we fight. Then I say stupid things, he says stupid things, and it goes in one big circle. We used to manage our differences better, but we had a huge fight right around when Haley came back to Citrus Cove. I ended up leaving for a few weeks to get away." Come to think about it, that was the last time I'd had a vacation.

"What was your fight about?"

I sighed, thinking back to it. It was stupid, which wasn't surprising. "I felt like it was time for him to retire. He fucked up one of our expensive pieces of equipment and it was just the final straw for me. That didn't go over well at all. The farm is everything to him, but it's everything to me too. I don't understand why he won't just enjoy his life."

"I'm sorry, Hunter. Maybe you could try something else to get through to him? Maybe write him a letter?"

I chuckled, feeling myself relax. "I don't think that'd go over well."

"It just could be a way to say everything you need to. Even if you don't actually send it. I've done it a few times when I was mad at my dad. I..." Her grip tightened on my hand. "I've taken some time over the last few days to think about him."

"Did you cry?" I asked softly.

"Not yet," she sighed. "Not yet. But I am starting to feel a little better. I reached out to the lawyers about Madden Enterprises. I'm still waiting on a response."

I frowned. The whole situation was still strange to me, but maybe I just wasn't familiar with corporate procedures. Donnie curled up, making me smile. He fit perfectly on my thigh, such a tiny little thing.

"I know I call him a rat," I said. "But I really like your dog."

"Despite the betrayal, he likes you too. Clearly," she snorted.

Silence settled over us, and she made a soft sound. "Can we call a truce for tonight?"

"Yeah," I whispered.

"Then can I use your shoulder as a pillow?"

"Yeah."

"Thank you."

I closed my eyes, and despite the horror of tonight, I smiled. "Goodnight, sparks," I murmured.

She let out the softest sigh. "Night, dimples."

CHAPTER TWENTY-EIGHT

emma

"EMMA... HEY, EMMA."

My eyes flew open and I sat up straight, wiping drool from my mouth. Hunter was kneeling in front of me, clearly exhausted. "They finished up the surgery. It took a little longer, but he's out."

"How did it go?" I asked. My voice sounded like I'd inhaled a pack of cigarettes.

He handed me a paper cup of water. "You snore a lot, just so you know. Should probably go to the doctor and get a CPAP machine."

I was mortified. "Are you kidding me?"

"Nope." He smiled. "What? There's nothing wrong with a CPAP machine."

"Hunter. I would look like a robot at night."

"As opposed to...?"

"Sleeping beauty?"

He barked out a laugh. "You drooled all over my arm, too. But even with the drool and a CPAP machine, you'd still be sleeping beauty."

I wrinkled my nose at the compliment.

I'd missed him. I'd missed him so much, I realized. The last few days had felt empty without Hunter in them.

"They're keeping RK overnight," he said. "Just to make sure he's okay. I'll pick him up tomorrow."

"What does RK stand for?" I asked.

"Roadkill."

"Hunter," I said flatly. "You cannot name your dog Roadkill."

"It's too late, I already signed the papers. He's going to have the best damn life ever. Also, I'm going to murder your ex-husband today. Maybe not actually murder, but kick him out of Citrus Cove and back to California."

"Good," I said. "I'm tired of this. He needs to leave."

"Agreed. Then we'll be done," he said, standing up. "I can't do this anymore. I'm done, Emma. I'm sorry."

Fuck. "Just like that, huh?"

"Just like that."

It was a knife to my heart. There was something so final about his tone. I'd taken a lot of time to think about what I wanted, and had come to the conclusion that I wanted Hunter.

But once again, I was certain he didn't want me. Not the way I wanted him.

"Fine," I said, standing up. "Where's Donnie?"

"I took him outside and he followed Katie around since she had treats in her pocket. He's with her."

"Speaking of," Katie interrupted.

We both looked up. She approached us with Donnie in her arms and a grin on her face.

"Here's your son back, he's as charming as your fiancé," she said.

"Thanks," I said blandly.

Katie raised a brow, but didn't say anything else.

"I'm gonna head home," I said, scooping up Donnie and my bag. I stood up and refused to look at Hunter. "See you later."

"Yep," he said.

"Bye," Katie said.

I smiled at Katie and went out the front door, my face immediately falling. I felt fucking miserable. I got in my car and put Donnie in the back, pulling out of the parking lot and hitting the road.

Fuck Hunter. Fuck this whole situation. I bit back tears as I drove, trying not to think about why it all ending made me feel so fucking sad.

My phone's ringtone blared and I sighed, pushing the button that would answer it on my car's speaker system. "Hello?"

"Emma?"

My heart dropped.

"Angela," I said. My stepmom. I couldn't remember the last time she'd called me.

There was a beat of silence. "Josh called me this morning to tell me you're engaged to someone else?"

I slowed the car and pulled off the side of the road, my heart beating so fast I felt like fainting. "I am," I said weakly. "Why didn't you call me about dad? Why didn't you call me about his funeral? What the hell is going on? And Josh tried to convince me to sell the company to him."

Angela snorted. "You're kidding. Josh would never do something like that. Now, he was pretty convinced the two of you would get back together. That's why he flew all the way down to the middle of... well, wherever you live."

I blinked back tears. "Do you even know where I live? Do you even know anything about me? Why didn't you call to tell me about dad?"

"I know you're supposedly engaged," she said, her voice

straining. "What's the meaning of this, Emma? You know Josh loves you."

"I don't love him," I said. "*Why* didn't you call me about dad? How did he even die? Josh said he didn't know."

She ignored my question again. "Well, sometimes we marry people we don't love."

"I'm not marrying Josh again," I said. "I refuse. And also, he's clearly lying to you. He tried to get me to sell."

Angela sighed. "Can you blame him? He's the one who's been here while you've been off gallivanting around."

"Are you fucking kidding me?" I seethed. "Answer me. *Why* didn't you call about my dad dying, Angela? *How* did he die? What the fuck?"

"Emma, your *language*. You're just being difficult."

I was fighting the tears so hard, I couldn't breathe. "I'm telling you the truth. But you don't believe me. You were never there for me. All you wanted was my dad's money."

She scoffed. "I don't believe you because I *know* Josh."

"You don't," I whispered. "You really don't. But it doesn't matter. I'm engaged and nothing's gonna change that. As far as the company goes, I guess I'll be talking to the lawyers. I hope you have a good life."

"What? You can't just—"

"You haven't spoken to me on the phone in years," I interrupted. "You don't know me. You have no interest in me."

"Now, that isn't fair, Emma. Of course I have interest. You're my daughter, for crying out loud."

"I'm not your daughter. If you cared about me, then you'd believe me about Josh. And you would have called me about my father *dying!*"

She sighed again. "Okay. Well, I can see we'll just have to agree to disagree. He could be just marrying you for the money, sweetheart. Small town and... Josh said he's a *farmer?*"

Fucking Josh.

"And of course I want grandchildren, but I don't want them if they're with a farmer—"

"You know what? You want to stop this wedding, then fly down your fucking self and do it. Otherwise, fuck off."

I hit the end call button and sank back, a sob breaking free. I squeezed my eyes shut as tears began to fall, my throat burning as my entire body shook. She never listened to me. She didn't even care about me. She didn't know me. The fact that she'd so blatantly ignored me made me feel like a small child again. All I could think about was my sister and how she'd always been the only person who listened to me growing up.

Donnie whined from the back seat, and I forced myself to breathe before I started hyperventilating. I kept crying as I pulled back on the road. There was only one place I could go right now.

Within a few minutes, I parked next to Honey's truck, got out with Donnie, and rushed up the steps. I knocked on the door, trying to wipe the tears away.

The door flew open, and Honey's eyes widened. "Oh, sweetheart. What happened?"

Donnie ran past me inside.

"I'm a fucking liar," I sobbed. "I'm a liar and I hate my family so much and my ex-husband is a goddamn menace and everything is falling apart and—"

Honey grabbed my forearm, and tugged me inside. "Go sit."

I kicked off my flip flops and threw myself on the couch, crying harder. I heard Honey come back to the living room and sat up, hugging a pillow as she sat down next to me, handing me a cold compress and pint of wild blueberry shortcake ice cream.

I stared for a moment and then started crying harder.

"Why are you so good to me? Do you always have emergency pints on hand?"

"Because I love you. And yes, I do. Got one for each of you in the back of the freezer. Now, whatever is happening, it's going to be okay. You are strong, you are smart, you have people in your corner. Okay?"

I sniffled as I took the compress, holding it to my face. The cold felt good against my cheeks. It took a few minutes before I could even speak, but eventually I let out a full body sigh and traded the compress for the spoon and pint.

"You're going to be mad at me," I said. "Everyone is going to be."

Honey gave me an all too knowing smile. "It happens, sweetie. Now spill the beans."

"I don't even know where to start," I said. Where was I even supposed to begin? The words bubbled up, all of the secrets spilling out in a string of chaos. "My family is rich. My dad started a computer chip company, right around the time when home computers became a thing. He had my sister and me late in life. When I was thirteen, she was driving me home from school and we were in a wreck. She died. And they blamed me for it."

"My god," Honey said. "Why would they blame you?"

"Because we were fighting," I said. "And I distracted her from the road."

Honey shook her head. "That wasn't your fault."

I shrugged my shoulders. I still felt like it was. We'd been fighting over something so insanely stupid. She'd borrowed a necklace without asking me, and I'd tried to grab it from her because I was mad. Then she swerved, and we were hit. To think that I'd lost someone I loved so dearly because I was stubborn still hurt to this day.

"Since then, I haven't been close with my dad or stepmom.

But they expected me to behave and act in a certain way. To follow the path they laid out for me. I ended up marrying a man named Josh when I was twenty. He went on to become an all-star in my father's company, and they wanted him to be more than just an employee. We were married for about fourteen months before I finally divorced him. I took off to Baltimore where I met Haley, and since then I haven't seen him."

"He sounds like a real asshole," Honey said.

"He is. So is Josh. When we got divorced, he never really got it in his head that we were actually done. Three weeks ago, he showed up on my doorstep."

"Here? In Citrus Cove?"

"Yeah." The tears started to flow again, and I sucked in a breath. "He told me my dad had died."

"Oh. Oh, Emma."

And I kept crying.

I was finally crying for him. A sob loosened in my chest and I closed my eyes, squeezing them tight as more tears started to fall. My hands trembled as I tried to spoon out another bite of ice cream, but I just couldn't.

"We weren't close," I sobbed. "We weren't. He didn't love me. Not the way he should have. I just... I miss the idea of him. I don't miss him, but I miss what could have been. All I ever wanted was for him to look at me with the same pride he had for my sister, but I was always a disappointment. I was always too much, or not enough. And fuck. I hate him. I hate him so much for that, but I also love him because he *was* my dad. But now he's gone. And I'll never have the chance to tell him how shitty he was. I'll never be able to tell him how I wished he was a real dad to me."

Honey gently pried the ice cream and spoon from my hands and placed them on the coffee table. Then she grabbed a pillow and placed it on her lap, patting it. I fell to the side and curled up next to her.

"Just let it all out, darling," Honey said softly.

My whole body shook as I kept crying until I couldn't anymore. I rolled slightly onto my back, horrified by the amount of snot. I'd always been an ugly crier.

"It gets worse," I whispered. "Hunter was over when Josh came by that day. And Josh made this stupid comment about how I should be done having my fun and it was time to get married again."

Honey shook her head angrily. "My god. The gall."

"Hunter happened to come up behind me and I introduced him as my boyfriend, because I didn't want Josh to think I'd ever go back to him. But then Hunter told him he was my fiancé."

"Oh." Honey's lips pressed into a line, clearly fighting a smile. "That's a peculiar twist."

"But Hunter hates me. So I don't know why he did that. And then I freaked the fuck out and told him we had to convince everyone we were dating this whole time. And he went along with it."

"I see."

"I told him it would just be until Josh left. But then he went and told Cam, who told Haley, who told Sarah, and then suddenly everyone knew. And Josh still hasn't fucking left. He's been lingering around town so we've kept it up, but then... Well, we had a party and got drunk. And Hunter and I ended up in the same bed."

Honey's brows shot up. "Oh my."

"I forgot to mention that Josh also tried to get me to sell the company to him."

"What a weasel. Surely you told him no."

"Of course I told him no," I said, shaking my head. "Things got... Well, Hunter and I..."

"Darling, I wasn't born yesterday. And Hunter is as cute as they come."

My cheeks could not have been more red. "Well, so things happened. But then we got into a fight because he found out about the letters."

"What letters?"

I let out a long groan, and covered my eyes. "You're gonna be mad."

"Out with it."

"Someone sent me some threatening letters, telling me to leave Citrus Cove. And they took photos of me. So when Hunter saw them, we fought about it. That was last week. And I told him we were done. But then, last night around midnight, Josh tried to run Hunter off the road and hit a dog. Hunter called me after it happened. The dog is okay and so is Hunter, but he went to the vet clinic. I drove over and stayed with him until we knew how the dog was after surgery. He's going to kick Josh out for good, and then said we're done. Then my stepmother called and I just... I just feel alone. This has been such a clusterfuck. I've lied to everyone I love. Haley is going to kill me when she finds out the truth."

Honey's face softened. "That's a lot to hold on to."

"Yeah," I whispered. "I just... Why does he hate me so much?"

"Who? *Hunter?*"

"Yeah. I don't get it. I know we fight. But the sex was really good. I mean. I want him in my life, but it's clear he doesn't want me. But..."

Honey let out a witchy cackle, and shook her head. "Darling, that man does not hate you."

"But he does," I said. "He's said it multiple times. And then he said we were done this morning."

"Mmhm. Thou doth protest too much, if you ask me. So he pretended to be your fiancé, and then told his brother about it? Hasn't he been pretending now for a couple weeks?"

"Well, yeah, but that doesn't mean he doesn't hate me. He's so frustrating." I scowled. "He installed a security system around my house. He tossed Josh out of my house like a bag of trash. Then he told me not to come around him if we're not having to act."

"Did you ever think about how he could have just told you no?" Honey asked.

I frowned. "What do you mean?"

"If he hated you, he would have just said no to this whole thing."

I pressed my lips together.

I hadn't thought about that.

"From where I'm sitting, it seems like Hunter made the choice to pretend to be your fiancé because he actually likes you. But instead of using his words, he's being a dumbass about it. And darling, I don't know how to break this to you, but sometimes men are like that. Dumbasses."

"There's no way," I said. "The first time we ever met, I tased him. Since then, he's hated me."

Honey burst out laughing and then covered her mouth. "Oh god."

I scowled. "If he liked me, wouldn't he just tell me?"

"Didn't you just say the two of you had sex?"

"Well yeah. A few times..."

"I see. Well, I distinctly remember him fighting Cam when they were younger because Cam was being mean to Haley. He's always taken up the mantle of being the one everyone goes to for everything. Always the one to stick up for the underdog."

She smiled. "You know, when Haley told me about the two of you, my first thought was *finally*. You should see the way he looks at you when he doesn't think anyone is watching."

My eyes widened. "What? There's no way." But maybe...

I thought about when I was with him. The rope, the whimper recording, the broken pipe...

Not very hateful of him.

"Then why would he help you? Have you ever seen what it looks like when a Harlow actually dislikes someone? Because he sure as hell would not help you out with a damn thing if he hated you."

"Am I being stupid?"

"A little," Honey sighed. "Love makes you stupid sometimes."

Love.

I swallowed hard and slowly sat up, wiping my eyes. I reached for the ice cream and took a bite, letting out a contented sigh. "This is so good."

"Good." She leaned back and grabbed a box of tissues, setting it next to me. "What are you going to do now?"

"I don't know," I said. "Go back to how things were, I guess."

"You think that's possible after everything that's happened with Hunter?"

Nope. There was no way.

"What would you do?" I asked.

"This isn't about what I would do. It's about what you want to do," she said. "But I do think it might be time you be the Emma we all know and love and confront him over this bullshit."

Hearing Honey cuss always made me giggle.

A weight lifted off my chest.

"As for that weasel ex of yours, I'm certain Hunter will run him out of town. That man is thorough."

She was right. Hunter *was* thorough.

"Yeah," I said, thinking about everything. "Are you mad at me?"

"Mad? No. Do I think this situation got out of control? Yes. And I don't think Haley will be too happy about being lied to. Or Sarah and Alice, for that matter."

I grimaced. "They won't be."

"I won't be the one to tell them. I'm going to leave that up to you."

"Thank you," I said. "For everything."

"Of course. That's what I'm here for."

CHAPTER TWENTY-NINE
emma

HONEY KEPT Donnie for me as a favor, and I decided to go straight to Haley's.

I wanted to confront Hunter. I wanted to find out what the hell was wrong with him, with us. But right now, I needed to fix what I'd broken with her.

I needed my best friend. I needed my sister.

I knocked on Haley's front door and waited. Cam's truck was gone. It took a couple of minutes before it opened.

Boy, she was not pleased to see me. Her lips pressed into a thin line and if looks could kill, I'd be dead. No one could give a dirty look quite like Haley could.

"Hi," I whispered. I immediately choked up, but bit back the tears. "I've been lying to you."

She released a slow breath and leaned against the doorway. "I know you have," she said, not a waver in her voice. "I've known you for years, Emma. I know everything about you."

"You don't," I said. "I want to talk. If you have time."

Haley stared for a moment, and then her shoulders softened, her expression melting. "I'm angry at you."

"You're gonna be angrier."

She raised a brow, studying me. But then stepped to the side and nodded her head towards her living room. "Should I tell Cam to take a hike?"

"At least for an hour, yeah. Then if you still love me, maybe he can bring us something sweet. Although I just had a pint of ice cream at Honey's. But I'm eating my feelings today, and there are a lot of them."

Haley winced. "Oh god. Did Honey give you an emergency pint?"

"She did."

"Then it's bad, isn't it?"

"Yeah, it is, Hal."

"Then come inside," she said. "Time to rip some bandaids off."

I shut the door behind me and kicked off my shoes, placing them in the shoe cabinet. I headed straight to her comfy couch and plopped down, hugging my knees to my chest.

This was going to suck. There was an elephant on my chest again and my ears were ringing. I was already exhausted from talking to Honey earlier, but she'd given me the strength I needed for this conversation.

All I could do was tell her the truth and hope she forgave me.

Her eyes flickered with concern as she sat down across from me. "Emma," she said softly. "What is happening? What is going on?"

A steady breath didn't lessen the sting in my throat. I started at the beginning. I told her about my dad's death, about Josh, about how Hunter and I had been pretending. I even told her about the party and how Hunter and I had ended up sleeping together the next day.

"I want more details on *that* later," she said. "But continue."

So I did. She didn't interrupt, she just listened, a talent she got from Honey.

I talked and talked and talked until my voice was hoarse and I'd revealed everything that I'd never let her know. About my family, my panic. I told her about my marriage to Josh and how those fourteen months had been my worst. My absolute worst.

"And then I met you, someone who believed in me. Who trusted and loved me. And I followed you to this small Texas town where I've met other people who trust and love me." My throat burned with my words. "And then I broke your trust. I asked Hunter to lie to all of you. I asked him to pretend to be my fiancé just to get back at Josh, and it spiraled out of control."

I'd been selfish because I couldn't face my own demons.

"I'm sorry," I croaked. "I'm sorry. I'm so sorry, Haley. I shouldn't have kept this all from you."

She sniffled and shook her head. "Why did you?"

"I didn't want to disappoint you," I cried. "I didn't want to lose you. I already lost a sister once and I can't do it again. I just can't."

"Emma. You're such a dumbass." Haley wiped her eyes and then moved closer, grabbing my hands. "Why would you ever think I'd stop loving you over all of this?"

"Because I lied. Because I've kept things from you. Because I've left you in the dark about my past even though you've always been honest with me."

Haley used the scrunchie on her wrist to pull her hair back and shook her head at me. "Yeah, and I'm pissed. I'm pissed you didn't lean on me. Since I've known you, you have always been there for me. You moved across the fucking country for me, Emma. And the one time I could be there for you, you didn't let me."

"It felt like too much. *I* felt like too much. I didn't want to scare you away."

She wiped away more tears and shook her head, a laugh bubbling up. "I had a serial killer go after me and that didn't scare you away?"

My vision blurred as I started to cry again, letting out a broken sound. "A serial killer scares me less than the idea of disappointing someone I love."

Haley cupped my cheeks and gave me a gentle shake. "Bitch, you need therapy."

"I'll get some," I promised. "Haley, I am sorry I've kept all of this from you. Not only did it pull us apart, I also haven't been there for you with what you've been going through."

She gave a slight nod. "I love you," she said. "And I forgive you. I'm still your best friend. You're my ride or die. 'Til death do us part, remember?"

"Thank you." I hugged her, crying into her shoulder. We sat like that for a while until I'd truly shriveled up. My body was out of water between confessing to Honey and now Haley.

"I'm sorry, Emma," she murmured. "I'm sorry about your dad."

"I am too," I sighed. "It just hit me when I was talking to Honey that he's really gone. We won't ever be able to mend our relationship. I don't think we could have anyway, but the chance is gone."

"I think it's valid to miss what could have been," she said. "I know we feel the same way about our moms."

I nodded slowly. Haley was the only person I'd ever been able to talk about that with because she understood. "Yeah. I think when she died, she took whatever warmth she had with her. My dad was never the same. And then when Evelyn died... I was just a reminder of them. And a disappointment."

"You're definitely not a disappointment. Remember what

you used to say when we were in college? Don't take criticism from someone you wouldn't want advice from? I don't want to be dismissive, but they didn't know you. And that is their loss because you're one of the best people I know. Even when you do silly things."

A soft smile appeared and I leaned back against the couch.

"I think we need a girls' night," Haley said and then she frowned. "Okay, so wait. Tell me about Hunter. Why did he do this?"

"I don't know," I said. "But god. I think I've fallen for the asshole."

She leaned back, her eyes widening. "Like for real?"

"For real," I said. "I can't fake this feeling. But I don't know what to do about it. He told me we're done."

"You skipped that part," Haley said.

Sometimes relaying info like this was hard for my brain to do in order. I told her about last night, about RK, this morning, and then what he said.

Haley snorted. "Oh god. Oh god, he's such an idiot. It's obvious he wants you. And now, looking back over the last three years, it's so fucking clear. He pulled a Cam."

"A what?" I asked.

"A Cam. He pulled a Cam. He had all these feelings and instead of being mature, he reverted back to acting like a dumbass."

"I don't know," I said. "I think he meant it. You should have seen his face."

"What did Honey say?"

I narrowed my eyes on her. "She called him a dumbass too, and said if he hated me, he would have never done this."

"Oh, he for sure does not hate you, Emma. That's why we've all been so fucking confused."

"What do you mean?"

Haley let out a nervous laugh. "Okay, so, confession. The entire reason we talked you two into working together for the festival was to try and make you like each other."

"*Oh.*" My mouth fell open. "This was all a ruse!"

"Yeah, and then y'all told us you were *engaged*! Imagine our fucking shock! We have an entire group chat dedicated on the side to making the two of you be friends. Alice, Sarah, and I have been plotting."

We stared at each other for a moment and then burst out laughing.

"Oh god," I gasped. "I'm going to cry again, but I can't because I'm dehydrated."

Haley wiped her face again, laughing until she cried too. We heard the door open, but couldn't stop our hysterics, even as Cam stepped into the living room.

The sheer panic on that man's face sent us both over the edge again.

"I can't tell if you're crying or laughing," he said, his voice full of terror.

"Both," I wheezed. "Both."

"I brought cheesecake, wine, and chicken wings."

"Great," Haley laughed. "Oh god. This is too much. Cam, I love you, but we need a girls' night. Maybe go check on your dumbass brother."

"What did he do?" Cam immediately asked. "Am I burying him? Did he upset you?"

Haley shook her head. "Nope. Not telling. Just go talk to him. And maybe don't punch him, I have a feeling he's not at his best right now."

"Fuck," Cam said. He rushed the bags to the kitchen and came to the back of the couch, kissing Haley quickly. "Okay. I love you, sunshine. Call me if you need anything."

"I will," Haley said.

We waited until he bolted out the door before melting into a fit of giggles again. Haley leaned against me with a sigh, sniffling.

"We should watch *Practical Magic*," Haley said.

It was my favorite movie. I nodded immediately. "Yes."

"And eat cheesecake and chicken wings."

"I'll drink enough wine for both of us," I said.

"Perfect," she chuckled. "No pressure, but when are you coming clean everyone else?"

"Not tonight," I said. "And well, Josh is still in town. And then there's the weird letters..."

"The *what*?"

Dammit. I'd forgotten to mention that. Most of the time my ADHD was my superpower, then there were times like this where all of my thoughts were scattered in the wind. "I started receiving threatening letters. Someone wants me to leave Citrus Cove."

"And you took that to the police, right?"

"I... did not."

Haley shook her head. "Hunter didn't make you?"

"He tried," I said. "It led to us arguing and then hurting each other's feelings. It's been a lot, Hal. I'm losing my mind."

"Okay. Tomorrow, we have some shit to deal with. And you still need to talk to Hunter."

"I'm not sure when," I sighed. "He's picking up RK tomorrow. God, I can't believe I have feelings for a man who named his dog Roadkill. What do I even say to him? I've caused him enough stress. I mean, Josh tried to run him off the road."

"Hmm. I think you need to talk to him, if you love him. Or think you love him."

I thought about it.

I wanted a chance with him.

A real chance.

I wasn't sure if he'd want it. I wasn't sure if he'd be willing to try. But even with everything that had happened, I wanted to try. I wanted to know if anything between us was real.

"Let's watch a movie and try to relax tonight," Haley said. "And see what tomorrow brings."

Even with everything I still had to face, I felt lighter knowing I didn't have to live a lie any longer.

CHAPTER THIRTY
hunter

CAM WALKED into my house without so much as a knock. I cursed as I jumped up from my couch and then sat back down, glowering.

"What the fuck?" I asked. "You can't just barge into places. I could have been *busy*."

"After walking in on Sammy and Colt going at it, I think I've seen it all," Cam said. "And besides, your door was unlocked. You know the rule."

I scoffed at my brother, but I didn't argue. The general rule was that if our door was open, you were welcome in. If it was locked or an emergency, use your spare key. And if it was locked and not an emergency, knock.

He planted his hands on his hips as he surveyed me, the entire chocolate cake on my coffee table, and the bottle of whiskey. The corner of his mouth tugged. "So, I just saw Emma at the house."

My stomach flipped, and I looked away. "Oh?" I couldn't even muster up the ability to act surprised. I leaned over and grabbed the whiskey, taking a long sip that scalded my throat. "I got a dog."

"Did you?"

"Yeah. He's at the vet. Emma's ex-husband tried to run me off the road and hit him."

"*What?*"

I nodded slowly, still pissed about it. "I'm not good company right now, Cam."

"Well, that's too bad. Emma and Haley have kicked me out of the house. I dropped off wine, cheesecake, and chicken wings for them."

"Well, aren't you a doll?" I drawled.

Cam snorted and kicked off his boots.

"Right, just settle in," I muttered.

"Damn, you are in a bad way, huh? Haley told me to go easy on you."

"Did she? Did she say why?"

"No, I was hoping you'd be the one to tell me that. Since I am your brother and all."

I sighed but scooted over on the couch, making room for him. Cam went to the kitchen and grabbed a plate and fork before returning, plopping down next to me.

"Should I order pizza or are you eating cake for dinner?"

"If you want to order some, I wouldn't say no."

"Alright." I pulled out his phone and placed an order. "So, are we gonna sit and brood? Or are you going to tell me what's going on?"

"What was Emma doing with Haley?" I asked.

"I don't know, man. I couldn't tell if they were laughing or crying. They said both."

I felt the same damn way. I wasn't sure if I should laugh or cry or just get in bed and sleep. I'd never been this miserable in my entire life. Not even after my first breakup with Allison in sixth grade, a girl I was convinced was my entire world. It was funny now, knowing what it really felt like to have someone who was your entire world.

"We fucked up," I said. "We lied to everyone. And it spiraled out of control and now we're in a big heap of shit. And you're all gonna be mad, Cam. Rightly so. But I just don't think I can deal with you being mad at me right now."

"I can't promise not to be mad, but I can promise I'll still love you."

I let out a slow, steady breath. The alcohol was starting to buzz just enough so I didn't feel like I was going to implode. "We've told a lot of lies, but one thing is true. I do love that woman. But I can't be who she needs me to be. I'm not worthy of her."

Cam grimaced. "Did she tell you that?"

"No. She didn't need to. I know it's true."

"Okay."

He didn't sound convinced. "I've loved her since she came to Citrus Cove. The first night we met, she tased me. And I think she must have broken something in me, Cam."

"So that really did happen?"

"Yeah, it did. I'll never forget it so long as I live."

Cam stifled a laugh and cleared his throat, trying to be serious. "Why didn't you just ask her out? Or be your normal self and be kind to her."

"Because she became so integrated into our family, I didn't want to pursue something."

"So it was easier to be an asshole?"

"Yeah," I sighed.

It was so fucking stupid looking back now. I regretted it. I'd done everything I could to convince myself that Emma wasn't right for me. But all the things I'd told myself were bad about her were some of the things I loved the most. I loved how stubborn she was. I loved how she added color to every room. I loved her crazy heels and jewelry and the way she could still flip me to the ground if she needed to.

And god.

Her smile.

I fucking loved Emma's smile.

Her greatest fear was that she was too much for me.

Mine was that I was too little for her.

"I recall you beating the shit out of me for such behavior in high school," Cam said with a prim sniffle.

"I sure did." I looked over at my brother and gave him a sad smile. "I don't know what to do now."

"Well... So are the two of you engaged or not?"

I shook my head slowly, then started at the beginning. I was vague about the sex parts, of course. But I told him everything else. Josh, Emma's dad dying, agreeing to lie for her. I told him about Pops telling me I wasn't worthy, and how I agreed.

Cam's jaws ticked. "Stop. Hold on," he said. "Hold on. I love our dad, Hunter. I love him. But he's got to stop this shit with you. It's gone on too long. You do so much for all of us. You always have."

"He'll never see it that way," I said.

Cam swallowed hard. "I'm sorry. I'm sorry you always got the brunt of that. You carry so much around and sometimes I don't feel like I do enough."

I felt guilty now, but decided to push through. Emma told me that I couldn't blame my brothers if I didn't tell them how I felt, and she was right.

"I've been mad," I said softly. "I've felt resentful at times, that you and Sammy didn't want to be at the farm. And I'm not saying I'm not proud of the both of you, you know I am. But several times I've felt like I'm the only one who cares, and I realized I put that on myself. It's not fair to either of you. But instead of saying something, I've just... I've just done what was expected of me."

"Is there something else you want to do?" Cam asked. "I just always assumed you wanted this."

I shook my head. "That's the thing. I know this is right for me. I love working the farm. I love working with the earth. I'm proud of how you and Colt have grown the business. And knowing Sammy has built on his own passions makes me proud too."

"Sometimes it feels like if we offer to help, we get in the way. But it isn't fair to you either." He leaned forward and cut a slice of cake, dragging it onto his plate. "I'm gonna talk to Pops."

"You don't need to do that," I said.

"I definitely do," Cam said. "And Sammy does too. If he's not going to listen to you, then maybe he'll listen to all of us. And for the record, you are good enough for Emma. I know all of this got out of hand, but I can see why you did it. God knows I'd do anything for Haley. If she would have asked me to pretend to be her fiancé when she first came back to Citrus Cove, I would have done it without hesitation."

I felt a sense of ease return that I hadn't experienced in weeks.

"You glossed over the whole ex thing," Cam said. "Is the bastard still in town?"

"I fucking hope not," I said. "I haven't tried to find him yet, but that motherfucker hit a dog right in front of me. Thankfully, Anna and Katie showed up to help."

"And Emma did too."

"Yeah. She did. She was the first person I called."

"And then you told her you were done."

I winced. "I just couldn't handle lying anymore, Cam. There are these letters that she's received telling her to leave Citrus Cove. She needs to go to the police, but she doesn't want to. And I understand why, but I just want there to be some sort of paper trail. *Something.*"

"Is that why you fought?"

"Yes," I sighed. "I couldn't understand why she wouldn't let me help."

"Did you ask her what she wanted to do?"

"What do you mean?"

Cam fought a snort as he took a bite of cake. "Did you ask her? Or did you do that thing where you swoop in like superman and take control?"

"Ouch," I muttered.

"She's just lost her dad. Which means she's truly without family, Hunter. Her ex-husband shows up and is being a creepy asshole, and then she asks you to lie to everyone for her. We both know that would weigh on Emma too. She's been carrying the same hurt you have. And then you tried to tell her what to do."

He had a point. "I was trying to help," I said. "Which I told her."

"There's trying to help and then there's trying to take over, and I've known you my whole life so I know that sometimes you do both at the same time, but Emma is used to taking care of herself. Haley is one of the few people she'll be vulnerable with because she's always trying to be independent."

I frowned as I took a bite of cake. "When did you get to be so wise?"

"Well, it started when I learned how to grovel to the woman I love."

I chuckled softly. "I don't think she wants me, Cam. I don't blame her."

"You're your own worst enemy," Cam sighed. "I think you should give it a shot."

"Aren't you mad at me?"

"I'm mad that this is definitely real and the two of you are being stubborn about it," Cam said. "And I'm mad that I've now lost twenty bucks to Haley."

I scoffed. "What did you bet on?"

"Who made the first move."

"It was me," I said.

"Nope. She said you were her boyfriend first."

"That doesn't count."

"It sure does."

I laughed despite everything and shook my head. "So you think I should talk to her?"

"I think you'd be the stupidest man in the world if you didn't."

CHAPTER THIRTY-ONE
hunter

IT WAS SUNDAY, and I hadn't talked to Emma yet.

I was a coward.

There'd been countless moments where I'd picked up my phone to text her or call her. I'd been annoying the hell out of Anna by asking for constant updates on RK, and wanted to tell Emma about it all. I wanted to show her the dog bed I'd picked out. I wanted to show her the collar and tags and ask her what kind of food Donnie liked best.

I wanted to share my life with her.

But what was I supposed to say? I'd fucked things up. I'd been so sure I wasn't good for her that I'd ended things between us.

It was a mistake. A mistake within a nesting doll of other mistakes.

Despite everything, I was still working. Anna had ended up keeping RK to monitor him over the weekend, and the plan was for me to pick him up on Monday morning.

I needed a distraction.

It was almost 5 p.m., and I was covered in dirt, completely exhausted, and beyond frustrated.

One of the guys had called out yesterday, so we'd been behind. I was finally caught up, but every muscle hurt. I was trying to get myself ready for having a pet. I planned to walk him every day, and once his leg was healed I wanted him to join me at the vineyard.

I walked between the rows of grapes and knelt down, studying the leaves. They were all looking good. Normally, that would please me.

But nothing felt right. Nothing could make me happy.

I straightened and rolled my shoulders, stretching for a moment. I let out a breath and put my hands on my hips. I was about done for the day. I needed to get some sleep, drink some water, eat some damn veggies since I'd definitely been living on cake lately.

I heard a yell and turned my head, frowning.

What is she doing?

Emma walked towards me wearing a crimson red dress and heels. Her long brown hair blew around her as she headed straight for me, her brows pinched together as she approached.

"What the hell are you doing?" I asked.

One of her heels sank in the mud and she jerked forward. I cursed, lunging to catch her before she fell face-first. Her hands braced against my shoulders as I steadied her.

"We need to talk," she said.

I released her and shook my head. I couldn't do this right now, not while she looked like a scarlet goddess coming to reap my soul.

"I told you on Friday—"

"Why do you hate me?" Emma interrupted.

"Wh—what?" I was taken aback. I stared down at her, my heart already racing.

"Why do you hate me?" she asked again. "Really? Not the bullshit taser thing. That was so long ago. If you hate me, why did you help me? Why did we have sex? A lot of really good, hot sex."

"Emma," I said. "I'm not doing this. We said we were done."

"If you hate me, then why do you know what kind of ice cream I like? Or what I drink? What kind of shampoo and conditioner I use?"

"Emma," I said again, my frustration growing. "Stop."

"No," she said.

Goddammit. I turned around to walk away, but she reached out and grabbed my hand, pulling me back.

"You're not running from me," she growled. "Answer me, Hunter Harlow. Why did you help me? Why was I the first person you called when RK was hurt?"

I pulled my hand free as if I'd been burned. "Stop. We agreed we were done."

I started to walk away again, but her voice carried across the entire vineyard.

"If you hate me, why did you pretend to be my fiancé?!"

Fuck.

I froze in place, my heart pounding.

"Why did you do all of this for me?"

I closed my eyes, my blood rushing in my ears. I felt her step closer, her words softened.

"Why would you ever agree to this if you don't want me near you?"

"You hate me back," I said gruffly. "The sex was just really good sex." *Lie, lie, lie.* "It's better this way."

"Why is it better this way?"

Because I'm fucking obsessed with you. Because I've ruined all of your dates. Because I watched you orgasm without you even knowing it, and that's terrible.

"Emma," I whispered.

"Why do you hate me? Tell me. Please. Is it because I like pink? Is it because I'm loud and opinionated? Is it because you think I don't belong here? Is it because I have a small dog? Or—"

I spun around. I couldn't do this anymore. Her eyes widened and she took a step back, but she wasn't escaping me.

Fuck me. I just couldn't do this anymore. I couldn't keep lying. I couldn't keep up the ruse. I couldn't keep acting like my entire world didn't revolve around the woman in front of me.

I moved in a blur. Emma squealed as I grabbed hold of her and threw her over my shoulders. She kicked and cursed as I carried her down the rows of grapes towards the barn.

"Hunter! Put me the fuck down! What the fuck are you doing?! You can't just manhandle me! Oh god, you're getting mud on my confrontation dress!"

Of course, Emma had a dress for confrontations.

My muddied hand ended up on her ass, but I didn't move it. Emma let out a growl before it bubbled into a laugh.

"My god, you're insane," she said. "You're getting mud on me."

"I am," I said. I glanced back at her with a smirk, despite the seriousness of what I was feeling. She shook her head at me, but then relaxed as if to accept her fate.

I held her tighter as I went into the barn. I pulled her legs around my waist and pushed her against the wall, breathing hard as I pinned her there.

She went still, her eyes widening. The sun was setting outside, filling the barn with pink light and deep shadows.

"I don't hate you," I whispered angrily. "I'm fucking

obsessed with you. Ever since you fucking tased me, I haven't stopped thinking about you night and day. Every waking moment, there you are, haunting me. All your little dates? Wanna know why they didn't work out? Because I ran them all off. Every single one of them. Every. Single. One."

Her lips parted breathlessly. "*What?*"

"Yeah, Emma," I gritted out. "Remember Kyle? Or Jaxon? Drake? Billy? Alex? Robert? I remember the look on each of their faces as I told them I'd make sure they never saw the light of day again if they didn't back off."

I released her, holding her until I was certain she was steady in those heels. I held up my hands, taking a step back to give her space.

Emma shook her head at me. "*Why* would you do that?" she asked. "I've been thinking I was cursed. That there wasn't a single guy in Texas who would ever want me. That there was something wrong with me."

"The only thing wrong with you is *me*. Ever since I've met you, I've acted like a caveman. A feral, stupid, unhinged caveman. For months, I've thought about touching you. Kissing you. *Fucking* you." I raked my fingers through my hair. "And then you spring a fake relationship on me?"

She pressed her lips together and crossed her arms. "That was... that wasn't planned. And you didn't have to go along with it. You made everything worse."

"I know that. But how could I ever say no when I've wanted you since the moment you fucking tased me? Waking up next to you that morning sent me over the edge. I couldn't keep my hands off you. I've wanted you so badly for years, and then I finally got to have you. But I'm not good for you. I'm not good enough for you."

Emma glared at me. "Who ever told you that, Hunter?

Who ever told you that you're not good enough for me? Because I never did. *I* never said that. And I'm the expert on who is good enough for *me*, not anyone else."

"But I'm still not good for you," I said. "After all the shit I've done?"

Her eyes searched mine frantically. "You really ruined all of those dates?"

"Every one of them. I also stroked my cock watching you masturbate on your security system." It felt both good and awful to get this all off my chest.

"Oh my god."

My heart thumped. I could feel the weight lifting from my shoulders, the truth finally out. After all this time, all of the little things I'd felt so guilty over—Emma finally knew the truth about me. "So yeah. There it is. There's the truth. I don't hate you, Emma, I could never hate you. But you have every right to hate me."

I started to turn to walk away, but her fingers clenched my shirt. "Don't you dare walk away from me, Hunter Harlow." She spun me around, craning her head back to look up at me. "I'm not letting you escape me."

"Emma," I protested. "You should hate me."

"I'm angry at you," she snapped. "I'm *infuriated* by you. All this time, I thought you hated me. I've been fighting to feel like I have a family and that I can trust others, but believing that you never liked me always hurt my feelings. Even if I acted like it didn't, it hurt. All of my past relationships have always ended up being messy. The guys I've dated have always thought I was too much work. And I thought you believed the same thing."

"No," I rasped. "No. Emma, I'm sorry. I'm sorry for how I've acted. I'm sorry for how I've hurt you. You're not too much work and you deserve someone who will be the prince you deserve. But I'm not a prince."

"I don't want a prince," she said. "I just want someone who looks at me and sees all of me. I just want someone who loves me, Hunter. I want a messy kind of love, a dopey kind of love. I want to be stupid together. I want to grow old together. I want to wake up knowing that whatever shit happens, I will still have that person beside me."

"I want that too," I whispered. "More than anything else."

She swallowed hard and looked away, her eyes shining with tears. "Do you want to know a secret?"

I sniffled and wiped my eyes. "Yeah."

"I fantasized about you watching me on the camera. That's what got me off." Her gaze sharpened. "And not only that—when you kicked Josh out? I've never wanted to fuck someone so badly. Ever."

"*Emma.*" I shook my head.

"Want to know something else?"

"Yes."

"I need you, Hunter. I want *you*. Even knowing how much you've fucked up, even knowing that you're the reason I haven't been laid in months—which sucks by the way—you're the one I want."

My mouth fell open. I searched for words, but she reached up and covered it with her hand, shaking her head.

"Let me finish. I've spent the last couple weeks wishing this relationship was real. I've wished that I was really your fiancé. More than anything else. And not seeing you this last week? I missed you."

"You missed me," I repeated. My heart pounded so hard I could hear my blood rushing. "None of what I've done is okay."

"No, it's not. We definitely need to work on boundaries and communication. We need to stop being stubborn. We need to let go of the hurtful things we've said to keep each other at arm's length." She released a long breath. "I told Honey. I told

Haley. I told them the truth, and I finally cleared the air. I still need to tell Alice and Sarah and everyone else, but I... Both of them made me realize a lot of things. One of those was that I was selfish for dragging you into this."

I shook my head. "I jumped in, Emma."

"Yes, but I also pulled you in. And I did so, not realizing I was throwing myself into a terrible situation with one of the best people I've had the chance to know."

My heart skipped a beat. "I feel like all I've done is fuck up."

"Me too."

We stared at each other, silence settling for a moment. "I want us to forgive each other. I can do that. Can you?"

"Yes," I said. "I can."

"And you should have told me about the camera thing. Why didn't you just tell me long ago that you liked me?"

"Would you have listened?" I whispered. I couldn't stop the tears, and didn't try to. "I made sure you thought I was an asshole. That you believed I was terrible. And it worked."

She thumbed away a tear before it rolled down my cheek. "I wish we could start over."

"I do too, Emma. I really do."

She leaned in closer. I closed my eyes for a moment, fighting for control over the emotions that warred in my chest.

I leaned down and pressed my forehead to hers. She swallowed hard. "I think we deserve a chance."

I nodded slowly. "I want that chance, Emma. I really do."

"Can we try? Can we give us a try?"

"Yes," I whispered. "God, yes."

"Then kiss me, you idiot."

I crushed my mouth to hers and lifted her, backing her up against the wall. All the secrets I'd been keeping turned to smoke, scattered by the sun that shone bright the second she gave me the chance to love her.

She knotted her fingers in my shirt, kissing me until I was breathless. I drew back with a pant, searching her gaze.

"The truck," she rasped. "Time to use that big truck."

"Yes, ma'am. Time to use that big truck."

CHAPTER THIRTY-TWO

emma

"IS THERE anyone who might walk up on us?" I asked.

"On a Sunday? No."

Hunter was a man on a mission. He yanked his truck's door open, barely allowing a breath between our lips before laying me on the back seat.

The way I needed him right now pumped through me. I arched against him, dragging my nails down his chest with a moan.

"Fuck," he whined.

I knew he liked that. I liked it too. I liked when he took control, but still let me do possessive things like leave marks. It satisfied me in so many ways.

"Damn this truck," he huffed. "It's not big enough for all the things I want to do to you right now."

I burst out laughing as the two of us struggled to get him on top of me. As tall as he was, it was a fight to get his long legs in the door, even with the truck being as large as it was. He reached back and slammed it shut.

"We fit," he announced triumphantly.

"Barely," I laughed.

He looked down at me and I swallowed hard, my smile melting into raw lust. I felt like the two of us had gone to hell and back for this new beginning, but it was worth it.

I wanted him. I *needed* him. *I loved him.*

"I missed you," I whispered. "I really fucking did."

"I did too. You have no idea." His throat bobbed. "I feel like there's so much more to say, but—"

"I want you right now," I interrupted. "We have all the time we need to figure everything else out. But I've been dreaming about touching you for days. I've felt like…"

"I've been going crazy without you," he whispered. "I couldn't breathe without you in my life, Emma. I need you."

"I need you too."

He brushed my cheek with his fingers, a gentle touch that burned hot.

"Please," I whispered. "Please fuck me." I sat up and grabbed his belt buckle, quickly unclasping it. He grabbed hold of my wrist and shook his head.

"Dress off," he growled, taking over on undoing his pants.

We were full of the same fire. I grabbed the edge of my dress and hiked it up, kicking off my panties as he yanked down his jeans. I didn't care that he had dirt on his clothes or smelled like sunshine and sweat, I needed him to fuck me.

I threw one knee over his lap right as he pulled his boxers down, his cock springing free. Pre-cum dripped from the tip, veins bulging along the shaft.

"Fuck," he grunted.

"Please don't tell me you're in an *I'm gonna take my time* mood," I whined. "Because I don't think I can be patient."

I slid my hand down to my pussy, feeling how wet I was.

He grabbed my hand and brought my two fingers to his lips, sucking them.

My mouth dropped. "*Hunter.*"

He let out a long moan. "You taste so fucking good. And fuck no. No, I'm not in a *take my time* mood. I need you on my cock *now*."

He grabbed hold of my hips and pressed the head of his cock against me, thrusting up.

I gripped his shoulders as I sank down. I'd never get over the feeling of him filling me, his cock spreading me. His arms wrapped around my waist, holding me as we began to move, our lips colliding with fevered desperation.

"Fuck," I whimpered.

It was clumsy. We were desperate for each other, for the reconnection. It felt like the first time all over again, soaking each other up.

His lips grazed up my neck, my nipples hardening as I shivered. I loved having my neck kissed. I groaned as he thrust hard and fast, the truck rocking with our movements. His beard was rough against my skin, his grip on me unyielding as he took what he needed. I sank my teeth into his bottom lip and he grunted, his fingers skating up my back until they buried in my hair, pulling hard as I kept rocking my hips.

I bit his lip harder until he sucked in a breath, thrusting up hard enough to make me yelp. "*Hunter,*" I rasped.

"You feel so good. I missed you. I missed you so goddamn much."

"I missed you too." His touch, his kisses, the way he demanded pleasure. I'd missed his laugh and his steadiness, keeping me afloat in the midst of a storm.

My head fell back as I rode him harder. He pulled down the straps of my dress, his lips moved down my chest as he pulled my breasts free. I whimpered as he sucked one of my nipples. My pussy throbbed with every pump.

"I'm so close," he rasped. "You feel so good, sparks."

Sparks. It was the only nickname I'd ever loved, the only one I'd heard that felt right.

Hunter was the only one who had ever made me feel like this.

I rocked once more right as my orgasm rolled through me, my pussy clenching around his cock with a long moan. Hunter gasped, holding me in place as he came, filling me.

He panted, relaxing beneath me. He pressed his head to my chest, his ear over my heart.

"That was..." he trailed off. "That was too quick."

A slow giggle left me. "Well, good news. My evening is clear."

"Ah, I see. You knew I was in love with you all along then?"

I grinned as he leaned back against the seat, looking up at me with those dimples.

"I thought you hated me," I said.

He shook his head. "Never. I could never hate you. I'm sorry it's taken me this long to get my head out of my ass."

I opened my mouth to tell him the same thing, but then I heard the sound of tires rolling over gravel. I immediately moved off of him with a squeak, his words flooding in a string of curses as he yanked his pants back up.

"For fuck's sake," he hissed. "This fucking family. I'm going to murder my family."

I fixed my dress quickly, my cheeks flaming as Hunter quickly got out of the truck and shut the door. My eyes widened as I peeked over the seat, watching as his mom got out of her car.

"Oh my god," I whispered to myself.

There was no fucking way I was ready to see Lynn after what Hunter and I had just done. I sank back down into the seat, praying to whatever universal force was out there that I wasn't going to have to pretend like Hunter and I hadn't just finished a quickie in the back of his truck.

Please do not come over here. I'm not here. I'm not—

The door opened, and I squealed as Hunter poked his head in. "We're being summoned for dinner tomorrow night and there is no way out of it, but she's gone."

"Jesus Christ," I hissed. "That scared the hell out of me."

"You and me both."

We stared at each other as the corner of his mouth slowly twisted up.

I grinned and covered my smile. I was humiliated. "Oh god. Could she tell?"

"Mama Harlow wasn't born yesterday, unfortunately." He shook his head as he braced his arms on the top of the doorframe. "What are you doing tonight?"

"You? Since we're official and everything now."

He raised a brow. "I think we should celebrate. I'd like to take you on an actual date."

"Tonight?" I asked, my voice pitching. "Hunter, I'm covered in mud and full of your—well, you know."

"I do know. Think you can be ready in an hour?"

"Fuck no I can't be ready in an hour," I laughed. "Two hours? It'll be late."

"I know a place," he said. "A nice place. It's in West Austin, and I'm friends with the owner."

"Of course you are," I sighed.

"I'll see you in two hours, then. Want me to take you home?"

"No, I drove here," I said. I was already moving off the seat.

He stepped back as I got out of the truck, my thighs clenching together.

"You're in a hurry," he teased.

"Two hours to get ready for a date?" I hissed. "See you later. Don't be early."

He chuckled as I waddled across the gravel to my car. I could still hear him laughing, even as I got in and drove off.

CHAPTER THIRTY-THREE
emma

TWO HOURS LATER, I'd managed to take a shower, do my makeup, my hair, and change into a dress that made me feel like a goddess. I'd picked out a black dress—you could never go wrong with the perfect black dress—with a lace corset bustier and a mid-length skirt with a split up my right leg. I was in heels, my long hair pulled back into a French twist, diamonds dangling from my ears.

Hunter's knock rang through the house. I double checked Donnie's food and water bowls, picked out a handful of treats for him, scattered them on the living room floor, and then opened the door.

Butterflies erupted in my stomach.

Hunter cleaned up really well. He wore a black button-down with black pants and boots. He smelled so good, my mouth started to water. He whistled softly as he looked me over, his eyes sparkling with a hint of mischief.

"You're beautiful, Emma. I thought the red dress was my favorite, but maybe I was wrong."

"Thank you." I reached up and grabbed hold of his cheeks,

drawing him down for a kiss. Red rubbed off on his lips and I snorted, quickly wiping it away. "Ope. No kissing tonight, I guess."

"I'll wear your kisses as a badge of honor."

I giggled and found myself just staring like an idiot.

This felt right. For the first time in my entire life, I felt like I was exactly where I needed to be with someone I wanted to be with.

"Are you ready?" he asked.

"I am."

I grabbed my purse, stepping out onto the porch and locking the door behind me. As I turned back around, I noticed a police cruiser slowly driving by. Hunter gave them a wave and then looped his thumbs in his pockets.

I already knew the answer, but I asked anyway. "Did you have them do that?" I asked.

"Yep," he said. "I sure did."

I couldn't say I was mad about that. I'd noticed them a few days ago, and felt a little bit safer knowing someone was at least driving through the neighborhood. I still wasn't sure what to do about the letters or the photos, but that would be a problem for tomorrow. I knew Hunter was right about showing someone, but tonight I just wanted to focus on us.

I was going on a first date with a man I was madly in love with. Or at least falling in love with.

"So. Where are you taking me?" I asked.

"It's a surprise." He held out his hand, and I slid mine into his palm. He raised my knuckles to his lips, kissing them gently before winking.

God, was it possible to combust from a wink? It sure felt like it. I followed him down the steps to his truck, where he opened the door for me. With a quick lift, he put me in the front seat, and shut the door before going around to the driver side.

I could get used to this, I realized. I buckled myself in, thinking about how this could have been us from the beginning if we didn't let our stubbornness get in the way. I'd spent so much time telling myself that he was rude, incorrigible, unlikable, a total asshole. And sure, parts of him were that way, but it's what I loved about him. And I also loved that he was protective and kind and always willing to do whatever he could to help others.

I wasn't used to having someone try to help me like this. For years, I'd been doing everything on my own. I worked to pay my bills, to save up and buy whatever I wanted. I found random hobbies and jumped into them headfirst until I was the best, and then usually moved on to something else.

Maybe that was part of why it'd taken me so long to open up to him.

That, and I realized now that when he offered to help, it wasn't because he didn't think I could handle myself.

When I was with him, it was easy to forget my problems. It was easy to forget about Josh and my dad, and the lies we've been spinning.

"We probably owe Honey and Haley drinks," I said. "Both of them are why I decided to confront you."

Hunter let out a soft chuckle. "I'll make sure to get them something. What did Honey have to say?"

"When I told her I thought you hated me, she told me there was no way you hated me, because then you wouldn't have helped me to begin with."

"Mm. Always so insightful. I love Honey. Although she kind of scares me sometimes. Can't get anything past her. Haven't been able to since I was a kid."

I grinned. "She's the best. She's the grandmother I never had."

"She's good at that. What did Haley think of it all?"

"She was angry," I said. "Rightly so. I've been a shitty friend. But I apologized. We talked through everything and she forgave me."

"I'm glad," he said. "I worried about keeping things from her. From Sarah and Alice too. I know how close you all are."

I nodded. "Still need to tell them."

"I told Cam."

"What did he have to say?"

"That I'd be stupid not to grovel. And he was right. I planned on it, but I was just..."

"Scared? Do I scare you, Hunter Harlow?"

He grinned slowly. "You *did* taser me the first time we met."

"I sure did." I smiled as I looked out the window, Citrus Cove passing by as he drove towards Austin. "What was it like growing up here? Aside from the stuff with your dad. This is such a small town, I can't imagine living my whole life here. Well, now I can, I guess."

"Do you like it?" He asked.

"I do," I said. "I plan to stay. You can't get rid of me."

"Good," he said. "As for growing up in Citrus Cove—I'm biased, but I love it here. I know I've complained about Pops a lot, and the farm, but I do love what I do. I like the seasons and the weather, I like being connected to nature. And beyond that, I like living in a small town. I like knowing who my neighbors are, I like seeing how their lives go. Their happiness is my happiness, and vice versa. You can't get that in a big city. I've taken long vacations, only to end up feeling homesick. Citrus Cove will always be my home."

I wanted it to be home for me, too. The longer I stayed here, the more it felt that way. Initially, the only reason I'd come out here was to be close to Haley. But then I'd met the rest of the people who would eventually become my own chosen family. And for that, I would always be thankful.

"I guess growing up here was maybe what you would expect. When I was in school, I was..."

"I bet every girl wanted to kiss you." I gave him a teasing air kiss. "Were you one of those guys? Mr. Popular?"

"I guess I was. Everyone says I was. I was also the guy who would step in if someone was getting bullied. I always hated that stuff. I remember when Cam was being mean to Haley because he liked her, instead of expressing his feelings. I guess the apple doesn't fall too far from the tree, huh?"

I started to laugh, recalling my conversation with her. "Haley said you pulled a Cam."

"God," Hunter sighed, shaking his head. "I sure did. I'm sorry."

"I know," I said, reaching over to touch his thigh. "We're moving forward."

"We are." His voice thickened. "If you touch me, I'm gonna get distracted."

Heat crept up my spine. I wanted to touch him more, but I also wanted to get to our date safely. I pulled my hand away and adjusted in my seat, focusing on him.

"I heard all about Cam before I even met him. When Haley and I met, we talked about him every now and then. It's funny knowing now how much they love each other and how much things have changed, especially after hearing all shit she talked about him. I think they were always meant to be together."

"Me too," he said. "Colt has always loved Sarah. Always. But you know how that went. As for Sammy, the three of them falling in love was a surprise to me, but they really work together, don't they?"

"They do," I agreed.

"And then there's us."

And then there was us.

"I think we have a shot," I said.

"Me too."

"Although, I have to tell you, if we end up together forever, I will be the one in charge of decorating. Although I suppose you can bring all your plants to my house."

"I will happily be in charge of all plants," he said.

"I noticed you robbed my back porch."

"I didn't see it as robbing you, more as rescuing your plants from certain death."

I giggled. "It wasn't that bad. They were still alive."

"They were holding on by a thread. I'll be in charge of plants and then you can boss me around. I love your house. All of the colors, the pink and blues, and things I would never think do to my own house. Every time I'm at my cabin now, I feel like it's bland."

"You should let me decorate it," I said. "I like going into thrift stores in Austin, it makes me happy. Home decorating makes me happy."

"I didn't know you liked thrifting. You should check out Mom's storage container in the back of the farm. It's full of all sorts of shit that has just sat there over the years."

"Well, we'll see how our dinner with them goes," I said.

He chuckled. "It'll be fine. I mean, I have a feeling we're going to be scolded about the fiancé thing... But she loves you, Emma. I think I'll be the one they're upset with."

I frowned. I didn't like the idea of anyone being mad at Hunter over this situation. I'd been the one to drag him into it.

"None of this has been your fault. They shouldn't scold you

for any of it. Plus, it's clear I can make my own decisions. And I'm choosing you."

"You're part of the family, Emma. Everyone loves you and cares about you. Historically, I don't just make rash decisions, so I'm sure there's quite a bit of confusion around the fact that they found out you and I were engaged because of a Facebook post. And she's given me some space on it, but I think I've run out of time."

"Well, we'll tell them the truth. And we can tell them we're dating now."

"We could also tell them you're still my fiancé."

I snorted. "Hunter, everyone is right about me not getting engaged without a ring. I *do* have high standards, you know."

"Oh, I know. It's one of my favorite things about you."

CHAPTER THIRTY-FOUR
hunter

THE STEAKHOUSE WAS PERCHED at the very top of a hill, offering a stunning view of the entire Hill Country. The stars twinkled in the vast skies above, making it a beautiful night out with the most beautiful woman I'd ever known.

Emma hopped out of the truck and I swept her against me, planting a kiss on her cherry red lips. I couldn't resist her. She moaned against me, and for a moment I thought about getting back in the truck and taking her straight home to my bed.

She drew back with a dreamy smile and dragged her thumb across my lips, wiping away her lipstick. "You're gonna have red lips all night."

"Happily."

Now that I finally had the chance to be with her, I wasn't going to fuck it up.

Love had been mentioned a couple times between us. We were both dancing around a real admission, but I already knew the truth. I'd been in love with this woman since the moment she tased me.

When I thought about the future, Emma was it.

From the very beginning, it had always been her. I knew that now. And even though we had a whole host of things that needed figuring out, and a whole bunch of problems to solve, I knew we'd be able to do it side by side.

Emma slipped her arm in mine as I guided her to the set of oak doors. The restaurant was busy for a Sunday night, but I had no doubt we'd get a table.

I spotted the hostess standing behind a hand-built desk. A local artist was often commissioned to build things like this. I'd know Olivia Stevens' work anywhere.

I admired it for a moment and looked up at the hostess with a smile.

"Reservation?" she asked.

"I'm a friend of Tom's," I said. "He told us we could stop by."

The hostess's brows furrowed and she opened her mouth to turn us down, but then I spotted Tom. He was an older gentleman with a handlebar mustache, silver hair, and hankering for good wine and ciders. He always wore a cowboy hat, always had a cigar in the front pocket of his shirt, and had rancher money that kept Texas running.

Colt made a reserve batch from our grapes each year, and I'd started sneaking Tom a few bottles around the holidays in exchange for steaks. It was a damn good trade.

What could I say? I was a simple man.

This place had the best fucking steak in all of Texas.

"Well, well, well," Tom called as he headed straight for us. "It's about damn time, Harlow. Who's your pretty lady?"

"My fiancé, Emma Madden," I said. His eyes immediately darted to her hand, and I mentally cursed. The damn ring was the bane of my existence.

Now that Haley knew the truth, I needed to talk her into helping me pick out the perfect one.

"Got a ring coming," I said.

"Good. Had me worried there for a second. Belle, put these two out on the balcony, and get em' taken care of."

"Yes, sir."

Tom gave us a toothy grin. "I expect some good wine this winter, Harlow."

"You know I save the best for you."

His laugh was a boom that echoed all the way up to the vaulted ceilings. "Y'all enjoy."

I smiled as he continued on, greeting other folks as he went on his way.

"He's like a Texan Santa Claus," Emma whispered, leaning into me. "You know everyone. It's crazy."

I kissed the top of her head as we followed one of the waiters outside.

The balcony had the best views. There was a soft hum of people chatting, and candles that cast a golden glow over the tables. I pulled Emma's chair out for her, enjoying the dance of excitement in her sweet hazel eyes.

I sat down across from her as a waitress darted over to us. "How's it going?"

"Good," we both chimed.

"Excellent. Water to start?"

"Yes," I said. "And I'll have a gin martini."

Emma's mouth dropped. "You're a martini man?!"

"I am," I drawled. "On occasion."

Emma fought a snicker. "I'll have a gin martini too. Can I also have a side of lemon wedges for my water?"

The waitress smiled. "Of course. I'll get that started. Olives?"

We both nodded then watched her go. Emma leaned forward, resting her chin on her palms. "Tell me something I don't know about you."

I smiled and leaned forward. "Hmm. Let's see. When I was four, I fell out of a tree and broke my arm."

"Ouch," she chuckled.

"Your turn."

I sat back as the waitress brought us our martinis and some water, along with a small bowl of lemon slices. Emma immediately snatched up a wedge and squeezed some of the juice into her water.

"When I was eight, I won a beauty pageant," Emma said. "And one of the competitions was costume and dance. I went as a cowgirl, but I wore all pink."

A grin split my lips. "Fuck, that's cute. And fitting."

"I wanted to be a cowgirl from the ages of five to ten because I wanted a horse, but then I learned how much horses shit and quickly changed my mind."

I laughed and took a sip of my martini. "It's not that bad."

"It definitely is. And I am also a little afraid of cows."

My brows show up. "Cows? But cows are so cute."

"They terrify me. That night you found me on the side of the road outside Citrus Cove? I thought one would eat me."

My cheeks hurt as I laughed. "Oh my god. Emma, I have a friend—"

"You always have a friend," she snickered.

"True. But I have a friend who has a cow sanctuary. You can cuddle them, pet them, give them a spa day. It's really cute. We should go on a date there."

"You want to cuddle cows for a date?"

"I want to show you that cows aren't vicious human-eating monsters."

She rolled her eyes playfully. "Okay, okay. We can cuddle cows, but that's more of a fourth date thing."

"Uh huh. Does dinner with my parents count as a second date?"

She wrinkled her nose. "I'm a little scared of how that'll go."

"You'll be fine," I said. "Can't say the same for myself. They're ready to throw me to the wolves."

"They'll be okay," she said. "I think I've asked this before, but really—how do you know everyone?"

"Small town living, baby," I said. "And also helping out when I can. When I'm not overworked, I am social and like going out. I've met people over the years or knew people from high school who have gone on to do cool things. Plus, I'm a Harlow. We're part of the community, you know?"

"I do," she said. "I'm a little envious. My family was never like that. We were known because of our name and money, but not for helping people in any meaningful way. After my mom died, I think she took whatever sense of community there was with her."

"I'm sorry, Emma. I can't imagine experiencing so much loss."

"It's okay. I... Okay, this is terrible talk for a first date, but I finally cried about my dad dying."

"Good," I said softly. "I was worried."

"I know my reaction was probably weird, it's just that he and I weren't close."

"I know," I said. "Well, I don't know. But I understand. I do know grief works in weird ways. Sometimes it blows in and hits you all at once, and other times it's a slow trickle."

She nodded. "It's exactly like that."

The waitress came back up to us and Emma cursed. "Need more time?"

I already knew what I wanted.

"I'll get whatever he gets," Emma said. "If you know what you want."

"I do, but I don't know if you'll like it. I'm getting steak."

"I like steak."

"A big-ass steak."

"I can eat," she said. "Believe me, I can put down a big-ass steak."

I believed it. I put in our order and leaned back, looking out over the hills.

"Are you excited about RK?" Emma asked.

"Excited and nervous," I said. "I'll pick him up tomorrow. I still need to shop for supplies."

"I'll go with you, if you want," she said.

"I'd like that. Does Donnie like other dogs?"

"He does, for the most part. He might be a little jealous if I pet RK, though, but I'm sure they'll become friends. Are you sure you're ready for a dog?"

"I definitely am," I said. "I've been wanting a pet for a while. And after what RK's been through, I'm not letting him go. Plus, it'll be nice to have a buddy to watch movies with."

She beamed. "What's your favorite movie?"

I felt a little shy about it. "*Practical Magic*," I said.

Her eyes lit up. "No way."

"It is," I said. "I love it. I love their family and the magic. It's perfect."

"It's mine too," Emma said excitedly.

"Really?!"

"Yes! I love it."

"We should watch it," I said.

"Another date." She grinned and so did I. God, her smile lit up the entire room.

I was finally going to have the chance to make her smile like this all the time.

My breath caught in my chest. I was finally going to get to know her. To love her.

Her expression softened. "When you look at me like that, I feel like I'm the only person here."

"You are," I whispered. "When I look at you like that, you're the only person who matters, Emma."

Her hand slid across the table and I took it, giving her a gentle squeeze. I'd never believed I'd get to do this with her, but now that I was, I knew this was it.

I knew she was the one, beyond a shadow of a doubt. A whirlwind of chaos and emotions had swept us together, but we were together.

"I'm trying to think of more first date questions," she said. "We kind of did things backwards, didn't we?"

"We did," I said. "It kind of works for us, though."

"It works perfectly for us."

The waitress returned with our food and I leaned back in excitement, watching two large steaks be put down in front of us along with bread, salads, potatoes, and that delicious sauce I loved.

"Anything else?"

"Nope," I said.

"We're good," Emma agreed.

"Excellent. Let me know if you need anything else."

I certainly didn't. I had a steak and the woman of my dreams.

As soon as she left, Emma let out a hum. "I have sex questions."

My eyes widened. "Okay. What kind of sex questions?"

"Hmm. Tell me something I don't know," she said with a sly smile.

I raised a brow as I cut a piece of steak. "Like about what I want to do? Or try? Or do to you? I feel like there's something you want, but you're trying to get me to say something first."

"Maybe."

"Tell me, sparks," I chuckled.

She reached for her knife and fork and started to cut hers into neat squares. Right as I was about to take my first bite, she looked up at me. "I want to peg you."

Thank god I wasn't chewing yet, because I would have choked. I still choked on air anyway and set my fork down, letting out a cough. "*Emma.*"

She smirked as she took a bite. "I'm just saying. Also, fuck, this is really good steak."

"It's the best steak." I fanned my face, my cock jerking in my pants at the thought of her wearing a strap-on. "I can't think about food now."

"If you let me peg you, I'll... Now you tell me what you want to try."

"Jesus," I rasped. "Can you let a man eat first?"

She grinned. "Just a thought."

"Mmhm." I grabbed my water and downed half the glass without breaking eye contact, and then took a bite. It was damn delicious.

Emma wiggled her eyebrows at me. "Have you collected yourself?"

I narrowed my eyes. "So much sass for me to fuck out of you later."

Her eyes lit up. "There he is. I thought I'd stunned the dominance out of you."

"Not a chance in hell, sparks." I cleared my throat. "We can talk about pegging. I'm interested."

"Does that mean I get to dominate you?"

"Sure. Go ahead, tell me what to do," I said casually. I already knew how this was going to go.

Her eyes widened and she sat back. "Well, maybe I don't want to tell you what to do."

I raised a brow. "But don't you want to be the boss?"

Her cheeks turned pink and she pouted. "Okay, so maybe I do like being submissive."

"You know what? You can peg me and still be submissive." I leaned forward and crooked a finger at her. She leaned in closer. "I can say good girl every time you thrust just right. We can also get a strap-on with a vibrator that sits on your clit."

"*Oh*," she whispered. Her cheeks were bright red. "I really like that idea."

"Me too."

She shifted in her seat. "Well, now I'm all hot and bothered."

"Welcome to the club."

CHAPTER THIRTY-FIVE
emma

AFTER DINNER, the only thing the two of us could think about was pegging. Which was not exactly how I thought our first date would end, but we were eager enough that we stopped by an adult store on the way home to buy everything we needed. We were now in my bedroom, staring at the bag of goods with a mix of excitement and trepidation.

Hunter put his hands on his hips. "I'm gonna take a shower and… prep."

"I'm going to figure out how to put this on," I said. "Then we'll meet back here."

"And we'll give it a go."

I nodded, now feeling a little nervous. But then Hunter tugged me close to him. I sucked in a breath, feeling his erection against me. "Fuck," I whispered. "You're so hard."

"I am," he murmured, kissing me. I parted my lips, our tongues meeting as he took me deeper. He moaned and drew back. "If neither of us enjoy this, there's a thousand other things we can do. So there's no pressure."

I nodded. "I know. Thank you for trying with me."

He kissed me again. "I've done some experimenting before, so I think I'm gonna like it."

"I think I'm going to like it too."

"I want missionary though, so you can look in my eyes while you fuck me."

Fuck. That alone turned me on. He smirked as he kissed my forehead and headed for the shower, taking one of the bags with him.

My phone buzzed in my pocket and I pulled it out quickly, seeing a picture of Donnie from Honey. I smiled and hearted it. She'd kept him for the night and he looked perfectly content.

Now, back to business.

I pulled off my dress, kicked off my heels, unclasped my bra, and then pulled off the lace thong I wore. I gathered my clothes and moved them to a corner, tossing my shoes on top.

Our bag of toys sat on my bed. I opened it up, pulling out the black harness we'd bought. We'd also bought the largest bottle of lube we could find, knowing we would definitely need to use a lot.

Nerves kicked up again. We were really going to do this. It was a sexual fantasy I'd had for so long, it felt like I was walking through an erotic dream.

I grabbed the harness and unclasped it. It took a couple minutes, but I managed to fit it on. Then, I pulled the bright pink silicone dildo out of the box.

Because of course, if I was going to peg Hunter, it was going to be with a pink dildo.

I grabbed one of my sex toy wipes from my dresser drawer to clean it, and tossed the wipe in the trash. Then I worked to get the dildo through the hole in the harness, secured everything, and looked down with a sense of wonder.

The power went straight to my head. And pussy.

I'd never worn a strap-on before, but I loved it. I moved my hips, waving it back and forth with a soft giggle.

This was amazing.

I couldn't believe Hunter was willing to try this with me. I hoped it would be something we both enjoyed. But like he said, if it wasn't, that was perfectly okay too. It was good to attempt new things, and know that if they didn't work for us, we could always try something else in the future.

I heard the shower turn off. I gave my hips an air thrust, giggling again as the dildo wobbled.

The vibrator. I couldn't forget the vibrator. I had a small one that would fit against me while I wore the strap-on. I opened my drawer, rooting around until I found it. It came with a remote too, which I would happily present to Hunter.

I pressed the button and it started to vibrate against my fingers, and I turned it off.

This was going to be hot as fuck.

I readjusted the harness and fit the bullet vibrator against my clit. I held onto the remote and turned when I heard Hunter's footsteps. He strode into the room with a towel around his waist, his chest dappled with water drops.

His eyes darkened as he looked at me. "Damn, baby. You're sexier than sin."

"I feel powerful," I said, waving my hips.

He chuckled and then crossed to me in a stride. He cupped my face and let the towel drop to the floor. "You are powerful," he said. "Are you ready to try this? I'm all cleaned up."

"Yes," I whispered. "I am. Are you?"

"I am."

I swallowed hard, suddenly nervous again. I felt like I was fumbling around, but this was *Hunter*, I reminded myself. He was my...

He was my fiancé.

Maybe not officially, but I'd let my mind go with that for the rest of the night.

"I have a present for you," I said.

"Oh?"

I gave him the remote to the vibrator. He smiled as he took it.

"Thank you," he said. "For your trust and for your orgasms."

"I can say the same thing," I chuckled.

Hunter kissed me softly and slowly backed me to the bed. My knees hit the mattress and I fell back, our kisses heating up as he crawled over me.

"I thought I was supposed to be on top," I giggled, giving his chest a light shove.

He wrapped his arms around me and rolled, seating me on top of his hips. We look down at my strap on, the pink dildo bright against his hard stomach. He held the remote to my vibrator in one of his hands, his thumb circling the button.

The anticipation was going to kill me.

"All right, sparks," he said. "Let's see what we can do."

I slid off him and grabbed the bottle of lube as he spread his legs. I licked my lips as I studied his cock. It was hard and ready and...

Before I could stop myself, I leaned down, bringing the head to my lips.

"Fuck," he grunted.

I took him deeper, sucking him slowly. His eyes glued to me as I bobbed my head up and down. The taste of his pre-cum sat on my tongue. I was hungry for more.

I wrapped my hands around the base of his cock, slowly jerking him as I sucked the tip. I cupped his balls, rolling them gently as I continued to pleasure him. His cock hit the back of my throat, working to take as much of him as I could. He was too big for me to ever completely deep-throat him, but I still tried, groaning around him.

"Fuck, baby. You're really good at this. Keep sucking."

His breathy command went straight to my pussy. It turned me on, and I was already wet from just these actions alone. I popped my lips as I pulled off of his cock and dragged my tongue down the underside to his balls. I sucked one of them into my mouth gently, enjoying the way he moaned.

I kept stroking his cock as I continued to suck on his balls, and he tilted his hips back, giving me access to his ass. I looked up at him, meeting his gaze before taking my tongue lower.

"Yes," he gasped. "*Fuck.*"

The tip of my tongue slowly circled his hole. I started off carefully, and then began to push, using more force as I rimmed him. Hunter's moans floated through the bedroom as I stroked his cock and fucked his ass with my tongue, my entire body throbbing with need.

There was something so sexy about knowing that Hunter, a tough handyman and farmer, was willing to be so vulnerable with me. It was hot and sexy, and such a fucking turn on.

Hunter arched, clearly fighting himself to not take control. He let out a frustrated breath as his cock throbbed. I pushed my tongue deeper, feeling his hole give way to me.

"Good girl. God, you're doing this so well. Keep going, baby."

His praise went straight to my pussy. I drew back, replacing my tongue with my fingers, circling him.

"Lube," he gasped.

"Yes, sir."

I leaned back and snatched up the bottle, flipping open the cap. I poured a large amount of lube over my dildo, stroking it up and down. Then I added more and circled his hole, slowly pushing a finger inside him.

"You have to relax," I said softly.

He let out a chuckle, and his muscles relaxed some. He blew a sharp breath as I pushed some of the lube inside him, using two fingers to gently stretch him.

"How does that feel?" I asked.

"Really good," he huffed. "You're doing such a good job. You can go deeper if you want."

I went deeper, thrusting them in and out slowly, then slowly rubbed down over his prostate.

Hunter immediately grunted. "Fuck!"

"Too much?" I asked immediately.

"No. Fuck. Emma, I'm going to come if you keep doing that."

"Do you—do you want to come?"

"Yes. *Make me come.*"

Whatever he said next was lost to a groan as I began to massage his prostate. His cock jerked on its own and within a few seconds, cum ejected from the tip, dripping down his length. My eyes widened as I realized I'd made him come without even touching his cock.

"Fuck," he panted.

I leaned forward, licking up the mess he'd made. His cum was thick and salty. I licked my lips and sat back, readjusting myself so the tip of the dildo rested against his asshole.

"Are you ready?" I asked.

"Yes, baby." His eyes lit up and I heard a *click*.

I gasped as the vibrator sitting against my clit roared to life. I'd forgotten all about it. I cried out, my head falling back for a moment. He turned down the intensity just enough to let my brain function again.

"Fuck." I could barely get myself together.

"Fuck *me*," he demanded.

I rested my hands on the backs of his thighs as I eased forward.

"Slow," he grunted.

I nodded, my breath hitching as he slowly took the dildo. The vibrations thrummed against my wet pussy, pleasure rolling through me. I trembled as I eased forward, giving him more.

"Good girl. Keep going. Nice and slow."

His voice was strained. His eyes fluttered on a soft moan and then I heard a *click* again.

I cried out as the vibrations kicked up in intensity. I rocked my hips, fighting to control myself. The dildo pulled back with me and then I slowly thrust forward, running my hands up my body to my breasts.

"Good girl. Play with yourself while you fuck me, baby."

My entire body was so sensitive. I whimpered as I began to pump in and out of him, circling my breasts and pinching my nipples. Electric pleasure thrummed with every thrust, the combination of pegging Hunter and the vibrator dragging me to the edge.

I was so, so close to coming.

I planted my hands on his chest and fucked him harder. Hunter's mouth fell open on a groan as I took him over and over.

"Oh god," I cried.

His cock had softened after coming, but it was hard again. He kicked up the vibrator another notch, drawing a cry out of me before dropping the remote and stroking himself. His eyes closed as he moaned, our bodies melding together.

"I'm going to come," I squealed.

"Come for me," he rasped.

I thrust into him a few more times before my orgasm washed over me. I froze, a cry trapped in my throat as my body tensed, the pleasure exploding. For a few blissful moments, everything was perfect. Everything was beautifully perfect.

I sucked in a breath as it ebbed. I panted as I looked down at Hunter, drinking in the hungry expression on his face.

"That was beautiful," he said.

I moved my hips and he nodded, still stroking himself. My heart pounded as he grabbed the remote, turning off the vibrator so I didn't completely fall apart again. I moved my hips, fucking him in long, deep strokes until his own cry echoed through the room and he came again.

He came for me. For me and me alone. More cum streaked his skin, his muscles relaxing as he melted beneath me.

"I love you," he whispered.

My eyes teared up and I leaned forward, kissing him hard. "I love you too, Hunter."

"I love you so much. I love you so, so much. I love you just the way you are."

I dragged him into another kiss as he thumbed away my tears.

I love you just the way you are.

I'd been waiting my whole life to hear someone say that to me.

CHAPTER THIRTY-SIX
emma

SUNLIGHT WOKE me slowly as it poured into my bedroom. My eyes fluttered as my dreams slowly evaporated and I let out a soft hum, warm and cozy.

Hunter's arm was around me, his breathing soft. I smiled to myself and wiggled my toes, ready to start my day while also wanting to remain next to him.

His arms slowly moved around me and he let out a soft groan. "I'm not ready."

I snorted. "I thought you were still sleeping."

"I wake up at like 6 a.m. every day."

I slowly rolled over and craned my head back to look at him. His eyes were still closed, but he was smiling. He slowly opened one eye to look at me.

"How's your ass?" I asked.

He snorted and shook his head, letting out another dramatic groan that had me giggling. He rolled onto his back and I moved on top of him, sitting on his hips and resting on his chest.

"A little sore," he grunted. "Manageable. Worth it."

"Good," I said. "I'll be thinking about last night forever."

"Me too." He tangled his fingers in my hair and started to massage the back of my head. I let out a groan and closed my eyes, relaxing into him.

"Mm. If you keep doing this..." I trailed off as I felt his cock harden against me.

"What'll happen?" he whispered, his tone teasing me.

"Fuck." I could barely think as he kept massaging my head.

"You make such pretty noises for me, sparks."

"*Mmph.*"

"I've got some time before I need to go pick up RK," he said softly.

I pushed my hips back, meeting his cock with my pussy. We'd both slept naked and every touch was turning me on. His fingers went from massaging my head to gripping my hair, and I gasped as he gave me a tug.

"Get on my cock," he grunted.

"Yes, sir," I rasped.

I reached down between us, moving the head of his cock inside of me. We sighed together as I sank back, taking the first couple of inches, and then sitting back more. Hunter dragged my mouth down into a kiss as I began to move my hips, grinding up and down on his cock.

A muffled curse was lost between our lips as I kissed him deeper, pleasure electrifying my entire body. I whimpered as I took more of him, every stroke going deeper until I was taking every inch with each motion.

He kept one hand knotted in my hair, the other on my hips as I rode him.

"Good girl," he rasped. "Fuck, you're taking me so well."

"I am." I felt a streak of pride mixed with euphoric lust. I loved it when he praised me for taking his cock. I loved it when he let me take some control while still dominating me.

His hips met me in a thrust this time and I gasped, leaning forward. He caught my breast in his mouth, sucking my nipple as he pumped up. I threw my head back on a long groan, my hips moving faster.

"I'm so close," I rasped.

All he could do was grunt. Both his hands held my hips as he fucked me harder, driving me to the edge. My cry echoed through the bedroom, sunlight dripping over us as I came. He kept fucking me through the waves of pleasure, every muscle tensing.

"Fuck," he grunted.

I felt the rush of his cum inside me, his hips jerking. I panted as I collapsed against him, his arms circling me. He kissed me gently before relaxing into the bed.

"Good morning," he chuckled.

I grinned against his chest. "Good morning."

It was the perfect morning. We laid like that for a few minutes before he let out a soft sigh.

"I've gotta run to the vet," he said.

"I have to pick up Donnie, but then we can stop by to meet RK," I said.

"Good. I want to show you all the things I bought for him to see if you approve."

"I'm sure it's all perfect."

He kissed the top of my head and then we slowly pulled apart. "Let's shower," he said.

"You just want to see me naked and wet."

"Obviously."

He gave my ass a spank as we made our way to the bathroom. I flipped on the hot water and we crammed inside, his arms caging me against the tile wall as he kissed me again.

I patted his chest. "If you keep distracting us, you'll be late."

Hunter sighed. "Okay, okay. We'll pick up our children and then resume this later."

I snorted at the thought of Donnie and RK being our children. He kissed me one more time before we got busy, scrubbing ourselves clean.

Within half an hour, I was making a cup of coffee and Hunter was about to head out the door. My hair was wrapped in a towel and I was naked, while he was fully dressed and clearly torn between staying and going.

"I'll see you later," I said.

He leaned in to murmur against my ear. "I love you."

I grinned. "I love you too."

One more kiss and then I watched as he went out the front door.

For the first time, I felt the blanket of contentment I'd been craving for so long.

I carried my coffee back upstairs and flopped down on my bed. I looked over at the indention in the blankets from Hunter's big body, and smiled.

My phone rattled on the dresser as a call came in. I took a sip of coffee and reached over, hanging off part of the bed as I answered. "Hello?"

"Ms. Madden? This is Nathan, your father's lawyer."

"Oh." My eyes widened and I put my coffee down immediately. "Hi. I've been meaning to email you."

"I've been meaning to get ahold of you, I apologize for taking so long. There's been a lot happening. Ms. Madden, I'm reaching out to you for several reasons, but the most pressing one is regards to your ex-husband, Joshua Martin. He is suspected to be behind the death of Michael Madden."

"What?" I whispered. The world froze around me. My heart hammered as I swallowed hard. "I... Okay. Can you tell me more?"

"Yes. A homicide investigation has been launched, and Joshua Martin is considered to be a person of interest. He might be behind the death of your father."

I winced. What the fuck was happening? "They think Josh killed him?"

"Yes. They do. Have you heard from him or seen him?" Nathan asked.

"Yes," I said immediately. "He's here in Citrus Cove. He showed up about three weeks ago and told me my father died. He tried to convince me to remarry him and sell the company to him. Obviously, I told him no. He also broke into my fiancé's house and attempted to run him off the road."

I stood up to grab a robe from the bathroom, sliding it onto my shoulders.

"Ms. Madden, did you go to the police about this?"

"I didn't. I should have, but it's been a stressful few weeks. I can reach out to them now," I said. Fuck. Why had I been so stupid? I should have done that. My eyes watered as I rushed downstairs to my front door, immediately twisting the lock.

I needed to text Hunter. I knew he was just going to pick up RK, but now I was nervous.

Nathan cleared his throat and then continued. "Please reach out to them immediately after this conversation if you're able to. I'll contact the investigator and let them know Josh has been seen in Citrus Cove. I would heavily caution you to stay indoors and away from him. If he approaches you, do not engage and call the police."

"I can do that," I said. Shock and rage combined into an overwhelming tonic. "Why didn't anyone call me when my dad died?"

"Your stepmother was supposed to. Did she not? She told us you refused to come to California."

"That's not true," I said immediately. "That's not true at all.

No one called me. I didn't know about his death until Josh showed up here."

"That's concerning." Nathan let out a low hum. "The entire estate and company was inherited by you. As his executor, I apologize it's taken so long to reach out to you. I filed the court documents, but with the investigation, there have been more matters to take care of. I'll be booking a flight to Austin this week so we can meet in person and get everything situated."

"Did my stepmom get anything?" I asked.

Nathan let out a sigh. "Your father left her with a small amount to live on. She was under the impression that she would receive more. She was not happy."

"Do you..." I trailed off. It was unthinkable, and yet I was going to ask anyway. "Do you think she could have worked with Josh to kill my father?"

"I'm unsure," he said. "I'd like to believe the best, but it's a possibility."

"How did he die? She wouldn't tell me. We spoke briefly on the phone a few days ago, but that was the first time I'd heard from her in ages."

"He was found in his office with pills and a letter. He appeared to have overdosed, but after further investigation, the medication that killed him was not prescribed to him. It was prescribed to Joshua."

I shook my head and went back up the stairs. I put the phone on speaker and started to get dressed. "My dad was not the type to do something like that," I said bitterly. "Any time he was sick or injured, it was a battle to get him to even see a doctor. I know we hadn't spoken in years, but that just doesn't sound like him."

"I agree." I could hear Nathan typing away in the background. "I've just asked my assistant to book my flight. I'll be there as soon as I can. In the meantime, I think contacting the police and getting somewhere safe is wise."

"I'll do that," I said. "I have people I can stay with."

Hunter would keep me safe.

"I'll be in touch."

"Thanks," I said.

The call ended, and I placed my hands on my head as my breaths turned rapid.

That son of a bitch. I'd always known he was awful, but this? I was in shock. This was heinous, even for him. I squeezed my eyes shut as I tried to process the information.

Hunter.

I grabbed my phone and called him. It rang and rang until it went to voicemail.

"Hey," I said, my voice trembling. "Please call me back immediately. The lawyer just called me about Josh. They think he killed my dad."

CHAPTER THIRTY-SEVEN
hunter

I BELTED along to the radio as I sped down the highway.

We'd said *I love you.*

And she'd pegged me. She'd rearranged my guts and my heart.

I really couldn't think of a better way to live my life. I grinned as I sang, counting my blessings. I was excited to get RK and take him home. Mentally, I went over my list of everything I'd bought for him.

It was going to be amazing. I got the dog, got the girl, now I just needed to get the ring.

My gaze darted to the rearview mirror, and my voice faltered. A familiar red car was trailing right behind me. I sped up some, but they fell back.

I was just being paranoid. I turned up the radio louder and sighed happily.

I glanced at the clock as I got closer to Anna's office. I'd need them to go over everything about caring for a dog with a broken leg. He was young and I think we all were confident he'd adapt quickly.

My foot eased off the gas when I spotted a woman up ahead on the side of the road, attempting to flag me down. Her car was parked in the grass with the hood up.

I was tempted to keep driving by, but I couldn't leave someone stranded. I glanced at the clock with a sigh. RK could hold on for a few minutes.

I slowed and steered off the road. I frowned.

It was a silver Lexus. I looked at the license plate. The numbers were the same.

But that wasn't Josh. Clearly. Maybe someone else had the rental now.

"Hmm." I put the truck in part and hopped out. "What's going on?"

"I think my battery is having issues, but I'm not sure," she called. "Can you take a look?"

"Sure," I said.

I took my keys out and put them in my pocket, leaving my phone on the dash. The red car I saw earlier drove past us. I spared it a glance and went up to the Lexus, giving the woman a grim smile.

"Thanks for stopping," she said.

"Sure," I said.

She had short dark hair and was tall and willowy. Probably in her upper thirties. Very much out of place, probably from Austin. I glanced inside the car, but the windows were too tinted to see anything.

"Did you rent this car?" I asked.

"Yes," she said hesitantly.

"Hmm." I went around to where the front hood was popped. I leaned over, looking over everything. I heard one of the doors open and shut.

I looked a little closer and frowned.

There wasn't a goddamn thing wrong with this car.

Cold, sharp steel pressed against my back and I stilled.

Fuck.

Fuck me.

"Shouldn't have fucking punched me."

"Josh."

God, I was a fucking idiot. The blade pressed hard enough to break skin, pain slicing through me. My heart pounded. If he stabbed me there, I would die. My kidney was right there and god knew what else.

"You should have left her," Josh snarled. "Should have never tried to get in the way."

"I should have done much worse than punch you," I growled.

I held up my hands though as the woman faced us. She pushed her sunglasses up, giving me a look over.

"Who are you?" I asked.

"Who do you think?" she asked bitterly.

"Josh's mistress?"

Her lips twisted in disgust. "Emma's stepmother."

"Ah," I said. The dots started to connect. "Let me guess, the two of you want the company. Or was it money?"

"We need to get off the road," Josh said. "Before someone sees us."

As he said that, the same red car I saw earlier drove by. I started to throw up my hands, but the blade dug deeper.

"Don't even think about it," Josh said. "I've already killed once for this, I'll do it again."

Fuck.

The woman in front of me rolled her eyes at him. "This entire little situation could have been done properly, but you fucked everything up. Get him in the car," she said to Josh. Her attention focused back on me. "If you try anything, you will die.

We just need you for a bit to get what we want. Do you understand?"

"Loud and clear," I said bitterly.

Josh grabbed my arm and shoved me toward the back door. I glanced around, looking for an out. I needed to be careful. He opened the door and shoved me in. I all the way to the other side and reached for the other door, but felt a sharp pain in my arm.

"Fuck," I shouted. I looked down at where Josh had cut my arm.

"We told you not to try anything," he said.

Pain lanced through me and I sucked in a breath, covering the wound with my palm. Blood swelled, dripping down and wetting my hand. I glared at him as stepmom of the fucking year got in the front seat and started the engine.

"So you killed Michael Madden?" I asked. "Together, I'm guessing?"

I eyed the knife in Josh's hand.

"I have a gun," she said, turning around. She waved it and then aimed it straight at me. My entire body turned to ice as panic set in. "I will use it if you try anything else."

"What's your name?" I asked.

"Angela Madden."

I gave a slight nod, trying my best to stay calm. If I played my cards right, I'd get out of this just fine, these two would go to jail, and Emma would remain safe.

"So what's your plan?" I asked.

"Shut the fuck up," Josh hissed.

I gave him a flat look. "There are not enough words in the English language to describe how much I hate you."

His vulture blue eyes darkened. "I don't know what she sees in you."

"Many things. What do you see in stepmom, huh? A fat

paycheck? For someone who was waxing and waning about me loving Emma for the money, it's a little fucking ironic."

"Shut him up," Angela growled.

She tossed a roll of duct tape back. Josh caught it and ripped off a piece, plastering it over my mouth. She kept the gun on me while he did that, and he tapped my hands.

"Wrists together."

I did as he asked and he used the tape to bind them together. Four layers of it. I could probably break it, but it would fucking hurt.

Angela turned back around in her seat. She pulled onto the road and floored the gas. I went silent, watching and thinking. I knew this area like the back of my hand. We were headed towards Austin, though, which I didn't like.

After a few minutes, she started to slow.

This is good. She pulled into the parking lot of a small motel.

Damn, I'd been wrong. They *had* holed up in a two-star, piece of shit place.

"Is money that tight?" I mumbled, but it was muffled by the tape over my mouth.

Angela pulled into a parking spot. Were they this stupid? It was broad fucking daylight on a Monday.

Josh immediately opened the door and got out, Angela following suit. I watched as he came around to my side. He opened the door for me and I got out, glowering at both of them.

This was gonna have to be it. I needed to act soon.

Josh walked behind me and Angela ahead, leading me to a door on the ground floor. It was painted green, number 009. She drew out a key, tucking the gun away.

The moment we entered the room, I took my shot. I struck out and managed to knock Angela forward, and then twisted around to punch Josh with my hands together. I gasped as the blade stabbed into my abdomen, slicing through me like butter.

Josh shoved me back, and the knife pulled free. I hit the ground, my vision dotting as the pain hit. I clutched my stomach, blood wetting my hands.

"Dammit, Josh," Angela sneered. "We needed him alive. We were going to use him to make her sign the fucking papers."

The pain was unlike anything I'd ever experienced. I looked down at myself, shock settling in. The knife had gone in right under my belly button.

Fuck, this can't be how I go.

My vision blurred as I fought to remain conscious. The pain was overwhelming.

This couldn't be it.

Not the day after I'd finally told Emma I loved her. Not after we'd fought so hard to start over.

This wasn't right. It wasn't supposed to be like this.

CHAPTER THIRTY-EIGHT
emma

I CALLED HIM FORTY-FIVE TIMES.

He didn't answer.

I was losing my mind.

Hunter wasn't picking up the phone.

I'd already called the police, Cam, and Sammy. They were gathering people, but everyone was a little lost without Hunter being the one to take charge in an emergency.

Bud had been notified and the entire town of Citrus Cove was turning over every inch looking for him.

They were doing their part, and I felt helpless.

I paced back and forth on my front porch, barely able to breathe. Haley's corvette was the first one to pull up. Her wheels screeched to a halt, and she jumped out, running up to me.

"He's not picking up," I said quickly. The panic was setting in, the fear taking over me. "He's not answering. He's not—"

"Listen to me," she said firmly. She grabbed my face, her eyes wide. "I need you to take a deep breath, Emma."

"What do you know?" I whispered, searching her gaze.

I could tell there was something. I'd known her for so long, it was clear something had happened.

"Hunter's truck was found on the side of the road right by the vet's office, but he wasn't in it, okay? Hunter is strong. He knows how to fight. If someone took him, he's going to be okay."

My entire world was shattering. A sob loosened in my chest and I shook my head, but Haley pulled me into a firm hug. "We're gonna find him. This is Hunter we're talking about, okay?"

"I love him. Haley, I love him so goddamn much. I can't lose another person I love. I can't. I just got him. I just got him in my life, I can't lose him."

"You're not going to," she whispered, squeezing me harder. "It's going to be okay. I'm here with you. Alice should be here any moment. We're all going into safety mode, okay?"

I could barely breathe. Tears stung my eyes, my throat closing up as I fought the urge to cry. I needed to find him. I needed to do *something*.

"I can't just stay here," I said.

"Tell me what the lawyer said," Haley demanded.

I nodded and repeated everything I'd told Cam. Haley listened and then shook her head.

"That son of a bitch," she whispered. "Okay. We're gonna make it through this. We've been through things like this, Emma."

"I can't," I rasped. "If I lose him, I just…"

"Emma," Haley growled. "Snap the fuck out of it. I need you to pull it together. We can fall apart once he's home."

I drew in a steady breath. She was right. I'd needed someone to tell me that, and now a steadiness settled over me.

I glanced up when I heard tires on gravel.

Alice's car pulled up behind Haley's and she got out. "Have you heard anything?" she yelled as she ran up to us.

I shook my head and wiped my eyes as she joined us on the porch. She pulled me into a hug and kept her arm around my shoulders. "Everyone is jumping into action. Sarah said Sammy is on the phone with everyone they know, and Colt is already out looking."

"Cam is working with Bud," Haley said. "We're gonna find him."

My worry was that we'd find him and it'd be too late.

"This is a nightmare," I whispered. "This is all my fault."

"It's not your fault," Alice insisted.

"No, it is. I should have told the police about the letters. About—"

"What letters?" Alice asked.

Haley and I winced. "There's been a lot happening," Haley said. "Emma and Hunter kept a few secrets."

"Ones we shouldn't have," I said. "And we did it because of me."

I drew in a deep breath, trying to keep my nausea at bay. My heart felt like it was going to beat out of my chest.

I gave her the most condensed version possible of everything that had happened.

"Oh my god, Emma," Alice said. She was clearly horrified. "What the fuck? Why didn't you tell us?"

"I didn't know Josh was a suspected murderer," I said. "And my lawyer is worried my stepmom is involved too. This is way worse than anything I could have imagined."

Alice pressed her lips. "I'm gonna yell at you later."

"Understandably," I said.

I swallowed hard and then frowned when a red car screeched to a halt.

"Who is that?" Haley asked.

We watched as a woman got out, and I realized I recognized her. She was the woman I'd seen glaring at me before. She wrung her hands together as she approached.

"Emma? I... Can we talk?"

"Now is not a good time," I snapped. "Who are you?"

"I've been sending letters..."

"Are you fucking kidding me?" I seethed.

"What the fuck?" Haley whispered.

Anger lurched through me and I marched down the front steps. "You're who's been sending those? The pictures? You've been stalking me?"

"Yes, but—but I can explain—"

Her eyes widened as I lunged for her. In one smooth motion, I knocked her to the ground and smashed the butt of my palm against her nose. It broke, blood gushing as she cried out.

"Wait! I know—"

Alice yelled at me, trying to pull me off her, but it wasn't gonna happen. I pinned the fucking stalker beneath me and she gasped out, trying to push me off.

"*I know where they went!*"

Haley and Alice managed to yank me back, all of our butts hitting the ground with a heavy thump.

The woman let out a sob and slowly sat up, clutching her face. "I saw who took him. It was a man and a woman. They took him to the motel outside of Citrus Cove. I just..."

"You were stalking him," I growled. "You were stalking Hunter?!"

"I know it sounds bad, but I wanted to try to convince him to leave you—"

"He's not going to leave me!" I yelled. "Why in the hell would you do all of this?!"

"Emma," Alice said calmly. "She said she knows where they went. We can focus on the other shit later."

She had a point. I forced myself to take a breath, trying to rein in my temper. Everything was happening so quickly, my emotions were going haywire.

"What did the woman look like?" I asked.

"She had dark hair and looked young—"

"Did the man look like a Ken doll?" I bit out.

"Yes."

Motherfucker.

Josh and my stepmom. It couldn't be anyone else.

"Are you telling the truth?" I asked, getting to my feet.

"Yes," she gasped. She held up her hands, blood gushing down her face. "I'm sorry. I should have never sent those letters or photos. I was being—"

"Shut the fuck up," I snarled. "You're lucky Haley and Alice are here. Which motel?"

"It's the Southern Inn."

I knew where it was.

And I wasn't going to wait another moment to get to Hunter.

"I'll call Bud," Haley said immediately. "We're gonna get him. We're going to find him."

"I'll call Sarah," Alice said, already pulling her phone out. "It's going to be okay."

That wasn't good enough for me.

I turned around and beelined for the house. I ignored Haley's call as I went inside, grabbed the baseball bat I kept in the corner in case there was a home intruder, and went back out. Haley's keys gleamed in the grass. I snatched them up and then ran to her corvette.

"Emma!" Haley shouted.

"I'm taking your car," I yelled back. "I'm going after him!"

"Goddammit, Emma!" Alice shouted.

I couldn't wait. I knew Josh and my stepmom didn't know self defense, but if they got the jump on Hunter, he was in real danger.

And if they'd killed my dad, then they could kill again.

I couldn't lose him.

I tossed the bat into the passenger seat, slid into the front, cranked the engine on, and backed out before either one of them could stop me. The tires screeched as it lurched forward and I gunned it down the road.

Living in a small town meant that the roads were easy to speed down, and I took full advantage. I rolled down Main Street going sixty, darting around other cars who honked at me and running red lights as safely as I could. I hit the highway and sped faster, straight for the motel.

Please be okay. Please be okay.

It was the mantra that kept me going. I just needed him to be okay.

The sign for the motel gleamed in the distance. I pulled into the parking lot and slowed.

The Lexus.

"Fuck me," I whispered.

I parked next to it, my heart hammering. I reached over and grabbed my bat then got out, surveying the rooms. The parking lot was mostly empty, aside from the Lexus.

A muffled shout echoed from behind one of the doors. Sirens reverberated in the distance, but they wouldn't get here fast enough.

My phone rang in my pocket, but I ignored it. It was probably Haley or Alice or someone else, but I needed to focus. I stepped onto the sidewalk, slowly approaching the door. I leaned in, pressing my ear to it.

I'd know my stepmother's voice anywhere.

Angela Madden.

Josh's voice followed her shrill yell, their words incomprehensible.

I took a step back. The last few years of all my martial arts training were here to help me now more than ever.

If my man was in danger, there wasn't a damn thing that was going to keep me from him.

CHAPTER THIRTY-NINE
hunter

THE LAST THING I ever expected to see was all five feet of Emma Madden breaking down the door with a baseball bat, screaming at the top of her lungs, her rage brighter than a neon sign.

Wood splintered as the door flew open. Josh and Angela both turned in shock and surprise.

Hell, I could barely see. I could barely breathe. I was clutching my stomach, the pain unbearable.

But she was crystal clear...

And that terrified me because it meant the person I loved was in danger.

"They have a gun!" I rasped.

Emma was quicker than Josh or Angela. I started to try to sit up as she launched herself at Josh with the fury of a woman scorned. My mouth fell open as she took out his knee with the bat.

His bones crunched, his screams pitching as she kicked him to the floor.

A wave of pain rushed over me. My breaths turned rapid, my skin covered in a layer of sweat.

Angela screeched and raised the gun, aiming at Emma.

No, no, no.

I used every bit of strength I had left to kick my leg out, knocking her off balance.

The gun fired.

Everything stopped.

The bullet flew past Emma, imbedding into the door frame. My ears rang from the shot, but I kicked again, this time knocking Angela to the floor. She screeched, but Emma moved fast, kicking the gun out of her hand and then doing what I could only describe as a wrestler smackdown on Angela.

Josh's screams pierced my ears. Fuck, I could barely see straight. I wheezed as I collapsed against the floor, curling into myself as I held pressure to my stomach.

Sirens grew louder, shouts followed. I closed my eyes, focusing on my heartbeat. I kept pressure on my wound and tried to breathe. It was all I could do now.

"Baby, baby." Emma's hands grasped my cheeks, her words panicked. "Oh god. I'm so sorry. I'm so sorry. Fuck. I'm too late, I was too late. Where did they stab you? Where are you hurt?"

"Stomach," I rasped.

Her hands slid down, applying pressure over mine.

"You're not allowed to leave me. You can't. Promise me."

"I can't promise that, sparks."

"*Please.*"

Please, please, please. I'd do my best. I wouldn't let go without a fight. Not after everything we'd gone through.

She pulled me over onto my back. The pain pulled me out for a moment, everything fading and then flooding back in.

"I love you."

I wasn't sure if she said it or if I did. But I knew it was true either way.

Everything blurred together. I felt myself being moved, and heard the shouts of people I loved blending with voices of strangers.

Everything hurts.
Everything is cold.
Everything went dark.

CHAPTER FORTY
emma

CAM HAD to physically pick me up off the floor. I couldn't stop sobbing as he put me in the truck and slammed the door, shouting for Sammy to follow. My vision blurred as I watched the ambulance take off, the lights flashing as they sped to the hospital.

He got in the truck and cranked it on, slamming his foot on the gas. He followed the ambulance, with Sammy close behind us.

"Haley is bringing you clothes. He's going to make it. He's gonna make it, Em."

My ears were still ringing from the gunshot and Josh's screams. Blood dried on my clothes and hands as shock settled over me. *Hunter's blood.* I hadn't felt this coldness since I'd lost Evelyn.

"We're all going to the hospital. We're all going to be there for him."

He kept talking as my sobs softened, but the internal screaming did not subside.

"The police are going to need to talk to you," he said.

"But—"

"Please stop," I whispered.

"I can't. If I stop talking, I'm going to lose it, Emma."

"Okay," I sniffled. "Then talk about something else."

"I'll tell you about a time Hunter saved a cat."

A broken laugh left me and I wiped my nose on my sleeve. "Okay."

"He was thirteen. I was ten. Sammy was seven and had been sneaking food to a stray calico who started coming around the farm. Well, one morning, we heard Sammy crying because he couldn't find the cat. We looked everywhere, but Hunter found her. She'd climbed all the way up a tree and was meowing."

"I bet he saved her."

"He sure did. He climbed all the way up until he got her, put her in his jacket. Skinned up his knees and hands. And then she scratched the ever-loving shit out of him as he climbed down. It was complete and utter chaos, but he saved the cat."

Quiet tears started rolling again. I didn't even bother to wipe them away. "That sounds like him."

"We took a vote and named her Princess Pain."

Another laugh bubbled up. "Princess Pain?"

"Yep. She had a litter of kittens a month and a half later that our mom made us take care of. Then we found good homes for them all. It was a good summer."

"What happened to Princess Pain?"

"She lived for another ten years. She had a long happy life on the farm."

I smiled as much as I could.

Cam let out a shaky breath. "My brother will pull through. He's a Harlow. He's gonna be just fine, Emma."

There'd been a lot of blood. I'd never forget seeing him like that. Everything replayed in my mind on a loop.

It'd been stupid for me to take off like I had. But I didn't regret it.

I wanted to know why Angela and Josh would do something like this. The money? The company?

"People do bad things sometimes," Cam said softly.

I hadn't realized I'd spoken aloud.

"There's no rhyme or reason. Sometimes, people just snap. I'm so sorry, Emma. I'm so sorry about your dad, too."

"I can't imagine it," I whispered. "I can't imagine doing something so terrible."

"The truth will come out. We've got people who will help handle things. The focus is on Hunter right now. Were you hurt at all?"

"No," I said. I wiped my nose with my shirt. "I had a baseball bat. I broke down the door, took out Josh's knee. Angela had a gun. She would have shot me, but Hunter managed to knock her off her feet. And then I tackled her, put her in a headlock until she passed out. Then I tried to help Hunter. The police showed up, and..."

"We're almost to the hospital."

He sped faster until I saw the sign for the emergency room. He turned into the parking lot and found the first open spot. My hand was already on the door handle. I jumped out as soon as the truck stopped and took off towards the building, Cam right on my tail.

I spotted Sarah and Colt with the boys in the parking lot and immediately turned around before they saw me. "I don't want the boys to see me like this," I said to Cam.

"Haley is almost here," he said quickly. "Do you want to go inside to the bathroom? I'll send Sarah over."

I nodded and darted to the doors. They slid open and I ducked inside, heading straight to the restrooms.

He'll be okay. He'll be okay.

I couldn't get the image out of my head. He'd been so pale and covered in sweat. And he was shaking. There'd been so much blood.

I went to the sink and gripped the edge. I forced myself to breathe, my ears still ringing.

"Emma, I'm here."

I felt Sarah's arms around me and turned around, burying my face against her shoulder. I let out a soft sob, but she just held me, stroking my back.

"We're going to get you changed and cleaned up. Lynn, Bob, and Honey are here. Hunter is in surgery already. He went into shock from the blood loss, but he's going to pull through."

"I feel like this is all my fault," I whispered.

"It's not. Do you remember how I felt when Haley was hurt?"

"Yes." I leaned back to look at her.

Sarah cupped my face and wiped away my tears. "It's just like that, okay? You didn't make this happen. You love Hunter. You would never hurt him."

I nodded, tears welling up again. "I need to pull myself together."

"You don't need to pull yourself together," she whispered. "You need to lean on all of us. We'll keep you together. The same way you've done for all of us, countless times."

The door to the bathroom burst open. Haley and Alice rushed in.

"I'm sorry I took off," I cried.

Alice shook her head. "None of that right now. You saved Hunter."

"Let's get this blood off you," Haley said.

The three of them worked to get me cleaned up, and I didn't fight them. I didn't have the strength to do this alone. I zoned out, trying to focus on holding myself together as Haley pulled my hair back into a bun and gently wiped my face and neck.

Once I was in clean clothes, Alice put the others into a bag and tied it off.

"I'll give that to Bud," Sarah said. "They might want it."

Haley washed her hands off and then nodded. "Alright. Emma, let's go to the waiting room."

I knew it was going to be the longest wait of my life.

CHAPTER FORTY-ONE
hunter

MY EYES slowly opened and I heard a gasp. I blinked a few times before I saw my dad.

"Thank god," he whispered. "I've never been so scared, son." He grabbed a cup of water and leaned over me, helping me take a sip.

"Hey Pops," I croaked.

He let out a soft sob as he put the cup down. "I'd better go get Emma and Mom. It's almost midnight. You were out for a couple days. But, I just... I need to say this."

I nodded and slipped my hand into his. "You don't have to right now."

"I need to. Hunter, I'm so sorry. I'm sorry I didn't listen to you. I'm sorry that..."

"Hey," I whispered. "I love you, Pops. I forgive you. I've also been difficult..."

He shook his head. "Emma told us everything about what's been happening. When I heard she'd lost her dad and that she felt like she'd never get to repair their relationship, it made me realize how damn stupid I've been. When we had our big fight, I regretted it, I just didn't know how to apologize. I know it's time for me to step back from the farm, but it's hard to. I'm working on it, though, I promise. You get your stubbornness from me, and I'm sorry. I just want you to know that I love you. And I'm damn proud of you, Hunter. I'm really, really proud of you."

"Thank you." I relaxed into the pillows and then winced. My entire body felt like it'd been run over. "Is she okay?"

"She is. You've found the right one."

I smiled at him. "I know, Pops."

"Let me go get them."

I breathed out as he left.

I'd made it.

Emma's voice echoed before she came through the doorway. She immediately leaned over and grabbed my face, kissing me hard. I kissed her back, drinking her in.

"I thought..." A soft cry left her and it broke my heart.

"Did you really think I'd leave you after everything we've gone through?" I whispered.

"I'm so sorry this happened, Hunter," she said. "I've told everyone everything. I talked to the police too, and—"

"Did they get them?" I asked.

She nodded and leaned back, wiping her eyes. "They got them. They weren't the ones who sent the letters, though. That was a woman named Louise."

My eyes widened. "Are you serious?"

"Yeah. But I didn't press charges because she helped us find you. If she hadn't been following you, I don't know if we could have found you in time."

The red car. I breathed out slowly. "I didn't expect that. I'm sorry. Louise was someone I saw briefly a while back, but I never thought she'd do something like that."

"I broke her nose. I also took out Josh's knee. And put my stepmother into a chokehold."

I snorted. "I'm used to being the one to save other people, sparks. But you saved me. I was almost passed out when you came through the door, but I still remember. You looked like an angel."

"An angel with a baseball bat."

I grinned. "A vision to behold. Thank you."

Emma's shoulders relaxed, and she took a deep, deep breath before letting it out. "I've been going crazy."

"Pops said I was out for a bit."

"Forty-nine hours and twenty minutes."

My smile softened into a wince. "I..."

She shook her head. "You're alive. And you're going to be okay. We're going to make it, Hunter Harlow. I'm in this forever."

"I'm in it forever, too."

Emma tucked her hair behind her ears and then smiled. "Let me go get your Mom. I swear, Hunter. We've had over a hundred calls the last couple days. Everyone in Citrus Cove wants to know if you're okay. I've met so many people that have stopped by to check on you. They've brought so much food that Honey and Lynn had to plug in an old freezer to keep some of the baked goods for later on."

"Really?" I chuckled. "Worried about losing their handyman."

She shook her head. "Worried about losing *you*. Also, Lynn said she'd give us five minutes alone before she comes in, and then will let everyone else in too."

"Well, I'm sure we can squeeze you in bed next to me."

"I'm never gonna leave your side."

"Careful, sparks. It almost sounds like you like me."

A soft laugh left her. "I *love* you."

"I love you too," I whispered. "Are we going to carve our names in the Harlow oak tree?"

"We sure are," she said. "We can pick a spot where there's room for our children to carve their names too."

My eyes widened. "How many kids do you want?"

"Three."

"Three!"

"Is that too many?"

"Hell no," I said. "I was thinking four."

She smirked. "We'll see. We're still doing things backwards, Hunter Harlow. We're not even officially engaged yet. Although I certainly let the hospital think we are."

"When I pick out the ring and ask you to marry me, it's going to be perfect," I promised.

"I believe you," she said. "Alright, baby. Our family needs to see you."

"One more kiss," I said.

Emma leaned down and gave me the best kiss I'd ever had.

I was the luckiest man alive.

CHAPTER FORTY-TWO

emma

One Year Later

"RK! DONNIE! GET YOUR BUTTS INSIDE!"

I planted my hands on my hips as I watched the two run around the yard at full speed. They took a sharp right and barreled straight for me. I stepped out of the way just in time for them to run inside, shaking my head.

I glanced at my watch and cursed.

The Wildflower Festival was today. Despite everything that happened a year ago, the event went so well that we'd all been asked to run it again. It was quickly on its way to becoming a tradition.

Hunter had left this morning to meet Cam, Sammy, and Colt downtown. I'd be meeting up with Haley, Alice, Sarah, and the boys before we all went our separate ways to do our parts.

I locked the back door and wasn't surprised to see RK

lounging in sunlight next to Donnie, two peas in a pod. It didn't matter that RK was at least six times the size of Donnie, they were best friends.

I leaned down to give them each scratches before straightening. "Alright. We'll be home later."

I grabbed my purse off the hook and stepped outside. The skies were bright blue, cotton candy clouds floating in the distance.

A lot had happened in the last twelve months. I'd sold Madden Enterprises to the Martinez brothers. Liam and Lucas Martinez were up-and-coming entrepreneurs with heart, which was what I'd wanted for the company. I'd almost sold out to a larger corporation, but that felt wrong since my dad had always refused to do so. Hunter, of course, happened to have a connection who introduced us to Liam and Lucas, and the rest was history. I knew I'd made the right decision by letting it go.

Both Angela and Josh went to jail. They'd confessed to giving Michael Madden the drugs that had killed him. Angela believed my father would leave her everything, not me. Josh believed he'd leave the company to him, not me. The two of them had agreed to work together to kill my father in hopes that they'd gain everything they'd wanted.

They'd both been wrong.

I'd been wrong about a lot of things too, and it took some time with Sarah's therapist (now my therapist too, she was getting all of our business at this point) to undo the knots I'd tied up.

Hunter had been there for me on every step of the way. We weren't married yet since we'd decided to take our time. We knew we were in this forever.

My phone rang as I got into my car. I pressed the answer button as I backed out of the drive. "I'm on my way," I said quickly.

"Hey, Emma," Haley said. "You're wearing your dress, right?"

"Yeah," I said, frowning.

"How does your hair look?"

"Good, of course. Why?"

"Just for photos for the paper. Also, how soon can you get here? There's an issue at the main tent."

"What kind of issue?" My voice pitched. I'd literally made sure every single thing that could possibly go wrong *wouldn't* go wrong.

"Just meet me over there. I'll see you soon."

"But—"

Haley hung up before I could ask anything else. I let out a frustrated sigh and sped up, making my way to Citrus Cove Cafe. It was where our group was parking, since it was close to the festival set up.

A few minutes later, I parked next to Hunter's truck. I hopped out and looked around, bewildered.

Where in the hell was everyone?

Part of Main Street was barricaded off. There was a tent at the center full of vendors and had a stage towards the back. I picked up my pace as I darted towards it.

Haley intercepted me, a ray of pregnant sunshine. She was about six months along, as healthy as could be, and happier than ever.

"What's going on?" I asked.

She grabbed my shoulders, giving me a look over. "Hold still, you have a mascara clump."

"Bitch, what is going on?" I hissed, closing my eyes so she could fix my lashes.

"Just trust me." She let out a soft snort. "Follow me."

My stomach twisted as she turned and headed into the tent. I followed behind her, then paused.

HIDDEN ROOTS

This wasn't the tent set up we'd agreed on. What the hell was going on?

But then I saw it.

Rose petals spread over a walkway leading up towards the stage, all different shades of pink. My heart skipped a beat as my gaze lifted to where Hunter stood. He was dressed up in nice jeans, a pressed button down, and his nice boots.

Behind him, there was a wall of vibrant colors and rich greens. Countless wildflowers sat together, creating a tapestry of beauty. In the center, there was a neon pink sign that spelled out 'Will you marry me?'

Tears sprang to my eyes and my breath hitched. I slowly proceeded down the walkway and looked to either side, realizing our entire family was here.

"All of you were in on it," I cried.

Gentle chuckles filled the tent from our loved ones, but my eyes were on *him*.

Hunter met me at the bottom of the steps at the center of the stage.

"Hi, sparks," he whispered.

"Hi, dimples."

He grinned and gathered my hands, bringing them to his lips. My heart pounded, all of my love for him welling up as I looked into his rich brown eyes.

Then he slowly got down on one knee.

"This is long overdue, but I wanted to do it right," he said. "You deserve everything good, Emma. All that you dream of, I want to give to you. I love you. I've loved you since the moment you tased me. I know we did things backwards, and I know I've taken my damn time, but..."

He slowly pulled a box out of his pocket and opened it. My breath left me. Everyone else in the room disappeared except for him and me.

The ring was perfect. A marquise cut diamond that gleamed on a white gold band, our initials engraved along the side. It was everything I'd dreamed of my entire life, and even more importantly—it was from the man I loved.

"Will you marry me, Emma Madden?"

"Yes," I cried. "Yes, yes, yes. I will. I'll marry you, Hunter Harlow."

He let out a shaky breath, tears shining. "I promised myself I wouldn't cry."

I laughed as he took the ring and slid it on my finger. I immediately threw my arms around him as claps and cheers filled the room, our lips finding each other in a hungry kiss. His arms wrapped around me as he lifted, sweeping me off my feet.

I sniffled as I pressed my forehead to his. "I love you," I whispered. "I love you so much."

"I love you too, sparks."

I knew he did.

I knew he loved me just the way I was.

Ours was the type of love that grew stronger like the Harlow oak tree, with roots that stretched and healed. It was the kind of love they wrote stories about, the kind that made us stupid. It was the kind that made us cry, the kind that made us laugh. The kind that made us change.

It was the kind of love that would last forever.

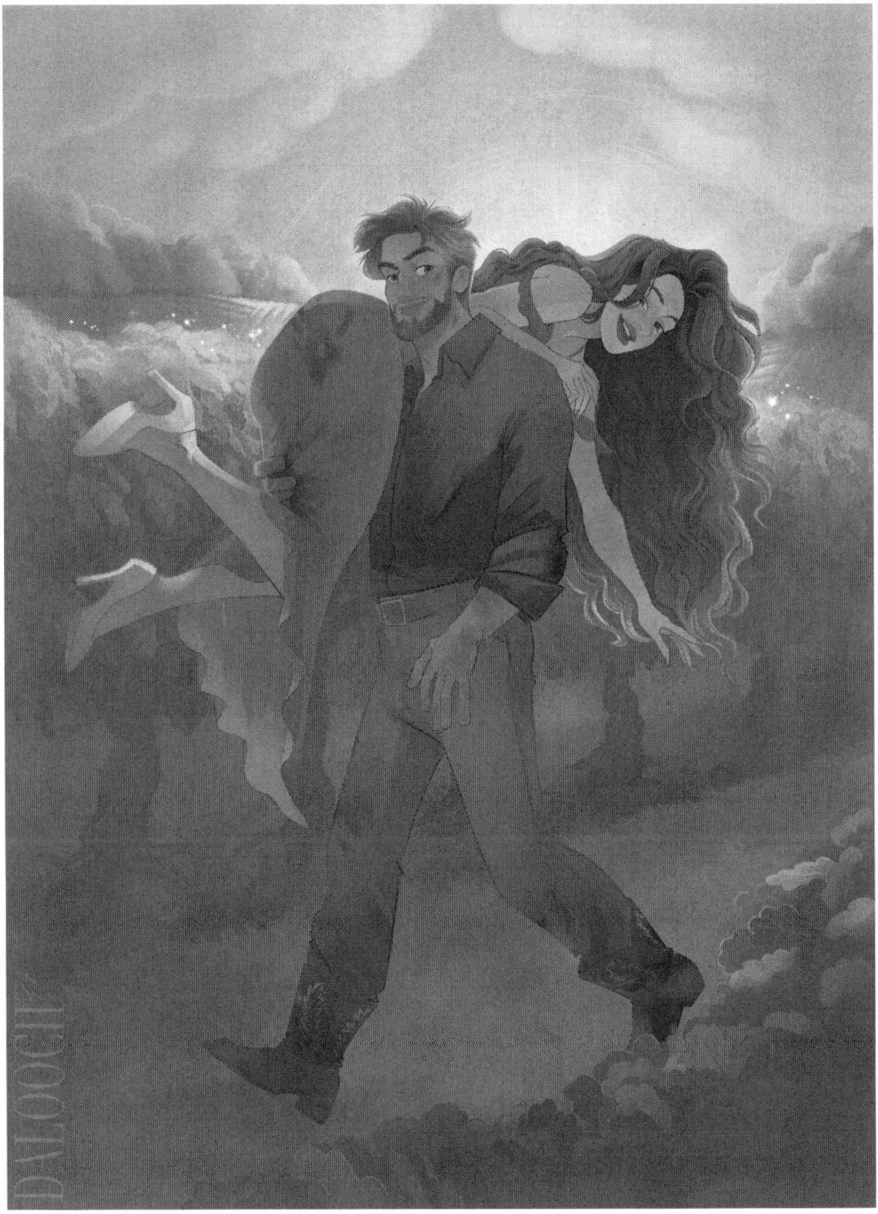

also by clio evans

Contemporary/Small Town Romance:

CITRUS COVE SERIES

Broken Beginnings (Citrus Cove 1)

Stolen Chances (Citrus Cove 2)

Hidden Roots (Citrus Cove 3)

STANDALONES

The Perfect Gift (Christmas Cuckold Novella)

Mine: A Reverse Age Gap Romance

Monster Romance:

CREATURE CAFE SERIES

Little Slice of Hell

Little Sip of Sin

Little Lick of Lust

Little Shock of Hate

Little Piece of Sass

Little Song of Pain

Little Taste of Need

Little Risk of Fall

Little Wings of Fate

Little Souls of Fire

Little Kiss of Snow: A Creature Cafe Christmas Anthology

Little Drop of Blood

Little Heart of Stone

Little Spark of Flame

Warts & Claws Inc. Series

Not So Kind Regards

Not So Best Wishes

Not So Thanks in Advance

Not So Yours Truly

Not So Much Appreciated

Freaks of Nature Duet

Doves & Demons

Demons & Doves

Three Fates Mafia Series

Thieves & Monsters

Killers & Monsters

Queens & Monsters

Kings & Monsters

Galactic Gems Series

Cosmic Kiss

Cosmic Crush

Cosmic Heat

Standalones

Nocturnal

about clio evans

A lover of myths, legends, BDSM, and queer joy in media–Clio Evans is the author of the Citrus Cove Series, Creature Cafe Series, Warts & Claws Series, and more.

From Austin but now living in Chicago, they can always be found drinking coffee or thinking about the perfect kinky happy ending for their books.

Join them on Instagram, Facebook, TikTok, or their newsletter for new releases, updates, and more!

www.clioevansauthor.com

Printed in Great Britain
by Amazon